A FAMILY
SECRET

Written by I.K. Baker

Print ISBN: 978-1-63616-178-5
eBook ISBN: 978-1-63616-179-2

Published & Illustarted By Opportune Independent Publishing Company

NOTES FROM THE AUTHOR

They say there's no better way of getting to know your true self than through adversity. And there is no better adversity than having a child. If you've already had one, you understand. If you haven't, just hear me out! Just imagine having to work harder than you've ever worked before on virtually no sleep at all. One might say, "Oh, well, I can't do that. That sounds too hard. Impossible, even." The funny thing is that you don't actually know what you're capable of. You don't know how much you can actually do until you have to do it. So, through your child, you are able to learn things about yourself you otherwise would not know.

Books are kind of like children. I look into the eyes of my daughter and see all the possibilities that she has within her. It is almost like looking at a blank piece of paper, so to speak. Like a book, the more time and effort you put into your child, the more you help shape their life story. You can fill them with ideas and actions. And before you know it, they are writing their own story, only needing your assistance from time to time. Books to me are organic, almost live things. When I started writing this story, I truly didn't know what I was capable of. How vast the inner workings of my mind were.

The whole book started out with an idea. An idea of a girl. She had no name, no story, but through the long hours I've spent with her, she acquired both those things and so much more.

Within each of us, there's a whole universe. This is where we store all our ideas, our hopes and dreams, our fears, and everything in between. This is the space where unborn books are found—stories of many different things for many different people. There is a storyteller within each of us.

Just imagine somebody handing you a newborn baby and telling you to raise the child: Make sure it is happy, well fed, and becomes a decent human being. Now, imagine somebody handing you a stack of papers and telling you to write a story that other people will enjoy just as much as you do. If you can do one of those things, then why not the other? Just start, and life will guide you. All your experiences will come forth to assist you. And when you can't find anything to call upon, just use your imagination!

Dear reader, I hope you will have as much enjoyment in reading this book as I have had in writing it.

TABLE OF CONTENTS

FAMILY TREES

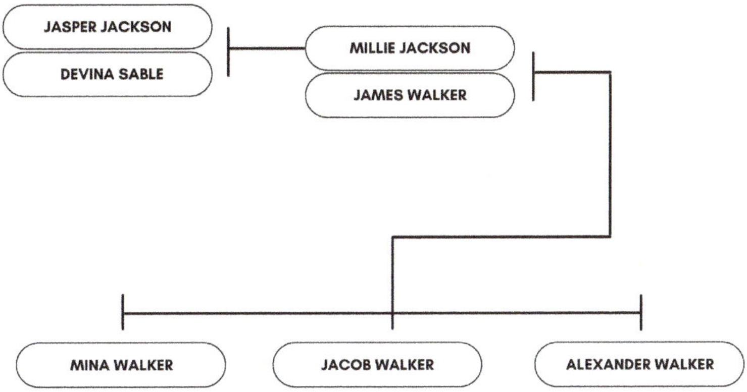

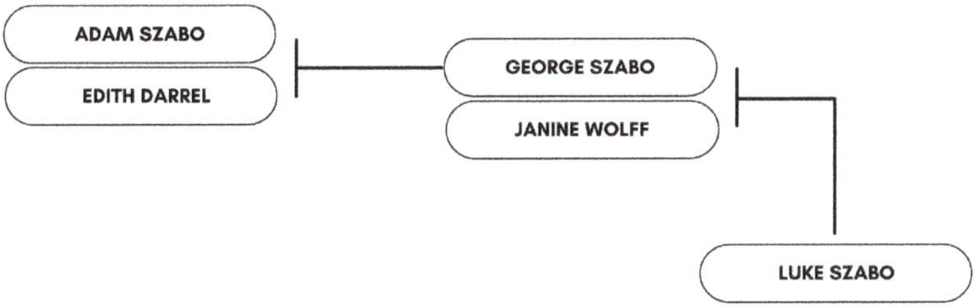

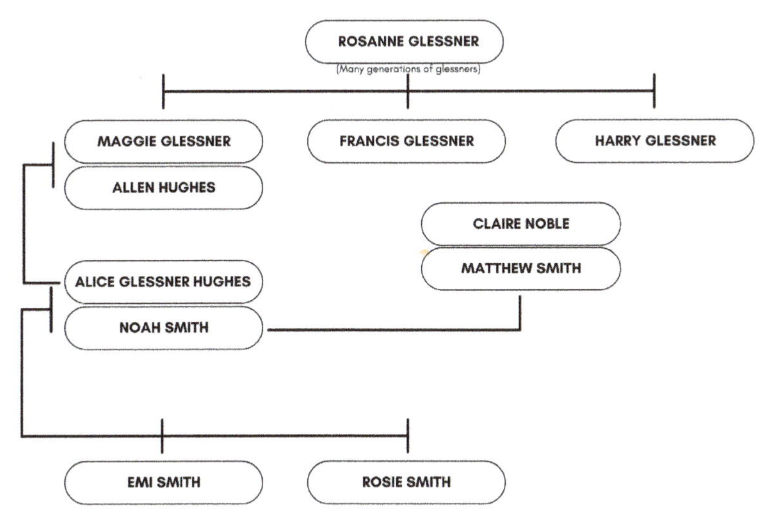

CHAPTER ONE

1998
JAMES

He turned the key, and the lock clicked open. The front door opened somewhat noisily, the hinges creaking. He would have to oil them soon. He told this to himself every time he came home late. Oddly enough, he never seemed to notice the complaining of the old front door when he opened it during the day. Only at night. When it was silent.

He turned and closed it as softly as he could, gravel and fresh mud crunching between his boots and the floorboards. He looked down, and to his surprise, he couldn't see his boots. Only boot-shaped mud. It was rough out there, but he hadn't noticed how muddy it was. All he noticed was the everlasting, unforgiving silence.

He wriggled out of his coat, but when he went to hang it up, it clung to him. It was stuck to him by dozens of burrs, the skeletal remains of late summer. He sighed heavily. His wife was in charge of taking care of his police uniform. This, along with his boots, would keep her occupied and most likely make her blow a gasket as soon as she saw them. He hung the coat, heavily laden with burrs, next to his daughter's maroon winter jacket. He almost turned away, but at the last minute, he paused, reached out, and gently touched the sleeve of the jacket, its soft, waterproof fabric a testament of his love for her.

Mina had fallen in love with it the moment she saw it through the store window. She accompanied him to Dallas on an errand. Being a true daddy's girl, she loved coming with him anywhere. They would drive long hours in the car, talking, shooting jokes. She loved hearing about the cases he'd worked on, and he probably told her more about them than he should have. He couldn't help it; he loved the way her hazel eyes sparkled when she gave him all her attention. Back then, she wanted to know everything about everything. The world had been interesting. He had been interesting. She was sixteen now. Their strong bond was starting to loosen already. Soon, she'd be moving away for college.

That day, though, she skipped along next to him as they walked from one store to another. Suddenly, he noticed she wasn't next to him anymore. He looked around and found her in front of a store a ways back. She was staring into a high-end clothing store like she'd just seen one of the many celebrities she was in love with at the time. She was pressing her angelic face to the cold glass, and the muffled sound of, "Daddy, look!" floated in his direction. He did look. What he saw was a cute—but pricey-looking—maroon coat on a skinny white mannequin.

He let her try it on. It had little black bows on the pockets. Black wool on the inside; smooth, almost shimmering maroon on the outside. It cost an arm and a leg, but it made his then-fourteen-year-old little girl look like a sophisticated young lady. Her eyes danced as she spun around for him. "It will keep her warm" was his reasoning for buying it for her.

At the end of the day, his wallet sighed with relief as all the cash had been lifted from it. He had to buy his sons something, too. It was only fair. But they agreed that the actual price of that coat would remain a secret strictly kept between the two of them.

He let his hand drop from the jacket. Would he have stopped looking if it was his daughter out there? Or would he look through the night and into the light of day?

He turned to face the inside of the house. He stood beside the stair landing. As if by habit, his eyes slid upward to where his children were sleeping. He froze. She was sitting midway up the stairs, watching him. She almost scared him straight out of his boots, which would have been a help because he wasn't sure how he would locate the laces. With her knees tucked under her chin, she looked like a curious little bird. Her mane of curly hair melted into the darkness around her, making it seem like her face was just floating there. She stayed up. She wanted to know. What would he tell her—"Honey, I'm sorry"? That wasn't good enough, and he knew it.

Her mouth slowly opened as one long leg extended downward to settle on the step beneath her. They heard a creak from somewhere in the house. She froze mid-motion, the unasked question stuck in her partially opened mouth.

His wife, Millie, stepped out of the dim kitchen at the end of the hallway, a mostly empty wine glass in her hand. She hadn't seen their daughter. He shot her a quick glance up the stairs that said, "Up you go, kiddo!" She did, fast and silent as a cat.

When he didn't make a move toward her, Millie approached with her usual slow and measured steps. The hallway light illuminating only half of her face gave her an almost predatory look. *A panther sneaking up on her prey in the underbrush*, he thought as goosebumps broke out over the back of his neck. It was only a cold breeze, he told himself. The door didn't shut right. It had nothing to do with him not wanting to talk to her about what happened. It was inevitable, though. She would get it out of him. There were no secrets kept around her.

He bent to untie his boots. He was trying to distinguish between mud and shoelace when her slippered feet came into view. He fumbled a bit longer.

"You might want to walk those outside and take the hose to them," she suggested dryly.

"You are probably right," he grunted, straightening.

He felt the familiar twinge of lower back pain that came and went with the cold. Soon, it would be staying permanently, like his wife's frown. Over the years, it had been steadily moving in, one sock at a time. Now, it seemed to be a permanent fixture on her face, like there was that one angry thought she just could not get rid of.

"So?" she asked, inquiring, her face smooth for the time being.

She sounded so innocent. Like she was just asking about his day. Like this was a day like any other. Like it had nothing to do with their neighbors. Pretending there wasn't a cloud of impending doom overhead, as if she wasn't just waiting for something like this to happen all this time.

He would just cut to the chase, hoping he could cut this discussion short. He had been on his feet for way too long. If he didn't lay down in the next few minutes, he would fall down.

"We found a bunch of footprints, but they seem to be going in circles. Going nowhere," he said, his voice sounding raspy and raw.

She blinked up at him, then slowly pursed her lips to one side. This isn't what she wanted to hear.

"Isn't that unusual?" she asked, moving the wine glass toward her lush lips.

She sounded testy, like someone had just delivered her pizza and it had the wrong toppings on it. *This isn't what I ordered. How dare you give me this?*

"Very unusual," he answered and went to bend quickly back to his still-tied boots.

She put a hand on his arm, stopping him. He looked at her hand, then into her dark, dark eyes. They bore into his, demanding more information out of him. When none came, she folded her lips into a thin line. He tried to slide his eyes from hers, but she squeezed his arm almost painfully.

"It has to do with what we know." She pulled him close as she spoke, so their noses were nearly touching. "The girl must have figured it out, and . . ."

"Do you honestly think this has to do with that?" He almost

growled at her.

He hardly recognized his own voice. It was suddenly so full of anger. He was just so tired of them beating this old, dead horse. It was already dead. It couldn't get any more dead than it was. Why keep poking at it? Why? His wife was obsessed.

"James . . ." his wife breathed. She had let go of his arm and taken a step back.

She was frowning furiously by now. One could mistake it for fear, but not him. He saw it for what it was. He wasn't the only one who had lost his temper. Millie straightened to her full height and did her level best to look down her perfect, round, little nose at him.

"You didn't tell the sheriff about it, did you?" It was a statement more than a question, and she obviously knew the answer.

"I don't believe it has any relation to what is going on right now. And we won't know anything for sure until . . ."

"That is your opinion! It doesn't make it true! The authorities need every single speck of information on that family!" She spoke in a loud, hissing whisper. "It could help fill in the missing pieces. It could . . . help . . . before it is too late," she finished lamely.

She was quite obviously flustered by this time. *You just want to air out their dirty laundry for everyone to see, thought James,* but he didn't say. That was a different conversation for a different night. He had to keep his head straight, concentrate on one problem at a time.

He closed his eyes and sighed heavily. Reaching out with both arms, he pulled her to him. She came without resistance, and he sagged against her body. She liked being needed, being useful. With a tired clarity, he realized that he did need her, too. The concerns he was having were too much for one man to deal with. He would talk to her, and not just because of her desire to know, but his to tell. But first, he would rest.

"I wish we would have found something, anything," he said wearily into her hair.

Her arms came around him, and within seconds, she was

rubbing circles on his back with one delicate hand.

"I'm sorry, Jim," she said softly by his ear. "You are ice-cold. Let's take these dang boots off and get you into the shower.

She held him at arm's length and looked into his face. The frown was still there, but resting for the moment. Her eyes caught the gleam of the hallway light, and now, he could see some caramel in them—and concern for him. She loved to fuss over him, and he needed that. That's why he married her.

Her eyes shifted, attracted by something. She reached out and unhooked a rouge burr that had escaped his coat and ended up on Mina's. She patted their daughter's coat, and a small, almost imperceptible smile appeared on her beautiful face. Yes, his wife, the glue of their household, the hunter of secrets. She knew exactly how much that coat had cost.

CHAPTER TWO

AUGUST, 1996
ROSIE

Her day started with a rooster crow. Right. Outside. Her window. She groaned as she arched her back, extended her limbs, and went into a full-body stretch. The timid early light of the sun poked gentle orange fingers through her blinds. Said fingers were trying to poke her eyes out. There came a second, even more enthusiastic crow, just in case the first one was ineffective. Moaning, she turned to her other side.

"Go away, horrible bird!" she croaked sleepily and burrowed deeper into her bed.

The rooster, who had been christened Napoleon when he was just a tender little chick for his no-nonsense attitude, was standing on an upturned red bucket under her window. This had become his favorite spot to wake the household from. He was a fierce protector of his flock from any animal or human threat, causing colorful exclamations from all members of the family when he sneakily attacked them from behind. Because of all these great qualities, they now referred to him as Leon the Terrible.

Despite all her early morning groanings, Rosie felt affectionate toward their loud rooster. She had once witnessed him jump high into the air and viciously karate-kick a hawk that had it in its mind to grab one of the hens. He had been magnificent. A warrior. A true knight in shining armor. His shiny feathers glinting in the sun, red wattles flopping about, he booted that hawk so gracefully out of the sky, it left her speechless. She could never look at Leon the same way again. Gone was the terrifyingly annoying waste of space, and in its place was this furious, yet adorable little creature.

That was the reason she hadn't moved the bucket. If he wanted to scream under her window at 6 a.m., so be it. It was for the lives of the hens.

She gave herself another minute or two, then slowly emerged from her covers. Her straight, strawberry hair stuck out oddly next to her face, where she assumed she had drooled at some point over the night. She brushed it away from her face and stretched luxuriously until her back popped. Leon, sensing her movement, peeked into her room with one orange eye from between the blinds. He clucked, satisfied with his morning's work. Rosie heard him flap his wings before he jumped off the bucket and strutted away. *See ya later, you little hooligan*, she thought, rubbing her face and yawning.

The upstairs bathroom was right next to her bedroom. She stumbled in there, still partially asleep, and began the morning routine of taming her hair. There wasn't much to it, really. Once she brushed it out, it was silky and slippery, with its golden strands. She ran her fingers through it and relished how soft it was. She knew a lot of girls who had straight hair and wanted curly or wavy hair, but not her. She loved her hair. The simplicity of it. The way her natural highlights caught the light of the sun. She had her mother to thank for it. Hers was the same; there was some gray in it now, but it was still beautiful.

She decided on a high ponytail for this morning and reached for her toothbrush and toothpaste. The cap was missing. She sighed theatrically. Her little sister was to blame. Emi, the forgetter of caps of all kinds. From toothpaste to milk containers, nothing was safe. It was as if she'd set booby traps for the family. Nobody could ever be sure if the beverage they picked up was safely closed. Sometimes, she just seemingly put the cap back, only for it to unexpectedly fly off and roll under the counter.

Rosie grumpily picked at the dried toothpaste. Emi was five—and kind of an airhead. Rosie wasn't really annoyed with her. She was used to it by now. Her stomach growled. She put the clogged tube of toothpaste down. She would come back to it after breakfast. A butter knife would make quicker work of the plug than her finger.

She came out of the bathroom, rounded the corner, and nearly fell on her face as said little sister burst out of her room and cannoned into her legs from the back. She leaned heavily on the wall she fell against and breathed softly in and out, waiting for the fright and pain to leave her knees. Emi, her timing impeccable for ambushes, flew past her down the carpeted hallway, her special sleeping blanket flapping behind her, shrieking like she was Leon the Terrible himself.

She stopped just before she reached the living room and looked back at her over her little bony shoulder. Her mouth wide, she gave Rosie a sweet little shit-eating grin.

"Your butt smells like cheese!" she said, eyes wide with all the naughtiness she thought she was about to get away with.

"That's it!" yelled Rosie. "I'm eating you for breakfast!"

Emi turned toward the living room and took off in a dead run, breathy giggles floating behind her. Using her much longer legs to her advantage, Rosie gained on her quickly. She caught her around the waist and pulled her back as she attempted to jump over the couch.

"You're not going anywhere now!" she said in her menacing monster voice. "Give me some baby back ribs!"

She pulled up Emi's pajama shirt and pretended to take a bite out of her side. She grazed the tender skin with her teeth, and Emi arched and bent like an earthworm on a hook.

"No!" she screamed. "No! No! No! Let me go! I'm chewy."

Rosie gave her a raspberry, and she kicked her little legs and giggled hysterically.

"You are right! I gotta cook you first."

She stood up with a load of wriggling sister under her arm and walked into the kitchen.

Her mother was already in there. Standing next to the stove, she was placidly buttering a piece of toast. Scrambled eggs sizzled in a pan next to her. The delicious smells of breakfast in the making filled the air all around her. Her mother turned her head to glance at them as Rosie carried in the mostly limp, but still laughing Emi. Rosie stopped next to her and bent down with ease, careful as to not lose hold of her squirming cargo. She pulled their giant red soup pot from the bottom cabinet. Her feet planted firmly on both sides of it, she proceeded to lower her helplessly giggling sister into said pot headfirst.

"Morning, my loves," said their mother, turning her eyes back to her cooking, a slight smile playing on her lips.

"Morning, Mom!" came the chorus of both girls, Emi sounding distinctly echoey from deep inside the pot.

"Can you not wait for breakfast, Rosie?"

"No, I must have some tender child meat right now," answered Rosie in her monster voice.

There came a long and desperate "noooo" from Emi, who was presumably doing a headstand inside the pot, her skinny little girl legs sticking up skyward.

Their mother snorted. Rosie looked up at her over her shoulder and saw that she now had a full-fledged grin on her face. Her mother had a good sense of humor—and also a sixth sense for stepping in just one second before one of them lost their temper while playing together. This uncanny ability always amazed Rose. How did her mother know the exact moment? It was as if she could smell trouble coming, like a bloodhound. She had a longish, pointy nose for it. Or maybe her ears were very sensitive. Rosie knew, for example, that Emi's tone of voice changed the second she had just about enough of something, but by that time, it was too late. The meltdown would commence, and both girls would end up in trouble, Emi for screaming and being "way too violent for the situation" and Rosie for pushing her sister too far.

Their dad did not have this talent for stepping in at just the right time, so in consequence, they got into more trouble when only he was watching them.

Suddenly, she felt her mother's hand on the back of her head. She ran her hand along her long ponytail affectionately just before she reached over her to grasp Emi's thin little ankles, hoisting her out of the pot. Emi's face was red, and she was no longer smiling, as if she was doing her dangdest to hold in a huge fart. Just one more second, and that fart, which was actually a scream, would have come out. Their mother gently laid her down onto the kitchen rug, where Emi stretched out placidly, looking like a satisfied starfish.

"Why don't you guys go wake up your dad? Breakfast is almost ready."

As if shot from a cannon, both girls popped up and took off toward the master suite. He heard them coming. As the girls burst through the door and leapt on him like two enthusiastic flying squirrels, their father curled into the fetal position to protect his soft parts. The struggle was epic. But like always, he had them in two separate choke holds within thirty seconds, Emi between his strong, hairy thighs and Rosie in the crook of his right arm.

"I can't breathe," croaked Rosie dramatically.

Something inaudible came from Emi, who was face-down in the covers.

"Ssss . . ." soothed their father, stroking Rosie's hair with his free hand. "Just go to sleep."

At this point, Emi made a valiant effort to escape her hairy prison, writhing and kicking, and really did let out a fart. Rosie and her dad gagged, and Emi giggled as all three of them scrambled from the bed.

Some of Rosie's friends didn't quite seem to like their parents. They weren't given enough allowance, free time, or attention. Their parents didn't get them. They were, at times, mean and too stern. Not Rosie's parents. Her home life was like a warm embrace. From the moment she opened her eyes in the morning to when she lay down at night, she felt nothing but love from them.

She was even okay with her annoying little sister. The truth was that Emi spiced things up with her booby traps and random assassination attempts.

Yes, of course, there were the occasional chores around the house, but that's how she earned her allowance. That's how it had always been. Her parents weren't unreasonable about it. They didn't make her get up in the middle of her favorite show and send her to collect eggs or load the dishwasher or anything like that, and she could pretty much come and go as she pleased. She had herself to thank for that, she thought philosophically as she bit into a piece of well-buttered toast. She was a good kid, so her parents treated her like one. Emi was a bit more of a spitfire, so she did force their parents to enforce the occasional time-out very rarely. This one time, she had put a live fish into Rosie's bed while she was taking a nap because she thought it would be hilarious if Rosie woke up next to "Fish Charming." She really didn't think Rosie would roll onto it, have a nightmare about something cold and slimy in her bed, and have an episode of hysterics when she finally woke up to scales and fish juice covering her back. She also didn't realize the fish would die. It was a shock to her that old Goldy Google-eyes couldn't just return to their family fish tank. He had to be flushed down the toilet. Emi mourned that fish. She sobbed uncontrollably the entire time she was in time-out, clutching the corpse of the fish to her chest and repeating, "I'm sorry!" and "Wake up!"

She was four at the time and hadn't quite grasped the meaning of death. It was actually quite funny, now that she thought back on it. Rosie's mouth turned upward, and she snorted a laugh around a fork full of scrambled eggs.

Her dad looked at her questioningly, but she just shook her head and rolled her eyes toward Emi, who was animatedly feeding one of her plastic dinosaurs. She didn't want to admit to the fish incident being funny in any way, shape, or form, lest Emi do it again. Her dad seemed to understand her silent gestures.

"You guys have any plans for today?" he asked.

Rosie thought for a second, scrunching her brow. Did she

have plans? These endless days of summer seemed to blur together. Nothing to do but have fun with her friends and explore the hidden treasures of their property and the surrounding wilderness. But summer was almost over. The thought squeezed her heart. She didn't mind school, but she didn't particularly like it, either. There was too much sitting around. All that listening and looking at the white board gave her a headache. She sighed inwardly. It would be back to the grind soon enough, but not today. Today, she was still free.

"Mina is coming over. We're gonna go ride," she said, sitting up straight.

"Oh! Oh! Me, too!" squealed Emi, almost jumping out of her chair. "I'm going to take Moonwalk."

Moonwalk was their grouchy elderly donkey, who had, for one reason or another, taken a special liking to Emi. Rosie suspected she was feeding him chocolate and candy when no one was looking. She didn't mind her sister coming along if it was just the two of them, but when her friends were coming, she preferred for her to stay behind. They couldn't run their horses fast if Emi came with. She wasn't steady enough for that. Besides, if the terrain got too rough or he simply got too tired, Moonwalk would just turn around and head back home. There was no convincing him otherwise when he decided the ride was over either. He would just give you a long, suffering donkey scream and show you his backside. Rosie didn't want to deal with that today. She wanted to ride for some uninterrupted hours with her friend, then come home all tired and smelling of horse, and possibly fall asleep in front of the TV. She was just about to interject when her mom spoke up.

"Emi, we are going to the doctor's today. Remember?"

"No!" Emi yelled dramatically with her head back at an alarming angle.

"Yes. We are going," her mom said calmly. "I want to get that mole on your leg looked at before we go to Nana and Pawpaw's this weekend."

Rosie let out a relieved breath. She wasn't on Emi duty this morning. Today was going to be great. Her little sister kept on protesting until their mom started clearing the table, at which point their dad picked her up bodily and took her to her room to get her ready.

CHAPTER THREE

1996
MILLIE

Millie took a long, suffering sigh as she and her daughter walked along the forest trail that led to their neighbors' house. It was only about a ten-minute walk, and it was actually quite nice this time of year. It was around 8 a.m., and the mid-August Texas sun was already shining powerfully down on the tops of their heads. Once they got under the trees, the temperature dropped pleasantly.

Alice and Noah Smith's property was technically neighboring theirs, but it was much bigger. While Millie and her husband, James, owned a quaint, well-maintained two-acre lot, their neighbors possessed a staggering sixty-eight. If their property wasn't so extensively, unnecessarily huge, the walk wouldn't be so long. She pursed her lips and looked over at her slouching teenage daughter. Mina looked utterly miserable. She was the one who promised her friend that she would feed her animals while they visited family down south. She had actually been excited about it—right up until a couple of days ago, that is. The girls had gone out horseback riding because, of course, the Smiths had about five horses and that awfully loud donkey, and Mina had come home with the oddest expression on her sweet, young face, like she had seen something she shouldn't have. She wouldn't talk about it, either. She normally loved boasting about all the outrageous and sometimes outright dangerous things they had done. But that day, she didn't say a peep. Her face and her normally chatty mouth were all closed up. She had taken one of her other friends with her, too, that day. What was her name? Millie searched her mind. Samantha? That's probably it. She should ask Samantha's mother if she knows anything. If her daughter was acting all out of order, too.

Mina did not want to go to the Smiths' house alone today. Actually, she didn't want to go at all. Not even when Millie finally told her she would go with her. She basically had to drag her tall, long-legged daughter out the door and start shoving her in the right direction. Mina said that her stomach hurt. Her head hurt. She just started her period. Basically every excuse in the book. Millie wasn't buying it. Her daughter had taken on this unnecessary responsibility, and by God, she was going to follow through with it. What kind of adult would she become if she thought it was okay to back out of any engagement just like that? It was Millie's job to groom her into a responsible young lady. So, she made Mina keep her promises every time—unless the promise was a ridiculous one, of course. Mina was flaky by nature, and Millie saw that as something that needed to be fixed. Or worked on, at least.

The Smiths' house came into view through the trees, and Millie felt her old hurt rising in her chest. Life wasn't fair, she thought again bitterly, like so many times before. Her daughter had to learn that valuable life lesson someday. Might as well be today.

They put out food for the cats and took care of the old, ratty dog. All that was left was to feed the chickens and make sure the horses were all right.

"You can do it," said Millie and gave her daughter a gentle shove. "Take care of the chickens, and I'll be right here."

Standing on the front porch, she shielded her eyes from the sun as she watched Mina reluctantly amble away toward the coop. It was maybe a hundred feet from the house. Now that she was alone, she could see to the real reason she offered to accompany her daughter. She just wanted to take a closer look at the house without any prying eyes. Well, the dog was with her, but it was probably mostly blind, anyway. It came back inside with her, slightly limping on its left hind leg. It was probably arthritis. The animal was around eleven, if she remembered correctly. Mina had told her once, but she had barely been listening.

The office was right by the front door. It had two desks facing each other. His and hers. Her lips pulled up in a sneer. These people were so disgustingly perfect. She could just see them doing paperwork together in the evenings, sharing pleasantries and laughing. The vision infuriated her. She turned out of the office and headed into the living room. She had been here a handful of times. Never alone, though. The property had been left to Alice by her grandmother when she passed. The whole interior of the house was the perfect balance of rustic and modern. They had expanded the original tiny house that sat on the property ten years ago, and they went all-out with it. It had all the modern amenities. Beautiful, sparkling gray granite countertops in the kitchen and the bathrooms. The floors were all a warm, inviting dark hardwood. The kitchen cabinets were painted a dark red, then distressed so they looked perfectly worn. Some of them had colored glass on the faces so you could just barely see the expensive china inside. The living room had a long, L-shaped light tan couch and a couple of leather recliners. She loved this house. And she hated Alice for having it. This should have all been hers, she thought as her eyes scanned over everything. Not the property, of course, just the home—and the man. Noah did most of the work on the home. The man was a jack of all trades. Great with a hammer, that Noah. She felt a strand of guilt tugging on her conscience. She did have a perfectly good husband at home whom she loved. James was a good man. Not handy, but very loving. The past haunted Millie. That was the problem. She just couldn't forget what had happened between the three of them. Her, Alice, and Noah. She couldn't forget it. And she couldn't forgive.

The girls' bedrooms were to the left, she remembered, and the master was to the right. She made a beeline for it. The room was dominated by a huge bed made out of logs, flanked by a chunky-looking nightstand on each side. Noah built these, too, of course, the handy bastard. His nightstand had a lamp and a pair of sunglasses sitting on it. Alice's was a lot messier, with books, earplugs, a picture of the younger version of the old dog and their two daughters, and a chocolate wrapper strewn atop it. She was probably a bad homemaker, leaving such a mess. Noah probably did most of the cleaning. Millie was a great homemaker. Her old two-story home was always spotless, and her cooking was exceptional, she thought with pride and defiance. She ambled over to Alice's nightstand slowly, letting her fingers run over the bedcovers. She picked up the books and read the titles. All sappy romance novels. Not Millie's style at all. She preferred thrillers and historical fiction. A lot more grown-up than reading about two nonexistent people falling in love. She pulled out the drawer, and inside was another book. No—actually, on closer inspection, it was a photo album. Did she want to see a bunch of pictures of their smug, happy faces and their so obviously beautiful blonde daughters? No, not really. She opened it anyway. It was exactly what she expected. She flipped through the pictures of family trips and school portraits, then snapped it shut. She was about to put it back when something fell out of it. It dropped to the floor with a metallic clatter. She bent to pick it up.

"Huh," she said. "How odd."

In her hand was a small silver key. Not big enough to be a door key. Bigger than the ones sold with those dumb lockable diaries girls nowadays loved so much. She examined it carefully, turning it in her fingers. In fact, it was the exact size of the keys belonging to the desk at the veterinary office where she worked. She held the shiny little key in front of her face and remembered the two desks in the office. Was this little key the guardian of a secret, perhaps? She heard the donkey braying in the distance. It was greeting Mina. She didn't have much time to dwell on this. Even before she made a conscious decision, her feet were moving at a quick pace, out the master, through the living room, and into the office. She tried Noah's desk first. She knew it was his by all the architectural paperwork stacked neatly in one corner. He was a roofer. Made damn good money, too, the swine. Out of the two lockable drawers, only one was locked. The other one held more office paperwork. She tried the key in the other one. No dice. She rushed over to Alice's desk. The woman was the definition of messy. She was a fitness teacher at the local YMCA. She had the body to show for it, too. The woman still looked like she was twenty-three, not thirty-three, even after two kids. Apparently, she was a great group teacher and an even better personal coach. "The pounds just flew off me," one of the moms at the kids' school had exclaimed. "It only takes a couple of times a week. Maybe three. You should try it!" she had said to Millie, smiling at her enthusiastically with her ghastly, uneven teeth. Millie had never been so offended in her life. The woman called her fat outright. She looked down at her frame as she tried the first lock on the desk. It was true that her behind had gotten a bit wider over the years, and there was a healthy layer of padding over her muscles. But she still felt sexy. Her husband loved the way she looked. He adored her. And she would rather pull her own teeth out than go to one of her . . .

The key turned, and the drawer opened. It was empty. Feeling slightly deflated, she quickly tried the other one. It opened, as well. It was filled with important family paperwork—passports, birth certificates. The woman should really put these in a safe. So negligent. It was only this, she thought. Just passports and birth certificates. No exciting or embarrassing family secret to be found. Nothing for Millie to store away for a rainy day. The Smiths were just your average, ordinary, grossly happy people. Nothing here to see.

Millie exhaled deeply, feeling strangely raw inside right then. She locked the first drawer. Before locking the second one, she reached in there with one desperate hand, like someone looking for a light switch in perfect darkness. Her fingertips touched paper at the very back of the drawer. It crinkled as she tentatively pushed against it. She pulled it out. It was an envelope. On the back of it was one simple, handwritten sentence: *In case of emergency.* It wasn't sealed. With her mouth slightly parted, she opened the flap and pulled out a white sheet of paper. It only held a few sentences of handwritten text. She read it quickly and hungrily. Her lips moved silently as she went. Her eyes widened. She read it again and again. She was just about to sit down in the desk chair, her brow furrowed ferociously, when she heard her daughter calling.

"Mom! Can we go?" There was a beat of science, and then she called again. "Mom? Are you here?"

She sounded nervous. Millie tried to stuff the piece of paper back into the envelope, but it wouldn't go all the way in. She tried again and again. Was there something else in there? She peeked into the envelope and saw a small, rectangular piece of paper at the bottom. Every fiber of her body wanted to look at it, but there was no time. If her daughter were to find her in here, snooping around, she would surely tell her friend. The girl couldn't keep a secret even if it was glued to her. She managed to force the paper back in the envelope, stuck it in the drawer, locked it, and pocketed the key. She almost tripped over the old dog as she hurried to her daughter. An almost tingling sense of anticipation washed over her. They would have to come back tomorrow. Maybe this time, she would let Mina stay behind. A growing girl like her needed her rest before the new school year began, after all.

CHAPTER FOUR

1996
ROSIE

Her grandparents' property off Lake Ray Roberts was located about an hour's drive from their family ranch. Her family had always spent one of the last weekends of the summer here. Rosie loved coming here. Usually. Her grandparents were kind and generous. The lake was always warm this time of year and full of adventures to be had. She helped Emi learn how to swim here with the assistance of her parents. She fished with her dad and once had rescued a baby deer with her mom. It got caught on the neighbors' fence. Rosie was about six. That was the year she met Luke, the sad and nerdy boy who was being raised by his grandparents. Rosie's grandfather, a vigorous elderly man who thrived on gossip, had told her all about the tragic boating accident that had claimed both Luke's parents. "Two boats collided at a much higher speed than permitted," he had said, patting Rosie's knobby little knee with one large, calloused hand. "It was horrible." He shook his head, looking down at his lap, and Rosie saw real sorrow in his old, weathered face. "Truly terrible."

Luke was a year younger than Rosie, a frail, long-limbed boy with thick black glasses sitting on his button nose. For years, Rosie had taken it upon herself to take Luke under her wing whenever they visited her grandparents. They would come pretty often, about five to six times a year. She would run straight over to the neighbors and demand to see Luke. As they aged, though, she caught him looking at her strangely. It was a bewildered and almost fearful stare. It made her feel . . . Well, she wasn't entirely sure how it made her feel. And that made her anxious. And then, there was that night they snuck out to go stargazing in the beginning of the summer. The night when everything sort of shifted. It made Rosie uncomfortable to even think about it. But even that was better than to let her mind drift to the morning of the ride with Mina and Samantha.

Rosie shifted her position. She was sitting on the swing bench facing the lake, her knees tucked under her chin. Up ahead, her sister and Luke were fawning over a fish he'd just helped her catch with a miniature fishing pole. Luke probably loved Emi as if she was his own sister. He acted as much. And for some time, Rosie thought he loved her as a sister, too. She looked down to her knees. They were so close to her face that she could see the grooves in her skin, the sparse, wispy, almost see-through hairs covering its surface. She had a scar from falling while riding her bike. It faded over the years. It had been crusty and painful for so long. Now, it was no more than a darker spot on her skin. Would her memories of that horse ride fade just like this scar? she wondered.

She had cleaned and saddled two of their horses. First off, there was the champagne-colored mare called Sand. Sand was her horse. She always rode her. She had picked their peaceful bay gelding by the name of Chai for Mina. He was Mina's favorite out of all their horses. She never told Rosie this, but she could tell by the way Mina looked at the horse. The way she encouraged him to go faster by whooping joyfully and patted his neck when she was pleased. Mina was great with horses. That was one of the reasons Rosie liked her. Her dad once told her that if a person liked animals, they couldn't be all bad. Rosie had some doubt as to the truth of that. She never contradicted him, though.

She heard footsteps and looked up with a huge grin on her

face. It was Mina, but she wasn't alone. The smile fell from Rosie's face. Mina was great, but she had the habit of spontaneously inviting some of her other friends without telling her. Rosie knew why. She wasn't an overly social person, and she could be awkward when meeting new people. Because of this, Rosie preferred to hang out with one person at a time. Mina knew this. She knew most things about Rosie because they grew up right next to each other. They had always gone to the same school, and they had been friends for at least ten years. And still, Mina just did as she pleased. That was one of things Rosie didn't like about her. She knew if she asked, Rosie would say no. So, she just went around her. She blew out audibly through her nose and went to clean one more horse.

Early into the ride, Rosie realized that Sam, their unwanted but polite and enthusiastic third wheel, was not such a great rider. She looked nervous and periodically jerked on the reins, making her mount snort and stomp. She'd already caught Mina rolling her eyes about four times when Sam made some kind of blunder. Why did she invite her in the first place, then? Sam's ride, a gray gelding named Pilot, was also giving Rosie looks which told her that, indeed, he was having a less-than-good time on this excursion, and he may just repay her for this by casually stepping on her foot next time she cleaned him.

"This is boring," announced Mina.

Rosie had to agree. They hadn't been able to run the horses because the first time they tried, Sam screamed and almost fell headfirst off Pilot. They were both pretty shaken by the experience.

"Any suggestions to remedy this?" asked Rosie with one arched brow.

If someone was going to suggest going back, it should be Mina. Rosie wasn't going to be the obvious party pooper. Mina smiled conspiratorially. She had that same almost sensual-looking pursed smile as her mom. They were almost exact carbon copies of each other. Except for her nose. That must come from her dad. Rosie met Mina's dad only a few times and only fleetingly, even though they were neighbors. He seemed to be working all the time.

She couldn't quite recall his nose, but she had spent plenty of time around Millie and could summon her face instantly. There was almost something regal about her. Something powerful and almost scary.

"We should go to the homestead," said Mina.

The homestead was a historic ruin, if you will. Oddly enough, this piece of property had belonged to Rosie's mom's family for the past two hundred years or so. A German immigrant called Rosanne Glessner had settled here with her new husband and made a life for herself. The family line could be traced straight back to her and beyond. Rosie had been named after her, and Emi after her daughter whom she had given birth to right here on this very land. It was kind of a big deal locally. Rosanne had also kept a journal, which was recovered from the ruins, translated into English, and being sold in most major bookstores. Of course, Rosie's family had one of the first copies at home. The Dallas Museum of History had the original one. It sat mounted in a glass case, open somewhere in the middle. She had seen it once and had felt an almost magnetic pull to it. She couldn't read the two exposed pages. She knew no German. None of her living family did. Her mother had said she heard Rosie's great grandparents arguing in German once. "It sounded harsh, " she had said. The ancient journal had something so familiar about it. It took Rosie to realize that Rosanne's handwriting was almost the same as her own. The shocking realization led her to beg her mother for German lessons. She lasted about four months. German, it turns out, is incredibly hard to learn.

Rosie loved going to the homestead. There was just something in the air over there, a sense of mystery and suspense. Mina liked saying that it was haunted, but it totally wasn't. There was an ancient cemetery about a quarter mile east of the homestead itself, and that actually may be haunted, but they could just skip going there. She was just about to say, "Hell, yeah! Let's go!", but there was one thing that gave her pause: The Red River bordered their property on the northwest side. And there was a really tall cliff there. Like, deadly tall. It wasn't too far from the homestead, which meant that if one of the horses were to lose its rider—she inconspicuously glanced over at Sam—it could technically run toward the cliff. And knowing how accident-prone most horses were, there was a strong chance it would fall to its death. She pondered this for a few seconds. She did want to go. She, in fact, never missed a chance to go. Walking around the old ruins was one of her favorite things to do. Mina saw the decision on her face, and her eyes twinkled with mischief. Rosie gave her a crooked smile. She couldn't stay annoyed with her for too long. Mina was too much fun.

"Let's try this again," said Rosie. She dug her heels into her horse's side.

They made it to the homestead in one piece. Sam had hung on for dear life. Now that they had finally come to a stop, she looked equal parts shaken and invigorated.

"I think I may be sick . . ." Sam croaked and slid off the side of her mount like a piece of Jell-O.

There, in a small, roundish clearing in front of them, stood the ruins of three buildings: the barn, the springhouse, and the main house. The springhouse was actually mostly just a hole in the ground with a few limestone bricks scattered near it. The barn, which had been built of wood, had only one whole and two partial walls standing. The rest was taken down by the elements and the termites. The house, built mostly from stone, still resembled its original form. It was L-shaped, a strange construction for its time according to Rosie's dad. He also said it originally had five bedrooms. They probably had a huge family. That was the thing back then: Have as many kids as humanly possible. Rosie imagined herself rocking a small child to sleep on top of a large pregnant belly. The room would have been lit only by fire light, and her husband would have been playing the harmonica or something. Maybe a banjo, if he hadn't been killed by a bear while using the outhouse. Then, she would have been a widow with kids at fourteen. Girls were married off and had kids at her age back then—according to their gross history teacher, that is. The thought that she would have had to have sex with some weird older guy whom her parents picked out for her was appalling. They could have picked someone who looked like her balding, big-nosed history teacher. Rosie shuddered. The bear was free to take him anytime. It sucked to be a girl back then. It really did.

They joined Sam on the ground, tied the horses to some sturdy pines, and left them to graze the lush, tall grass of the clearing as they headed toward the house.

As they walked, they got a strong gust of wind from behind. It threw Rosie off balance for a second. She staggered and glanced at the others, but they seemed not to notice. The waist-high grass around her rippled with a northern gust, pushing her toward the house. She looked behind her. Two of the horses were placidly chomping away, their tails swishing and their hides shivering periodically as they shook off biting insects. Sand raised her head and nickered at her. She arched her neck and shook her big head, as if she was done with this place already. *We'll be quick*, thought Rosie, and she jogged to catch up with the others. When they passed by the spring house, Mina gave a playful "Hellooo!" at the mouth of the hole. Sam giggled, and she did it, too. Their echoes bounced back at them from the seemingly bottomless cavern. Feeling slightly silly, Rosie bent and let loose a whoop into the opening. She straightened and frowned into the darkness.

"What's wrong?" asked Samantha, suddenly seeming nervous.

"Nothing!" said Rosie quickly, throwing her a withering smile. "It just sounded like there was water down there."

"So?" Mina asked mockingly. "What are you, the water police?"

Rosie gave her a flat look. It hadn't rained for weeks. It would just be strange to find water in there. The hole was way too deep and dark for them to see the bottom. Rosie picked up a small rock and tossed it in there. It landed with a dry thump. Rosie scrunched her mouth to one side.

"Stop making that face! You'll get wrinkles," Mina scolded

her and shoved her from behind playfully.

Rosie was standing only a step away from the mouth of the opening. She put her arms out to catch her balance. Mina snorted, and Sam put her arms out, ready to grab Rosie if need be.

"You hoe!" Rosie exclaimed. She turned on her heels and grabbed Mina by the waist. They struggled, giggling and grunting, with Rosie trying to pick her friend up and Mina doing her level best not to get thrown in the hole.

The few pounds Mina had on her friend due to her height won her this one. She got away. Laughing, she ran toward the house, with Rosie on her heels and Samantha a bit slow on the draw, a little ways behind them.

They stopped by the front door, bending over with hands on their knees, gasping dramatically. There was no actual door. It had disappeared over time, along with part of the roof. The girls looked up to where the stones of the house came to a peak, then back down to the empty mouth of the doorway.

"Let's go in," Mina said.

"Ya know we're not supposed to." Rosie mock rolled her eyes, hands on hips. She already knew they were going to go in.

She also figured out why Mina brought Sam along. They did this thing from time to time where they would bring another kid along just to scare the crap out of them. It was almost always Mina's idea, but Rosie usually went along with it. It was all in good fun. Nobody actually got hurt—except for that one time when that cocky little dweeb, Marcus, tripped on a rock running out of the house and did a faceplant. He broke one of his teeth. His parents would have been furious if he had told them how it happened. But lucky for them, he was too embarrassed to admit two girls had scared the living daylights out of him. Instead, he told his parents he fell from his bike. That was the last time Mina had brought someone here for a while. Today, Rosie wasn't really feeling the idea. Sam seemed so innocent and fragile. It seemed wrong to mess with her. It was enough that she almost fell off the horse. Twice. They were getting too old for this kind of stuff, anyway.

"Is it safe?" inquired Sam, still roaming the exterior with her eyes.

Mina and Rosie looked at each other.

"Nah," they said in unison and headed inside.

The whole house seemed to creak around them as if they had walked into something alive. Like it was the mouth of some big, ancient creature. The floor was covered with leaves that had fallen in through the opening above and blown in through the open window and door frames. They were in the big family living space. To their right was an opening to a small room. Right across the living area stood the old stone fireplace. It was black with decades of use, its chunky stone chimney going all the way up the wall and through the roof.

"This is so creepy," Sam said in awe. She was scanning what remained of the roof, her mouth wide open.

"Careful," said Rosie. "Sometimes, these big old spiders drop from the roofbeams."

Sam snapped her mouth shut and brushed nonexistent spiders from her hair. Okay, maybe Rosie would poke a bit of fun, but that was it. They moved forward slowly and close together.

"They say it's good luck to pet the fireplace," said Mina.

"Only you say that." Rosie rolled her eyes and looked at Sam. "She says that because it's far from the door."

"I do not!"

"She wants to scare you."

"Hey! I so do not."

Her plans spoiled, Mina crossed her arms and pouted, her bottom lip sticking out childishly. Now, they were past the hole, and there was an actual wood ceiling above them. There came a creak, and they all looked up, their faces pale in the gloom.

"What . . ."

Mina's voice cut off when the ceiling creaked again. A shower of dust and dirt fell down on them as the boards above creaked for the third time. Rosie blinked rapidly to avoid the dirt falling in her eyes, her long eyelashes sweeping up and down. None of them could avert their eyes from the ceiling. They huddled close together, and Sam pulled her long, wavy hair in front of her face. She peeked through the strands as if they could protect her from harm. One more creak. Some more falling dirt. Was someone up there? Walking around?

"What's up there?" Sam asked in a small voice. She sounded like a dormouse.

It was the question they had all been thinking. Nothing like this had ever happened before.

"Just . . ." Rosie's voice failed her. She cleared her throat. "Just the attic."

This was when it happened. Rosie's memory was fuzzy, and it really made no sense at all.

On instinct, she let her face fall forward, and she saw something that wasn't there before. There was an old woman standing next to the fireplace. She was gently patting the smooth stone with one gnarled hand. Pat, pat, pat. Time seemed to slow around Rosie. She tried to see the woman's face. To ensure herself that she was just some normal trespasser. That she was just a regular human and not a ghost. But she was covered by long strands of wavy gray hair that almost reached the ground. Rosie let out a breath. She saw it puff out white in front of her face. She noticed that all the small hairs on her body were standing on end. The air had become icy. She was dimly aware of fear blooming inside her body like ice crystals. They penetrated all her cells. Her lungs were full of it. She couldn't breathe. She opened her mouth in slow motion to let it all out. To rid herself of it. But no air, no sound came. She felt weightless, yet pinned to the floor, as if she was stuck in this strange, airless, timeless void. The stillness of it was a fright of its own. Was she dying? Was she already dead? How many seconds had passed since the last load of dirt landed on her face? Since the last time she took a breath? The woman took her hand off the fireplace and lifted her chin to show yellowing teeth through the tangle of hair covering her features.

Rosie's voice finally came, but it didn't actually sound like her. It sounded like an animal in agony. The two girls moved on either side of her, pulling her out of the void so the three of them could flee together. She wanted to run. She was going to run. But her feet, her legs, her whole body betrayed her. Her torso twisted to turn away from the threat, but then she simply fell down like she was just one of the leaves that had made it into the room. She fell softly, slowly, ambling toward the floor. She didn't actually feel the impact. She seemed to just hover there above all the others, the faces of the leaves staring at her like many lost souls. There was peace. There was silence and warmth before it all came crashing down on her.

The first thing she felt upon her return to reality was her jaw. It was clenched so tightly that her teeth threatened to crack. Then, she felt her neck, her shoulders, her back arched like a bow before they all relaxed. She was dimly aware of some frantic noise. Once her ears adjusted, she could make out the girls screaming. They were dragging her by her arms, her body just limply going along for the ride. They were both yelling at her to "Wake up! Get up!" In another second, she could distinguish their two voices from each other. Mina seemed scared out of her mind as she yanked on her deadweight, and Sam was sobbing uncontrollably. Rosie blinked tiredly. Her body jerked as they pulled her through the threshold of the house. She groaned and pulled her knees up. As soon as she gave this sign of life, the girls let go of her arms and urged her to get to her feet, pushing and shoving her upper body. Rosie felt dizzy. Their loud, quickly spoken, halfway whispered orders and words of encouragement blurred together until they became indecipherable gibberish. She tried to stand and fell right back down. Her body ached. Her muscles felt like she had just finished some intense workout. Her stomach was the size of a pinprick, and her heart was racing a mile a minute. She turned onto her hands and knees and vomited scrambled eggs and toast onto the pine needles covering the ground.

All four shoving hands were removed from her as she did this. They let her retch and heave. When she was finally done, she had tears, saliva, and runny boogers all over her face and slowly dripping to the ground.

Somehow, they had made it to the horses. Rosie couldn't remember how they got her to stand up or exactly how they arrived at the other side of the clearing. She only possessed fragments of memories. Feet moving fast as the others ran and dragged her along. Tall grass swiping at her face, arms, and legs. Grunting, moaning, and panting. They may have all fallen together a couple of times. Since she was still pretty disoriented, Mina helped her climb into her saddle by pushing on her butt. She then extensively wiped her hands on her shorts, looking absolutely disgusted. Come to find out, at some point during these proceedings, Rosie had peed herself. She was utterly mortified. Thank God nobody was home when they got back. The girls had quickly dispersed, leaving her to tend to her many scrapes and bumps by herself. She had thrown her soiled clothes in the washer and sat in the bathtub until the water went cold. This was the single most frightening and confusing event of her entire young life.

She was going to tell her mom about it when she got home from the doctor's with Emi. But then, no matter how hard she tried to put things into words, she simply couldn't. It wasn't quite that she couldn't find the exact words to describe things, although that was part of it. But it was more like she had some kind of blockage made of shame, confusion, and numbness within her. And that was what was making it impossible to talk about it.

She did take a nap that day and had strange dreams of water in a deep, deep hole.

Luke sat down next to her on the swing, startling her out of her daytime nightmare. He had this almost comical concerned look on his face. His eyebrows looked like wings when he did that, arching up weirdly at the ends. Rosie wished he would stop looking at her this way. In fact, she was suddenly sick of it. Why on earth did he keep using this face on her? It was unnecessary. It was annoying.

"What?" she said moodily.

"Rosie, you . . ."

He reached out and touched her shoulder. As soon as his

fingertips made contact, he instantly pulled his hand back, as if her shoulder was a hot stove or something. He could be so dramatic. She was hoping they would be able to recover from what happened between them earlier this summer, but if he kept being so weird, there was just no way. Irritated, she glanced at his hand that he was now cradling with the other. His fingertips were black. She blinked and shook her head slightly. No, they weren't black. His hand was perfectly normal. She was seeing things. She needed to take a nap. She had been so tired lately. So, so tired. She was still looking at his hands. He was saying something. Her ears wouldn't focus on the sound. She looked up into his face. His lips were moving, but she couldn't help but stare dazedly into his eyes. He did have the prettiest hazel eyes behind those black-rimmed glasses. Surrounded by thick, dark lashes, his eyes were almost feminine. He grabbed her by both arms so urgently, her whole body jerked. His hands were as cold as ice. She tried to say so. She wanted to say, "Hey! Let go! Your hands are way too icy," but her lips felt chapped and numb. No, it wasn't just her lips. Her whole body was numb. What was going on? One moment, she was just sitting here with one of her best friends. The next, she was about to float away. The only thing holding her in place was Luke's viselike grip. The world shifted as her head rolled on her shoulders. Her vision was gone. Everything was gone, leaving nothing but the sound of the water.

CHAPTER FIVE

1996
ALICE

Sitting in her mother's kitchen on the lakefront property, Alice enjoyed the pampering one could only get as an adult when they went home to their parents'. Her mom, Maggie, had made her tea with honey and cinnamon buns. The sweet scents of carbs and sugar filled the air. Alice put her feet up onto the cushy bench next to the breakfast table and leaned against the wall, hot cup of tea in hand. She always strived to be a mother equal to her own. Maggie was the most wonderful parent anyone could ever wish for, and she was an even better grandmother. As she fussed over the cinnamon rolls, Alice looked out the big bay window she was sitting next to and sighed, feeling perfect happiness fill her from head to toe. Luke and Emi were fishing, Rosie was relaxing on the swing, and Noah was talking animatedly with her dad. Her father had been a great parent, too. He was just a bit of an airhead. He would often be too distracted with whatever he had going on to notice what his family needed. But he did have a great sense of humor, and her kids loved him.

"That mug was my sister's favorite, you know," Maggie said, sitting down across from her with a tray of rolls.

Alice inspected the mug. It was a depiction of an octopus.

Time had worn some of the pink glaze off of it, but it still held liquid just fine.

"I think you've told me that before. She got it at the town market, right?"

"Yes, yes. At the Sunday market. There was this lady there who made them by hand."

She smiled wistfully, her old face crinkling in all sorts of places. Her mother had looked like a little china doll when she was young. Her perfect, big-eyed, round face was portrayed on a painting in the living room. She must have been five or so, her sister about seven, and their little brother around four. Alice adored that picture. It was hard for her to think of her parents as children, but the painting was proof. They didn't just emerge into the world as adults. They grew up just like Alice did. Just like her children were doing now. In fact, her mother looked very much like Emi, and her sister, Francis, was the spitting image of Rosie at that age. Her mother still looked cute, with her wide brown eyes and thin, but always smiling lips.

"So, my sister, she really wanted one. And then, one Sunday, we had watched her make the octopus, and she ran to Maa crying. She dropped on her knees and begged her with her hands clasped just like this."

She imitated young Francis, shaking her clasped hands and looking upward theatrically.

"And you know what my mother said?"

Alice had remembered the story by now, so they said the line together in unison. "What on earth do you need a damn octopus for, Franny?" They chucked together, both looking at the googly yellow eyes of the octopus in question.

"She wouldn't buy it for her, and Franny's pocket money wasn't enough." She reached out and stroked one yellow eyeball with affection. "But I had some change, and when we put our little money together, it was just enough."

She removed her finger, and sat back in her chair, clasping her own mug with two hands. Her smile faded.

"She was a good sister, you know. Before . . ."

"I know, Mom." Alice reached out and clasped one of her mother's hands.

"We got the mug for her maybe a couple of years before it started. I think she was around eleven. And then, the thing that happened with Harry . . . Everybody blamed Franny for it, but they never could prove a thing."

Alice wished she could take away her mother's sorrow as she sat there squeezing her old, weathered hand. Francis started behaving unusually at an early age. She had soon become violent toward her family and was finally diagnosed with schizophrenia and placed in an institution. Alice had visited her a few times while she was still alive. To her, it was always a dreaded thing that needed to be done. The older Francis got, the less the medications seemed to have an effect on her. Each visit would be interesting at best and shockingly terrible at the worst. She recalled now the last visit she had with her aunt. It was while she was pregnant with Rosie. Harry, the youngest of the three, had disappeared when he was ten. He was last seen walking into the forest behind the family home alongside Francis. They never found any trace of him, and Francis, far gone in her illness by then, just kept talking in circles. They never got anything useful out of her. The police suspected that Harry had somehow fallen off the cliffs by the edge of the property and was swept away by the Red River. They wanted to blame it on Franny but had no proof.

Alice shuddered involuntarily and took another sip of her hot tea. She glanced out the window. Emi had now joined Noah and Grandpa, effectively stopping them from having an adult conversation, and Luke was . . . She scanned the yard until her eyes landed on the swing. She leaned closer to the glass and squinted. At first, her mind didn't quite register what she was seeing. Luke seemed to be cradling Rosie's upper body in his arms. They seemed strangely intimate and, to her motherly eyes, wildly inappropriate. Did they actually have a relationship like that? How did she not notice? Was it even possible? She was fourteen, and he was . . . what?

Thirteen? They were kids. Kids didn't hold each other like that. She lifted a hand, ready to bang on the window and yell, "You two, stop that!", like they were misbehaving dogs. When Rosie's head tipped back, her mouth was wide open, a black hole on her face, and her eyes were completely white. She looked lifeless. Alice jumped up involuntary, as if struck by lightning, rattling the table and spilling her tea. At the same moment, Luke looked up and scanned about for a second until his eyes locked with Alice's. His expression was one of pure panic. He wasn't cradling her; he was stopping her from falling to the ground.

Maggie said breathlessly, "What's wrong?", and also jumped up from the table. Her small hands hovered in front of her nervously, ready to soothe, grab, hit, or do anything to fix this unknown crisis threatening her child.

"It's Rosie!" yelled Alice. She was already running for the door.

She dropped to her knees in front of the bench and took Rosie's limp, unresponsive body from Luke.

"What happened?" she demanded almost accusingly.

"I . . . I . . . I . . . think she fainted," the poor boy stuttered.

He was white with shock, his thick glasses sitting askew on his thin face. Alice instantly felt bad. This wasn't Luke's fault. He loved Rosie like a sister. He was there to catch her when she fell. Alice smoothed the hair away from Rosie's face. Well, most of it. She had long strands stuck to her forehead. She felt hot and sweaty. This wasn't good. *Meningitis.* The phrase came to her from the deepest depth of her brain. A lady had told her casually after one of her aerobics classes that she had lost a child to the disease. Alice couldn't remember how they had ended up at the topic, but she had listed some of the symptoms. Fever, vomiting, loss of consciousness. "We thought it was the flu. He stayed in bed for a few days and didn't get any better. By the time we took him to the hospital, it was too late. But that was twenty-odd years ago . . ." Alice didn't quite know what to say to her at the time. What do you say to someone who lost a child?

She now went cold with fear. She whipped her head around and screamed, "Noah!"

He was on his feet in an instant and running toward them. She looked down at Rosie's splotchy face. No. Not her child. Not today.

CHAPTER SIX

1981
MILLIE

Millie was hugging her best friend to her chest. Alice was leaving to go to college in Houston today. Millie already had a part-time job as a receptionist at the Whitesboro police station. She had no plans of going anywhere. This would be the first time they would be separated in eleven years.

Millie was around nine when she and her family had moved to Whitesboro, a sleepy little town in the middle of nowhere. As it happened, they moved just down the street from a family with a little girl the same age as Millie. The two little girls became fast friends. And the rest, as they say, is history.

Her parents had told her they moved because Whitesboro was a better place to grow up than Dallas. But Millie knew the truth. She heard them talking at night. She had snuck out of her room, sat behind the big leather couch, and listened. She imagined she was a little mouse. Small, sneaky, and with big, all-hearing ears.

"I think we should do it," her father had said. "We're gonna lose the house soon if we don't do something."

"You're right," her mother said softly. Millie could only see the round of her cheek from her vantage point; the rest of her was blocked out by her huge, round mane. "But the town . . . It's . . . There isn't a Black community there. We'll stick out like a sore thumb. Millie will get picked on in school."

"It's not ideal; I know that. But the store is going under. We can't afford the mortgage anymore. Nobody can, and that's why nobody is buying shoes."

Millie's family couldn't have known that just a year from then, the housing market would crash. The interest rates—and, therefore, mortgage prices—were steadily going up until they were simply unaffordable. People were losing their homes left and right. And they were about to become one of them. Her parents ran a shoe store together. Her dad actually made some of the shoes they sold. Millie was strangely proud of that fact.

The day before this conversation, Millie's dad had gone up north to try and borrow money from his cousin yet again. They were just about to shut off their electricity because they couldn't afford to pay for it for so long. The cousin turned him away. He drove home devastated and really not knowing what to do next. At a red light, he clasped his hands on top of the steering wheel and prayed with his head down. He prayed for some miracle so that he and his family wouldn't end up on the streets. When he looked up, unshed tears dampening his eyes, he saw an empty storefront on the main street with what looked like an apartment on top of it. Two people, a man and a woman, were moving furniture out the door. Hoping this might be his miracle, he stopped and inquired about the building. The two people turned out to be a young couple. The building had belonged to the husband's father, who had recently passed. They were looking to sell and sell quickly and under market price. They were moving to Florida the next month, and they wanted it out of their hair. Plus, they could use the money, the wife had said, petting her rounding belly.

By selling everything they owned in Dallas, they could afford it. So, they had made the move.

They did encounter some looks, but after a bit of time, the townspeople learned that they were decent folks and had embraced them into their fold. Jasper Jackson's handmade shoes became something the town was known for.

Millie had made a few good friends, but none of them were closer to her than the kind and funny Alice. And then, there was Noah Smith. He lived next door to Alice and had spent a lot of time at her house, so Millie saw him often, too. When they met, he was a sad, shy little boy with an abusive father and an alcoholic mother at home. He had found refuge at Alice's home.

When they were twelve, Noah's mother finally died of liver failure. It was an incredibly hard year for him, and he practically moved into Alice's house. Her parents were nice and very understanding, and they welcomed him as if he were a long-lost son. The three of them also became incredibly close. One would never go anywhere without the other two. They all loved and needed one another. And from the outside, their little trio seemed simply sweet. In reality, though, nothing was ever simple. About a year after his mother's passing, Noah went through a miraculous change. Urged by Alice and her parents, he joined the football team at their high school, and it turns out that he was pretty good at it. In seemingly no time at all, from the shy young boy emerged a more confident young man. And it was around that time that Millie's feelings toward him started to change. She had always liked him as a person, although at times in the past, she did find him kind of gloomy. But now gone was all the gloom, replaced by muscles. She started to watch his body move when they were hanging out together and found that she really enjoyed looking at him. By the time they were fifteen, she knew she had a crush on him. That crush, however, soon evolved into almost an obsession. She thought about him constantly and saw his face in strangers; he was in her dreams when she slept. Millie always tried to look for excuses to hang out with him one-on-one. And although she did succeed from time to time, it seemed that her feelings toward him were tragically one-sided. She thought the most probable reason for this was that she was not pretty enough. But when she confided in her mother about all her feelings, she patted her on the back and told her something that dumbfounded her. It wasn't that Millie wasn't attractive enough or funny enough or the wrong color—because she did fear deep down inside that her being Black might have to do something with it. The real reason was Alice. Noah loved Alice. At first, Millie didn't want to believe this. They fought and played like brother and sister. But her mother, with her all-knowing adult eyes, had seen things Millie could not at the time.

After that conversation, she paid closer attention to the interactions between her two friends. And after some time, to her surprise, their feelings for each other became clear as day to her. She now saw how Noah clung on to every word out of Alice's mouth. The soft eyes he looked at her with. How Alice would touch his arm often and shove him playfully but generally treat him like a friend. Only a friend. She didn't give him wistful looks like he did her.

So, he was in love with her, but she didn't feel the same way. To Millie, this was ironic but not very helpful to know. The biggest problem was that they were both her friends. She may have been in love with Noah, but she loved Alice, too. She couldn't just spread an awful rumor about Alice to make Noah reconsider his feelings for her. She just couldn't do that to her. There was no way to push them apart. Also, ruining their perfect but not-so-perfect trio seemed like sacrilege. It was an impossible situation.

Millie lived in this weird limbo for the next five years. She tried to date other boys, but nothing lasted more than a few weeks. She loved Noah, and no matter how she tried, she just couldn't stop. It would have helped if he wasn't so damn nice to her. But he was. And he just kept getting hotter and hotter. Alice and Noah didn't date anyone in high school. It baffled Millie. She could understand Noah, but why wouldn't Alice date? They talked about boys quite a lot. She seemed to like boys. When they were seventeen, Millie had asked her straight-up, "Girl, are you a lesbian or something?" Alice laughed until she fell on the floor. She wiped tears from her eyes as she gasped for air. Then, she tried to grab Millie's face to give her a kiss. They wrestled, rolling to and fro, a tangle of long legs and tumbling hair. "Come here! Be my lesbian lover!" Alice had grunted, trying to get a handful of Millie's boobs. When they finally tired, they lay next to each other on Alice's bedroom floor. "Don't worry, I like penis," Alice said and rolled her head toward Millie's on the pink carpet. "I just don't want to tie myself down."

When they graduated high school, Alice and Millie went out for milkshakes, leaving Noah behind, and Alice told Millie she was leaving for Houston. "I got a scholarship!" she said, grinning ear to ear as she clasped Millie's hand on the tabletop of Mike's Ice.

Her friend had, yet again, surprised her. She was leaving. It was totally unexpected. She was always planning on leaving. That's why she didn't date anyone. A sad and slightly bewildering thought occurred to Millie. Not then and there in the milkshake place, but a day later. She was brushing her hair in the one-bathroom apartment her family lived in and thinking about Alice leaving. *That's why she didn't date*, she thought again and admired the immense self-control that must have taken. Her hand suddenly stopped mid-brush, and she looked at her reflection. To her own eyes, her face looked too long, maybe a little asymmetrical, too. Alice was so pretty with her freckles and gold hair. She could have anyone she wanted. Did Alice actually love Noah? Like, *love* love? Like, *in* love? And she just wouldn't date him because she wanted to leave to attend college somewhere else? She didn't want him to tie her down? Was it even possible to be in love with someone and be so close to them day after day, to know—for she must have known that he felt the same—and not do anything about it? She put the brush down and just stared at it, unseeing. She thought back on her friend's interactions yet again. Alice squeezing Noah's arm. Them hugging for just the appropriate amount of time for friends. There was love there for sure. And restraint? Maybe . . . Maybe not.

She put both palms on the vanity and leaned in until her face was just inches from the mirror. She looked into her almond-shaped dark chocolate eyes, her thick black lashes, her full lips. She was pretty if you looked close enough. Alice was leaving. And Noah would need her. Millie would be there for him. And with time, who knows? The memories of Alice would fade. Noah would move on, and Millie would be right there.

They spent most of their time together, the three of them. They went roller skating and to the movies. They hung out after hours at the old playground in their neighborhood, laughing and teasing each other, each of them careful not to mention the fact that Alice was leaving. But the day of her departure came along seemingly in the blink of an eye.

After both Noah and Millie hugged Alice, she got into her parents' car and waved to them tearily. The car pulled away from the curb, blowing black smoke at them. And then, she was gone. Both of them felt the hole inside them left by their friend, and they stood close together for support. Millie looked up at Noah. His face was hard as stone, his lips a thin line, his eyes still staring at where the car had just disappeared around the bend in the street. Millie reached out and took his hand.

"Come on. Let's go get some fries!" she said gently. "I could use some comfort food."

Noah didn't say anything. He just let her lead him away, unresisting, like someone walking through a dream.

CHAPTER SEVEN

1996
ALICE

They had finally pulled up in front of their house in the early morning on Sunday. They were supposed to stay at her parents' home until Monday, but with everything that had happened, they decided it would be best if they came home early.

It wasn't meningitis. The doctor at the emergency room had assured them for the third time, looking extremely annoyed with Alice for questioning him. It looked like Rosie had contracted some kind of bug. She was a bit low on iron. That, along with the high fever she had, could account for her fainting and tiredness. The hospital had sent them home with some fever reducers and antibiotics. Alice did notice that for the past few days, Rosie seemed kind of out of it. She thought she might have overdone it with the horse riding. She was probably sore. And she often stayed up late reading some book or another, so she hadn't been worried. Rosie was a teenager. She was bound to get moody from time to time. She couldn't stay her perfect child forever. In reality, she had already been coming down with something.

Alice felt like a bad mother. A failure. She should have pressed Rosie to tell what was wrong. Instead, when she saw the dark circles under her eyes, she just asked, "Are you all right, my little rose bush?" And Rosie had answered, "Yeah, Mom, just a little tired." And that was that. She needed to pay more attention. She was way too focused on her fitness career. That was her father coming out in her. She had to dial it back a bit. She would cancel some of her afternoon classes. That way, she would have more time with the kids, and she herself would be more rested, more attentive. She settled the kids on the couch in front of the TV and went back outside to help Noah with the bags. He was just coming in from the car, a suitcase in each hand. He gave her a kiss on the lips as they passed each other in the doorway. She smiled at him and squeezed his arm gratefully. Noah was a great father and an amazing husband. He was always there for them, knowing what to say, acting quickly in a crisis. She couldn't imagine her life without him. It's hard to imagine she almost missed out on being with him altogether.

There was maybe one more bag in the car. She went to get it. Bending precariously, she excavated the bag from the deepest depths of the trunk. When she stood up, to her surprise, she saw Millie walking down the footpath toward their house. She had emerged from the woods graceful and proud, like a deer. Then, when she saw Alice, she also looked quite like a deer in headlights. Her eyes widened, and her step faltered—only for a second, though. She quickly composed herself and quickened her pace to reach Alice.

"Back so soon?" Millie said, smiling at Alice.

"Yeah, we had a little incident at the lake. Or I'm not sure what you would call it."
There was a beat of silence where Alice was searching for words to tactfully describe the happenings at her parents'.

"Rosie fainted," she said finally, lowering the heavy bag she was holding to the ground by her feet.

"Oh!" exclaimed Millie with a strange mixture of concern and intrigue.

"It's nothing serious!" said Alice, quickly flapping a hand in the air. "We went to the emergency room, but it turns out that she just contracted some kind of virus."

Millie let that sink in for a second. Alice watched the woman play multiple different answers in her mind before choosing one to put on the table. She was usually great at reading faces. And her friend and neighbor had a very expressive one.

"There must be something going around," she said. "Mina isn't feeling quite herself, either. That's why I'm here instead of her. Maybe I should take her to the doctor's."

Alice looked at her blankly for a moment. Why would Mina be here? It did occur to her for a second that it was odd that Millie just showed up. She seemed to pick up on her confusion and added with a sympathetic smile,

"Rosie asked her to feed the animals."

"That's right! That's right!" Alice looked over at her house and back again. "That's absolutely right. I'm sorry! I am a bit spacey. It's just . . . What happened . . . I guess what I'm trying to say is that it was scary," she finished lamely.

She felt tired to the bone. Millie removed one of her delicate little hands from her shorts pocket, wiped it on the denim, and reached out to touch Alice's arm.

"Well, I should get going. I hope your daughter feels better!" Millie said and gave Alice a smile.

As she walked away, Alice pondered the somewhat strange interaction they just had. Millie's expression was somehow odd. The smile she gave her didn't seem to reach her eyes. They appeared cold, darker than usual. And there was something strange about what she said. She had put extra emphasis on the word "your" in her last sentence. *Your daughter.* Was it only her imagination? It may very well have been. She was about five minutes from falling over. She didn't get any sleep the night before. She would give Rosie her medication and then take a short nap, she decided.

"Mom, where is the journal?"

"What, my love?"

Rosie was lying on the couch under their fluffy maroon blanket, her upper body propped up on one elbow.

"Rosanne Glessner's journal. I want to read some of it."

She looked pale and weak, her skin developing that almost translucent look you sometimes get after a high fever washes you all out.

"Are you sure you want to read? Aren't you tired?" Alice leaned over her and placed a hand to her forehead. Her fever was gone. "Maybe you should try taking a nap."

"I don't feel like sleeping," she said, looking up at her with her beautiful, angelic face.

Alice walked over to the bookshelf next to the TV and, after a minute of searching, located the old, well-worn copy of their family's history. It had been a while since she read it herself, and she didn't quite remember the details. Maybe she should get into it. Or maybe they could read it together. She let this thought linger for a couple of seconds and then remembered how bone-achingly tired she was. It was one thing if Rosie didn't want to sleep, but Alice's bed was calling her name. Rosie would fall asleep eventually, Alice thought. The journal wasn't that interesting.

She handed Rosie the book, and her sweet, lanky teenage daughter smiled up at her gratefully. Alice's heart squeezed. She loved Rosie so much, so completely. She loved Emi, too. She loved her entire family with all her heart. But Rosie was her first baby. She was the one who had transformed her into a mother, into an adult, into the new and very much improved person that she was today. She not only loved her; she was grateful to her.

"Thanks, Mom! You're the best," said Rosie.

"No, you are," Alice replied. And then, she finally heeded the call of her bed.

CHAPTER EIGHT

1996
ROSIE

She had read some of the journal before. Years ago. It hadn't been very interesting to her at the time, and it was full of words she couldn't yet comprehend. Fancy, old-school words. Ever since she had gone to the homestead that last time, she had this strange desire to read it again. She wanted to understand Rosanne, to get into her mind. Part of her suspected that the old woman she saw there next to the fireplace was her. Her ghost, that is. Maybe she had reached out to her specifically because she had unfinished business that only Rosie could help her with . . . She settled deeper into the cushy couch and leaned her head back against the armrest. She felt much better than she did earlier. The medicines must be doing their job. She turned the book over in her hands. The front read *Journal of Rosanne Glessner,* and underneath, *A Rise from the Ashes.* On the back was a summary and the brief story of how and where the journal had been found. They would be covering the journal in her history class this year, so she might as well get a head start on it. She opened it and thumbed through the pages, looking for her bookmark from ages ago.

She vaguely remembered what she read before. Rosanne

came from some noble family. Her mother died when she was a small child, so she was raised by an army of nannies. Instead of marrying for wealth like her father wanted, she married for love. Rosie could understand that. She herself wouldn't want to marry some old fart, no matter how much money he had. She would much rather live in poverty with a handsome and loving husband. She thought briefly of Luke and his serious hazel eyes behind his glasses. She felt a blush coming on, so she stuck her nose in between the pages, hoping her sister wouldn't notice. *Enough of that. Concentrate on other people's problems!* she ordered herself vigorously. So, Rosanne had married some guy named Eric Glessner. He had promised her that he would come up in life, and they would end up rich, and blah, blah, blah. In reality, he was just some good-looking, poor asshole with a bunch of empty promises. They had a baby. A girl. Heidi. And he knocked her up again, and that time, she was so done because they lived in a shack, and all they had to eat was moldy bread. She threatened to leave him. Then, he came up with the great idea of going to America so they could get some free land to slave away at. And then . . . There it was. Her bookmark. A gray, polka-dotted guinea fowl feather.

August 18, 1742

My grandmother would roll in her grave if she knew I had come to England. She had always hated the English. God rest her soul. When I saw the ship today, I was somewhat reassured that the voyage wouldn't be as horrific as people describe. It is truly massive. I wouldn't have thought something this big could actually float. The beast is called the Susanne-Darling. Apparently, it's customary to name ships after women. It's good luck, they say. I hope it is. I've never been at sea. I was terrified this morning but also excited, as was Heidi, and the baby in my belly seemed to be, too. It was kicking away like a storm. Eric told me we would have our own cabin. Ha! What a joke. When it was time to board, they herded us into the belly of the ship like we were cattle. All eighty-nine of us passengers were going to be traveling in one cabin, and a not very big one at that.

There are people from all over the continent in here. I have heard more new languages than ever before in my life. There are Russians, and Polish, and a few more I didn't recognize. We are all on top of each other. At one point, I had almost fallen on my great big belly. A woman with a kind face caught me. She spoke to me in heavily accented German. Eric was nowhere near me when this happened. He would let me get trampled, the pig.

They will close the upper doors soon, I'm told. And then, we will be left in the pitch-black. I write this in the last few minutes of light we have. Heidi is scared. She's been crying as other people shove and step on us. I'm scared, too. But I cannot cry yet. I'll do it when she is asleep.

CHAPTER NINE

1996
LUKE

Luke Szabo was a peculiar boy. He always had been, ever since he was born. From a young age, he seemed to hear and see things that other people didn't. When he was a baby, he would often stare at the thin air so intently, like a cat looking at an almost invisible insect on the wall. When he got a bit older, he would babble to a corner of the room or out the window, having full-fledged baby conversations. It always looked like he was looking at or talking to a person, someone in particular. The only thing was, there was never anyone actually there. His mother, Margaret, was into the spiritual and supernatural, so ever since the beginning, she embraced Luke's different behavior. When he was finally able to actually tell his parents about what he was seeing, his mother acted like it was completely normal. If Luke were to say, "Oh, look, Mommy! There's the little girl again!", his mother would smile and wave at the air emphatically. His father, on the other hand, did his very best to ignore this peculiarity altogether. It wasn't until Luke tried to involve other children in his "delusion," as his father would call it, that his mother was forced to have a talk with him about the matter.

He had called a little girl over to a bush by the playground near their house and told her to look at the black cloud underneath it. The other child didn't understand what she was supposed to be looking at, soon got tired of it, and tried to walk away. Four-year-old Luke would not be put off so easily. He grabbed her arm and yelled at her, "Look! Just look at it! It has hands, too! Can't you see?" At this, the little girl ran screaming to her parents, the pigtails virtually scared straight off her little blonde head. As she wailed, curled against her mother's leg, her parents had strong words with Luke's mother. "Why would your son say that? We just got her to sleep in her own bed! Now, she is going to have nightmares!" cried her mother. She picked her up and held the little girl to her chest as if she were an infant. She was probably around six or so. Luke's mother had tried to defuse the situation by explaining that Luke was just "a little different, is all," he could "sometimes see spirits," and the father of the little girl roared, "If your boy is a fucking lunatic, just keep him at home!"

So, when they were driving home, they had the talk. His mom spoke while staring straight ahead, teardrops hovering on her blonde lashes. "Sweetie," she had said, "it's best not to tell anyone else about the things only you can see. You can still tell Mommy! You can always tell Mommy anything. But some things might scare other kids because they've never seen them before. Okay? "Luke looked up, bewildered, at his mom's profile from behind his thick glasses. It was quite obvious that he had done something terribly wrong. It was okay with him. These new rules were completely fine with him. The problem was that he couldn't quite tell which were the things that only he could see and which were the things that everyone could see. In consequence, slowly but surely, he cut himself off from other people. He talked as little as possible to anyone, be it spirit or human. His mother had always blamed herself for this obvious change in his behavior. His dad also blamed her. They were arguing the day of the boat accident. Six-year-old Luke had made a blunder. Sitting in his grandparents' kitchen, he all of a sudden cracked a huge smile and cheerfully exclaimed, "Look, Nana! Your mom is here!"

Nana dropped the irreplaceable Szabo family china plates she had been holding. They had been passed down in their family for the past God knows how many generations. The first of their kin to immigrate to America had brought them with her from Hungary. Now, their hand-painted shards lay at Nana's slippered feet.

Luke had forgotten that his great grandmother Eszter had been dead for two years now. The apparition that materialized in the kitchen next to his Nana and gazed at her with such abundant love looked just like Great Grandma when she was alive. At that moment, Luke had forgotten all about the funeral and all the crying. All he could think about was how good it was to see Great Grandma again and how happy Nana would be once he told her she was here.

"And there goes the fucking china!" screamed his dad.

Luke curled into a little ball on top of the chair he was sitting on. He had done it again. He felt hurt and ashamed at the same time. It wasn't his fault that he was like this. He couldn't stop being like this. And one day, his parents would stop loving him because of it. But that day would never come. Because this day was the last day they were alive.

His father stormed out to the dock, followed by his pleading mother. They got on the boat together, still talking furiously. They often did this when they fought. They would go off somewhere together, then come back once they had made up. Luke's grandfather told all the neighbors that it was the other boat's fault. The person on it had been on holiday. He wasn't a local. He didn't know the lake. But it wasn't that man's fault. His father had been in a rage and wasn't watching where he was driving.

After their deaths, his mother would come to him a few times. Usually, when he was already in bed, she would just walk into the room and look at him with a tender smile and love in her eyes. She never spoke, but then again, spirits rarely did. That same awful, awful year was when he had met Rosie.

His grandparents were watching TV, and Luke was playing

with his LEGOs on the living room carpet. The reporter was just saying how they finally located the body of the missing young man back in Luke's hometown. They had been looking for him for over two and a half years and had finally uncovered his body from under a bush next to a well-used playground. Apparently, somebody's dog had dug up a shinbone. They were interviewing the owner of the dog when they suddenly heard this awful scream that did not sound human at all. The three of them had rushed out to the yard, and on the far side, they saw their neighbors trying to wrangle a young deer that had gotten itself tangled on the fence.

There was this little girl, with her messy blonde hair sticking out in all directions, grabbing onto the deer's front hooves and whispering soothing things into its velvety ears. Her mother finally got it loose, and it took off running as soon as its feet touched the ground. The girl had looked straight at Luke with a huge jack-o-lantern smile and exclaimed with all the excitement of one who just performed a miracle, "Did you see that?"

To Luke, she was shining, like a little gap-toothed angel. Rosie treated him like her best friend from day one. She didn't care that he was shy and afraid to do most things or that he didn't talk much. She had forced her friendship on him in the loveliest manner possible. Soon, Luke started to open up to not just her but to everybody around him. He had made some new friends at school, too, to his grandparents' delight. But without fail, he would anxiously await Rosie's return to the lake. She was his rising sun.

He couldn't quite remember when he started noticing it. At first, he thought it was something stuck to his glasses. A speck of dirt or something. But when he cleaned them and put them back on, it was still there. A little black spot hovering just above Rosie's left shoulder. It followed her everywhere she went. Always tiny, always in the same spot.

Spirits came in all shapes and sizes. It was actually really rare to see a full-body spirit, and even more so to have them interact with you at all. Normally, they didn't really see you. They just went about their business like they were still alive, just to dissolve into nothing from one moment to the other. More often, though, spirits were something shapeless, like a puff of white or black smoke or a speck of light. If he could get close enough to make contact, sometimes, he would get a vision of the person they used to be. But not all the time. There seem to be no clear rules on the manifestations altogether. They were real to him, though—very much so.

Over time, he came to recognize the little black speck as just a part of Rosie. He accepted it like he accepted the color of her eyes. Only thing was that recently, it had seemed to have grown in size.

In the beginning of the summer in 1996, Luke visited Rosie's family up near Whitesboro. He had done this before a few times. He loved going to Rosie's house. It felt like a real home with real parents. Not that his grandparents weren't doing an excellent job in raising him; they were. They loved and understood Luke just like his mother had. But when he went to Rosie's house, he felt like he was a part of something bigger. Their fun banter cushioned him and made him feel at ease.

He went this time because he hadn't seen Rosie in about five months. It had been way too long. When he arrived, though, he was surprised to see that she had changed. She seemed to have gone through an evolution of sorts. She was thinner, her hips wider, and her chest . . . It had boobs on it. He caught himself staring at them for a little too long one time. That wasn't the worst part, though. Rosie had caught him, too. She had crossed her arms in front of her budding chest and looked at him with marked disapproval, which made him go the color of a ripe tomato. She didn't hold a grudge. That wasn't like her. Within minutes, she laughed it off, put an arm around his shoulders, and told him that they were going to do something fun that night.

They rode out in the late afternoon. Luke was a terrible horseman, but that didn't stop him from going on this mystery mission with his best friend. He slipped and slid all over the saddle, sitting on his testicles multiple times and pinching them painfully. When Rosie wasn't looking, he reached into his pants and adjusted his boys so they were sitting more comfortably. When she looked back at him, he straightened up and tried to look confident and dignified.

They got to the homestead just as the sun was setting. It threw a beautiful orange light at the ruins. The sight almost took Luke's breath away. He turned in his saddle precariously to look at Rosie, and his heart almost stopped. She sat there, her eyes closed, the evening breeze lifting her hair gently, the light of the setting sun shining gold through the strands. Perching atop her champagne-colored horse, she appeared to be absorbing nature itself. She was truly heartbreakingly beautiful at that moment. Had she always been like that? How did Luke not notice? She looked like she belonged here. Like she was one with the land.

He got goosebumps just looking at her. Was this love? he wondered with awe.

She breathed in deep and opened her eyes.

"Come on!" she had said, already turning her horse. "We're going to the cliff."

She helped him tie his horse to a tree. As she did, her hand brushed against his. They looked at each other for a heartbeat. Her blue eyes reflected in his hazel. She brushed a strand of her hair behind her ear self-consciously as her eyes shifted away. They walked out onto the edge of the cliff where the trees opened up and it overlooked the valley below. They had sat down in the lush green grass and eventually lay back to enjoy all the many hundreds of thousands of stars the Texas sky had to offer.

"So, what have you been doing?" Luke had asked when the silence had become unbearable.

Rosie had shrugged. He couldn't actually see her doing it, but he could feel her shoulders move against his.

"Just a whole bunch of horse stuff, I guess," she said meditatively. "I think Sand is going to have a baby. We bred her to this beautiful buckskin stallion a few months ago."

Sand was her horse, of course. The girl lived and breathed horses. At this very moment, Luke had wished fervently that he was a better horseman. Maybe he could ask his grandparents to enroll him in some lessons back home. He wanted to impress her.

"I wish my grandparents owned some horses," he said out loud. The thought actually had never occurred to him before.

"Oh, that would be so awesome! We could go riding around the lake. Maybe we could even make them swim! The riverbed is way too muddy over here to do that."

Her instant enthusiasm warmed his heart. It was so easy to make her happy. All you needed was horses. If only everything was this easy. One magic word, and all worries are gone.

"If I was a better rider, it would be more fun for you," he said wistfully.

"Ah, you are plenty fun," Rosie answered in a nonchalant tone.

She sat up and arched her back, gazing upward. She looked like a cat basking in the moonlight.

"You are also smart and funny," she added without looking at him. "Not everyone has to be good at everything. That just wouldn't be fair."

She always knew how to make him feel better. She always

. . .

He sat up quickly and pointed upward.

"Look, a shooting star!"

The white arc of it whizzed across the sky, leaving all the other stars twinkling in its wake.

"Make a wish!" she said, looking up where the shooting star had just been.

Luke looked at her curiously. She was acting just a bit odd. She normally always looked him straight in the eyes, laughing and teasing. What was up with her?

"Nah, this one is yours." He did his best to match her not-a-care-in-the-world attitude.

There was a beat of silence that was almost too long. She then finally turned her head to look at him, her eyes dark holes in the starlight.

"I wish you were just a bit braver."

Luke's heart skipped a beat. Whatever did she mean by that? He almost couldn't take a breath. Something was definitely up with her. It wasn't just what she had said but how she said it. She sounded almost like she was nervous. But that couldn't be. Rosie? She was never nervous about anything. She jumped right into things without thinking. Now, she was looking at him expectantly, her eyebrows arched. Luke's mouth opened slightly. He was breathing through it. He snapped it shut self-consciously and swallowed, his Adam's apple bobbing. Rosie was chewing on her bottom lip. Looking at her, Luke had this idea. But it seemed so absurd, he almost couldn't believe he was considering it. He thought she might want him to kiss her. His heart rate picked up at the thought. Him kissing Rosie? It was totally unfathomable. And yet, in this very moment, it seemed almost inevitable. He leaned toward her almost imperceptibly, and she matched him, leaning close. Was this really happening? Surely, at any moment, Luke would faint and head butt poor Rosie and probably break her nose. But no. Their faces just kept getting closer and closer until he could feel her breath on his cheek. Their lips touched lightly, and there was a spark of electricity between them. They both leaned back, startled. Rosie touched her lips and giggled softly. Luke couldn't believe this actually happened. He couldn't believe it. He had kissed Rosie. The world had shifted. He could actually feel the movement of it. Things realigning, adjusting. He realized he was smiling ear to ear. He wanted to try it again. He looked at his Rosie. His beautiful, wonderful . . . There was a pair of eyes staring at him from next to her head. He was so startled that all the air had gone out of him. There was a woman squatting right behind Rosie—only it wasn't an actual woman. The edges of her body seem to swirl and shift, like sand falling in water. It was an apparition. Her big, round eyes were fixed on him. She had intelligent brown eyes and light brown hair fixed in a bun at the nape of her neck. As far as he could tell, she was in her thirties. She died relatively young. She had lifted a hand and placed one thin finger in front of her lips in a shushing gesture. Luke went pale. She saw him. She was actually communicating with him. He could feel his body leaning away from her and away from Rosie. Just because he could see ghosts didn't mean he liked them. All the hairs on his body were standing on end. He could see Rosie lift a hand from his peripheral vision. He could hear her say something. He couldn't move. He couldn't speak. He couldn't even strain his ears to make out Rosie's words. The woman had him like a fish on a hook. He couldn't get away.

She stood, and Luke saw she was wearing a long dress. It almost looked like she had just stepped out of an old Western movie. She looked down at Rosie and smiled. Reaching out, she caressed her hair, although Rosie obviously couldn't feel it. Then, she spoke, and Luke's world shifted yet again. "My dear Rosie," she had said in her echoey spirit voice. She looked once more at Luke, and he could see her mouth moving, but this time, no sound came. Then, she was gone, swept away by the light breeze of the river below the cliff.

Time had started again, and all the noises of the real world returned. Rosie had a hand on his arm and was shaking him violently. He had leaned so far back, he was almost lying on the ground.

"Luke! What's wrong? Answer me!" She was screaming at him, her eyes wild.

He couldn't tell her what really happened. That was completely out of the question. She would think he was nuts.

"Sorry," he said, his voice sounding raw. He cleared his throat. "I have asthma, and sometimes, I can't breathe."

"Asthma?" Rosie asked. Luke saw the disbelief on her face. "Since when?"

"Recently. Very recently."

It was a lame excuse, and he could tell she wasn't buying it. She said no more about it, though. They got back on the horses and rode back home, the forest as silent and cool around them as an empty church. The rest of his visit was awkward, to say the least. Rosie did her level best to avoid him. So, he spent most of his time playing with Emi. It was totally miserable. All Luke could think of the entire time was that he had messed up his first kiss. And not just any first kiss. Rosie would never want to kiss him again, and it was all that damn ghost lady's fault. Every time he thought of how he spazzed out, his face went a bright shade of red. He could almost feel smoke coming from his ears. It would have been better if he'd had a stroke and died. It was a relief when his visit was finally over.

He had hoped that by the end of the summer, Rosie would forget how terribly he messed up and give him another chance. No such luck, though. When she and her family finally made it down to the lake, she was very noticeably gloomy and would not talk to Luke at all. She even avoided eye contact with him. His life was officially over. He could literally die, and it would be okay. He even thought about walking solemnly out into the woods and digging himself a grave to lie in. He could also sob dramatically while he did it. He would starve in a week or so, he guessed. Then, some friendly crows could peck his eyes out, and the local coyotes would scatter his bones. It sounded like a much better prospect than being rejected by Rosie day after day. And he would be giving back to the wilderness. Win-win, right?

He looked at the shiny blue eyes of the fish he and Emi just caught. They were just the same color as Rosie's. He was about to cry. It must have shown on his face because Emi was looking at him questioningly.

"Why are you sad?" she inquired in that blunt, little-girl way of hers.

Luke sighed dramatically and felt his body shrink and shrivel like a raisin. He really didn't want to talk about it. Instead, he pushed his glasses up the bridge of his nose and started working on freeing the unfortunate fish from the hook.

"Are you and Rosie fighting?"

"Damn it, Emi!" He was starting to get cross with her. "We are not fighting, and I'm not sad. Now, we have to let this fish go before it dies."

With his luck, the ghost of it would haunt him for the rest of his days. The hook was really in there. He twisted it this way and that, but it didn't want to come out. The fish wasn't helping, either. It was insistently flapping its slippery little body and poking his fingers with its barbed fins.

"Your face says otherwise," Emi said.

"What?"

"Your face says you are sad," Emi said solemnly.

"Well," he grunted as the hook finally came loose, "my face is lying."

He tossed the fish into the lake with some relief. He was so done talking to a five-year-old about his feelings. He was just about to come up with an excuse to get away when Emi let out a dramatic sigh.

"You are sad; Rosie is sad. I wish you guys would just stop."

"Rosie is sad?" Luke interrupted her pandering, his worry for his friend flaring.

"Yeah. She has been really sad," she said solemnly. "All she does is sleep. I asked Mom, and she says it's . . ." She paused to think. "Adesense."

"Adolescence?"

"Yeah, that's it. Mom says she'll get over it. I wish she would hurry."

Rosie was sad? She wasn't mad at him, but sad? That was a new and slightly less distressing concept. That meant that maybe, just maybe, if he apologized and told her that he really, really liked her, she could feel better. And they could move on from this. And maybe they could kiss again. The thought of it quickened his heart and prickled his skin. He could fix this. He was just about to send Emi on some made-up errand when she popped up and took off toward where her dad and grandfather were talking. Luke stood up, too. He wiped his fishy hands on his shorts. Maybe he should go wash them. No! No time. He had to go talk to her before he lost his nerve.

She was sitting on the swing bench with her knees tucked under her chin. She looked like a little bird. A sad little bird. She did look profoundly sad. Oh, dear God! Did he cause this? He quickened his pace. Was she wearing a scarf? In this heat? He stopped. Not because he wanted to, but because his feet would not move. They grew roots and anchored him heavily to the ground. Rosie had something hovering around her shoulders. It was like a dark, angry little cloud, shaped like a boa. It resembled some of the apparitions he'd seen before. Where on earth did that come from? Was it? Could it be? His feet came unstuck, and he sprinted to her. He sat down next to her, hoping to be able to examine the thing. Was that the black speck? That couldn't be. It was so big. But it had to be. The speck was gone, and here was this . . . thing. It moved, puffing out here and there. It looked malicious. A horrifying thing occurred to him. Was this what was making her sad and not the kiss? Sometimes, spirits were able to move objects or change the temperature around them. He'd experienced things like that firsthand. Was it possible that this one changed Rosie's emotions? This was disconcerting on so many levels, many of which he didn't even want to think about.

They talked for a couple of minutes, but Rosie didn't seem like herself at all. She looked tired and annoyed with virtually everything. The skin on the back of her neck was a strange ashy color, as if the thing was draining her color. If only he could just get rid of it for her. Maybe that would help her mood, at least. When he tried to put a hand on her shoulder, the little cloud zapped him. He saw what appeared to be a tiny strike of lightning come out of it. It was as painful as a wasp sting. He pulled his hand back, but it was too late. His fingers were turning black. He cradled his throbbing hand in his lap and tried not to cry. He'd never seen anything like this in his entire life. He'd come across many spirits, but none of them came even close to doing what this thing just did. If he was honest with himself, it had scared the shit out of him. He looked at his Rosie's lovely, familiar face and knew that whatever this thing was, it was the cause of her feeling the way she did. His sixth sense told him so. He had to figure out a way to banish it. But how? Holy water? He could try that.

As if the cloud had read his mind—and it was entirely possible that it actually did—it puffed up around Rosie's shoulders as if enraged. Small blue sparks flew from it before it changed shape, becoming skinny and eel-like. To Luke's amazement and horror, it constricted around Rosie's neck like a rope.

Eyes big as saucers, Luke reached for the thing, only to be stopped by an invisible barrier just an inch from it. His fingers slammed painfully into it and bent at odd angles. Not seeming to care about the blinding pain, he grabbed Rosie by the arms instead. Her body seemed to be vibrating, her skin hot to the touch like live coals. The skin on the palms of his hands screamed for him to let go. But he wouldn't. He had to help her. He had to save her. But despite all his efforts, Rosie's face drained of color. Her eyes rolled back, and her head tipped forward, followed by her upper body. Luke hung on to her for dear life, his hands practically sizzling. He wasn't enough. He was just a thirteen-year-old boy. He wasn't at all enough to fight whatever this was. He looked around wildly for help and had locked eyes with Rosie's mother, who was inside the house by the big kitchen window. Alice seemed to immediately understand that there was trouble. As soon as she came out of the house, Luke could feel her fear for Rosie. Her energy hit him like a wave, sweeping across the lawn and washing over him. It was the single most powerful experience of his young life, as if by searching for help, he was able to tap into Alice's life power. The wave traveled into Rosie through his arms and hands, and the thing loosened around her neck. Alice called for her husband, and when he ran over, his wave of energy put out the little cloud altogether. It had reverted to its original state, maybe even a bit smaller than it had been. It hovered placidly around Rosie's shoulders once again as she lay on the grass, breathing evenly.

They had taken her to the hospital, of course. As Noah picked up her unconscious body, Luke slowly sat back down on the bench and stared down at his hands in his lap. His skin wasn't burnt at all like he thought it'd be. He expected to see no skin at all with how hot Rosie felt. He thought his hands would come away from her arms looking like blackened, charred claws. They, in fact, looked almost completely normal. The tips of his fingers were still a bit gray, but his normal color was coming back by the minute. He watched as his fingers slowly returned to a rosy pink. One of his fourth fingers was crooked. It was either broken or dislocated. It would probably need to be looked at later. He couldn't even think about that right now, though, for in just a few minutes, a brand-new world had opened up in front of him. A world where entities could not only interact with the living but harm them. A world where he, skinny little Luke, could actually do something about it. Because he did! He harvested Alice's energy. He felt it, as if in his desperation, he had opened some kind of door. Not all the way, though. Only a crack. Right now, sitting here, feeling mentally and emotionally exhausted with his injured hand in his lap, he was equal parts intrigued and terrified of what would happen if he were able to open the door all the way.

PART 2

CHAPTER TEN

1998
JAMES

He walked, bleary-eyed, into the police station at around 6:30 a.m. and headed straight to the staff room, where the coffee machine resided. He needed caffeine. Loads of it. He had fallen into a dreamless sleep as soon as he got home in the early morning, but his partner phoned him about three hours later. He had to come in.

They had a break in the case. If it didn't involve his neighbors, he probably wouldn't have bothered. He would have told Jeffrey to shove it and gone back to sleep. But as it was, he was way too involved. So, he got out of bed, feeling like he was rising from the dead, all crusty-eyed with his back aching and joints cracking. He spent hours trudging through the unforgiving North Texas wilderness the day before, so the fact that his thirty-eight-year-old body was protesting wasn't surprising, only inconvenient. Millie had brought hot coffee to his bedside by the time he was pulling on socks. She had sprung out of bed the instant the phone rang and dashed into the kitchen to make a fresh pot. Was he this vigorous at thirty-four? he wondered. Perhaps. Millie had a sort of unhealthy interest in this case he knew. But as long as she managed to turn it into something constructive, like making fresh coffee, he didn't mind that much. Millie had her reasons for being the way she was. He'd always known that. But in spite of how her past influenced her decisions in the present, Millie was and always had been a loving and loyal wife to him. He respected her for that. And more importantly, he understood her.

He made his way to the interrogation rooms. Jeffrey had popped, weasel-like, from a hallway James was passing, almost making him spill his scorching mug of coffee. Droplets of it landed with expert precision on his tie and yellow shirt. A bad omen. This day was going to be shit even before it began. He took a tentative sip so the cup wouldn't be so full and burned his tongue. He could feel his blood pressure rising. He tried to shake off his aggravation and focus on the task at hand.

"Where is he?" he barked at Jeffrey.

The man looked hurt by his tone, his mouth curving down on his thin, weaselly face. For God's sake, this wasn't Jeffrey's fault. The man was just doing his job.

"He is in number three, sir."

Jeffrey had been assigned to him for training five months ago. He was fresh out of the academy. James remembered those days. He himself had been so eager to make a difference in the world. He had thrown up copiously when he saw his first dead body. A young woman washed up in the Red River. Her discolored, bloated face was etched into James's mind. It was a reminder of why he became a cop. They did catch the bastard who did it. They made sure he would never kill again. He was put on this earth to stop scumbags like that man. He wished he could have stapled a permanent sign to his back that read *RAPIST*. There were plenty of men in the penitentiary who would give him a taste of his own medicine once they knew what he had done.

Jeffrey had yet to pop his cherry in the corpse department. James really hoped that this case wouldn't be the first time for him.

"Who found him?" he inquired, a tad more delicately this time.

Jeffrey visibly relaxed.

"Nobody, sir. That is, his wife did, I suppose."

James gave his young partner a flat look. They had been over this multiple times. Jeffrey tended to go in circles around the actual facts. James wished he could give him a good smack on the back of the head every time he did that. He'd learn a lot quicker. Jeffrey saw the intent and flinched.

"Sorry, sir!" He quickened his pace to keep up with James. "His wife says he just walked out of the forest by their house."

"What do you think?"

"Sir?"

"Do you believe her?"

Jeffrey considered the question very seriously.

"He looks like he spent the night out there. So, yes. Yes, sir, I believe her."

James nodded. He wiped coffee off his mustache with his bottom lip.

"Okay, then. Let's see what we are working with!"

Noah Smith was sitting alone in the third interrogation room. The reason for this was that number two had a dripping water leak, and number one was currently housing their local vagrant, Harry, who was sleeping off one of his legendary benders.

James went in with Jeffrey on his heels and sat down across from his neighbor. The man looked beat-up. He had an array of scrapes and bruises all over his exposed skin, as if he was just running through the underbrush without any attempt to miss the branches. He also had mud caked on the left side of his face and on the front of his coat and jeans.

"Looks like you took a tumble, Noah," James said.

He was going to start this off friendly and neutral. Noah had an empty coffee mug and a half-empty water bottle in front of him. He pushed the bottle aside a few inches meditatively with a fourth finger. It had a deep gash running across it, and the nail was missing. James saw Jeffrey shift uneasily from his peripheral vision. The kid wasn't the best around injuries involving blood.

"A few," Noah said, his voice no more than a whisper.

James leaned forward, putting his elbows on the table to take a closer look at him. More than a few of the cuts on him would need stitches. Should they treat him before the interrogation? The neighbor in him said yes, but the cop just shook his head solemnly. Noah may be his neighbor, and he may be hurt, but he was also their number-one suspect. Time was of the essence here.

"Listen, Noah. You look tired, so I'm just going to cut to the chase."

Noah looked at him with bloodshot eyes. There was something about his expression. Like he already knew what was coming. Like he knew the answer, too.

"Where are the girls?" James asked frostily.

He had abandoned his pretense of being nice and neighborly. The night had been cold, in the forties. If Mina had to spend the night out there, she would get hypothermia in just a few hours. The Smith girls were no different. They were out there feeling lost and freezing. His blood boiled at the thought. *If they weren't dead already*, said a tiny voice in his head.

"You should be out there looking for them," Noah retorted accusingly.

"We have officers, firefighters, and volunteers out there. They are combing through the woods as we speak. They will find them eventually, but it would be a lot faster if you would just . . ."

"If I would just what?" Noah snarled, showing his perfect white teeth. "I went out there to look for them! You know that! My wife told you! I told your partner!" He was shouting. His voice was like gravel, his words hitting James's face like rocks.

Jeffrey had flattened himself against the far wall. He was right to be a little afraid. Noah didn't seem like himself at all. He was like a detained wild animal. He wanted to get back out there. But whether that was to keep looking for his daughters or to cover his tracks was yet to be determined. Noah seemed to be very angry. He was quite possibly the angriest James had ever seen him since they'd known each other. James could see the fear underneath. If he was innocent in this, he would be afraid for his girls. From one parent to another, he could see and feel Noah's pain. As a cop, though, he could see something else through his experienced eyes. It was in the shift of Noah's eyes, the clench of his jaw. The way his foot kept tapping on the tile floor of the interrogation room. *Tap, tap, tap.* James's senses had been honed through the fifteen or so years he'd been working in this field. Noah was holding something back. He could feel it in his bones.

"Have you looked into that woman?"

James's mouth folded into a thin line. Alice had told the first responding unit that she had seen a woman in the woods behind their house the day before the girls had gone missing. By her description, it may have been an old homeless person who had wandered onto their property by accident. This sighting could have been real. Or it may just be her attempt to take the heat off her husband, giving the police another suspect to look at. James had some doubts about the sincerity of her statement.

"We only found four sets of footprints on your property, Noah. They all belong to your family."

"My wife said . . ."

"Your wife said the trespasser had been barefoot. There would have been no mistaking her prints for any of y'all's."

Noah looked pleadingly at him. All the anger seemed to drain from him, leaving him looking older than he really was.

"I didn't hurt my kids, James. They are out there somewhere. I want to help look for them. Please allow me to do that!"

He seemed sincere, but if the years of police work had taught James anything, it was that looks can be deceiving. Someone was lying. Whether it was the wife or the husband, he wasn't sure yet.

"I can't let you go. I'm sorry, Noah."

James stood up from the table and headed for the door.

"Check by the cliffs!" Noah yelled after him.

James's skin prickled. He had the sick feeling that Noah just revealed to him where he would find the bodies without actually saying so. He turned back halfway and gave his prime suspect a long, hard look.

"I didn't make it that far last night." Noah's voice broke. Was that guilt? There was only one way to find out.

CHAPTER ELEVEN

1996
MILLIE

Millie lay on her bed wide awake, James placidly snoring next to her. Not a care in the world. It was somewhere around 3 a.m. She could not sleep for the life of her. In fact, it was possible that she would never sleep again. She didn't return the key. She was going to put it right back into the photo album—just after she figured out what the little square piece of paper in the envelope was. She thought she had a couple more days to read the handwritten note again and bask in the glory of her findings. She thought she had a whole forty-eight hours to return that damn key to its hiding place. It turns out she thought wrong. The Smiths came home early, throwing her whole life into chaos. They really didn't need to come home after just one day. That Alice most likely sensed that Millie had been snooping around in her house. That floozy slob of a woman probably had a sixth sense for such things. It wouldn't surprise her one bit. Alice did look like a keen fox when she squinted her eyes just right. A fox can always smell a rat. Now, Millie had to wait for an excuse to be alone in their house again and hope Alice wouldn't look for the key in the meantime. It was a ratty thing she did, going through their things—and taking something from the house, too. Millie should have been ashamed of herself. She wasn't. She was full of a righteous urge to expose something bad about her neighbors, the people who were once her closest friends. The thought of Alice figuring out that she had taken the key and read the note did make her slightly nauseous. The thing was that she couldn't figure out if it was caused by fear or anticipation.

She thought of the note again. It was Alice's handwriting for sure. Millie had matched it to some of the other paperwork on her desk. She visualized it yet again like so many other times in the past few days. In her mind's eye, it floated in front of her face as she lay there in bed.

In case of my and my husband's deaths or a medical emergency, please contact the following person. He is my daughter, Rosanne Emily Smith's, biological father.

The name was Nathaniel Davis. He was born June 3, 1960. There was also a Houston address and a phone number.

Millie could feel her arms break out in goosebumps. Alice had a secret. And it was a big one. A life-changing one. Nathaniel Davis. Millie had never heard Alice mention the name, not even fleetingly, which meant she wanted it to stay a secret. She had most likely met him when she attended the University of Houston, and apparently, she had gotten pregnant from him. The timeline checked out. Now, there was only one very important question. Millie could feel her whole face break out in a deliciously wicked smile. Did Noah know about this? Or did he think the girl was his?

1981

Millie was definitely sad about Alice's departure. But she got over it in a week or so. She had focused all her attention on Noah. The problem was that he didn't seem to be getting any better. He had reverted to his gloomy past self. He even quit football and went to do roofing with his father. It wasn't like Alice had died, yet he seemed to mourn her like he did his mother. Millie tried to be understanding, but it was getting kind of old. She was ready to settle down and have her own family, and she wanted to do it with Noah. She already had the receptionist job at the police station. She was making her own money. She was almost twenty and all grown up. All the men around her seemed to notice. All except Noah. In fact, a couple of the younger police officers even asked her out. It had been two months since Alice had left, and she was starting to consider saying yes to one of them. This one called James Walker was handsome enough. Only a few years older than Millie. She had seen him eyeing her from under his thick brows. But he was no Noah.

Millie had to switch tactics, she decided. So far, she had only been there for Noah as a close friend. She needed to make sure he understood that she wanted more. If he knew, he would be able to look at her as a potential girlfriend. So, she planned it all out. She persuaded him to go with her to a drive-in theater. They had just started showing *Quest for Fire*. According to one of Millie's girlfriends, it had a lot of saucy scenes. Millie went bright crimson at the thought of watching something alone with Noah. She had told him it was an adventure movie involving cavepeople. He was sold on it. All men, big or small, love prehistory. Give them dinosaurs and saber-toothed anything, and they will light up like Christmas lights. This had been step one. Now for step two.

She spent hours getting ready under the watchful and knowing eyes of her mother. She had to make herself into an irresistible young woman. She wore red lipstick and one of her mother's more daring dresses. It showed off the tops of her breasts. Normally, she was a lot more conservative, so she kept tugging on it nervously, feeling like she might show nipple if she bent over.

After much begging, she was allowed to borrow her dad's car, and at 6:30 p.m. on a Friday, she drove off to pick up Noah from his house.

The movie was a lot more interesting than she expected, and she ended up glued to the screen. Then, all of a sudden, a caveman grabbed a cave woman, and they were doing it. Right there. In front of everyone. Millie seemed to liquefy. She scooted down in her seat and drank deeply and noisily through the straw of her soda. There were giggles and hoots from the other cars. She chanced a glance at Noah from under her lashes and saw, to her delight, that there was a red wave creeping up his neck. He had a hand in front of his mouth, as if he were contemplating the secrets of the universe. Millie smiled to herself, holding the straw between her teeth. Step three of her plan was done. She had gotten him to think about sex in her presence. The final step would be the hardest to achieve, though. She wanted him to kiss her by the end of the night. Did she have the nerve to suggest it if he didn't? She wasn't sure.

"That was a really interesting movie," Noah said as they walked down Main Street.

They had parked the car and gotten some ice cream at Millie's suggestion.

"It was different than I expected. It was very . . ." She trailed off and took a meditative lick from her strawberry cone. "Well, I didn't expect so much caveman sex."

She went just about as pink as her ice cream. It was a daring thing to say. But it was worth it. Noah laughed out loud.

"Yeah, there was definitely a lot of that." He smiled sort of shyly down at her. "It caught me a bit off guard."

There was a beat of silence. It was time for Millie to make her move. The mood was right. The time was right. She opened her mouth to say, "I think we should just call this a date and be done with it," when Noah spoke.

"I bet Alice would have liked it. She would have thought it was funny."

Millie shut her mouth quickly before she screamed. *Alice? Alice!* Things were going *so good*, and then he just *had* to bring up Alice. He also had that dumb, wistful, faraway look on his face. He was thinking about Alice. He was probably thinking about her the whole time they watched the movie, wishing he could do to her what those cave people were doing to each other for most of the movie. Millie had a bitter taste in her mouth. This was stupid. This was pointless.

"Are you okay?" Noah asked. "Your ice cream is melting. It's running down your hand."

She looked dazedly down at her ice cream. It was melting. It ran down the cone, then her hand, and finally dripped slowly from her wrist, leaving fun pink droplets on the sidewalk. She looked back up at him. He was examining her with a sort of brotherly amusement.

"Here!" he said and wiped her hand with his napkin. "If you weren't going to eat it, why did you ask for it?"

He was smiling. He was being nice, just teasing her in a friendly way. She had failed. She did everything she could and failed. She threw her cone in a nearby trash can.

"Millie? What's wrong?" He sounded confused.

Fuck it! Fuck all of it!

"I wanted to make today a date," she said flatly.

He looked taken aback, as if the thought of them going on a date had never before occurred to him.

"But Millie . . ." He searched for words, lifting his arms. Noticing that his ice cream was melting, he chucked it in the trash and stuck his hands in his pockets. "We are just friends, the three of us. You, me, and—"

"This is just about you and me, Noah! This has nothing to do with her!" Her anger flared with her desperation. She had raised her voice. She had never yelled at him before.

He stood there. Just stood, saying nothing. She squared her shoulders. She was going to finish this tonight. No more guessing. No more hoping. No more waiting. She was so sick of it all. She had waited long enough.

"I like you, Noah. I have liked you for a long time, more than just a friend. I was hoping you would see that, but you didn't, so . . . So, here it is."

She let her arms fall to her side. She looked into his eyes and tried to channel all her feelings, her hopes, and her dreams into her own. She wanted him to look at her and understand that she was his. All he had to do was take her. He swallowed, took a step toward her, then stopped. His face fell.

"Alice will come back," he said in what was almost a whisper.

Millie had lost. She held her tears back by lifting her chin. Well, if she was to lose, at least she would keep her dignity.

"If you're not going to date me," she said in a clear voice that sounded much more grown-up than her own, "you will lose me as a friend. I'm done waiting for you."

She turned and started walking to her dad's car. She wasn't even going to drive him home. He could walk; it wasn't that far. She looked back at him, her hand on the door handle.

"And Alice isn't coming back."

Her voice rang out on the almost empty street. Then, she got in and drove off, wanting to leave her love right there on the sidewalk with him and knowing she couldn't.

She looked as cold and as hard as steel when she left him there on the street. At least, she hoped she did. In reality, she was lukewarm and mushy. She cried that entire weekend, only leaving her room to eat and use the bathroom. Her mom sat with her for a time, attempting to tactfully pull information out of her and reassure her at the same time.

"Honey, it's okay. It's not the end of the world," she would say, patting her back as she lay face down on her bed. "You'll meet someone better. You'll see! He's just one boy. There are so many out there."

She was right. Millie knew she was. She was crying to purge herself of all the feelings she had for him. All the good memories. She would start as a whole new person on Monday. She would leave Noah behind and date someone new, starting preferably immediately. Maybe that cute, young cop with the wispy mustache, James. He looked like he was up for the challenge.

When she was feeling especially miserable, she would read *Gone with the Wind* to prove to herself that things could always get worse—much worse. It put things into perspective.

Monday came, and she was ready. She had walked into work

feeling especially lovely. She wore a pink scarf around her head to keep her unruly hair from encroaching on her face, and pink lipstick she had borrowed from Maa. "You can keep it," she had said with a cheeky smile. "Looks better on your pretty young face, anyway."

She smiled to herself. She loved her mother so much. She was her rock. When she reached her desk, she gasped. There was a beautiful bouquet of flowers waiting on it, all pinks and whites. They matched her outfit perfectly. She looked around and caught James's eye. He smiled at her like he always did. She smiled back and gave him a little wave. It had to be him who had gotten these for her. He was so thoughtful. There was a card in the flowers. She opened it and hoped that she would be able to blush prettily after she read it, not just turn a splotchy red.

Dear Millie,
Please give me another chance!
Noah

She dropped the card, the color draining from her cheeks.

CHAPTER TWELVE

1981
NOAH

He had been four when they bought the house on Mossy Oak Street. Allegedly, his mother and Alice's mother had been good friends at one time. That was before her drinking got out of hand. He didn't remember it. But he could see it in his mind's eye: the two women sitting on the side of the sandpit in the park at the end of the street. They would have been talking about their husbands, laughing, the late afternoon breeze lifting their hair and making the ancient swing set creak, their two small children playing placidly in the sand. They would have, of course, joked about Alice and Noah getting married one day. They got along so great. They were the same age. They were beautiful children who would become beautiful adults. It made sense. They would smile at each other and think to themselves, *One day, we will become in-laws and probably drive each other crazy.* None of them would have guessed that Noah's mother, Claire, would one day be unable to stop drinking. At that time, she still gazed upon the world with her hazel eyes and her freckled face with wonder. She had thought at the time that her husband's abuse would not get any worse than it was. The shouting and occasional shoving were a part of every marriage. That was how men showed dominance. That was how her father had been. Her mother never told anyone and forbade Claire and her sister to say anything, so they didn't. So, now that it was happening to Claire, it didn't even occur to her to confide in her friend. To cry for help.

Matthew Smith was an intimidating man with his big hands, a broad back, and booming voice. He seemed to have this all-encompassing discontent surrounding him no matter where he went or what he did. The truth about Matthew was that he was never truly happy. Everybody seemed to get ahead in life much faster than he did. His friends and neighbors always had newer model cars and better TVs. Their wives cooked better, had bigger breasts. He always seemed to make the wrong decisions—the decisions that would set him back, not bring him forward. Noah didn't see at the time how sad he actually was. He only saw the anger brought on by his sadness.

He remembered the first time it had happened—the day his father had hit his mother so bad, it left marks on her frail body. Noah was six. He and his mother were bent over a book. Noah had difficulties understanding what he was reading. Dyslexia, the grownups called it at school. So, his mother would practice with him every afternoon after school. Claire was making chicken and rice for dinner. She flipped the chicken breasts in the skillet, then went to sit next to him. There was a word he couldn't get past in the story.

"The rabbit was chased by the fox. A c-crafty carnivale . . . carvorie . . ." Noah's tongue twisted in a knot. Whoever came up with these words was truly mad.

"Let's see, darling!"

His mom stuck her head close to his. Her curls tickled his cheek.

"It's car-ni-vore. A crafty carnivore."

"Oh," said Noah, unimpressed.

"Go on!" ordered his mom, ruffling his hair.

He kept reading under her watchful eye. Suddenly, his nostrils flared, irritated by an unpleasant smell. Claire jumped up, knocking her chair over backward.

"The dang chicken!" she cried.

It was only bad luck that Noah's father chose just that moment to walk through the front door, a six-pack dangling from one hand. He smelled the burning food right away, and an eerie expression that looked almost like anticipation crept onto his face. He made his way to the kitchen table, where Noah was sitting with his book, his heavy work boots shaking the entire house with each step. Then, he saw the chair on the floor, and his face folded up like a fist. Noah's stomach clenched, as if preparing for impact. He scurried from his seat and into the living room, where he took cover behind his father's old leather recliner.

"You broke the fucking chair, Claire!" Noah heard his father shout.

He placed his hands over his ears, but he could still hear him.

"Our stuff means nothing to you, huh? My hard-earned money means nothing! Look at you! You burned the fucking chicken, too. I'm not eating that shit!"

In reality, the chair was already damaged when they bought it secondhand. A couple of the spindles were loose on the back. One of these had fallen out when the chair hit the floor. Noah would learn later on in life how incredibly easy it was to fix such things. To his father, this was unacceptable for some reason. He bellowed at his mother like a raging gorilla.

"I'm sorry, Matt! The chicken is just a bit charred. It'll still taste good. I'll fix the chair . . ."

"Fix it!? How are you going to fix it, you dumb cunt? You can't do anything right!"

"We have that wood glue in the . . ."

Noah heard a sickening thud, like a meat hammer hitting a piece of steak. The kitchen cabinets rattled. He heard his mother make a strange, almost gurgling sound. He instinctively knew this fight was worse than all the others that came before. He had to do something to help his mother. She sounded like she was hurt. Collecting all his courage, he peeked over the armrest of the recliner.

His mother was on the kitchen floor, cowering from his father on her hands and knees. He loomed over her, spewing obscenities.

"Why can't you be a normal, good wife? You make me do this. I'm sick of it!"

There was blood coming from Claire's mouth and nose. It dripped, thick and gooey, onto the white kitchen tiles. Her hand slipped in it as she tried to crawl away. She searched the home with desperate eyes like a doe that had just been shot, looking for her fawn just to see it one last time. Her face was turning an angry dark purple. She finally saw him and mouthed "Go!" at him with her swollen pink mouth. He did go then, even though he knew he should have stayed. He ran on all fours to the back door, where he crawled soundless through the dog door. They never actually had a dog. The house just came like that when they bought it.

Once outside, he ran over to Alice's house and tapped on her window. She was home, thank God. Noah would never know how lucky that had been. She opened her window and frowned when she saw his face. She had paint smeared all over her yellow shirt.

"What's the matter?"

"My d-dad, my mom . . ." he sobbed, unable to make a coherent sentence.

Looking alarmed, Alice climbed out of her first-floor window.

"My dad is in the backyard. Let's go get him!"

"No!" Noah screeched.

His dad would tell him over and over, once he was done raging, that he was not to tell anyone what was happening at their house. "They will take you away, and you'll never see me or your mother again." His dad wouldn't have been a great loss, but he couldn't imagine being separated from his mom. It was a terrible, horrible thought. Just telling Alice that something was wrong was a big no-no. A complete violation of the rules. But she was his best friend.

"They will take me away if anyone finds out."

Alice stared at him defiantly, her small chin creasing with

concentration.

"He's hurting her, isn't he?"

Noah nodded, looking scared.

"How did you know?"

"I hear him yelling a lot."

She looked toward his house, chewing her bottom lip. Suddenly, she took off toward his front door, her blonde pigtails flying. Noah gasped. He felt the blood drain from his face. He should have run after her, but his feet were rooted to the ground. Alice opened the screen door and rapped quickly on the door with one small fist. Then, she was running back, taking big jumping steps like a rabbit. They both ducked under the bushes by her window, and just a moment later, the fox emerged from its hole. They saw Noah's dad look angrily around from between the leaves. He mumbled something along the lines of "Fucking kids!" before he ultimately went back inside.

That night, after his bath, Noah watched her mother's reflection in the mirror as she brushed his hair. Her face was ugly and swollen, like a pumpkin that had been rejected from the patch. There were also dark marks on her neck.

Noah and Alice would never know that they had saved her life that day. Matthew had been so enraged, he was going to throw caution to the wind and finish her. He would figure out what to do from there. He was simply done playing house. He was in the process of choking Claire when Alice knocked on the door. It scared him. He may have not wanted to take care of his family anymore, but he definitely did not want to go to prison. Getting caught in the act wasn't an option for him. He'd rather die himself. So, he was more careful after this. He would still continue to hit his wife and also his son when he eventually tried to stand up to him. But only in places where the bruises could be covered by clothes.

In the end, Claire's demise was the thing she used to numb the pain of her marriage. In many ways, it was better this way. In many ways, it wasn't. Her addiction to alcohol took many years to grow and blossom. This allowed her to slip away slowly. She was less and less present in Noah's life, until one day, she was gone altogether. Only God knows how long she would have lived if she tried to leave Noah's father instead of turning to alcohol. Only God knows if she would have succeeded. The threats were there: "I'll kill you if you ever try to leave! I'll kill that damn kid you love so much, too!" Matthew would tell her these things periodically to keep her in line. They never had to find out if there was any merit behind all the threats, however. Claire never tried to leave.

Throughout his childhood, Noah had one constantly positive thing in his life. Alice was like a beam of sunshine that cut effortlessly through the gloom of his days. She and her family allowed him to be a boy, a carefree child, if only for the few hours he had to spend with them. He loved Alice ever since he could remember. There was no beginning or end to it. His love for her was an endlessly flowing river that he could always get a bucket of feel-good from. Alice was bossy and, at times, straight-up mean. They would mostly play what she wanted, which was almost always the husband-and-wife game. They had seven kids because that's how many dolls she had. All girls. One would think eight girls in one house would drive a boy mad, but Noah handled them like a man. To him, figuring out how they would transport all seven of their make-believe daughters to the playground was a lot more relaxing than being at home and waiting for his father to go apeshit. And no matter how difficult Alice could be, she always had Noah's back. Her courage surprised and, at times, terrified him.

His mother had baked him a chocolate cake for his eighth birthday. As usual, his father went into a state over it. He did this every time he and his mother did anything remotely nice. "The cake had cost too much" was his mantra for that day. After they cut and tasted it, the flavor wasn't as good as Matthew had expected. Therefore, it was a waste of his money. He had pushed Claire so hard she fell on the coffee table and broke it. She had had a few gulps of sherry at that point and didn't even attempt to catch herself. When Noah tried to help her up, he got a boot to the bum. He staggered and rubbed at his sore behind, letting despair and hatred fill his small body. What was even the point of having a birthday? Or a family? This was the worst day of the year. He was supposed to have fun, but it was never really allowed. His father yanked his mother up by one arm. She shoved at his gripping hand clumsily, groaning in pain. His father sneered at the both of them. He was just about to go into round two of the birthday abuse when a small voice rang out from the kitchen. All their heads turned in that direction at once. There in the kitchen stood Alice, wearing denim overalls, her hair hanging in two braids over her shoulder. *Shit*, said Noah inwardly. He had promised her he would come to her house for dinner. He turned his wide eyes to the clock above the TV. It was half-past 5 p.m. He had lost track of time. But why on earth did she come in? She knew. She knew what must be going on. She did look absolutely terrified.

"Good evening, Mr. and Mrs. Smith!" Alice said politely, her voice trembling only a little.

She walked over and took Noah by the arm. It seemed to him that all three of his family members forgot how to breathe, as if there was no air in the room. Matthew was still holding Claire's arm. They all just stared at little Alice, speechless, like she was some beautiful, yet deadly thing.

"He promised to come over for dinner."

And then, Alice started to walk him out, just like that. It seemed to go against nature for Noah to be able to escape this situation so easily. His father spoke out when they were almost to the door. They froze. Of course he couldn't just go. What was he thinking? What was Alice thinking?

"He's not going anywhere! Go on! Out! Off with ya, little brat!"

They almost made it out. Noah could feel his heart sink all the way down to his toes. He made an attempt to slip his arm from Alice's grasp, but she would not let him go. Her face was set. Noah recognized the expression immediately and almost laughed out loud. She made this exact stubborn face when she planned on doing the exact opposite of what was requested of her by her parents.

"We are having spaghetti," she called back over her shoulder, yanking Noah with her out the door and down the porch steps.

Noah would never, ever even think of pulling such a thing with his dad. He would kill him. Without hesitation. But Alice wasn't his kid, his property to do with as he liked. He wouldn't risk hurting her. Alice's family would destroy him, and he knew that perfectly well. He didn't come after them.

At Alice's house, they had store-bought strawberry shortcake, and Noah received a football as a collective gift from the whole family. It was so incredibly nice. They played Activity, and Alice's dad gave the best impression of a charging buffalo Noah had ever seen. The man was a boss when it came to board games. Noah spent the night there, too. With Alice snoring quietly on her bed and him taking up the guest mattress on her bedroom floor, he pondered the stark difference between the two families. Alice's parents built each other up. They worked together to create a better home, while Noah's parents seemed to barely tolerate each other.

After dinner, it was Alice's father who did the dishes. Noah had never heard of such a thing. A man doing dishes? It was absurd. He saw Noah watching him open-mouthed and grinned. "Well, Maggie made the dinner, after all. It's the least I can do." Noah vowed to himself that when he grew up, he would do the same. He would have a happy home with happy children and a happy wife just like this. He wished his mother could have been a part of his birthday dinner over here. He wished for it even though he knew it was impossible. His father would never allow it. Also, his mother had gotten unusually drunk tonight. It was disturbing to watch her giggling and falling like a small child. It gave Noah a desperate, hollow feeling, as if he should be taking care of her. He should have told her after her second shot, "That's enough, Mom! You can't have any more." It was all backwards. She was the parent. She should be thinking like this. Not Noah. He then wished desperately that one day, his dad would not come home. Not for him to die, but to simply disappear into the world. He envisioned bright light filling the house and his mother telling him that it was just the two of them now. He drifted off to sleep on that lovely thought.

CHAPTER THIRTEEN

1996
ROSIE

Her day had started with a rooster crow, and she knew that today would be the day they ate Leon the Terrible. Rosie awoke to a splitting headache, and in consequence, the rooster had sounded like an air horn. She did not want to go to school that day, but it was only early September, and she had already missed a whole week. She threw her legs over the side of the bed and immediately stepped on their elderly dog's tail. The dog yelped, and she almost fell backwards. She caught herself, one hand on the bed, her offending foot in the air, and the other balancing on her tiptoes.

"Ollie! Get out of my room!" she yelled at him crossly, but he was already doing his limp scurry into the hallway.

She immediately felt bad for lashing out. She liked it when Ollie slept in her room. She yelled at him so heartlessly. He was so old, too. What was wrong with her? She uncaringly pulled mismatching clothes onto her body. She would give Ollie part of her breakfast. That should ease her guilt and put her in his favor. She wasn't that hungry, anyway.

Mina was already at the bus stop when she got there. They hadn't really talked about what happened at the homestead.

Rosie had told her friend about the other fainting incident at her grandparents' and how she most likely caught some virus. Mina just reacted in her usual Mina fashion. She gave Rosie unasked for advice: "Take some vitamin C, and drink hot tea," she had said, and that was that. Like tea and vitamins would fix anything. She didn't really act the same around Rosie. There was an almost polite distance between them now. She supposed she would feel awkward around Mina if she had dropped to the floor in front of her without warning and peed herself. Rosie hoped the strangeness would go away on its own with some time.

"Hey, lady!" Rosie greeted her breathlessly. Everything nowadays seemed to wear her out. It was ridiculous.

"Hello, milady!" Mina curtsied.

When they were little, they used to pretend that they were forest princesses. Rosie's dad had built them a little wooden house by the stables. They used that as their castle. They called each other "milady," spoke in horribly butchered old English, and twirled around in long dresses all day long. Those were the days.

Mina looked her up and down, like she thought Rosie might have something contagious.

"How are you? You don't look that good."

As much as the observation hurt her feelings, it was the plain truth. Rosie wasn't sleeping well, and in consequence, she had dark circles under her eyes.

"Yeah, well, I feel like washed dog shit, so I'm glad my looks match," she said moodily.

"Geez. Sorry for asking!"

Mina dug the toe of her tennis shoe into the dirt, twisting her ankle round and round. She was clearly uncomfortable. It wasn't even 7:30 in the morning, and Rosie had already had enough of herself. Why did she have to react this way? She was such a bitch. She needed to just turn around, go home, and go back to bed. All she did nowadays was go around hurting feelings. She just couldn't seem to help it. Someone rubbed her the wrong way even slightly, and she was instantly pissed. The next moment, the feeling would pass, and she would feel terrible.

"I keep having this strange dream," she said, picking up the conversation since going back home wasn't an option. "It wakes me up, and I can't go back to sleep."

Mina peered at her, her eyes narrowed and head tilted. Her lips puckered into her signature smile.

"It's a sex dream, isn't it?" she said, grinning idiotically.

"No! It's not a sex dream, you wild pig!" Rosie retorted in mock disgust.

"I bet it's all nasty!" Mina continued dreamily. "Who are you doing it with?"

"It's not a sex dream, you half-wit!"

They were both giggling now. Rosie felt much better. She shoved her friend.

"I bet it's Mr. Hallar."

Rosie recoiled as if Mina were waving shit on a stick at her. Mr. Hallar was their balding geography teacher. He was in his early fifties, and he had long gray hairs sticking out from his nose that he had no intention of doing anything about, even though basically everyone made fun of him for it. The teasing may be more effective if they did it to his face, Rosie thought. They were snorting with laughter and holding onto each other.

"Stop! I'm gonna barf on your new shoes." Rosie bent over and gagged playfully.

This was good. This was them. Besties for life. Spirits lifted, Rosie let go of her friend and drew a deep, refreshing breath of the morning air. She felt like she had forgotten how to breathe for a minute there. She heard two blue jays bickering in one of the trees up above. From further away came a mockingbird call. She sighed with pleasure. *Today may actually turn out to be a good one.*

"So, what is it about?"

"Hmm?"

"The dream.'

"Oh. That." Rosie had already forgotten about how they got to the topic of sex dreams. "It's kind of weird. I dream that I hear the tap dripping."

"That's it?"

"It sounds so real. I keep getting up and checking the sink in the bathroom. It's never really on. But I am almost sure I can hear it when I wake up. It drives me crazy."

"That is kind of weird."

The day dragged by slowly, the minutes lasting forever. Rosie could feel a tension building within her as they neared the last period.

She stared sleepily out the window by her desk, desperately wanting to be outside. She wasn't meant to spend so much time indoors. She leaned on one elbow, wanting to doze off so badly. She needed to run free, her lungs expanding with meadow air, just like her horses. Sand liked to lie down and take a nap in the warm sunshine, her big belly rising and falling, legs stuck out straight. Her bottom lip always fell to the side, revealing her giant teeth. She was so incredibly cute. Her head was slipping, her upper body slowly making its descent onto the desk. There! Her head rested on her book. Just five minutes, and she would be all rested.

"Rosie!"

She snapped to attention. Ms. Lesbith was looking at her intently. Her history teacher was intimidating, to say the least. Her eyes were an unusual light brown and sort of scary-looking. She used them to stare holes into her students' souls. It was like trying to play Who Blinks First with a hawk. You were going to lose. And you would get eaten.

"Here I was, boasting about how we have a local celebrity in our class, with your family's history and all, and here you are, falling asleep."

Muffled snorts and giggles came from all around her. She sank down in her seat, attempting to become smaller. This was absolutely mortifying. She wished she could disappear.

"I . . . I'm sorry, Ms. Lesbith!" she croaked, her voice scratchy with sleep. "It won't happen again."

Ms. Lesbith chuckled and looked around her class.

"I know history is sometimes boring, but come on, Rosie! Your family is the source of the legendary journal." She brandished the school's copy of Rosanne Glessner's diary. "Have you even started reading it?"

"Yes, Ms. Lesbith, I have."

Why wouldn't she just leave her alone? She was acting like Rosie had meant to offend her personally by falling asleep. It was an accident. She was just tired. Couldn't Ms. Lesbith see that? She was looking down at Rosie in exaggerated disbelief. Her glasses were in the shape of a cat's eyes. She really did look like a predator of some kind. Rosie felt like an insignificant little mouse who was about to become a meal. She just sat there with what she knew was a pitiful expression on her face, unable to look away from those hawk eyes. Finally, Ms. Lesbith shrugged, like she didn't just ruin Rosie's entire school year by humiliating her in front of everyone, and said:

"Okay, then. Everyone, please turn to page twenty-nine. Rosie, read the entry for us!"

Rosie fumbled with her book. Her hands were shaking. Her voice would be, too; she was sure of it. There was too much adrenaline coursing through her veins from being put on the spot. Ms. Lesbith turned her wrist and looked at her watch. She pursed her lips and tapped her foot, making sure everyone knew that Rosie was a total fuck-up. Rosie finally found the entry. She recognized with some relief that she had already read it a few nights ago. It was not a particularly uplifting entry, and for some reason, that made an unusual calm settle over Rosie. *Poor Rosanne*, she thought. And suddenly, her teacher's scrutiny didn't feel that demolishing anymore. When she started to read, her voice rang out strong and clear in the quiet of the classroom. She saw Ms. Lesbith give her an annoyed look from her peripheral, but then she was swept into the story, and it was just her and Rosanne.

August 27, 1742

I lost the baby in the night. At least, I think it was night.

We have been stuck in a storm for days. It's dark. The hatch above remains closed. Giant waves throw the ship and the people in here with it. It feels like we are being ground up in the mouth of some large beast. They don't give us enough water, either. Eric held Heidi while I suffered through the miscarriage. Afterward, a kind woman called Kata helped clean me up. Her husband had broken his neck the day before. His body was thrown overboard. She is from Hungary, she tells me. But she does speak pretty good German and some English, as well. I had asked her to take care of my Heidi in case I, too, perish in this watery hell. I know Eric wouldn't take proper care of her. He may just bet her on cards, the swine. Kata herself has no children, but she looks like she would make a good mother. She has a kind voice. And she took care of me, using her husband's clothes to wipe the blood from my body. I thought I might bleed out, but luckily, the bleeding stopped. I feel weak and parched.

Heidi is complaining about her arm. She received a small cut in the worst of the storm. I think it may have been from a nail. I bandaged it for her, but it still oozes. I pray to God that her wound may be healed quickly. I also pray for all our souls in case we all have already died and this is purgatory.

Ms. Lesbith called Rosie back as she attempted to escape out the door quickly after class was over. Mina, who was scurrying just ahead of her, looked back with sympathy and some alarm.

"I need to have a word with you," said Ms. Lesbith, reading some paperwork in her hand and not looking at her.

Rosie and Mina both winced. Mina gave her a grimace, mouthed "Sorry," and took off. She didn't want to be anywhere near when Ms. Lesbith gave one of her legendary speeches. She had a habit of tearing into her students if they displeased her, and more than one had left her class in tears. Today, it was Rosie's turn. Dragging her feet, she walked back inside and stopped a few feet from her teacher.

"I do not tolerate such disrespect in my classroom, young lady."

Rosie groaned inwardly. She didn't will herself to doze off. It just happened. Why didn't this lady get it? She needed to get out of here. She would just stay small and humble, and hopefully, the history monster would keep it short.

"I haven't been sleeping well, Ms. Lesbith. I am so sorry."

There was a moment of silence as Ms. Lesbith tapped a finger on her desk and seemed to take a long, hard look at her.

"Is there anything going on at home? Because if there is, you have to tell me! You know that, right? Any mistreatment needs to be reported."

Rosie thought her teacher meant to be kind. Maybe she was a hard-ass on the outside but well-meaning on the inside? The thing was that her stare on Rosie remained cold and calculating.

"Most teachers wouldn't bother," she continued, "but I care about my students, Rosie. And I can't just stand by if . . ."

"No!" Rosie heard herself yell.

Her gut clenched. This wasn't right. Ms. Lesbith wasn't being kind. She didn't actually care about Rosie. This evil wench was just looking for the next person to make miserable. She was trying to get her parents into trouble. Her sweet, innocent parents. This lady was the devil! If Norma Lesbith was annoyed before, she looked thoroughly pissed off now, an angry red rising on her cheeks under her glasses.

"Don't you dare raise your voice at me! If your parents have not taught you any manners, I'm just going to have to do it myself."

Rosie flushed hotly at this. *How dare this lady! How dare she?* Rosie thought of her mom bringing her medicine and smoothing down her hair. Her dad carrying her into a hospital. Holding her tightly against his broad chest, as if she weighed nothing. This wasn't right. If Ms. Lesbith started a rumor about her parents, people might just believe her. If Ms. Lesbith claimed they abused her, would the school call the police? Mina's dad would be the first to know. She wouldn't want to be friends anymore. This couldn't happen. She had to do something. Rosie's hand shot out, totally without her control, and grabbed Ms. Lesbith's bony arm.

Her vision had a pulsing blackness around it. She saw a young woman with bright light brown eyes dimpling at a man with deep smile creases on his face. They were happy. So full of hope. "I want to have a large family," she was saying to him. The image blurred, and a new one emerged: the same woman at a doctor's office, the paperwork in her hand reading *Norma Lesbith* on the top. "I'm sorry, ma'am," the doctor was saying. "We need to remove the mass. If we don't, it will cost you your life." Now, Rosie was inside the woman's body. She felt her lips tremble as fat tears rolled down her cheek. *But I won't be able to have children*, she thought. Her heart was breaking. Rosie could feel it—a huge crack going straight through the middle of it.

Time and space had warped, and she found herself in a bathroom. Ms. Lesbith was leaning on the sink, staring into the mirror. She was older, lines creasing her forehead, her long hair cut into a short bob. She had mascara running down her splotchy face. Someone banged on the door.

"Norma, open the door!" boomed a man's voice.

Ms. Lesbith tuned and kicked the door so violently that it shook.

"Jesus Christ!" came the man's voice again. "Stop, honey! Come out and let's talk, okay?"

"Talk?" she screamed. "You want to talk about how you fucked my friend and got her pregnant? Is that what you want to talk about?"

She became hysterical, scrubbing her contorted face with her palms and running them through her hair. She paced back and forth in the small room, with Rosie hovering somewhere above her. The man finally wrenched the door open. It was the same man from before. Her husband. He came to her, palms up in surrender. She was having none of it. She grabbed the hairdryer and swung it at his head. His eyes wide, he managed to duck at the last second, and she ended up smashing the mirror with it. Rosie saw her teacher's distorted face depicted on hundreds on shards. They were on the ground, in the sink, and still in the frame of the mirror. All the little

Normas looked equally sad and defeated, their mouths moving in unison.

"I want you out of my life, you disgusting pig," she panted.

Rosie was, yet again, transferred. She now saw Ms. Lesbith sitting alone by a window, hugging her knees to her chest. The chair was the only piece of furniture in the room. She was sobbing quietly. Rosie floated into her body and felt what she felt. Saw her thoughts. She was mourning for the children she would never have. The family she could never build. Her husband who had left her. She mourned all her hopes and dreams. Her life to be, which crashed and burned in front of her very eyes.

Rosie saw and felt all this in the split second she was holding her teacher's arm. Then, Ms. Lesbith wrenched her arm violently from her grasp, and she was left empty and numb.

"You little witch!" Ms. Lesbith was snarling at her. "You can't grab a teacher like that! I will have you expelled!"

She was rubbing her arm where Rosie had touched her. Her skin was colorless and gray there. Rosie looked into her face. With her lips pulled back and teeth showing, she reminded her of some exotic cat. Her teacher was still talking to her—screaming, in fact—but her voice was all echoes and vibrations. Suddenly, Rosie could feel this dark liquid substance fill her body. She was pushed out by it, like a wave crashing into her. She saw the two of them standing there, facing each other in the classroom. There were books on the teacher's desk, leftover writing on the whiteboard. She observed these things with detached interest, as if they had nothing to do with her, as if she were just a bird in a tree above. She saw herself open her mouth and speak.

"I see now. I see how it is, Norma."

Ms. Lesbith stopped her sputtering and stared at her, aghast.

"What did you just call me?"

"You are full of envy. So, so full of bitter envy. I'm surprised that your thin stick of a body can even contain it." She sounded calm and matter-of-fact, like a professor introducing some simple math problem. Ms. Lesbith opened and closed her mouth like a fish.

"But you can't. Can't you? Not really. It does overflow sometimes."

Rosie's body was walking around the teacher's desk, dragging the fingers of one hand on the top nonchalantly. She now leveled her gaze at her teacher.

"You punish your students. Your poor, innocent students. Like me."

Rosie chuckled softly, and Norma went rigid.

"We are going to the principal! I will have no more of this filth."

She tried to grab Rosie, but she danced back quickly, smiling and weaving her body like a little girl.

"It's not our fault that you can't bear children, Norma. It's not really your fault, either. But the way you act about it, well, that's completely on you."

"Shut up! You'll pay for this! Terrible child."

She reached for Rosie again, and this time, she stayed put, allowing Norma to grab one of her arms. She let go immediately, gasping and shaking her hand.

"Oops!" said Rosie, giggling. "I wouldn't touch me when I'm like this. Sorry, I forgot to tell you. It could be dangerous."

Ms. Lesbith held her hands to her chest and took a step back. Rosie could see confusion and fear mixing within her. They were swirling, the two feelings fighting each other for the upper hand.

"What's wrong with you?"

Fear was definitely winning.

"Me? What's wrong with *me*?" Rosie smiled at her crookedly. "No, Norma. It's what's wrong with *you*. You see, *you* are damaged. Missing a key element. Your uterus, right?"

Norma's mouth dropped open.

"Yes! And without that, you are not really a woman. You are just a dried-up husk. A stick figure. An imitation of a woman, forced to teach other people's stupid, snotty kids, knowing you can never have your own . . ."

The slap rang out harsh and loud in the classroom. Ms.

Lesbith was a lot quicker on her feet than Rosie thought possible. One second, she was a few feet away, looking bewildered, and the next, she was standing right in front of her, her palm smashing into Rosie's cheek. She was, all of a sudden, back in her body. Sucked in, like water down a drain. She felt the sting of the slap. Her vision went blurry as tears gathered in her eyes.

"Norma! What on earth!?"

In the doorway stood the short, squat figure of Mrs. Espinoza, the Spanish teacher. She held a cardboard box in front of her chest containing her teaching supplies. Rosie turned to look at her, and a tear escaped her bottom lid. It left a wet streak down her cheek.

"Dear God, Norma! What did you do?"

She rushed forward and dropped her box on the desk. She took Rosie's chin gently in her hand and turned her face this way and that. Rosie was so incredibly confused by everything she had just gone through that she just stood there like a mannequin, letting her body be manipulated, her eyes glossy and her cheek on fire. The Spanish teacher turned her attention to Ms. Lesbith, her face red and her little dark eyes shooting sparks of fury.

"This is a disgrace!" she spat at her with her heavy accent. "You should be ashamed!"

"You weren't here, Celia!" Ms. Lesbith retorted, finally finding her voice. "She said these awful . . ."

"It doesn't matter what she said! You hit her! Somebody else's child. At your workplace."

"Celia . . ."

"You hit her in the face!" Mrs. Espinoza shouted, the volume of sound much too great for her small frame.

There were curious students gathering in the doorway, Mina among them. They were whispering, their necks arching to see over each other's heads like many curious turtles. Celia glanced at them and then back at Norma.

"Go to the principal's office!" she ordered, lowering her voice. "I'm taking Rosanne to the nurse. We'll meet you there."

CHAPTER FOURTEEN

1981
ALICE

Alice lay on her dorm bed with her head propped up on her arm. Nate was buckling the belt on his faded jeans. He bent over, looking for his T-shirt in the mess that was the dorm room floor.

"You should really do some organizing, babe."

He was giving her an excellent view of his perfectly shaped rump. Alice giggled, feeling delightfully naughty. She had just had sex with her boyfriend in her dorm room while her roommate was out. She was the definition of a college cliché, and she was perfectly okay with it. This is what she came here to do: to see new things, to meet new people, to experience the world outside of her sleepy little hometown. She was hitting all her goals.

Nate came over and gave her a kiss on the lips.

"Gotta go, babe. See ya later!" he called out to her from the door, bag in hand. "Be good!"

The door closed behind him with a quiet thud. Alice flopped onto her back and gave a huge sigh as she took in the texture of the ceiling. The blinds were down, and the room was dark and quiet now. A wave of relief washed over her, and her body flattened into the mattress. She always felt this odd release whenever Nate left her, and she wondered, not for the first time, if they were just too wrong for each other. Nate had a handsome, angular face and a lean, well-sculpted body. She had lost her virginity to him a few weeks ago. He had been gentle and understanding with her. Sex with him was great in general, although Alice had not much to compare it to. But she seemed not to be able to connect to him on an emotional level. Even when they were having conversations, Alice found herself drifting away almost all the time. She often caught herself thinking about her friends and family back home while Nate spoke animatedly to her about something else. There was a disconnect there, as if she left reality behind and this was some strange make-believe. Nothing was actually real. Things had no consequences, not like back home. She thought a lot about Noah and whether what she did was the right thing after all. She thought now of all the things that happened to her in her lifetime that had brought her to this very spot. All the decisions she had made, thinking they were the right ones.

She was around ten years old when she had a very pivotal visit with her aunt. She and her mother would go every few weeks to see Aunt Franny at the special hospital she lived at. Sometimes, her dad would tag along, too, but he generally had found Aunt Franny "way too creepy." So, he skipped visiting whenever he could. Her mother treated the visits as if they were work. She just had to get them done, and that was that.

So, it was somewhere around 1971, and she and her mother had just sat down in the hospital cafeteria to have tea and homemade sandwiches with Francis. The conversation was going well at first, but that's how it always was. At first, Francis would compliment their outfits and comment on how big Alice was getting. They would chat about school and work and what the other inhabitants of the hospital were up to—and then *bam!* Her aunt would say something totally out of left field and shocking, and the next thing Alice knew, she was being dragged from the building by her red-faced mother. Alice could say that this visit was just the same as the others, but it wasn't. What Aunt Francis said to her that day shaped her life in ways she wouldn't have been able to imagine at the time.

"So, Margaret from room twelve told me that Mr. Gaines from room eight was having an affair with one of the nurses," Francis said, winking at Alice with a conspiratory smile.

"Not in front of Alice!" Her mom shook her head good-naturedly.

Alice smiled into her mug. Sometimes, Aunt Franny was just the right amount of outrageous. At times like this, Alice was able to remind herself that her aunt was a regular person behind her illness. She had once been a normal little girl with dreams of a normal future. It was sad that she had been denied all of it—having a car, a family, a dog. She wasn't even allowed to keep a hamster in here ever since one of the patients ate the fish from the community aquarium. *It must be awful to live out your days all locked up like this*, Alice thought.

Franny took a sip of her tea and grimaced.

"Oh, dear, this is more bitter than Satan's heinie."

Francis shuddered dramatically.

"Let me see if I can find some more sugar," Alice's mother said.

She looked about, spotted some at the far end of the large room, and made a beeline for it. As soon as she was a few feet away, Francis reached out and touched Alice's cheek with a tender hand. She looked lovingly at Alice, who tilted her face into her palm. She did love her crazy aunt.

"Such a pretty little thing you are," Francis said. "You look quite a bit like your father. But don't you worry; you still have time to turn out just like your old Aunt Francis."

Alice's smile faltered. She giggled nervously. She was pretty sure her aunt was being sweet, but she did live in a mental hospital. Alice doubted very much that it would be a good thing to turn out just like her. It would be quite terrible, actually.

"Oh, don't look so concerned, my little darling!"

She was stroking Alice's cheek with her thumb.

"Just think of all the lives you will ruin when you grow bigger. You and that beautiful little one of yours."

Alice felt a sharp sting on her cheek. It was almost like Francis's hand was a live wire. She jerked away from her. It was happening again. A switch had been flipped, and Aunt Franny went from charming to nuts in only a fraction of a second.

Her mother returned a moment later to find Alice looking down into her tea with a hand on one cheek.

"Alice?" she said, looking back and forth between her and Francis, suspecting that something had happened but not sure yet.

"Did you tell her already that there's a good chance she'll go crazy, too?" asked Francis in a cheery, conversational tone. "It's all in the genes, you see. You go back in our family tree, and you'll find crazy all over the place," she continued.

"Francis!" her mother warned urgently, but it was as if Francis didn't hear her.

"Our grandmother was totally cuckoo, for instance. Remember, sissy, how she tried to stick a knife in Grandpa that one time?"

"Francis, stop it, or we'll leave right now!" her mother pleaded, her face going from pink to red at an alarming rate.

Aunt Franny laughed heartily at this.

"At the end of the day, you're going to leave me alone in this shithole, anyway. What do I care if it's right now or an hour later?"

She turned to Alice and continued to speak rapidly to her.

"Some adjustments had to be made. At one point there, Heidi was supposed to be the next one, you see? But with everything that had happened, that just wasn't possible."

"Francis!"

Her mother slammed her palms down on the table so hard that it almost tipped over. The room went silent, and all the heads turned in their direction. It was definitely time to leave. Francis looked about her, a wide smile on her face. She seemed not to comprehend what she had just done. It didn't click that the things she said were terribly distressing to the ones closest to her. She picked up her cup and attempted to sip from it, only to find that her tea had spilled. She frowned into the cup, put it back down on the saucer, and smiled radiantly at the two of them. Not a care in the world.

Alice had taken some time to absorb this new information. So, according to her aunt, the family had a genetic disposition for mental illness. It could strike at any moment. Francis started going nuts somewhere around thirteen, if she remembered correctly. So, there was a chance, a very real chance, that Alice would become schizophrenic, too. The thought made her ill. She didn't want to hurt the ones she loved. She did not want to end up living out her days in a loony bin where her relatives only came to see her out of obligation. She wanted a normal life.

A day after their visit with her aunt, Alice sat down in the kitchen, where her mom was doing the dishes, and mentally psyched herself up for the interrogation.

"Mom!" she said severely.

Her mother whirled around, yellow rubber-gloved hands dripping suds held out in front of her.

"Jesus, Mary, and Joseph! You scared the daylights out of me, child!" She looked at her crossly. "Why on earth are you sneaking around like that?"

"I'm not sneaking. I just didn't make any noise."

"Well, you should! Announce yourself when you enter a room or something."

She was just about to turn back to her dishes, but Alice called out to her again.

"Was what Aunt Franny said true? Do we really have crazy in our family?"

She saw one of her mom's rubber-gloved hands tighten on the lip of the sink. She shook her head slightly, picked up a plate, and started scrubbing it in slow circles.

"You know most of what your aunt says is hogwash."

"This wasn't, though, was it?"

She put the plate back in the sink, looking irritated. Alice could see her scanning the kitchen to avoid her eyes and possibly find something to change the subject with.

"Did Great Grandma really attack Great Grandpa with a knife?" Alice kept pushing.

"For God's sakes, Alice! Why do you want to know these things?"

She could see her mother getting upset. It was clearly a touchy subject for her. But it was Alice's right to know, wasn't it? She took a deep breath and blew it out.

"I want to know because if there really is a chance that I can end up like Aunt Franny, I would maybe like to do some things a little differently."

There was a catch in her voice on the last word. Her mother's eyes softened. She took off her gloves and came to sit with Alice by the table.

"What things, my love?" she asked gently, taking Alice's hand in hers.

"I would maybe like to see more of the world. I've never been skiing. I'd love to try that. And maybe, just maybe, I'd like to have a dog before I become crazy and forget to take care of it."

Her mother laughed softly and shook her head.

"Is this just a ploy for us to take more vacations and get a dog?"

Alice smiled a little sheepishly, looking down at the table.

"No. I really just want to know the truth." She paused, chewing on her bottom lip. "But if knowing the truth comes with a few benefits, I'll take them."

Her mom's smile faded a bit. She patted her hand and stood up. She walked into the living room and came back with their copy of Rosanne Glessner's journal. Scooting the chair closer to Alice, she sat back down and started flipping through the pages.

"Our copy is different from all the rest of them," she said. "They printed our family tree on the last few pages. Do you have a pen?" she asked.

Alice twisted around in her seat, pulled out their kitchen junk drawer, and excavated a pen from it.

"Let's see here!" Her mom took the pen from her and bent

over the book.

Alice stood up and peered interestedly over her shoulder. The pages revealed an intricate system of names and connecting lines in a fancy font. Only the last few of them were handwritten.

"Look! There's you." Her mom poked at the last name on the page with the pen.

Tracing the names with her pinky finger, she went higher and higher on the rows until she located Aunt Franny. She placed a little X next to her name. She did the same with Alice's great grandmother. She repeated this a few more times under the watchful eyes of her daughter.

"Here!" she said in a businesslike manner, clicking the end of the pen. "These are all the cases I know of, but I may be wrong on a few. After a certain time, it's all just stories of the past. I don't really know what is truth and what is fiction."

Alice examined the book carefully. There really weren't that many. Sometimes, it skipped one, even two generations. But it was definitely there. Embedded in their genes. Now, she knew. And knowing was half the battle. She leaned closer, squinting. They were all women. Only women.

In the coming years, Alice made some decisions about her life based on what she knew. She had no idea at the time that this would lead to one of the biggest dilemmas in her life. Noah. Because she loved him, she was sure of this, just as she was sure the sun would come up every morning. It was all fine until around age fourteen. She had come to the horrifying realization that he loved her, too, and definitely not just as a friend. If she gave into the almost overwhelming desire to date him, well, that would have ruined everything. She couldn't tie herself down. Not to her hometown, not to Noah. Not to anyone or anything. So, she resisted. And she resisted some more. She did notice that her other best friend, Millie, was crushing hard on Noah, too. It made her feel so jealous that occasionally, she became sick. Literally. She had run into the girls' bathroom at school and vomited into the toilet one time she saw Millie give Noah wistful Bambi eyes. It got easier over time, and eventually, she hoped they would date so Noah would stop pestering her to go out on date-like excursions with just him. They never did, though.

After high school, her break finally came. She got into the University of Houston. It was a truly bittersweet moment. She did it! She was going to leave on the journey that would be her life. Now, she just had to tell everyone she was leaving. She had to tell Noah. Even the thought of that made her stomach clench. She could already see his face. The way it would crumble. His warm brown eyes becoming glossy. She couldn't do it. Maybe she would just leave without saying anything. No. She couldn't do that, either. As she was mulling over her options, someone rang the doorbell. She glanced out her window. It was him. Of course it was him. Destiny wouldn't make it easy on her. She was alone at home, too. It was a perfect time to tell him. She got off her bed with lead in her arms and legs and slowly shuffled toward the front door.

She really didn't know how to break it to him. They were sitting on her bed in her bedroom, the setting sun illuminating everything in a cozy orange glow. It was a way too romantic of an atmosphere to give such bad news in. Noah was sucking on his bottom lip, so he had something to say. He always did that when he was just about to say something meaningful. He looked at her in that cautious manner of his. Alice had a bad feeling about this. She reached behind her and touched the letter from the university that lay on her bed. She had to be strong and go through with her plan.

"Alice . . ." said Noah nervously. "You told me before that you weren't going to date until after high school."

Alice's skin prickled. She had a sick feeling about where this was going. She had told him that she wasn't going to date while in high school to ward him off. She was planning on leaving right after, so it didn't matter. She didn't think he would actually bring it up right after the last day of school.

"I know you like me," he continued doggedly, "so . . . so I want you to be my girlfriend!"

And there it was. Why couldn't he just forget about her and

date somebody else? Alice didn't want to break his heart. It would have been so much easier if he did it to her. So much cleaner.

"We could still be best friends," he said desperately when she didn't say anything. "That wouldn't change."

Tears welled in her eyes. She wiped them away angrily. Why did he have to do this? Why couldn't he just let her go to live her miserable, lonely life full of adventure? It had to be done. The Band-Aid needed to be ripped off. She grabbed the letter and handed it to him. He looked utterly confused. Reluctantly, he took his eyes off her and read it. Then, he read it again. When he looked at her again, the hurt in his eyes was unmistakable.

"You are leaving?" He didn't quite say it as a question.

"Yes," she answered and felt her chest tighten familiarly.

"You didn't tell me you were applying. If you did, I would have . . ."

"I want to go on my own."

Now, he was looking at her like she had just slapped him. She sighed.

"I have to do this."

"Why?" Now, he sounded almost angry.

Was he going to go through the whole array of human emotions before this was over?

"Because I do!" she said definitely.

"I love you."

He said it. And the inside of her chest tore. She felt the physical pain of it. Her flesh came apart on the inside, like overstretched fabric. She knew he was in love with her. It was hard to miss. But he had never said it out loud before.

"If you don't feel the same way, just tell me! I'll understand."

So, all she had to do was lie. Brutally break his heart to protect her secret, the reason behind all her decisions. She never told her friends about her aunt, about her faulty genetics. She didn't want pity or worry from them. She wanted to be treated as a completely ordinary girl for as long as possible. He gave her a frail smile that was meant to encourage her to speak. She just had to tell this one lie, and it would all be over. He wouldn't even miss her with a broken heart. He would hate her. He would finally move on. Date someone else. Marry someone else. Have kids with someone else. Her face crumpled. She could feel hot tears roll embarrassingly down her cheeks. She saw him open his arms through the veil of wetness. She went to him. Crushed into his chest. His arms closed protectively around her, one on her back, one on the back of her head. She couldn't lie about loving him. So, she told him her secret instead. She told him about what her aunt had said. About the history of mental illness in her family. About her fear.

"I want to see something else of the world besides this town. If I'm going to go crazy one day, I want to have experienced different things first."

She was calming down slowly, the tension seeping out of her like air from an old balloon.

"If I become schizophrenic, I can't have my husband or my kids seeing it, dealing with it. I don't want that. I'd much rather be alone."

"Alice, it doesn't . . ."

He was just about to say it didn't matter. But it did. He would see it over time. What if they had a daughter, and she turned out to be ill? It would ruin them. She was only nineteen, but this much she knew. So, she cut him off with a kiss. He went still, his hands flying from her back. But only for a second. Then, he melted into her. Her hands gripped his shirt as she gave into the temptation that was him. Their tongues found each other, and their breathing became rugged. She let all those years of sexual tension loose on him. This was going to be the one and only time. She lay back on her bed, pulling him down with her. She would let him do whatever he wanted, if only for just the one time. This was her goodbye.

So, she lied to Nate. She told him she was a virgin and pretended. She didn't do it for Nate's benefit. She did it because it was a lot more bearable to pretend that she had lost her virginity to a new and unimportant boyfriend than live with the guilt of knowing that was her last gift to her best friend. Because Alice wasn't going to go back home. Not if she felt even the least amount of chance of going crazy. She had already decided that if she were to notice any sign of it, she would tuck tail and run. Her loved ones would never see her again. If, by any chance, she did not go crazy by the time she was . . . forty, maybe, then she might move back home. But by that time, Noah would be long gone. Married to somebody else. Raising children with somebody else. He would be able to be a father to completely normal kids without a chance of it all going to hell.

Alice lay there in her dark dorm room. She was completely still but for a lone teardrop slowly making its way down her temple. She would forget about Noah eventually. She would forget about that wonderful golden afternoon when she had given herself to him. She would make herself forget about it all. But first, she would relive all of it in her mind one last time.

CHAPTER FIFTEEN

1996
NOAH

They were sitting in the car in front of Norma Lesbith's house. It was a mistake coming here. They both knew that. But neither of them had the ability to stop the other one from getting in the car.

This woman had hurt their daughter. Noah wanted to punch her teeth in. Just the thought of anyone putting even a finger on his beautiful daughter put him in a rage. He thought that if it ever were to happen, he would go to prison because he would kill the bastard. But it had to be a woman. And not just any woman. A poor, sad little stick like Norma Lesbith. The woman looked like a stronger gust of wind would take her. He couldn't hit her. He had watched his dad hit his mom for years and years until she finally drank herself into an early grave. He swore to himself that he would never hurt a female no matter the circumstance. He glanced over at his wife and knew by the look on her face that she had made no such promise. Her jaw was set for battle. It would have been an even bigger mistake letting her come on her own. The kids still needed her. She was feisty, even in the best of her moods. Who knows what she would do to Norma if she was left alone with her . . .

So, both of them came. And now, they sat in the car, silent

and angry. The calm before the storm. There was no concrete plan of action. They wanted to talk to her for sure. Noah wanted to hear her side just so he could tell her it was stupid. Rosie was such a good kid. She never even gave back talk to anyone. She didn't deserve this . . . this humiliation. This abuse. He hoped Norma would get fired. He wanted her to never be able to work with children again. He wanted to let her know, really firmly, that she had messed with the wrong student. By the way Alice was eyeing the mailbox, he had a strong suspicion that she wanted to rip it out of the ground and break down the door with it, then maybe apply it to the head of Norma Lesbith once they were inside. He could help her with that. Breaking the door down wouldn't be a direct assault on the woman herself, just some mild property damage. His conscience could definitely handle that.

The front door of the tiny shotgun-style house opened, and the abusive harlot stepped out. She had a glass of something in one hand and a pinched expression on her face. She crooked a finger, beckoning them to come. She then turned and walked back inside, leaving the door open. Noah and Alice looked at one and other, each of them wearing matching expressions of "What the fuck?" on their faces.

"I'm glad both of y'all are here," Norma said without preamble as they walked into her sparsely furnished kitchen. "Saves me the apology trip to your place."

The home looked sad and empty on the inside, with just the bare minimum furnishings. No pictures on the walls. Not even a cat on the sofa. It gave Noah the distinct feeling that he wasn't just looking at the inside of her house, but the inside of Norma herself.

"Were you really going to apologize?" Alice asked with notable skepticism.

Noah had his own doubts. The woman wasn't the apologizing type.

"Of course!" Norma said way too heartily. It made Noah think the liquid in her glass wasn't just grape juice. "They banished me from the school for a month. Without pay. But our lovely principal said I would be let go permanently unless I apologized, so I wanted to get it out of the way."

"You got some nerve!" Alice said with malice, her eyes squinting, foxlike. "You slap our daughter and act like this is all just a huge inconvenience to you!"

She put extra emphasis on the "you." Noah agreed with her. Norma didn't look shameful or apologetic at all. She looked pissed. And drunk. They should just walk out right now and let the principal know what they saw here today. He wasn't quite done with her, though.

"We still haven't heard that apology, by the way. Why don't we start with that?" Noah interjected, seeing smoke signals emerge from Alice's ears.

Norma swirled her drink around in her glass thoughtfully.

"Do either of you know a man named Alexander Cowell?"

Both Alice and Noah looked at her blankly.

"So, you are not going to apologize?" Noah asked with visibly clenched teeth. He could feel a vein pulsing in his temple. This lady was something else.

"I'm working up to it."

"Bullshit!" Alice cut in. "You despicable human being! Our neighbor is a cop, you know. His daughter is in your class. How about I pay him a visit and tell him how you treat your students?"

The corners of Norma's mouth dipped down, making not-so-appealing frown grooves appear on her face. She was trying to appear unaffected, but Noah saw her concern in the shift of her eyes behind her glasses. Would James do anything? he wondered. Does he already know what happened? If Mina saw, she would most definitely have told him by now. If he were James, he would probably pay Norma a visit and brandish some cop power in front of her. Tell her that he could have her locked up if she ever slipped up again. Or something of the sort. Scared the damn woman a little bit, at least.

"Just please answer the question!" Norma cleared her throat and shifted her weight.

She looked thoroughly uncomfortable. Noah glanced at Alice. She looked up at him, eyebrows arched. Her beautiful face was smooth. So, she had no idea either where Norma was going with this. This was turning out to be a most absurd situation. They came over here to do what? Scare her? Give her a piece of their minds? He wasn't quite sure, but definitely not to be interrogated. Alice gave a little shrug.

"What was the name again?" she asked.

"Alexander Cowell."

After a pause, they looked at each other again. The name wasn't familiar at all. Who was this guy? And what did he have to do with Rosie?

"No," said Noah.

"Who is he?" asked Alice, her rage dissipating.

Norma stared holes into both of them with her intense eyes. Was she trying to decipher if they were telling the truth?

"He is my ex-husband," she said coldly.

He could feel Alice go rigid next to him. A hot flush went up his own neck. Either this lady was straight-up messing with them, or this situation somehow involved a grown man they did not know. Either way, he didn't like it.

"Lady," Noah said, barely controlling the anger in his voice. "You better elaborate because I'm on the verge of losing my shit! Okay?"

Norma sighed and took her glasses off to rub the bridge of her nose. Her face looked strange and naked without them. Her eyes seemed smaller. They were an unusual light brown Noah noticed for the time. They were sort of pretty in an odd way, like a wolf's.

"I am very sorry I slapped your daughter the other day. It is true that I am not the most patient of all the teachers, but I have never in the past raised a hand to any of my students. What happened was just as shocking to me as to anyone else."

Alice crossed her arms and scoffed. Norma looked at her sharply.

"Now, I haven't told anyone the reason that I slapped her,

nor would anyone really listen, anyway. Now that I have the chance, I feel like I should tell you that the things that your daughter said to me were highly inappropriate."

"Oh, yeah. She cursed at you, and you hit her. Is that right?"

Noah felt like a pot full of boiling water. If somebody didn't do something soon, he was going to explode.

"She didn't curse. Not exactly. She threw some very personal information about my life in my face."

Alice let out a strange noise of audible frustration. Noah placed both of his hands on the back of his neck and back down again. What on earth was she talking about? Very personal information? He saw Alice move in his peripheral vision. She took a step back and leaned against the kitchen counter.

"I feel like we're going in circles here," said Noah. "I feel like we are at a shrink's office."

"What do you mea—"

"What did she say?" Alice interjected, her voice ghostly.

Noah turned to her, his brows furrowed. It wasn't like her to cut him off like that. She was as white as a sheet. Norma ran her tongue along her front teeth and tapped on her kitchen table with one manicured hand. She suddenly straightened up, her decision made.

"When I was younger—much, much younger—a life-saving operation was performed on me to remove a cancerous mass from my body. The mass was on my uterus, so unfortunately, that had to go, too."

Noah recoiled. It felt somehow wrong to use the word "uterus" in his presence. And definitely in relation to his own daughter. This conversation was just one left field ball after another. Norma saw his reaction and smiled faintly.

"I've never told this to anyone, so imagine how confused I felt when your daughter brought it up."

"Rosie . . ." Alice let out a breathless whisper behind him.

"Rosie knew this?" Noah said with thick disbelief.

"Uh-huh." Norma nodded slowly. "She had said a few other very hurtful things, as well, but this is the one thing I've never told anyone. The only person who knows about it is my ex-husband. As far as I know, he lives in Canada now, but when Rosie brought up my surgery, I thought that . . ." She trailed off. "I actually don't know what I thought. And I lost it. I am terribly sorry."

There was silence in the small room, in which Noah could hear his own heartbeat. This all didn't make sense. How could Rosie know these things? When they questioned her about the incident, she kept repeating, "I don't know! I don't know what happened! I don't remember!" They thought that she was just embarrassed. They assumed she would talk when she was ready. But this? They should have pressed her harder for information.

As they were driving away from Norma's house, Noah contemplated the best course of action. They should probably have Rosie see a psychologist—if she is unwilling to talk to them, that is. Alice was chewing on her thumbnail in the passenger seat. She had this faraway look on her face. He knew what she must be thinking, and it broke his heart. He thought back to that long-ago conversation they had in her bedroom. She had been terrified by the mental illness that supposedly ran in her family. She told him something about her aunt constantly saying strange things. He had to admit that his memories were a little fuzzy on that because of what happened right after. They had glorious, awkward sex. It was both of their first times, and the situation itself had been so unexpected that sometimes, he doubted it even happened. He had been so nervous that he almost missed his aim. He rubbed a finger over his top lip, remembering it now. He glanced over at Alice. The love of his life. How full of twists and turns their life had been—and still was, as it turns out. This had to be something other than mental illness. Rosie had heard some weird information about her teacher somewhere and decided to brandish it as a weapon when cornered. It was wrong of her to do that, and the teacher overreacted. It was that simple. Now, he just had to make sure Alice didn't overthink the situation.

"It's not that," he said to her quietly, putting a hand on her thigh.

"But what if it is . . . ?"

"We will get to the bottom of this. She will go through some stuff in her life, but it doesn't mean she's going to turn out like your aunt."

There was silence from next to him. He chanced a glance at her, shifting his eyes from the road. Her face was turned to the window. She looked so lean and fragile at that moment, like a little girl who had just lost something precious. He saw the line of her spine through her white T-shirt. Her tan arms. He knew the feel of her so well. How smooth her skin was, how toned the muscles underneath were. Suddenly, he was overcome with how much he loved her. Her sadness was almost unbearable. He wished he could take it away. He wished he could make her understand that everything would be all right. He would make it all right. She just had to trust him.

"Maybe we should take her to a psychologist," he ventured.

Her shoulders went up to her ears.

"No," she said. "Just not yet. Please . . .". . ."

CHAPTER SIXTEEN

1996
ROSIE

She was dreaming of brushing Emi's hair. Probably because she did actually brush it before they went to bed. They had gone out riding that day, and the wind had put terrible tangles in her angel hair.

"We have to do a hundred brushes before bedtime," she said, sitting cross-legged behind her. "One, two, three . . ."

And on it went until her hair turned to strands of gold. But that was normal. That was what was supposed to happen. That's how dreams were. Something totally off the wall would happen, and your sleeping brain would rationalize it immediately: Nothing to see here. Just gold hair. Move along, people. It got shinier and shinier with each stroke. She ran her fingers through it, and the strands made a sound like little chains bumping against each other. Then, one of them cut her finger.

"Ow! Emi! Why did you do that?"

But Emi was disappearing into the floor. It was made of water. She could just see the top of her golden head as she went under. She looked about her. How did she not notice that she was sitting in water? She put one hand in it, then her arm, all the way to her armpit. Suddenly, she fell forward, as if pushed, and went into the abyss. She sank slowly to the bottom, where the fine silt billowed out all around her. And there, in the midst of all of that, was something shiny. She dove for it, her feet kicking furiously, until finally, she closed a hand around a smooth and shiny pearl. It was as big as an avocado seed. Rosie was mesmerized by it. Within the pearl was Emi. "Would you look at that!" smiled Rosie. "Look how small you are. You little terror." The pearl started to vibrate. It made a strange humming sound, like live electricity. It turned dark, changing from a shimmery white to oily black. The blackness spread from it like ink. It covered her hands and spread rapidly around her. She dropped it, Emi still inside. She was screaming silently and banging on the inside of the pearl. She should have gone back for her, but suddenly, she was out of air. She swam for the surface, the darkness biting at her heels. She was almost there. Reaching and pulling, she swam with all her might. She could see light above her. The fingers of her right hand were just about to break the surface. Something grabbed her ankle and yanked her down. She screamed, losing all her air, black water filling her lungs. She kicked and punched at her invisible enemy until it finally released her. Her head broke the surface. She took an enormous gulp of air and pulled her soaked body out of the water. To her surprise, she was on her bed. Still gulping air, she looked around, but everything seemed normal. All her things neatly lined up on her selves. Her desk covered in textbooks. It was all there. Her heart rate slowed. She lay back onto her pillow, intending to fall asleep, when she heard it. The rhythmic *tap-tap-tap* of dripping water. This was going to drive her mad. Irritated beyond belief, she hopped out of bed and marched out of her room. The bathroom tap was dry, of course. She could still hear it. It was coming from somewhere else in the house. She walked slowly down the hallway, passed her parents' room, and listened. Was it the kitchen tap? She walked into the living room and listened once more. No, not the kitchen. She tilted her head this way and that, like a dog trying to understand its master. *Tap, tap, tap.* It was in the office. But that wasn't right. There was no running water in there.

She peered into the dark room from where she stood. In the gloom of the office, a pair of small blue lights flickered alive. Cold fright washed over Rosie's entire body. It was a pair of eyes. She knew it even before a person's silhouette separated from the darkness. The small porchlight shined through the window next to the front door, and in its light, Rosie recognized the long, tangled hair of the old woman from the homestead. She resisted the urge to scream. Clamping her hands over her mouth, she backed up slowly. The woman's cracked lips moved rapidly. She was speaking a language she didn't recognize. It sounded like angry gibberish. She glided smoothly from the office, her feet not showing under her tattered sack of a dress. She headed straight for Rosie, quickly picking up speed. She backed up rapidly and stepped on the remote that was left carelessly on the floor by her sister. Flopping backwards with her arms splayed to the sides, she went into a freefall. She fell through the floor and found herself sitting up in her bed. She looked around her room wildly, expecting the old crone to materialize from a dark corner any second. She didn't, and in a few minutes, Rosie's rapid breathing slowed to almost normal. *It was all just a dream*, she told herself as she slid under the covers. A highly elaborate, very stressful dream. Adrenaline running high in her veins, there was no way she was going back to sleep. Not for a while. She looked at the alarm clock on her nightstand. It was in the shape of a grazing cow. She got it for her seventh birthday. The cow told her it was almost 4 a.m. She reached over and pulled the string on her night lamp. It illuminated just enough of the room to chase away any wandering ghosts. Rosanne Glessner's journal was sitting on her nightstand next to her clock. She hesitated for a moment, then reached for it.

September 16, 1742

Heidi is gone. The cut on her little arm festered. It was all black and blue, and it oozed this vile humor. The conjure man on board offered to cut it off. He said she would die if he didn't. And she did. I couldn't let him do it. When that rusty blade had touched her swollen flesh, my baby howled like a tortured animal. I couldn't bear it. I snatched her up and ran as far as the ship would let me. She died in my arms a day later while her father gambled away the rest of our money. Passengers are dropping like flies, and the drunks still play cards. The world is twisted beyond my comprehension. I wouldn't let go of her until she started to smell. Kata had helped me wrap Heidi in one of my petticoats so we could throw her into the sea. We watched her drift away together, a part of me going with her. She told me she would have done the same, that she might have died even if I let the man take her arm. Her words were lost on me. My heart feels as if it has a wound such as on Heidi's arm. It is extremely painful, but I welcome it. I deserve it. I hope it, too, festers until it takes me.

I slept with my drunken slob of a husband the same night. Wishing, willing God to bless me with another child. For if He does not, I fear this wound in my heart will not stop growing until it swallows me whole. The desperately pitiful creature that I am, I cannot decide whether I wish to live or die.

September 17, 1742

Kata wishes to teach me English to pass the time. She insists I will need it and will welcome the use of it. I resist her attempts to teach me. I ache from within and wish to do nothing but sleep. Sleep will not come. There isn't much else to do in this hellhole. So, I finally gave in. It's a wretched language, although I think that of everything nowadays.

Kata carries a small wooden case with her everywhere she goes. There is a carving of a woman on it. She wears a splendid gown with many flowers. It's about the size of a breadbox. When I asked her what it contained, she just smiled and said she could not tell me. She fears if word got 'round, the other passengers would try to steal it. She did tell me, however, that her husband had made it as a wedding gift, and she herself was the woman in the gown. When she let me take a closer look, I, too, smiled. It was my first one since Heidi had left me. It felt foreign on my face. The carving looked exactly like her. There was no mistaking it. It was such fine craftsmanship. Such effort and time had been put into it. My bruised heart ached for her, for her late husband must have loved her dearly to know her face so well even before they had wed. I watched her for a time as she stared out into the sea and wished that I could pine for my husband like she must be pining for hers.

CHAPTER SEVENTEEN
1996
MILLIE

Millie was thoroughly ticked off this morning. The school had called in the middle of her packing lunches for her three kids to inform her that the school bus had broken down. So, she would have to scramble to get her kids to school and herself to work on time. She looked at her reflection in the small decorative mirror hanging above the trash can. She looked tired and washed out. If she didn't do her makeup, she could pull it off. She'd just have to endure everyone at work asking her if she was sick. "No, you blind bitch! I'm just old!" She'd love to say that to Rachel, the head veterinarian. She would lose her job. That's a given. But it would be worth the expression on Rachel's dumb, degree-wielding face. Then, Pamela Briggs called her, too. She was Samantha's mother. Millie had paid her a house call last week, bearing a loaf of banana bread. Pamela had broken her ankle and thus provided an excellent excuse for Millie to go over to her house for a chat. She wanted to know if Samantha had mentioned anything to her about the ominous horse ride that had left both Mina and Rosie acting out of sorts. According to Sam, the girls rode up to the old homestead, which was clearly haunted, and Rosie somehow fell and hurt herself. "Sam was convinced that Rosie fell because she had seen a ghost." Pamela laughed heartily. "Imagine that! I think the girls are just a bit spooked."

Ghosts! Millie had snorted on her way home from her information expedition. Her trip had been a waste of time. Now, Pam was calling Millie to ask if she could possibly pick up Samantha on her way and drop her off at school. She herself couldn't drive at the moment, broken ankle and all. The woman was mistaking her for a friend just because she had given her some banana bread. Asking her favors all willy-nilly. Next thing Millie knew, she would be calling to ask if she had an extra kidney. She had looked at her somewhat revolting reflection once more. If she didn't do her hair, she would have enough time. This was her thing. She made herself be nice to people. She did the things they'd ask because of one little thing her dad kept saying while she was growing up: "You never know who you'll need a favor from." It turned out to be the single best piece of advice she had ever received. Turns out that people will do things for you if they think you like them and if you help them out from time to time. So, when the garbage man slipped on ice in front of her house, she got out and helped him instead of driving off like she wanted to. She was three minutes late to work that day, thanks to having to listen to his life story. A few weeks later, though, when one of the wheels popped off her garbage can, a brand new one had appeared on her driveway the same day. Indeed, she had collected countless useful favors over the years from people who otherwise wouldn't have had to help her. And all she had to do was one nice thing that one time.

So, she was now driving four unruly kids to school, makeupless and with a festive scarf over her bed head. Her two boys, ages nine and twelve, were hitting each other in the face with their karate belts, and the two girls were doing this unnaturally high-pitched laugh over "how cute" this one celebrity was. Their combined noise was slowly wearing away at her eardrums. Mina, who was sitting superiorly in the front passenger seat, twisted her nimble young body unnaturally to be able to whisper something to Samantha.

"I'm going to ask her today," Mina said in a hushed tone.

"I don't think you should. We should just leave it alone!"

whispered Sam.

Millie's selective hearing kicked in immediately as she sensed that the girls may be harboring a secret. She turned the radio down just a smidge and leaned all the way back in her seat for better hearing.

"But I want to know if she saw her, too," Mina hissed.

"There was nobody else there! You imagined it."

"Says you!"

"I just don't think we should bring it up to Rosie. She wouldn't want to talk about that day."

Mina sighed, frustrated.

"It's not the first time someone accidentally peed . . . Mom! Are you eavesdropping?"

They were stopped at a red light, and Millie had accidentally let her head turn in her daughter's direction.

"You are always doing that! It's so annoying!"

Mina plopped back into her seat and crossed her arms in a way that made it clear to Millie that she wasn't going to hear any more of this secret of theirs. She was quite delusional in this. She should know that a daughter could not keep secrets from her mother. At least, not for long.

1981

Millie

Tonight was going to be the night. Noah was taking her to a New Year's Eve party at one of his friends' houses, and Millie was going to sleep with him for the first time. They had been dating for around three weeks, and it was due time. She wasn't that nervous, not really. It wasn't like she was a virgin. Pete Miller had taken care of that in eleventh grade. Millie smiled at her reflection as she applied mascara. Pete had been good. He had been the only one she had considered dating seriously besides Noah. It's a shame his mother was terrible. She hated Millie, that bitter old hag. She had overheard her talking to Pete one time when she went to dinner at his house.

"When are you going to get serious and date an appropriate girl, son?"

"There is nothing wrong with her, Maa. I really like her."

"But Petey, think about your mother, your family! What will people say if you give me brown grandbabies?"

Millie's mouth dropped open. She had gone to the bathroom and was now eavesdropping in the hallway leading back to the living room. She heard them talking and figured she may hear something juicy if she listened for a bit. She didn't expect this, though. The nerve of this stuck-up wench. She stepped out of the hallway, holding her head high with righteous indignation. They both looked taken aback by her sudden appearance.

"You should be so lucky, Mrs. Miller," she said coolly to the woman who would never, ever, ever become her mother-in-law.

Mrs. Miller went bright pink.

"You, you . . . you!" she spluttered, her small mouth taking on all sorts of strange shapes.

Millie had leveled her gaze at her. Say it! she willed her. Say it, and I will slap you right back to last Tuesday. I will slap you harder than my mama slapped me when I stole Daddy's car and ran over the neighbor boy's bike. She could still feel the burn of that slap when she thought about it. Her mother had some mighty palms on her. Unfortunately, the well-bred lady within Mrs. Miller won this fight, and she only said:

"I do not approve of you!"

"Well, that's just fine! Jolly, even. 'Cause your son ain't good enough for me."

She regretted it the moment the words left her mouth. Pete's young face folded up on itself like a fist. He was going to cry. He had been so sweet to her, and she threw it in his face. She knew he was his mother's most prized possession, and she wanted to hurt her so bad that she forgot Pete was even there.

She had left that house covered in shame. Not because of what Mrs. Miller had said. Oh, no! She was raised better than that. She was proud to be Black. Her parents had told her time after time that if anyone treated her differently because of the color of her skin, that just proved how utterly stupid they were, and to tell them right away so they could put things right by whooping some ass. No, she was ashamed by how revoltingly she had treated poor Pete. Her pride had been hurt, and she had taken it out on him. Deep down, she also believed that this was somehow Noah's fault. If he just quit loving Alice and dated her, she never would have gotten involved with dear, sensitive Pete in the first place.

That was ancient past, however. Now, she had what she wanted all along, and she couldn't be happier. At the beginning, Noah was very timid. He kept reverting to treating her like a friend over and over. She had to remind him that they were dating. Recently, however, he had become more passionate. A lot more. He kissed her deeper and for longer. He touched her more intimately. When they had gone to the movies the other day, he snaked his hand up her shirt and cupped her breasts. She was so incredibly aroused by this that she would have let him take her right then and there if it weren't for all the other people. It was time to make things official. Well, more official. She had told her parents two weeks ago that Noah was now her boyfriend. Her father had cheered, a twinkle in his eyes. Her mother, well, she had a sit-down with her.

"Are you sure you want to date him, darling? You know he has the thing for your friend."

"She's not here, Maa. Relax!"

Millie took out a bottle of pink nail polish from her drawer and started working on her toes. She was a grown woman. She knew what she was doing. And how better to show that she wasn't at all concerned than by doing something relaxing while they talked about it, like painting her toes? Her mother wasn't done yet. Frowning, she sat down on the bed and took the polish from her hands.

"I'm just concerned that if Alice comes back, he'll go to her. I just don't want you to get hurt."

"Don't worry, Maa!" she chuckled, taking the polish back from her. "He is falling for me fast and hard. By the time she comes back—if she comes back—he will have forgotten about her entirely.

She proceeded to paint her nails with a calm, steady hand, as if her mother didn't just reveal her deepest, darkest fear.

On New Year's Eve, she went ahead with her plan. Noah had

been amazing. He showed eagerness and passion like she had never experienced before. He had given Millie her first orgasm. Afterward, as they lay in bed in the spare bedroom of his friend's house, Millie took a minute to gloat. She was nestled in the crook of Noah's arm. He smelled deliciously primal. Alice had been a fool not to date him. She should have at least slept with him. It was too late now. Too bad for her.

CHAPTER EIGHTEEN

1996
ROSIE

Rosie was cleaning her horse whilst lost in thought. She kept running the brush over her side again and again. At the end of each stroke, more and more dust fell to the ground. There was always more dust. It was incredible how much of it a horse's coat could hold. It was like a sponge; the more you squeezed it, the more suds it made. Suddenly, she felt a push against her hand. She lifted the brush and saw to her delight that Sand's stomach bulged out in one spot, then slowly retracted. She smiled ear to ear.

"Sand! It's your baby!"

She pushed against the spot where it had happened and was rewarded with another movement. Sand grunted, clearly not as amused by this intruder in her body. She turned her head back and gave a low, trumpeting snort. She touched her own belly with her dexterous upper lip. The foal moved again. Sand looked at Rosie questioningly. She had never had a foal before. Rosie wondered if she knew that there was a tiny horse within her or if she thought it might be colic.

She would make a great mother; Rosie just knew it. She patted Sand's belly affectionately and resumed her cleaning. Her plan was to visit the homestead today. She really didn't want to, but she had to find some answers. If Rosanne was really haunting her, as she suspected, she might find some clues there as to why. What was this unfinished business she needed help with? That's the only reason ghosts haunted, to her knowledge.

"Ow!" she screamed as a heavy weight descended onto her foot.

Their gray gelding, Pilot, had ambled over to where she and Sand stood in the pasture and casually stepped on her foot.

"You sizeable asshole!" she moaned, shoving Pilot in his broad chest.

He lifted his weight painstakingly slowly off the offending leg, like he had all the time in the world. Rosie yanked her smashed food out from underneath as soon as it was possible. She examined it. Some horse poo on her shoe and bruised toes; nothing too serious. She had a scratch on her ankle on the same leg. They now throbbed in pain together. She rubbed at both the foot and the scratch, feeling a little less sure of herself. Maybe she shouldn't go to the homestead. This could be a bad omen. Sand reached over, bending her long neck gracefully, and bit Pilot solidly on the rump. He squealed and kicked, narrowly missing Rosie, who flattened against her horse, and took off in an angry trot. Rosie leaned heavily against Sand's protruding stomach. Her head felt like it was full of air. She had been getting these strange dizzy spells lately. They passed quickly. *Lack of sleep*, she thought. She was going. She had to do something. She had the disheartening feeling that things weren't going to get better on their own.

"Rosie!" her sister called, running down the path to the stable where she was saddling her horse.

Moonwalk, the grouchy old donkey, brayed with delight at the sight of her.

"What's up, Potato?" Rosie asked, holding up her stirrup with her head while fastening the cinch.

Potato was the nickname she gave Emi shortly after she was born. She had been a chunky little baby, full of rolls.

"I'm coming with you!"

"No, you're not!"

"Mom says I have to!"

Rosie let the stirrup drop against Sand's side and turned to look her sister in the face.

"Did she really say so?"

Emi crossed her arms in typical stubborn Emi fashion. She had more in common with the donkey than she realized.

"Okay, no. But I say so!"

"Not today, Emi. I really have to do this on my own."

"Do what?"

"Go to the homestead."

Emi scrunched her face up, looking like an angry little gnome.

"You never take me anymore."

"Well, I want to get there fast, and you and Moonwalk are anything but."

"I'm going!"

She grabbed the donkey's halter from the wood peg it rested on and let out a loud whoop that was meant to summon the wretched creature. It worked. Moonwalk came galloping down the slope of the meadow, screaming his reply enthusiastically.

"Emi, no!"

"If you don't take me, I'll tell on you."

"Tell what? I don't do anything."

She grabbed the halter in Emi's hand and tried to wrench it from her grasp. A not-so-graceful tug of war issued, in which Rosie lifted Emi off the ground. She wouldn't let go.

"I'll tell Dad you have a boyfriend!"

"What?"

Rosie released her hold, making Emi fall on her butt. She popped back up, unfazed.

"Yeah! I saw you at Nana's house."

"What are you talking ab—"

The memory of her and Luke kissing came to her even before

she could finish the sentence. She felt her face flare immediately.

"Ha-ha! You lobster!" Emi cackled.

But they were at the cliff. She couldn't have possibly seen them there! There was no way! But then she recalled that one time Emi had been grounded for doing something absolutely stupid, and she snuck out of her room by climbing out her window. The little rat!

"You little shit!" she said without much merit.

The battle was over. Emi had won this one. Rosie could have countered by threatening to tell on Emi about sneaking out at night. But she couldn't do that without exposing herself. It was a checkmate. Even the freaking donkey seemed to be laughing at her defeat.

Emi saddled her accomplice, looking smug and periodically making this horrible kissy face that made her puckered mouth look like a butthole. She also sang "Kiss from a Rose" by Seal just to drive her point home. She effectively butchered the song by only knowing the words to the chorus. The rest of it she hummed and mumbled.

The two of them rode out in good spirits. Once she stopped seething, Rosie found she was relieved she didn't set out alone. The weather was fair, and the two animals *clip-clopped* amiably side by side as their riders chatted and sang. They trotted and galloped a bit where the dirt path was even and straight.

"Why did you want to come so bad?" Rosie asked when they were almost to their destination.

"Because I love you, you idiot," Emi said, exasperated.

Rosie snorted.

"I love you, too, Potato."

There was a minute of silence during which Moonwalk huffed and puffed. His long ears bobbed back and forth as he struggled to keep up with the much bigger horse. He was just about done, Rosie thought. Any minute now, and he would want to turn back. Good thing they were already there. The beautifully rustic ruins of the homestead emerged in front of them. The donkey let out a long, suffering bray that made all the crows within one mile take flight. They called mournfully to them as they lifted from the trees and the remaining roof of the old house.

"I hope they don't poop on us." Emi shivered and squinted up at the sky.

Rosie surveyed the clearing with her eyes. Everything looked to be quiet. She wasn't going to get off her horse. There was no way. Those days were over.

"Let's go look at the house!" she said, gently steering Sand with her heels.

"Uh-uh." Emi shook her head vehemently. "It's creepy here today. I'm gonna stay here."

"Okay, but don't wander off!"

"I can't. Moonwalk is eating."

She gestured at her mount, who was loudly chomping away at the lush, green grass. He wasn't going anywhere for at least a few minutes. Once he found a good patch of grass, it was almost impossible to move him.

Rosie pointed Sand's head toward the house and clicked her tongue.

It was really a lovely day to do this. The fall winds rattled the trees, releasing thousands of colorful leaves into the air. They swirled and danced before settling down, each on their chosen spot. Rosie felt her heart beat in unison with her horse's. This was when she was the happiest, when she felt like she became one with the nature around her. She saw a couple of does standing frozen at the far edge of the clearing. She stopped her horse and waited for them to make their move. The bigger one stamped one foot, releasing vibrations through the forest floor and letting any others nearby know that there were trespassers on their land. The other one, slightly smaller, must be her fawn from last year. Eventually, they decided it was time to go and slowly walked into the woods, their dusty brown coats a perfect camouflage. Within seconds, she lost sight of them. She urged Sand forward until they stood within the triangle of the spring house, the barn, and the main house. She looked over her shoulder, searching for her sister. She and Moonwalk were still in the exact same spot. She saw her little mouth move silently as she talked to the donkey. As she turned her gaze back forward, her eye caught movement from just ahead. She was expecting another forest critter but instead saw the back of a long dress disappear behind a giant oak. She felt her pulse quicken. She was waiting for a person to step out on the other side of the oak. The forest became silent and still. It took her a minute to realize the wind had dropped. The uneasy feeling of being watched crept over her, like fingers drumming on her spine. She heard a twig snap to her right and jerked her head in that direction, only to see a small white hand disappear behind the bark of another tree. She swallowed hard, taking a firmer grip of the reins. Multiple different scenarios ran through her mind. Could this actually be a ghost? Was it Rosanne's ghost? Or was it maybe an actual person or multiple people? Was she in danger? She heard a door slam and jumped in her saddle. It was the front door of the old house, but it had no door. It hadn't had a front door in ages. And yet, there it was, thick and solid like the tree it had been carved out of. She felt a pull toward it. From behind her came a whisper. She couldn't turn her head, her spinal column having become a solid rod of iron. She felt somebody's breath on her cheek.

"Don't go!" said a woman's voice.

The house was changing in front of her very eyes. The stone bricks that had fallen over the years were now lifting back into place as if somebody had hit rewind on time. The rest of the roof, along with the shingles, materialized out of thin air. She flew toward the front door as weightless as a feather. She went through it, the solid wood no barrier for her, and found herself standing in the entryway. Only it wasn't the house she knew.

This one was new and full of life. To her left, in the old office, stood a bulky wooden desk with a man bent over it. His long black hair was tied back at the nape of his neck. He was scribbling something on a piece of paper with a long colorful feather that Rosie recognized as the tail feather of a turkey. A toddler with shaggy blonde hair ran past her, almost bumping into her leg. She followed him, drifting into the living room, where a huge fire was roaring in the old fireplace. There were a lot more people in here. There were three kids total, two boys and a girl. The girl and one of the boys appeared to be really close in age, around nine or so. They were kneeling by a wide log that they used as a table to play some game involving dice. There was the little boy, who looked to be two or three. He ran up to a young woman who was knitting by the fire, the already done fabric draping over her enormous pregnant belly. At the other side of the fireplace, adjacent to the pregnant woman, sat an old lady who had apparently fallen asleep in her chair. Her head was resting on one shoulder. Wisps of her graying brown hair escaped her bun and fluttered in front of her face as she snored softly. They all wore old-school western-style clothing and seemed to be unaware of Rosie's presence. She examined all their faces and concluded that she had no idea who they were. As perplexing as her own presence here was, she knew she was seeing these people for a reason. The biggest problem was that she had no idea what Rosanne actually looked like. There were no paintings or photographs of her either at home or in the museum. She also hadn't seen enough of her personal haunter's face, as it always had hair in front of it, to be able to tell if any of these people were a younger version of her. The little boy finally gave up on trying to climb into the young woman's lap. There was too much stomach in the way. He instead toddled over to the old lady. Roused from her nap, she lifted the delighted youngster onto her knees and rocked him back and forth. They all seemed so peaceful and happy. The scene strangely reminded Rosie of her own family, all huddled together in front of the TV on a cold winter evening. Her lovely vision was shattered instantly when she saw the figure in the corner of the room. The old crone was squatting in the darkest corner, just left of the fireplace. The room instantly felt colder. The pregnant lady shuddered and pulled her shawl tighter around her shoulders. The crone stood slowly, her small frame unfolding like a crumpled piece of paper. She stepped out of the darkness straight in front of the fire. Nobody reacted. They couldn't see her. Without realizing she was doing it, Rosie started to take rapid gulps of air. She felt dizzy and lightheaded. The crone walked over to where the two older children were playing and placed a gnarled hand on the back of the girl's neck. She shuddered, her breath coming out white. The apparition lifted her other hand and pointed straight at Rosie.

"You!" she creaked. "You're the one!"

"What?" Rosie breathed.

She wanted to understand. She needed to know what to do to be done with this haunting business once and for all.

Her world tilted, and she found herself back on her horse. A crow had landed on Sand's neck, making her jump. They were outside between the triangle of the buildings, and everything was normal, the structures nothing but ruins. The bird cawed at her loudly and took off flying. She followed it with her eyes. It flew in the direction where she had left Emi. Only she wasn't there. Fright washed over her, cold and prickling.

"Emi!" she called.

No answer. She called again, louder this time, letting her growing panic penetrate her voice. This time, she received an answer, but not from her sister. A long, echoey donkey cry broke the silence of the forest.

"Moonwalk!" she yelled with relief.

The donkey answered again, his cry seeming more alarmed than annoyed like usual. Rosie tried to pinpoint where his calls were coming from while her own mount danced agitatedly under her. It sounded like they were at the cliff. She wasn't quite sure, though. Sound traveled strangely in the forest. It tended to bounce off rocks and trees and had the ability to lead an inexperienced person in the wrong direction. Sand was ready to go, though, and Rosie decided to trust the horse's instinct to find her friend. They took off in a quick thundering gallop toward the cliff. Sand was experienced when it came to forest trails, so she nimbly dodged saplings and jumped over logs without slowing down. When they got close to the cliff, the trees fell away, and Rosie saw her sister immediately. She was sitting on top of her donkey, both facing the drop-off. They were dangerously close to the edge. Moonwalk stomped and brayed as he heard them coming but didn't turn to them. It looked like he was stuck. Caught on something, maybe a small tree. She brought Sand to a sliding halt and jumped from her saddle even before the animal stopped moving completely.

"Emi!" she cried, running up to her sister.

Suddenly, Moonwalk became unstuck. He turned rapidly toward Rosie, throwing Emi in the process. Rosie caught her glazed-eyed sister mid-fall as she slid out of her saddle like a bag of potatoes. She kneeled on the ground with Emi in her arms. Her eyes were open but unseeing. She looked to be sleepwalking.

"Emi! What's wrong? What happened?"

Her sister reached out with one small, grubby hand and touched Rosie's face.

"You found me," she said, still staring into space.

"Wake up, you annoying little turd!"

Rosie shook her violently, and that seemed to do the trick. Emi blinked a few times, and her eyes focused on Rosie's face.

"What happened?" she asked groggily.

"Thank God!" Rosie exclaimed, hugging Emi to her chest. "I told you not to wander off, you idiot!"

On the way back, Rosie insisted on having Moonwalk on a lead. Emi didn't fight her on it. She didn't remember how she and Moonwalk made it to the cliff. The most reasonable explanation was that she lay down in the saddle and had fallen asleep. This would have given her donkey the opportunity to make his way to the cliff. It was a weak explanation, no matter how reasonable. It was highly unlikely that she would have stayed asleep the entire way there, even if she did doze off. And Moonwalk's default setting was to go home, which was in the opposite direction from the cliff. But they could not come up with anything better. The other strange thing was that the donkey seemed to be unable to turn around when Rosie got there, yet there was nothing there that he could have gotten his reins stuck on.

Something else was scratching at the back of Rosie's mind.

Something that had happened recently. She couldn't remember it until they got home and she was in her room. Her eye caught the dreamcatcher Luke had made her in summer camp one year. It was hanging above her bed.

She and Luke were sitting in the exact same spot on the cliff where she had found Emi today. Luke had also acted very strangely. It could have just been a coincidence, but Rosie had the feeling that it wasn't. She had gone to the homestead hoping for some answers but ended up leaving with more questions than she had started out with.

CHAPTER NINETEEN

1996
ALICE

They had driven down to the lake on the first weekend of October. She had told Noah that she thought Rosie could use a little getaway, a change of scenery. He agreed readily enough. The real reason Alice wanted to come was to have a very serious talk about Aunt Francis with her mother. She didn't mention this to Noah. Something was nagging at her memory ever since they sat Rosie down in her bedroom to get the truth out of her after their visit with Norma.

She and Noah took a seat on either side of her, effectively caging her in on her bed.

"We just want to hear your side of it," Noah had said, delegating.

"I don't know what happened!" she exclaimed, leaning back against the wall with her arms crossed.

She was using a tone of voice with them recently that she never had before. It was cold and harsh and made Alice feel like she had no right to know anything about her daughter anymore. That everything that came out of her mouth was annoying. It was incredibly distressing.

"You have to say something, honey!" Noah kept pushing. He was being way too nice, in Alice's opinion. This was serious stuff. They had to be more assertive. "What did you say to her just before she hit you?"

Rosie seemed to fold deeper into herself.

"I said I don't remember!"

She pulled her knees under her chin and turned her face away from her father, so now, Alice had a clear view of her face. She looked scared. Alice touched her arm gently. It was time to get to the point. She was done beating around the bush.

"Ms. Lesbith said you told her something that you were not supposed to know. She had surgery to remove one of her organs. How did you know that?"

The word "uterus" hovered at the tip of Alice's tongue. It seemed like an inappropriate word to use around a fourteen-year-old even though it was such an essential part of a woman's anatomy. She decided not to say it at the last moment. Rosie squirmed. She squeezed her eyelids shut, but Alice could see her eyes moving back and forth rapidly behind her eyelids.

"I," she began and stopped, her tongue hovering inside her open mouth as if she didn't have the words for what had happened. "I saw it."

She looked pleadingly at Alice and then at Noah, willing for them to understand something she clearly didn't.

"It was like I was there. And then I just said it. I don't know why."

Her chin quivered. Her wide blue eyes filled with tears. She launched herself at Alice, who squeezed her to her chest. It felt like ages since she was allowed to hold her like this. Not since . . . not since they took her to the hospital. Noah picked up one of her bony little feet and rubbed it gently with his thumbs.

"Why is Rosie crying?"

Emi had walked into the room without either of them noticing. Rosie let out a huge, raspy sob at the sound of her sister's voice. Emi's eyes went as round as saucers. Her bottom lip jutted out, and she, too, burst out crying as she ran to her sister.

"Rosie!" she wailed. "Don't cry!"

Alice could feel her own eyes getting hot. She valiantly held back her tears as she and Noah sat there rocking their two crying children. Noah wouldn't cry. He was a man's man who didn't like showing vulnerability in front of people. Alice hadn't seen him cry since he was a little boy. He held it together, even at their wedding, his tears never escaping his bottom lids. He was the strong one, both physically and emotionally, and he held on to that role with an iron grip. But just then, as Alice looked at him across the sobbing bodies of their girls, she saw him turn his head slightly and rub the corner of an eye with one finger.

She "saw it," Rosie had said. Like she was there. Alice had this nagging feeling that she had heard something like this before. She racked and racked her brain, and suddenly, out popped this memory of a conversation with her father. She had been sixteen, and her parents were arguing about the upcoming visit with her aunt yet again. Her dad really just wanted to get out of it, and her mother had put her foot down.

"It's Easter!" Her mother stamped her foot for emphasis. "We are all going as a family!"

Afterward, Alice had sat down next to her father on the couch. He was rubbing his forehead with both hands, looking utterly miserable.

"Why don't you wanna go, Dad?" she had asked, her curiosity piqued.

"Oh, it's a long story, my love. And it's not for the ears of a little girl."

"Dad, I'm sixteen."

Her dad had looked taken aback, as if a few years of life had passed without him noticing. He took in her budding womanly shape, her growing breasts and widening hips. He coughed, shifting his eyes away from her.

"Where did the time go . . ." he said, shaking his head slowly.

"Dad!"

"All right. Well, you know your aunt has a . . . talent for saying embarrassing stuff, right?"

"Yes . . ."

She drew out the word. "Embarrassing" was a very mild way of putting it, in her opinion.

"I don't know where she gets her information. Frankly, none of us have ever found out over the years. But somehow, she seems to know all the worst things that have happened to you in your lifetime. And she will say those things out loud, too, in the most inopportune moments, of course. And I just don't want her to ruin another Easter . . ."

He trailed off and reached into his pocket for his pack of cigarettes. At this point, Alice did remember that last Easter, they had also gone to visit her aunt. They had taken her father's sister and her two kids with them, as well. Aunt Macy had a pair of rambunctious eleven-year-old little boys. She had always told Alice, very tiredly, that having twins is the worst possible thing that could happen to a woman. Anyway, she had gone to the bathroom at some point, and when she came back, they had left immediately. There was no explanation as to why. Alice hadn't given it a second thought at the time. But now, a year later, her parents simply refused to tell her what happened. So, wickedly, and somewhat guiltily, she called her aunt and asked her. At first, she didn't want to tell her, either. She just kept laughing nervously through the phone, starting sentences and leaving them unfinished. Finally, after much wheedling, she had said, whispering, that Aunt Franny told everyone her father had gotten an erection at church on Easter Sunday when he was the same age as her boys.

Here and now, in the present, Alice giggled at the memory. But back then, she had felt nauseated by the mental image. She kept on washing her face, wishing she could wash her brain instead. It was quite possibly the worst thing that ever passed her ears. Words like "Dad" and "erection" should not be allowed in the same sentence. There needed to be a law against it.

She did recall then that there may have been a few times

when Aunt Franny knew more about her than she should have. Strange, embarrassing things, like when her period was due, or that she had peeked through the keyhole one time when Noah was changing at their house. But she always thought that maybe her parents had told her things behind her back. Her thinking had been so innocent, so naive.

The lake was still warm enough to swim in—if you were a masochist, that is, which most kids seemed to be. They had some cold showers come through during September, and the water temperature dropped quite a bit. The kids still waded in at least knee-deep. Emi latched onto the rope swing like a little wet monkey after she was done trying to catch small fish with her butterfly net. Alice kept hearing her screaming demands of, "Swing me! Swing me!" from where she sat in the sunroom. Rosie was taking a nap upstairs. With Noah on rope swing duty, Alice was hoping for no interruptions. Her mother breezed in, carrying a tray of homemade eclairs. She had gotten a haircut since the last time Alice saw her. She was looking cute with her chin-length silver bob. She was a great baker. Alice didn't inherit this from her. Maybe she should try harder. She could learn how to bake this good. Maybe if she baked, Rosie would be magically healed by all the sweetness. Alice herself had always loved to come home to the smell of fresh baking. Maybe her mother's baking was what had kept the evil away from her. You never know.

Maggie pushed the tray of eclairs in her direction on the coffee table. She was so happy about their surprise visit; she hadn't stopped smiling since they arrived.

"Isn't your face getting tired?" Alice asked and took one of the offered pastries.

"As a matter of fact, it is." Her mother dimpled at her, rubbing a hand against one cheek. "But I just can't seem to stop."

"Well, maybe I can help you with that . . ."

Her mother's smile faltered. Alice felt like a true asshole. Did she really need to involve her mother in this? She may not have any useful information. And then, all Alice would be doing is giving her sleepless nights. Maybe she should try solving this on her own first. She had Noah, after all. Noah, who wanted Rosie to go to therapy. Alice's fear was irrational; she knew that. She was afraid that if Rosie went to a psychiatrist, she would immediately be diagnosed with something terrible. They would insist she'd be put in an institution or be doped up on drugs. The thought of either of these scenarios coming to pass almost paralyzed her with fear. She needed more information to be able to make the right choice. She needed some good old-fashioned parental guidance.

"Mom, I'm worried about Rosie."

"Oh, dear . . ."

Her mother wrung her hands nervously.

"I knew there was something going on. She's not herself these days, is she? It's not just when she visits?"

"No, Mom, she loves coming here."

"I just thought . . . Well, it seemed like she and Luke had a falling out, the way those two have been avoiding each other."

Alice thought about sweet, skinny little Luke Szabo and smiled to herself wistfully. Those two definitely had something going on. Young love, perhaps? She thought of Noah and herself at that age. How long ago it was that those first sparks of romance appeared between them. How vehemently Alice had resisted them. And all for naught. They still ended up together, as if governed by fate.

"They will be fine, Mom. Don't worry! Actually, maybe just worry a little bit, but not about Luke."

And so, she told her mother all she knew. The sleeplessness, the irritability. Her moodiness and back talk. She left the thing with the teacher for last. Her mom seemed to be shrinking with every word she added. Alice felt like she was sucking all the happiness out of her through a straw. She felt like a truly bad person. An incompetent mother.

"My God," her mother said finally after she had stopped talking. "Why didn't you tell me sooner? Why didn't you call me?"

She should have. All sorts of answers came to mind: *Because*

I was busy. Because I didn't care enough until recently. Because I just had to wait until it got out of hand. Because I was trying to blame somebody else. She thought about Norma, the history teacher who was so sad and lonely on the inside, so cold and hard on the outside. She had slapped her daughter, and Alice still managed to feel bad for her.

"I was afraid," she said. "I keep thinking this is how it starts."

Her voice broke, and her mother instinctively put out a hand toward her.

"Oh, honey, no! Hush, now!"

Alice wiped away the first tear of the day. She had been finding times to seclude herself from her family and let out a good cry each day ever since they had that talk with Norma.

"How did it happen with Francis? Was it similar?"

She blew her nose noisily in a tissue offered by her mother.

"It all happened so long ago . . ." Her mother trailed off. "It's hard to remember the details."

"Don't be kind to me! Not right now!" Alice shook herself and tried to internalize her feelings.

There would be a time and place to let them out. Not right now. They had too much to discuss. Her mother compressed her lips and nodded solemnly.

"Perhaps there are just a few similarities," Maggie ventured, "but that doesn't necessarily mean that this is schizophrenia. It could very well be something totally different."

"Should I take her to a professional?"

She wanted her mother to say, "No, absolutely not!" or maybe a lighter version, "Just wait a bit longer, honey, and see what happens!" The longer she managed to keep her head turned the other way, the longer she could keep the fantasy of a perfect family alive.

"Yes, dear. I think that would be best."

CHAPTER TWENTY

1996
LUKE

He was reading a book called *Hauntings*. It was one of thirty-three books from the *Mysteries of the Unknown* series. He felt he needed to do some research in order to better understand just what he was dealing with when it came to Rosie's speck. He ended up with two dislocated fingers after his encounter the last time, with no real explanation to give to his grandparents about how it happened. So far, the book was pretty good, but some of the stories were outrageous enough that he suspected they were made up. Somebody just wanted some attention. Five minutes of fame.

His bedroom setup was pretty cozy. A few years back, his grandfather, with the help of Rosie's dad, had installed a loft that his bed now sat on. Underneath was his desk and a bean bag alongside a bookshelf. The lake house itself was small, and so was his room. This loft had made excellent use of the space.

He was lying on his bed, holding the book in front of his face, when his grandpa opened the door.

"Hey, kiddo! The Smiths pulled up!"

He sat bolt upright, banging his head on the slanting ceiling.

"Son of a turd nugget!" he groaned, falling back against his pillow and rubbing his hands against his very sore forehead.

"Didn't mean to startle ya, son!" his grandpa said, chuckling. "Reading something fun up there?"

"No, Grandpa! Just a boring mystery book."

"If ya say so."

He gave him a knowing smile, a rogue twinkle in his eye, and closed the door softly, backing out. He had caught Luke one time with a *Hustler*, and from then on, he always assumed Luke was reading some dirty magazine when he was alone in his room. He was such an old dog. Luke wished he'd stop treating him like a normal teenager. He was so abnormal, it should be illegal. Luke wondered what the naughty old fart would say if he knew the first naked woman Luke had seen was a ghost. He had been eight and deeply affected by the experience. He'd gone biking around the lake with his grandparents. He rode ahead, and when he rounded a bend in the road, *bam!* There she was, in all her pale, misty glory. Luke was so startled, he fell off his bike and skinned the side of his shin painfully. He didn't go bike riding after that for a long time. And he wouldn't even walk that route until years later. He was pretty sure the naked ghost lady had been a murder victim.

His second naked lady was Grandma. Luke had surprised her late at night as she was raiding the fridge for the rest of the chocolate cake from his tenth birthday the day before. Luke had snuck into the kitchen for the exact same reason. He had bumped into a chair. It made an ungodly screeching noise. Grandma had whirled around. Her robe wasn't tied. End of story. He wished he could have washed his eyeballs.

The third time was the *Hustler*. One of his friends from school had lent it to him. He really didn't want to take it home, but he also didn't want to refuse when it was offered to him. He didn't want the other boys to think he didn't like girls. So, he took it home, intending for it to stay hidden in his school bag until it was time to return it the next day, but curiosity got the best of him. And that was the time his grandfather caught him. With all the shock and embarrassment involved, Luke actually didn't mind if he never saw a naked lady ever again.

He had no idea the Smiths were coming. It normally would have been a delightful surprise, but with everything that happened recently, he was nervous. As he made his way over there, he hoped the speck had somehow disappeared.

No such luck there. It was billowing around her shoulders, snapping and reaching like a tiny Cape.

"Rosie!" he called out to her, closing their backyard gate.

To his surprise, she hopped up from where she was sitting on the grass with her sister and ran to him. He barely had time to open his arms and catch her. She crashed into him so hard that they almost toppled over. His ribcage cracked under her tight squeeze.

"It's so nice to see you!" Her muffled voice came from his shirt.

She looked up at him, beaming, and for a second, his heart stopped. This was the old Rosie. His Rosie. She was back! For a second, he was so overcome with happiness, he couldn't speak. He heard the faint sounds of the thing crackling and snapping, though. Its energy ran through him, making his hairs stand on end. It wasn't a completely unpleasant feeling. But every fiber of his body warned him that there was danger coming.

They once showed a clip of a boy in the news who had been struck by lightning and survived. His hair had stood up in a halo around his head, his mother explained. "He was smiling before it struck. None of us knew it was coming."

Rosie stepped back and inspected him at arm's length.

"Did you grow an inch?" she asked, her eyes twinkling. "You are, like, six inches taller than me now."

"Or maybe you just shrunk."

He patted the top of her head affectionately and was rewarded by a tiny zap from her Cape. He wasn't that happy about all the growth he had achieved this past year. He felt gangly and uncoordinated. When he looked in the mirror, he felt his knees were way too big for how thin his legs looked. He took up track in school, and that made him feel a bit better. Now, his long legs actually had a purpose. Plus, they were starting to shape up slightly, so they weren't just white limp noodles attached to his pelvis.

"Your birthday is next week, right?" she asked, taking his hand and leading him toward the back gate.

"Did you remember, or did your mom tell you?" he asked with his version of a shit-eating grin.

"That is irrelevant," she retorted, her nose stuck high in the air. "Come on, you snail trail! I have a surprise for you."

They walked into the small wooded area behind the houses. There were a couple of mossy boulders back there, ideal to sit on. When they were small, they used to build a fort between them. They pretended Rosie's dad was a dragon. They would fend him off heroically, poking at him with small sticks and throwing pinecones at his back. Now, they just sat down on them across from each other, Luke sticking his not-so-noodly legs out in front of him.

"Here!"

Rosie handed him a red polka-dotted gift bag.

"Where were you hiding this?" Luke asked, truly baffled.

"Up my bum," she said cheekily. "I know you don't turn fourteen until next Tuesday, but we're not gonna be here, so happy early birthday!"

"Thanks!"

The bag revealed a copy of Rosanne Glessner's journal. It was shiny and new. Luke knew the story of Rosie's heritage, but he'd never actually read the journal before. He was delighted.

"Thanks, Rosie! I've actually been meaning to read this."

"Well, it's sort of a selfish gift, really."

She looked at him from under her lashes sheepishly. Luke saw her cloud cape fair as if hit by a strong gust of wind.

"I'm going to tell you something, okay? But you have to promise not to laugh at me!"

Rosie sat up straight, folding her legs crisscrossed under herself. She took a deep breath.

"Are you okay? Are you in some kind of trouble?"

He furrowed his brows at her. She seemed to have forgotten

all about their unfortunate kiss on the cliff. She was acting all normal with him, but it was still kind of odd. Something was off.

"Not exactly," she said. "Now, promise you won't laugh!"

"Okay, okay. I promise."

"Okay!" She took another deep breath. "I think I am being haunted."

The thing crackled and threw small blue sparks in all directions. *OH! You may be right about that*, Luke thought with trepidation. He searched his mind for something to say. Something meaningful. Supportive, even. But all he could think was, *There is a small, angry storm cloud on your shoulders, and I think it may be a demon.*

"Oh," he said lamely.

"Something happened to me at the homestead at the end of August . . ."

And so, she told him a story that he would have considered a hundred percent made-up if he hadn't experienced her strange electric appendage personally. Having unusual dreams, feeling drained, and seeing things were her symptoms of ailments, with some daytime visions on the side. At this moment in time, Luke was so incredibly grateful that he could see ghosts. Otherwise, he would have to consider his best friend a lunatic. It sounded surreal and scary, and it explained everything.

"I think it is the ghost of Rosanne. She probably has some unfinished business here on earth and needs my help. I actually got you her journal so you could read it and help me look for clues."

She finished and, unfolding her long, tan legs, stretched them out in front of her. They were so incredibly shapely that, for a second, Luke just stared at them, forgetting to speak. Was it even fair for someone to have such nice legs? His mouth went dry.

"Hello! Earth to Luke!" She waved a hand in front of his face.

"Sorry!"

He snapped his gaze up to hers. She had the loveliest blue eyes. They were like the lake on a clear day. It was near impossible to think about anything else when she was looking so lovely right here in front of him. Within reach.

"So, what do you think? Do you think I'm crazy?"

"Absolutely not!" he said much too quickly.

He cleared his throat. This would be an excellent time to tell her about his peculiarity. A perfect time. Possibly the only time. He could just say it. He could say it out loud for the first time since his mother died. It would be such a huge weight off his shoulders. It would be absolutely terrifying. She might believe him. Or she might not. She may think that he was trying to make fun of her for what she had just told him. She may think that Luke was making things up because he thought she was making things up. Telling her could send them into a downward spiral yet again. It could make him lose her for good. He swallowed the bitter ball of frustration that rose within him.

"I'll help you," he heard himself say. "Whatever is going on with you, we'll figure it out together!"

She gave him the widest smile, her shoulders slumping.

"Oh, my God!" she said, covering her mouth with both hands. "You don't know what this means to me. I have been feeling so down. So alone. But I knew you would believe me! I feel so much better!"

She hopped off her rock and hugged him.

"Thank you for being there for me," she whispered in his ear.

Her breath tickled. It made a delightful wave of goosebumps run down his arms and up his spine. She leaned back and their eyes met, and for a moment, he was conscious of all that was them. He could feel her hands gently pressing against his sides. Her hips barely touching his outstretched thighs. Her hair brushing against his arm as it hung down and framed her face in gold. She was a mythical forest creature, and he a mere human who just happened to be at the right place at the right time. His gaze flickered down to her lips. She had a perfect Cupid's bow. His breath hitched. Did he dare? Did he dare try it again? His body made the decision on its own. As if drawn to her, he leaned down to her face. She closed her eyes just before their lips touched. He could feel her. The essence of her. She held so much power, and she didn't even know it. The speck was in the background, its angry energy hovering menacingly just behind hers. It had nothing on Rosie. She was too bright to be taken down by such an insignificant thing. Try all it might, it would not take her. It didn't stand a chance.

CHAPTER TWENTY-ONE

1996
ROSIE

Sometimes, things unravel in such strange ways that it's hard to believe it's reality. The further along Rosie got in the journal, the more she wondered what she would write in her own. If she kept a diary, she might write something like:

My name is Rosanne Smith, but people call me Rosie. I am an ordinary girl from an ordinary family. I have a little sister, whom I love. I also have an old dog called Ollie. I have a secret crush on my best friend. Nothing really interesting ever happens to me.

Or maybe she would write the truth:

My name is Rosie Smith, but people call me loony. I am a sad girl with parents who don't understand me. I have an annoying little sister, and my dog will probably die any minute. I have no real friends. I am pretty sure I am slowly going crazy.

After the terrifying dream she had, Rosie was afraid of going into the office. She wasn't consciously aware of this until her dad asked her to grab something from in there. Standing on the threshold, her legs had turned into cement. She couldn't do it. She couldn't go in. It was utterly ridiculous. She kept seeing those awful blue eyes in the dark corners. Cold sweat broke out on the back of her neck. She ran and jumped on the couch, where she hugged a pillow to her chest. Was she going to let despair take over her life? She thought about what a rough life Rosanne Glessner had had, losing her daughter and unborn child. If Rosie had led a miserable life and then died, she may end up becoming a scary ghost, too. Rosanne's spirit was just sad and misunderstood. That's all it was. She had to help her move on. When she came to this revelation, her fear had gone away. In the next few days, she had come to have a more positive outlook on life. She became more productive. That was why she returned to the homestead. It hadn't been a particularly helpful visit, but she didn't let that discourage her. The one thing she was grateful to learn was that Luke probably had some kind of experience there on the cliff. Just like her sister. So, it wasn't his fault that things got awkward. She made the decision to tell Luke about what was going on with her. He always had her back. Her positive attitude seemed to have kept the nightmares at bay. She was actually sleeping through the night, so by the time she saw Luke on the first weekend of October, she felt more like herself than at any time in the past month.

She was surprised to see that Luke had grown a bit. She just saw him a month or so ago, and she didn't notice. She had been really out of it last time they visited. She must have not been paying attention. He looked more grown up as well as taller. Even his legs looked less skinny. She was surprised to notice that her heart rate picked up when she took him by the hand. She thought her fledgling feelings for him were squashed after their kiss this past summer. He had acted so completely out of sorts, Rosie had felt wrong for initiating it. She was older by almost a year. It was a possibility that Luke hadn't been ready. Or he just didn't feel the same way. After that kiss, she had felt wrong on so many levels. She just wanted to forget about it. It was a great relief to think that wasn't the way it was at all. It was the place, not the boy. The place had something wrong with it. The cliff had a secret.

As she told him her dark secret by the boulders in the forest, though, she felt something new between them. Something exciting. She watched the muscles flex in his tan arms as he shifted his weight, his thick eyebrows furrow as he listened to her. She found that she was attracted to him. She had known him for so long, it was almost unfathomable. The first kiss, well, that was sort of an experiment. She liked him a lot. They were alone under the stars. So, she gave it a go.

Now, she found her eyes slowly drifting to his lips again and again. He had a nicely shaped mouth. Maybe a bit fuller than Rosie's, in fact. When she hugged him, the heat of his body had moved something within her. Something primal. Their second kiss was delightful. No awkwardness like the first time. No strange looks. Just them.

That day, life had been good. Full of hope and sunshine. If Rosie had known that this would be her last day like this, her last day of being normal and happy, she would have kissed him again.

That night, she settled contentedly into the bottom bunk bed and prepared to read the journal. Emi was already out above her, one little foot carelessly hanging over the edge of the top bunk. She watched her little toes spread and flex as she dreamt. The bottom of her foot still had some dirt on it. She always forgot to scrub her soles, the dirty little piggy. Rosie smiled with affection, then scratched at her ankle absentmindedly. The scratch she had on it had become very itchy. She found herself scratching at it whenever her mind went blank.

She opened the book and gazed down at its pages in the soft yellow glow of the little desk light her grandma had given her. Luke was probably reading his copy right now. They were now connected to each other through this book and Rosanne Glessner's ghost. She could just see him lying back on his loft with the book in front of his face. She touched her lips with two fingers, slowly running them back and forth. A hot flush spread across her cheeks. She felt suddenly embarrassed and wondered if her parents suspected what they had been up to in the forest. She imagined her mom casually asking her how her second kiss had been. She would just about die of embarrassment. Her skin was on fire now. She shook herself and shimmied into her pillow. Nothing better that some nice seventeenth-century tragedy to cool her boiling blood.

October 19, 1742

A lot has happened since I last wrote. It had been a dreadful and confusing time. Our ship had finally touched ground at a strange place called Charleston. I arrived here with Kata and you, my precious journal. Eric had mysteriously disappeared from the ship sometime at the end of September. I would have scarcely noticed if not for some angry men who came to assault me in the night. They were looking for money. Three of them. They were holding a knife to my throat; they demanded it. Eric owed them after losing so many times at cards.

Since I had nothing of value on me, they took my body. One by one. As I lay on the wooden boards, being ravaged, I saw Kata's eyes shining in the darkness. She was gripping her small pocketknife, ready to pounce on the man with his back to her. I shook my head at her. It wasn't all that bad, after all. I was still so wracked with guilt over Heidi, I scarcely felt a thing. In fact, I laughed softly to myself, for I had marked all three of them with the blood of my moon. The last decent thing Eric could have done was give me a child, and he couldn't even manage that. Good riddance to him! Maybe one of these men will be more successful.

In Charleston, us single women were treated like livestock. We were rounded up and quickly put up for auction. With no husbands or adult sons to vouch for us, we couldn't do anything about it. The ones who protested hard enough or tried to run were killed right there in front of everyone. And nobody did a thing. Kata and I held hands as they lined us up on the market square to be inspected by potential buyers. They asked how old I was, and I told them I was nineteen, for I had celebrated my birthday on the deck of the ship. I was surprised to hear that Kata was twenty-eight years of age.

Twenty-eight, and no children to her name. Not for the first time, I wondered if she had a secret or two up her sleeve.

People came and went, Black and white. A Negro man once asked me if I was literate upon seeing me clutch my journal to my bosom. I told him I was, of course, that being the only useful quality I possessed. A little while later, I was informed that I had been purchased by the man's master. I pleaded with the man to ask his master to buy Kata, as well. He laughed in my face. An ugly barking sound. He told me the old hag was not worth a penny. It was then that I knew that I wasn't only bought because I could read and write. I was once considered to be beautiful. I turned heads left and right back in my hometown, with my long, wavy chestnut hair and small, heart-shaped face. Eric had once told me that my eyes were as beautiful as a newborn fawn's. I had not seen a mirror in months. From what I could imagine, I most likely looked like my own ghost. But my new master apparently had some imagination. They tossed me onto a wagon with two Negro women and some goats, and off we went. Kata and I watched each other until she was out of sight. I cried bitterly. It was as if I lost my sister. A sister whose last name I don't know, nor she mine. With all the grief aboard the ship, I had never asked her. And now, I may never again get the chance. How would we find each other? I howled into the open space between us, "My name is Rosanne Glessner!" and hoped it would carry across the trees to her. I chose to use my maiden name, for Eric was no more.

Now, I could be anyone I wished, even if I was a slave, for that's what I was purchased as. One of the women pulled my head into her lap and ran her fingers through my hair, whispering words of reassurance I could not understand.

My new home is to be a ranch in Texas. My new master is called Abel McCullum. He had traveled to Charleston to gather supplies and train goods, I was told. I have seen only glimpses of him, for he rides in the front of our convoy, and I in the back with the animals and the other slaves. I am the only white-skinned person back here. At first, I was most uncomfortable. I had never met a

Black man before embarking on this journey and wasn't sure if they are civil. To my surprise, they are quite nice people. Especially the women. They sing as they walk and even when they work. They spend their downtime on the wagon, mending clothes or splitting beans.

Their songs have a strange foreign melody that is as pleasing to my ears as it is alien. There is only one wagon for us to rest on. The women are allowed to take turns sitting on it while the others walk behind. We move from sunup to sundown. My tender feet are blistered and raw, and we have only been on the road for four days. Most of the Blacks don't speak any language but their own, but the one who arranged my purchase told me it would be near a month before we reached our destination. I was dumbfounded. I'm not even sure if it is possible for a human to walk for a month straight. My muscles are weak from the ship ride. My lovely satin shoes have broken. They now dangle, useless, from my belt. The English-speaking Negro's name is Nono. When I asked him why, he smiled and said that was the first thing he learned in English. "No-no!" This made me think of Kata. It is because of her that I am able to communicate with these people at all. Her insistence that I learn English is proving to be more useful than I ever imagined.

Nono is a lot more compassionate than I gave him credit for. I can see that he pities me for my soft feet and weak body. I am not offended by this. I pity myself, too.

He asked to see my broken shoes the other day. When I gave them to him, he spoke to one of the women in that strange foreign tongue of theirs. He gave my shoes to her, and in a couple of hours, she gave them back to me, only they didn't look like my shoes anymore. She had stitched hide over the satin. The hair on it is white and brown. I asked her where it came from. Somehow, she understood my question and pointed to the goats. They had killed one of the billy goats two days ago for meat. I had no idea that its hide had been cured, and so quickly, too. My amazement must have shown, for the woman laughed. She has a pleasant, jingly laugh. I told her my name, and the way she said it made me and the other women around us cackle. When I attempted to pronounce hers, even the men were rolling with mirth. I am not even going to attempt to write it down . . . Ta-ttengi, or maybe Tuatangi. There, my dear journal. I gave it a go for your benefit.

Both the colored men and the women tend to treat me like I am a young girl. I don't know if this is because I don't speak their language or if they genuinely think I am younger than I am. In any case, it feels good. Strangely enough, it reminds me of my childhood.

I have just been told by one of the white drivers that I am summoned to the master's quarters tonight. I had a suspicion that this may happen eventually. We all know why I am to go there. The women prepare me by brushing the tangles out of my hair. They give me two long French braids that dangle prettily down to the middle of my back. They also hand me some herb that I am to rub on my skin. I saw them doing it before, so I mimic their movements. The juice it releases smells spicy and earthy. It masks my odor somewhat. I am generally grateful for this, for I haven't bathed in over three weeks, the last time being aboard the ship when Kata and I took advantage of a rainstorm. We washed each other's backs with the last of my soap and danced around in the pouring cold rain like two silly little girls.

I miss my friend, but I have to say, in this very moment amongst my new dark-skinned family, I do not feel unhappy.

Rosie dreamt of a moonlit sky. She was walking out to the lakefront in the backyard hand in hand with her sister. They were being naughty. They were going for a midnight swim. Emi was a fairy with brightly colored see-through wings; Rosie was a mermaid with legs. She didn't question how that was possible; she just went with it. The starry sky melted into the lake on the horizon until she couldn't tell where one ended and where the other began. She didn't bring her sister's floaties. They didn't need them. Rosie, being a mermaid, could easily hold Emi up in the water. She would just sit on her back, and they would swim and swim and swim some more. Rosie would take her to see the other mermaids. That was the plan. They walked out onto the dock, still holding hands. When they reached the end, they grabbed the edge with their toes. There was nothing between them and the water but air.

"Are you ready?" She gazed down at her sister lovingly.

But Emi was gone. She looked around for her and finally spotted her in the sky. She was hovering as gracefully as a butterfly above the lake, glowing with her soft inner light. *She got a head start on me, the little devil*, she thought. That was okay, though. Once she jumped into the water, her legs would transform into a mermaid tail, and she would catch up to her in no time. She bent her legs and leaped, her arms wide. She heard a loud thud, and at the same time, her head snapped to the side. Then, she received a full-body shock as she submerged into the chilled lake. She flailed her arms and gasped, inhaling black water. At this point, she was fully awake and came to the horrifying realization that she, indeed, did jump into the lake. It wasn't just a dream. As she reached the bottom, she kicked it and shot up to the surface. She emerged, sputtering and coughing. Her forehead, face, and arm were pulsing with blinding pain. She must have bumped into something headfirst. It was pitch-black around her, so she picked a direction randomly and swam for it blindly. She bumped into her grandparents' docked boat almost immediately. She moved alongside it, reaching with her hands in a fanning motion until her fingers finally found the bottom of the ladder. She went weak with relief. So weak, in fact, that she couldn't pull herself up. When she tried, she had a shooting pain going from her left shoulder down her upper arm. She screeched and almost let go.

"Mom!" she screamed weakly. "Dad . . ."

She sobbed quietly against the boat, holding on to the ladder with one hand. She let the waves rock her gently.

A flurry of bubbles emerged to the surface about ten feet from her. As she watched in horror, the top of a head surfaced, revealing two electric blue eyes. Her face still obscured by her sopping hair, the old woman slowly climbed out of the water until she stood on the surface. Just like Jesus.

Rosie screamed. A long, agonizing howl tore out of her, as if someone had torn off one of her fingernails. She tried to pull herself out of the water with one arm, her legs feebly kicking and sliding against the bottom of the boat. The woman took a slow, measured step toward her, then another.

"Mom! Dad! Help!" Rosie wailed desperately, churning the water.

The lights came on in the house, and just before the thing reached her, someone opened the back porch door. Yellow light spilled out and onto the lawn. It reached the water and cut between Rosie and the woman. Rosie blinked rapidly, blinded for a moment. The woman was gone. She could hear footsteps on grass and people calling for her. In a minute, a pair of strong arms grabbed her under the armpits and pulled her up and out of the water. As her family gasped and fussed over her, brushing back wet hair from her face and finding a blanket to cover her with, Rosie looked out onto the water and, in the distance, saw a pair of blue eyes slowly dip back under the surface.

CHAPTER TWENTY-TWO

1996
MILLIE

Millie slipped the little key into the desk drawer lock and sighed with relief as it clicked open. She thought she would never get the chance to do this again. She thought the Smiths would eventually find out that she had taken the key and would confront her on her own doorstep. Her anxiety about having the key with her had given her gray hairs. But it was all okay now. Alice had called her the day before and asked if she and her daughter could come take care of the animals for a couple of days. Millie had been way too enthusiastic when she said yes.

Mina did come with her earlier in the day to check on the horses. Now, she was out with some friends, so Millie had free range to explore the house.

She read the letter again, even though she remembered it word for word. Then, she slipped her fingers down to the bottom of the envelope and took out the small square piece of paper. It was a photograph, just like she expected. It looked like it originally came from one of those photo booths that took three photos in a row. This one had been cropped off from the others. Millie could see what appeared to be Alice's arm and some of her hair in the edge of the picture. The man in the middle seemed to have pushed her out of the frame playfully. He was smiling a wide, white-toothed smile. He had light hair and blue eyes that went well with his angular face. *Quite a handsome man*, Millie thought to herself grudgingly. She held the picture up to her face and squinted at it. Did Rosie look anything like this man? Perhaps she did. Around the eyes and nose. Then, something occurred to her. Alice had slightly slanted light brown eyes that Millie thought made her look like a fox. Noah had big, wide, dark brown ones. Long lashes, too. Their younger daughter—or, should she maybe say, their only daughter—Emilia, had Noah's eyes. She looked like a small, girly version of her dad. And Rosie . . . Well, Rosie had blue eyes. You couldn't miss it; they were striking. The image in front of her was too small for her to tell if this man's eyes were the same color blue as Rosie's. Also, you could get a blue-eyed child from two brown-eyed parents. But working with the information that she had, she doubted very much that the letter she had found was a hoax.

She sat down in Alice's chair, still holding the picture between two fingers. So, what should she do? She had to figure out if Noah knew. That was the main thing. He may know. But if he didn't . . . Millie smiled, her lips pursed. Then, she would make sure he found out. He would regret doing to her what he did all those years ago.

1982

Millie

A gust of fresh January air ran through the streets of Whitesboro. It almost knocked Millie's hat off. She squished it to her head, squealing, and leaned into Noah's shoulder. He gave her a kiss on the top of her head and squeezed her hand.

"Come on! We're almost there."

"It's freezing!"

Millie's teeth chattered. Her birthday was coming up in two days, and Noah was taking her birthday shopping. He didn't tell her where they were going, but she suspected the small jeweler's on Second Street. They were going in the right direction for it. He wouldn't get her an engagement ring. It was too soon for that. But he may get her a promise ring or a nice gold necklace. Her skin prickled at the thought. She would one day become Mrs. Millie Smith. It had a nice ring to it. Way better than Alice Smith.

As if summoned, she appeared in front of them. Millie was so shocked, she forgot how to breathe. Alice was standing in front of the Green Street Bookstore, about fifteen feet away. She was gazing at the display with her profile to them, oblivious to their presence. Millie jerked her eyes up to Noah's face. He hadn't seen her yet. He was inspecting a deep cut on the palm of his hand he had gotten at work the other day. Millie panicked. If they continued on their route, they would walk right up to her. She couldn't let that happen. She wasn't ready. Alice didn't even know they were dating. Maybe she was only in town for the day. If Noah didn't see her today, he may not even find out she was here. They would turn around. Yes! She would tell Noah she had to go to the bathroom, and they would walk back to the restaurant they had just passed. By the time they came this direction again, Alice would be gone. She stopped and pulled on his arm.

"Hey, Noah . . ."

Her hat flew right off her head on the back of another gust of wind. It cascaded through the air. Both she and Noah followed it with their eyes. It bumped against Alice's shoulder and fell on the ground by her feet. She looked down at it and seemed to recognize it—of course she did; she had seen Millie wear it a thousand times— then she looked straight at them. Millie gasped. Her face! She had two black eyes and a busted lip. She looked dazed, as if she wasn't really seeing them. Then, recognition hit, and her eyes widened in her racoon mask. She turned and ran, disappearing quickly into the crowd of people.

"Alice . . ." Noah said in a whisper.

His whole body had gone rigid, and he was ready to spring. If Millie hadn't been anchoring him down by his arm, he would have run after her without a second thought. Cold fear filled Millie's body from head to toe. This was too soon. They hadn't been dating long enough for their relationship to withstand this. Whatever had happened to Alice, Noah would want to go help her. To rescue her. He would forget about Millie in a second. She wanted to cry.

They ended up searching for Alice for the rest of the time they were out. Millie couldn't persuade Noah otherwise. They, of course, couldn't find her. She didn't run from them because she wanted to be found. Millie would never find out where Noah planned to take her for birthday shopping. Her birthday—no, her entire existence had become irrelevant in Alice's presence.

Noah dropped her off at her house after dark. He was going to run straight to Alice's house when he left here. This was Millie's last chance to make a difference. She might not get him back once he left. All the effort, all the time, all the love she had spent on him would go to waste. The whole town would know what happened in a few days. She would be lonely, miserable, and humiliated.

"Noah . . ." she started and stopped.

He was already looking down the street to where Alice's house was. Millie squared her shoulders.

"Don't go to her!" she heard herself say. She was almost appalled at how wrong it sounded.

She was their friend. Clearly, something bad had happened to her. They should both go to her. Millie didn't want to. Even though she loved Noah, she had always felt he was rightfully Alice's. She had taken something of hers while she wasn't here. She wasn't going to just knock on her door and face her. And she didn't trust Noah with her, either. He hadn't made any promises to Millie yet. He could just leave her today, and she would have to be okay with it. He didn't say anything. He came to her, folded her in his arms, and kissed her on her forehead. Then, he was gone. Just like that. He stepped off the porch and walked into the darkness. Millie felt helpless, bitter tears gather in her eyes. *Fucking Alice! Stupid, pretty damsel in distress Alice! Terrible friend Millie. Selfish, ugly little girl.* She couldn't stop her mind racing, just as she couldn't stop the tears that were dropping, unguarded, from her staring eyes. The street was dark and silent, with nothing but the occasional sweep of the wind. That hug and that kiss, they felt like goodbye.

CHAPTER TWENTY-THREE

1996
ALICE

The doctor held the radiograph up to the light of the lamp in his office.

"You can see the fracture right here."

He pointed at a short, thin line running through the middle of the humerus, the bone of the upper arm.

"It's only a hairline fracture, so it won't need a cast. You just need to keep your arm in that sling for a couple of weeks."

Rosie looked gloomily up at the doctor from her perch on the patients' reclining chair, her left arm cradled in a sling. Her forehead and the left side of her face were an angry bluish-purple. Alice wrung her hands to occupy them and avoid nervous movements. She reached over to brush the hair back from Rosie's face. Rosie turned her head, avoiding her touch. She was gravely embarrassed by what happened, Alice knew. Still, she couldn't help but feel hurt by this show of obvious rejection.

"Thank you, doctor, for seeing us on such short notice."

She was just talking out of nervousness. They came to the same emergency room as the last time when Rosie had fainted. As luck would have it, they also happened to see the same doctor.

"Of course! Of course!" the doctor said, nonchalantly looking over Rosie's file. "We are here anytime you guys need us. May I ask again how this happened?"

Rosie squirmed in her seat. She looked out the window, her face turning a vivid red under the bruises. She had asked Alice not to tell the nurses, but that was unfortunately not an option. They can't be coming back to the emergency room with an injury like this and no explanation. Alice had to give them something. So, she told them what had happened with as little detail as possible. Now, Alice was about to retell it again to the doctor. She saw Rosie swing her legs off the chair from the corner of her eye.

"I have to use the bathroom," she said and slid off the seat.

"Second door to your left," the doctor instructed.

As soon as Rosie left the room, he looked inquiringly at Alice with his piercing blue eyes. She cleared her throat.

"She said she had a dream that she jumped into the lake. She apparently sleepwalked down to the dock."

"So, you're saying that these injuries are from her jumping into the lake?"

His eyebrows were almost at his hairline as he said this. He was making no attempts to hide the fact that he didn't believe a thing Alice had told the staff.

"Not exactly," Alice said defensively. She could feel heat rising in her face. "My parents' boat was parked by the dock. We are thinking she bumped the side of it."

"So, she didn't see the boat floating there?"

"She said she was sleepwalking."

It was a Herculean effort to keep herself calm. The doctor was implying that something, if Alice was understanding correctly, was foul play. Child abuse . . . Even the thought of it disgusted her. Someone thinking that either she or Noah would hurt their kids sent her into a spiraling rage.

"Ma'am, you have to understand that this story seems a bit . . . far-fetched. That, coupled with your daughter's demeanor and the fact that this is the second time . . ."

"Stop right there!" Her voice quivered along with her arms. She was holding her temper in, but for how long? "We don't hurt our children! Not me. Not my husband. And definitely not my parents. I know how this looks. I know the story is odd. But this is what my daughter told me, and I believe it to be true."

She exhaled deeply, her nostrils flaring. The doctor put Rosie's file down and crossed his arms.

"There's no need to get angry! I'm just following protocol."

"I am not angry," Alice said through clenched teeth.

The doctor compressed his thin lips and ran a hand through his white hair.

"Does Rosie have a history of sleepwalking?"

"Yes," she lied, straight-faced.

It seemed like the only way to get this busybody off her back. He arched one gray eyebrow at her.

"And why have you not seen a doctor for this?"

"Nothing like this has ever happened before . . . I didn't think something like this could happen . . ." She was fumbling, drowning in that one little lie.

The doctor seemed to switch gears. He sat down at his computer and started typing away vigorously.

"I'm going to give you a referral to take your daughter to a child psychologist."

He looked up at her from behind his computer screen. His eyes and creased forehead were telling her that this was a good compromise, and she should take it. She did.

Rosie ambled back into the room as the doctor was finishing up the referral. She stood in the doorway, rubbing one ankle against the other with true teenage awkwardness.

"Do you want me to take a look at that before you guys leave?" the doctor asked, tilting his chin toward Rosie's feet.

Alice looked down and, to her horror, saw a nasty-looking wound on Rosie's right ankle. And the mother of the year award goes to . . . definitely not Alice. She squatted and took Rosie's sneakered foot into her hands, tilting it this way and that to examine the atrocity that was the wound. It looked like it may have started out as a simple scratch, but now, it was crusty with a rash around it. It looked angry and infected.

"Where did you get this?" she asked Rosie almost angrily.

She couldn't help it. Why didn't she just tell her that she was injured? It seemed to Alice that Rosie wasn't telling her anything anymore.

"I don't know."

She turned her cheek and looked out of the room, desperate to get out of here. Alice felt the judgment of the old doctor on the back of her neck. She took a deep breath. They would get the wound treated today, and it would get better. Yes!

"Please do look at it, doctor." She straightened up and gave him a terrible fake smile. "And thank you for all your help!"

A bit later, they were sitting in the car, driving back to the lake house to collect Emi and Noah. He had had to stay behind with Emi because she had been in hysterics. She ran outside with all of them and witnessed her sister being pulled from the lake. She didn't want to stay with her grandparents. She wanted to accompany them to the emergency room. Rosie kept on insisting she was fine and she didn't need to go anywhere whilst cradling her injured arm and patting her face periodically. It was, altogether, a grand shitshow. So, Alice ended up taking her on her own, leaving Noah to deal with Emi. It was a rushed decision she had made and had regretted almost immediately. She felt so small and helpless talking to this doctor who was accusing them of child abuse. It was ridiculous. It was scary. She didn't feel capable of handling the situation at all.

"Rosie, my love . . ."

"Hmm?"

She was resting her head in the palm of her hand with her elbow against the door. She looked so tired and broken with the one arm in the sling and the odd, vacant expression on her bruised face.

"You know you can tell me anything, right? If you actually got hurt doing something other than sleepwalking, or if somebody hurt you, you can tell me. You will not get into trouble."

Rosie didn't move. Was she even listening? She was acting so incredibly strange lately, Alice hardly recognized her. Her daughter was bubbly and witty. Not this tragic mess. *Alice, you're such a bitch!* she chided herself. Rosie was clearly going through some stuff. She needed to be there for her, not judge her.

"Rosie . . ."

"Don't worry, Mom!"

Rosie turned to her suddenly, this huge, wide smile on her face. It looked wrong somehow. Her face was crinkling in all the wrong places, like it wasn't her smile but someone else's.

"It will all work out at the end, just like you and Daddy."

Daddy? She hadn't referred to Noah as that since she was six. She normally just called him Dad.

"What are you talking about?"

Rosie didn't answer. Instead, she turned back to the window, this eerie smile still plastered on her face. She started to hum. The melody was instantly familiar to Alice, but it took her a second to recognize the song. All the hairs on her body stood on end. Her memory flashed back to that awful night in 1982. The night when her faith was at a turning point once again.

1982

Alice

Her life was over. It was time to face it. And she couldn't blame anyone but herself. She was the one that ruined it. She lay on her bed in a sobbing heap, with a harsh early January wind howling outside.

She came home from Houston. She had to. She wanted to be around people who loved her. And then, she ran into them. Noah and Millie were clearly together. It was so obvious. They probably started dating as soon as she left. They could hardly wait for her to be gone. She thought that Noah would wait for her. Even though she made it clear they didn't have a future, she, deep down, still expected him to wait. And now, things were different. She needed him. She wasn't sure in what shape or form, but she needed him. And he couldn't be there for her if he was dating someone else. He wouldn't want to. It was all shit. She was stupid. So, so stupid. She had ruined her own life thinking she was protecting everyone else.

She went to her little radio and flipped the cassette. It started playing a song that had been etched into her memory ever since that night. It was "The Chain" from Fleetwood Mac. It was a fitting song for the mood. She reached out and picked up the bottle of sleeping pills she'd lifted from her mother's nightstand earlier. She just wanted some help falling asleep. There was too much on her mind. But now . . . what was stopping her from taking the whole bottle? She would just drift off, and this whole nightmare would be over. She rattled the bottle to the beat of the song. It would be a mercy to everyone in her life if she left for good.

She caught some movement outside from the corner of her eye. She got off her bed and went to the window. Her breath came out in a ragged sob. It was Noah. He was standing on her driveway, the cold wind whipping his hair and coat. *He came!* She opened her fingers, and the pill bottle dropped to the floor. With the song still blasting from the radio behind her, she ran from her room and ripped open the front door. The wind hit her body, trying to push her back inside. She ran to him, her long hair flying, their destinies colliding once more.

Rosie was humming "The Chain" from Fleetwood Mac. *Why?* Why that song in particular? It was a possibility that she had heard it on the radio. But that comment . . .

Alice started forward, her knuckles white from gripping the steering wheel and her arms shaking. She was looking at the road, but all she saw was Noah's young face illuminated by the streetlight, and all she heard was Fleetwood Mac.

PART 3

CHAPTER TWENTY-FOUR

1998
JAMES

They vacated Harry the vagrant from interrogation room one and brought Alice in for questioning. James knew of the animosity between Alice and his wife—or more like the animosity Millie harbored for her. He didn't think Alice was aware that Millie never actually forgave her for what happened between them in the past. James didn't know the details. He knew Noah and Millie had dated, and it ended when Alice came into the picture. He never wanted to dig into this thing that had caused his wife so much pain. He had hoped that Millie would forget about it with time, that the happy family memories would replace the old, sour ones. James wasn't one to dwell on the past. Bad things happened, and the faster you got over them, the better. Noah may have done Millie wrong in the past, but it all worked out. James got the girl in the end, and that's all that mattered. Millie was a doting wife to him and a loving mother to their three children. Life was good. And still . . . every time Millie saw any member of the Smith family, she would straighten her spine into a rigid line, as if becoming taller would repeal the hurt still present.

James himself had no personal problem with the Smiths.

They were decent people as far as he could tell. The older girl was a handful from what he heard, but that was all teenagers, wasn't it? He himself had had to endure his fair share of back talk and eye-rolling from Mina.

Alice seemed like a completely average woman. Not bad to look at, but James would never say that out loud. His wife would hear about it by the end of day and castrate him in his sleep.

"Good day, Mrs. Smith!" he said, stepping into room one and closing the door behind him.

He decided to leave Jeffrey to watch Noah in case he said or did anything incriminating while alone in his room. But more than that, he didn't want to overwhelm Alice by having two men question her at once. He alone was more than adequate for the job.

"You can call me Alice, James! We have been neighbors for how long? Fourteen years?"

James nodded solemnly. That they were.

"All right, then. Where are your kids, Alice?"

His abrupt change of tone seemed to shock her a bit. But they weren't here to be neighborly. She let out a strange sound. Somewhere between a laugh and a sob. Her tears fell seemingly without her notice. Was it guilt or simply devastation? To tell himself the truth, James personally hoped that she wasn't involved. He had a soft spot for women. He hoped that none of the parents were to blame here. He hoped the girls were just lost in the woods and the family would be reunited. He wished for these things for the sake of all involved. But wishing would get him nowhere. As his father used to say, "You can wish in one hand and shit in the other and see which one gets full first!" Alice shook her head.

"It wasn't . . ." Her voice broke. "It wasn't us! Noah and I, we are good parents! They are just gone! We have to find them!"

"Calm down!"

He handed her a tissue, which she ignored. She was staring straight down at the table, but he could tell she wasn't seeing his hand with the tissue in it. He knew that look. She was reliving something in her head. He had to make her talk now.

"Tell me what happened!"

"I already . . ."

"Tell me again! Maybe we missed something."

So, she did. Looking only at the table, she told him, word for word, her rendition of the events.

They noticed around 9 p.m. that Rosie wasn't in her room. They had heard a noise from in there. She couldn't describe it. It was just some noise. They looked for her a bit first in the home and outside around the house before checking on the other daughter. She wasn't in her room, either. At this point, Noah had told her to call the police. He went out to check the stable and the chicken coop. Alice did as she was told. After getting off the phone, she walked the house again. She looked in the attic and the basement, too. After finding nothing yet again, she went to stand on the porch to wait for either Noah or the police to show up. Noah didn't come back. His story had been that he thought he saw movement in between the trees, so he took off into the woods.

Alice looked up at him finally, her red-rimmed eyes pleading for him to believe her. He did. She could be innocent in this.

"Have you found the woman?" Alice asked, taking the tissue from his stilloutstretched hand and applying it to her face.

James frowned at her. This would be her downfall. She said she had seen a homeless-looking lady in the woods by her home the day before the girls went missing. They found no trace of her and, to be honest, he didn't think she existed. Alice loved her husband very deeply. Even a blind person could see that. This mystery woman was most likely a cover, a scapegoat to take the heat off her Noah. If so, then it was also false information given to the police. If either of these missing girls turned up dead, Alice could be charged for her attempt to derail the investigation, even if she had nothing to do with the crime itself. James took a long, calculating look at her. Did she love her husband more than her own children?

"James?" Alice spoke, and she sounded like a hopeless little girl.

"There is no woman," he said and watched her face closely.

She looked taken aback. Her mouth opened and closed, but no sound came. She blinked hard a few times and rubbed at her watery eyes.

"But I saw . . . It could have been a man. Her face was covered by hair. She had long hair, but she may have been a man."

She was backpedaling, trying to change her story to make it work. It didn't.

"There was no man," he said calmly. "We found no evidence of another person being present on your property."

"Just because you didn't find any evidence doesn't mean she wasn't there!" She raised her trembling voice at him.

So, now, her true colors were emerging.

"We found no footprints belonging to an extra person. Just the ones belonging to your children and your husband. Evidence doesn't lie. People do!"

She went silent. Her slanted eyes darted from one corner of the room to the other like a trapped animal.

"I want a lawyer," she said abruptly, crossing her arms in front of her. "And I want you to find my children!"

He couldn't get anything else out of her, so eventually, he left the room to take a break. He needed more coffee. A lot more.

As he sipped his dark, life-saving Manna, he asked himself again if he was truly going into this investigation unbiased. He told himself he had no hard feelings toward Noah for hurting Millie all those years ago. He didn't feel like he did. However, there was something telling him that Noah was to blame here. That he had something to do with the disappearance of his girls. James, at first, believed that it was his cop's instinct telling him this, but now, he wasn't sure. Millie was his wife. His to love and protect. Could it be that he did want Noah to be punished, not for this crime but for breaking Millie's heart? This just happened to be a convenient way to make it happen. It was sickening to think that he may put an innocent man behind bars out of what? Pettiness? Over something that really shouldn't concern him. He needed to take a step back and look at the big picture, he decided. He would go back to the Smiths' property and take another look at the tree line around the house. With all the rain they had gotten, any footprints should be visible, but it was a possibility that the vagrant woman, if she really existed, was able to hide her tracks. Some backwoods people were quite cunning and capable of such things, only stepping on rocks, leaves, and fallen branches to avoid leaving their mark in the soft earth. If he found even a partial footprint, that would be something. It would make a difference. It would most definitely change the direction of the investigation. It would mean that Alice was no liar after all.

As he prepared to head out, another memory suddenly came to him. Something about a case from a long time ago. His old partner, Sam Smart, had told him about it some years back. He had since died of a bad heart, the crafty old geezer. It was a case that had never been solved. Sam had to retire knowing that he would probably never know the answer to what had happened. A child had disappeared near the same area where the Smiths' property lay. They never found him. A family member had been the main suspect, but there wasn't enough proof to prosecute. James couldn't recall the details, only that it had happened sometime in the fifties. There was something about it, though, that may have some significance to the Smiths. He just couldn't remember what.

He stopped by the receptionist's desk on his way out and asked Lizzie, their young, chatty receptionist, to pull all their files on any unsolved cases from that time period.

Then, he was off to find himself a homeless lady if there was one to be found.

CHAPTER TWENTY-FIVE
1996
ROSIE

She was floating in darkness. Above her was a circular opening through which she could see the moon and the stars. It felt like ages since she had seen anything but pitch-black. She floated slowly upward toward the opening. The moon was so bright, it almost blinded her. She reached out with one hand to touch it. It seemed so close now. She could hear crickets. Such wonderful music. For so long, her only melody was the sloshing of water and the continuous *tap-tap* of condensation dripping from the ceiling. Or was it the bathroom tap? The sound of dripping water was suddenly so loud, it was like a hammer hitting her eardrums. She placed both hands over her ears and squeezed her eyes shut. The noise was abominable. It got under her skin. With time, it slowed and receded into the distance, becoming a soft beat. She opened her eyes a crack and found she was now in the hallway between the bedrooms in her house. She hovered there, body upright, feet not touching the floor. She felt weightless as she slowly glided forward. Looking down, she spread and wiggled her toes. Was she always able to do this? Just hover in the air and move without walking? She must have because it came so naturally to her. She glided out into the living room. So far, this had been fun, but now, a bit too late, she realized where she was headed and that she had no control over effortlessly gliding body. The door of the dark office stood ajar, just waiting for her. *No, no, no, no! Shit!* She arched her back and reached with her toes, trying to make contact with the floor. It was no use. The opening of the office kept getting closer and closer until it was right there in front of her, its dark depth calling to her. She hovered there, unable to make out anything within. Suddenly, the dripping sound stopped, and its absence was even worse than the sound itself. There was complete, utter silence, out of which emerged a woman's voice.

"You don't know," it said, creaking in a sing-song tone. "You didn't need to know. It's better if you know. You should know . . ."

Out of the darkness emerged the old crone, her beady eyes flashing blue. She didn't use her legs, either, Rosie noted. She was feeling absolutely horrified but glided up to her as effortlessly and smoothly as a leaf on water. She was frozen with fear, her body rigid and helpless. There was no way out of this. She was going to come right up to her and do something unimaginably terrible. She just knew it, and every cell in her body protested against this unwanted contact. The woman stopped right in front of her and lifted up a bit so they were nose-to-nose. Rosie saw that her skin was the color of ashes behind her tangled mess of hair. With one hand, the woman lifted her mask of hair, giving Rosie a full view of her face for the first time. She expected her to be ugly and scarred, maybe with the flesh of her face falling away from her skull. In fact, she looked quite normal and, to Rosie's surprise, strangely familiar. Who was she? Could she be one of the women she saw in her vision at the homestead? It was hard to tell. She saw them so fleetingly; her memory was unsteady. The crone tilted her head and opened her mouth. Out of it came the almost unbearable loud sound of dripping water. Rosie could feel her heart hammering in her chest. She sucked in air through her flaring nostrils like a frightened rabbit in the claws of a hawk. The woman smiled at her, an eerie, crooked grin exclusively reserved for the mentally disturbed. Things happened kind of quickly after that. The woman placed a hand on Rosie's chest and gave her a shove that sent her flying backward through the house. She went through the living room and into the hallway to then come to a jerky stop in front of her parents' bedroom door. The door in front of her opened with a creak without her touching it, and her legs finally, gratefully, lowered to the ground. When she settled on the hardwood boards, it was as if she had entered another dimension from before, as if now, at just this moment, she came out of sleep. She heard the cicadas outside, the small sounds of the house at night, the gentle breathing of her parents. She hadn't even been aware until right now that these sounds had been missing. She was awake now; she was sure of it. Not daring to look back in the direction of the living room, she quickly walked into her bedroom and closed her door with a soft click. She looked at her cow clock on her nightstand. It was only 1 a.m. If she managed to fall asleep quickly, she could still get a decent night's rest. Ignoring the call of Rosanne's diary next to her clock, she crawled into bed and firmly shut her eyes.

Sleep eluded her for a long time. When she eventually did doze off, she was almost immediately awakened by Leon the Terrible's cheerful screaming from just outside her window. She felt she had only been asleep for five minutes. In reality, it must have been longer. It had to have been longer. There was no way she was going to survive the day on such little sleep. This was the last straw. She had had it with the fucking nightmares, the bloody insomnia, and that shithead of a rooster. She had had enough of all of it. She jumped out of bed, burst out of her bedroom, and ran through the house to the back door, passing Emi and her mother in the kitchen.

"Rosie?" her mother called after her.

She didn't stop. This had to end today. She marched outside and around the corner of the house to her window. Leon was still standing on the upturned bucket. When he saw her coming, he gave a few clucks of alarm but didn't move from his perch. He had no reason to fear her. All Rosie ever did was feed and take care of him. The ungrateful bastard. Rosie tore the bucket from under him, making him land ungracefully on the ground in a flurry of flapping wings and flying feathers. He collected himself quickly and squared off with her, chest puffed out, clucking loudly with rightful indignation. She lifted the heavy red bucket up above her head and brought it down on him without hesitation. His clucking ceased abruptly, yet Rosie didn't stop. She couldn't stop. She struck him with the bucket over and over until Leon was nothing but a bloody, feathered pancake. Rosie heard herself grunting with each blow. It was as if something had been unlocked within her, and now, she couldn't close it back up.

"Rosie! Stop!" she heard her mother scream from behind her.

"Leon!" This was her hysterical, annoying little brat of a sister.

She dropped the bucket and turned to face them, her eyes bloodshot and rolling in their sockets. The little shit was crying. Over what? This annoying fucking bird? All she was doing was getting Rosie in trouble with her damn wailing.

"Shut up!" she heard herself scream.

And then she was running. She was headed straight for Emi. If she didn't shut up, Rosie would make her. She was intercepted by her mother, who had grabbed her around the waist. Rosie twisted her upper body and swiftly elbowed Alice in the face. The blow knocked her mother backward; she let go and fell on her ass like a sack of potatoes. This was when Noah had made his entrance. He engulfed Rosie in a bear hug from behind just as she was about to grab Emi's long nightshirt. He pinned her arms to her side so all she could do was kick her legs. She windmilled them in an effort to get him in the crotch. She couldn't. The angle wasn't right. She howled, her neck arched upward, sounding distinctly unhuman. Her voice echoed across their land. She screamed until she felt something tear in her throat, and suddenly, she was out of air. Just like that. No more fuel for her muscles or her brain. Her body went limp. She let her father lower her to the ground, both of them breathing ruggedly. She regained her own person slowly, for this, this thing that had just attacked the rooster, wasn't her. It was as if she had been worn down enough by sleeplessness for something else to come in and take over. It was terrifying. How could she even begin to explain this? How could she ever make it right? She hardly even remembered the past few minutes of her life. What did she do? What had she been thinking? She turned her head slowly and looked at the gnarly heap of flesh and feathers that had once been Leon. One of his yellow legs stuck up out of the heap at an odd, crooked angle. She felt her face morph into an ugly mask of anguish. A long, undulating cry came from deep within her as she began to rock back and forth in her father's arms.

CHAPTER TWENTY-SIX

1996
MILLIE

Indecision and forbearance were wearing Millie down slowly, like a chisel against a brick. She had this incredible information in her possession, and she did not know what to do with it. Noah wasn't Rosie's biological father. Her just knowing this wasn't going to move mountains on its own. Noah needed to know. The town needed to know. The real father, this Nathaniel Davis, needed to know. She wanted to put it on billboards, the local newsletter, just something! She also wanted to remain anonymous. Nobody else needed to know where this information was coming from. She frowned furiously at her ledger. She was sitting at her desk at the vet's office. They were slow, which allowed her mind to wander.

"Is everything okay, Millie?"

She looked up to be met by the falsely concerned eyes of one of their veterinary technicians. Barb was a terrible gossip. She always wanted to know if Millie was "okay" whenever she let her face slip. Barb just wanted something juicy she could then share with anyone who would talk to her. She thrived on other people's misery. Millie often overheard her talking about various pet owners and their personal business. Normally, Millie didn't mind her. She was intrigued by gossip herself, but she despised Barb when she tried to weasel stuff out of her. The woman should know better. She was now curiously peering into the ledger in front of Millie. No shame. She was like a child smelling cookies.

"Everything is fine," she said, infusing her voice with as much Southern sweetness as she could manage. "I just overbooked a time slot was all."

"Oh. All right, then."

Barb turned, her ponytail swinging, and walked to the back, probably to tell the other techs about Millie's incompetence as a receptionist. But that was all right. Millie would just put salt instead of sugar in her coffee one day this week.

Back to her own thoughts, Millie wondered if there were any legalities in a case like this. Was Alice legally required to let the father, Nathaniel, know that he had a child, for example? As she pondered this, it occurred to her that he may already know. What if Alice was secretly collecting child support from him? Or, better still, what if she and Nathan had some sort of secret relationship? She wished she remained closer to Alice over the years if only to have inside knowledge on her life. Would she even tell her? There were so many unknowns, they were giving her a headache. She could ask her husband about some of it. The legal parts, at least. He was her closest confidant, after all. She called him up on her desk phone and asked if he was free to meet her for lunch.

An hour later, they were sitting at the local burger joint just a couple of blocks from the veterinary office. It was the perfect place, really; she could walk there, and burgers were Jim's favorite. He was packing away his plate with gusto, shoving three or four fries in his mouth at the same time.

"Working hard today, I see!" She dimpled at him.

"Nothing gets past you," he chuckled, his mouth full. "So, what was it you wanted to ask me?"

Millie shifted in her seat. She was pushing her pea salad around on her plate. She had been thinking about the best way to ask without revealing who she was talking about. She wasn't entirely sure how Jim would feel about her snooping around their neighbors' home. Because if she told him she was talking about Alice and Noah, the next question he'd have would be: "How did she know?" She would prefer not to have to lie to him.

"Hypothetically," she started cautiously, "let's say you had an old girlfriend who got pregnant with your child. Would she have to tell you? Legally, I mean? Would she have some kind of obligation?"

James blinked at her. This definitely wasn't what he had been expecting. He smiled, shook his head, and popped another fry into his mouth.

"You are so good at catching me off guard, it's scary. Is there an illegitimate child of mine out there somewhere that I don't know about?"

He flashed her a cheeky grin. His front teeth were a bit crowded, making his canines slightly turned. This gave them a bit of a fang-like look. Millie had secretly found this sexy ever since James had smiled at her for the first time. It gave him a unique, slightly dangerous look.

"Don't be silly, you skunk!"

She shook her head, grinning at him mischievously.

"This isn't about you or me. I just wanted you to be able to imagine yourself into the situation."

"Okay, okay. I get it! So, the answer is no. A woman does not legally have to tell a man if she is having his baby. She can try and raise it on her own, and nobody can say boo about it. It's rude and foolish, if you ask me, but not illegal."

"And what if she is raising your child with another man?"

James leaned back in his chair and surveyed her with some suspicion.

"Who is this about?"

"Just hypothetically!"

She spread her fingers out on the tabletop. Her nails were perfectly manicured and painted with purple nail polish.

"Does this hypothetical man know he is raising somebody

else's child?"

"Maybe . . . Maybe he doesn't."

She had separated her peas from the rest of the salad and lined them up in a straight line with her fork. She looked up at James and saw he was examining her line of peas with a thoughtful look. When he looked into her face, his blue eyes bore into hers. He was hesitant to give her an answer.

"Who are we talking about? Do I know these people?"

She shifted her eyes from his to look out the front window of the burger place.

"Millie, could it be that these things are none of our business?"

"Can you please answer the question?"

She pursed her lips at him. He knew that look well. This was her way of telling him she was displeased with something without actually saying it.

"If the man doesn't know and he finds out, he can pursue legal action against the woman. She can be charged with fraud and owe him money. That's basically it in a nutshell."

"I see," said Millie, leaning back in her chair.

"Now, will you tell me who we are talking about? And don't tell me it's just a hypothetical person 'cause I know better."

He knew her too well. It was a blessing and a curse, really. When it came down to it, he knew exactly how to comfort her, where to rub her back at the end of a long day, but he also knew when she was lying. Most of the time.

"It's the Smiths. Rosie isn't Noah's."

She exhaled deeply through her nose. She almost couldn't believe she said that out loud. Her special little secret. It was like finally showing someone a valuable, precious stone that you had been holding on to.

"What . . ."

James coughed explosively. He must have choked on a fry or something. He gripped the side of the table with both hands, his eyes bulging.

"Are you sure? How do you know?"

His voice was scratchy, but he regained his composure quickly.

"I . . . may have stumbled across a document while at their house."

"Millie!"

He threw his arms up in exasperation.

"Look, it doesn't really matter how I found out. I already know. Don't you think Noah has a right to know, too?"

"He doesn't know?"

Millie paused to collect her thoughts.

"I'm not sure."

James's lips folded into a thin line, seeming to disappear into his mustache.

"You know what I'm sure of?" he said finally, slapping his hands on his thighs. "I'm sure this is none of our business. There is a good chance that Noah Smith does know, and if he doesn't, you're not going to be the one to tell him!"

This had been an order. She was not to do anything. The thing was, Millie really didn't do well with orders.

That day, after work, Millie sat down at her kitchen table with a pen and two pieces of paper. Her children were upstairs doing their homework, and James hadn't come home from work yet. She, in fact, didn't expect him home for another couple of hours, so she had some time to herself.

She had the whole rest of the day to think about what her husband had said and to consider all the routes she could take. She could take her husband's "advice" and do nothing. But that, to her, seemed like a waste of an opportunity. This may not be any of James's business, and to him, it would seem like it wasn't Millie's, either. But it was. This was something she didn't know she had been waiting for all these years. This was her chance to show Noah he had made the wrong decision. He should have chosen Millie. Because he didn't, he had spent all these years caring for somebody else's child. Spent money, love, and affection on her. Thinking about it made Millie angry. It made her much angrier than it should have. She imagined herself in his shoes. She would be furious. She would fly off the handle and break things. She would divorce Alice and leave her to take care of the little bastard on her own. She would tell her she was a slut. She may actually do that if she got the chance. If the right opportunity rose for some slut-shaming.

So, no, she couldn't just leave this alone. She had to at least stir things up a bit. After much thinking, she decided that writing a letter would be the best way to go. They would never figure out who sent it. She would send a letter to the Smith house and another one to the Houston address written on Alice's secret paper. This way, both men would know the truth, and they would be able to do with it as they saw fit. It was a good plan. The perfect plan.

So, she spent the next hour and a half working on her pieces of art, choosing each and every word carefully and making sure to change her handwriting. She thought about using their computer to do it, but Mina was working on it. She wanted to get this over and done with. There was no way Noah would recognize her penmanship, anyway. They went to school together and exchanged notes plenty of times, but even Millie couldn't recall what his letters looked like. She was safe.

That night, she had made love to her husband. She initiated it out of guilt at first. She felt bad for blatantly disobeying him. But it turned out to be the best sex they'd had in a while. Millie's mind was crisp and clear, her body wound up with delicious anticipation of the drama to come. She relished in the feel of James's body in a way she had forgotten she could. It wasn't until after the act itself that she had some time to think about why this had been. Alice may just lose her husband over this, while Millie got to continue her peaceful, stable life with hers. She fantasized about Noah crawling back to her and begging her to leave James and be with him instead. She would laugh in his face and tell him to fuck right off, of course. She wouldn't leave James. Not in a million years. She loved him dearly. But the fantasy of being able to say no to Noah left her lightheaded. Such power! The ecstasy of it.

The next day, she dropped those two letters in the mailbox and had walked away with a new and much more confident stride she didn't know she had in her. Her high heels clicking on the sidewalk, she lifted her face to the sunshine and relished all the new and exciting days still to come.

1982

Millie

She didn't see Noah for five days after that dreadful windy day when they accidentally bumped into Alice. He missed Millie's birthday. He probably forgot about her altogether. He was a terrible, selfish asshole, and so was Alice. By the fourth day of his total absence, Millie doubted the encounter with Alice had been an accident at all. She knowingly ran into them looking all sad, knowing that Noah wouldn't be able to resist her. He would feel obligated to check on her, and she would take care of the rest with her "charm." She was a witch! A horrible, man-stealing witch! "Oh, Millie, I didn't want him, but now that you have him, I simply must take him from you!"

She was a dirty, lying slut. That bruise on her face was probably painted on, too.

She was sitting at work, hating the world. It had been raining for the past two days, so the weather was matching her mood perfectly. Heavy raindrops were drumming so loudly on the tin roof of the police station that it sounded like a shooting practice was taking place up there. James Walker came in through the front door, shutting it quickly behind him to keep the weather out. He was sopping wet. There was water running on his face and dripping from the brim of his hat. He hung his wet jacket on the coat hanger by the door, making it lean precariously to the side. He put his hands out to catch it but ended up leaving it as it was when it didn't fall.

"Hey there, Millie dear!" he called, walking up to her.

"Hello, James . . ." she answered, not looking up from all the work she didn't have.

She didn't want him to be nice to her out of pity. She'd

rather suffer in silence.

"Look, I wasn't going to say anything, but . . ."

"Then don't!"

She wished she could just stay at home until she was able to put her face back into order. She knew she looked a mess. She didn't want people to think she was weak, but she also didn't want to lose her job. James was drumming his fingers on his desk. The sound was irritating beyond belief. She reached out and placed a quick hand on his to make him stop. His skin was cold from the rain. The feel of his rough hand sent a shiver down her spine. He had such big, manly hands. She let her hand linger for too long. Realizing this, she removed it quickly.

"I'm fine, James," she said quietly, still not looking him in the face.

"Do I have to kill the bastard?" he asked severely.

That made her look up. She met his eyes. He had a masculine face. All sharp angles. But his eyes were a pretty blue, like the August sky. She smiled at him bitterly.

"Yes," she said and, to her surprise, laughed. "Oh, Lord! Please don't take me seriously! I'm a mess."

James reached for her hand and took it in his. Her breath caught—in a good way. His touch felt like a cold balm on sunburn.

"He doesn't deserve you. You know that, right?"

"James . . ."

She was shaking her head, but he wasn't letting go.

"Kick him to the curb and let me take you out!"

Her lips parted. She saw his eyes drift to them, and within them, she saw his want. He wanted her. In that moment, there wasn't Noah somewhere out there. There wasn't an Alice with all the past memories. There was only Millie, her hand in his. Connected. She couldn't see the past, only the future they could have. He would bend over backward to make her happy. Only her. There was no other woman between them. In that moment, Millie desperately wanted that. To just let go of her past. Never see Noah or Alice again. Start anew with James, and not even give a reason or excuse to anyone. Especially not Noah. Then, he let go.

"Just think about it!" he said, and with that, he turned toward the door.

He put on his sodden jacket. There was a thunderclap from above as he was shrugging his shoulders into it. For a second, the electricity went out, leaving them in perfect darkness before it came back. He was a real man, braving the dangers of his job even during a thunderstorm. Telling her what he wanted. No guessing. No games.

"I will!" she heard herself say as he walked through the door.

He put a hand on the brim of his hat and gave her a small nod.

The next day, the weather broke. Noah was waiting for her outside of the station at the end of her shift. There was a small creek that ran along the back of the building. There was a walking trail and some pretty trees. At his suggestion, they went for a walk. There wasn't much talking at the beginning, which was fine with Millie. She needed some time to collect her thoughts. At the moment, she had no idea what she really wanted. She longed for what James could give her, but she also didn't want to let go of Noah. If she could just morph the two of them together, it would be perfect. She felt betrayed and hurt. She should just let him go. Be done with it. Move on. Her pride wouldn't let her. She couldn't just give him an easy way out. If he was going to break up with her, she wanted him to suffer through it. He would be the bad guy. Not her. People would call him a two-timer and a cheat. In this case, Millie would be okay with being the victim.

"I saw Alice," he said finally.

"I know you did."

He looked at her with an expression somewhere between alarm and anguish.

"I'm not stupid," she said, knowing she had an ugly, bitter frown on her face. She didn't care. Let him see how much he hurt her.

"I'm sorry, Millie . . . I . . . I'm really sorry."

"Did you sleep with her?"

She didn't actually want to know the answer; she just wanted to make him squirm.

"Yes," he said, so simply and bluntly she could hardly believe it.

That one little word was like a punch to the gut. She searched his face. Was he lying, knowing she would not be able to forgive him for this? His face blurred as hot tears gathered in her vision.

"Oh, Millie . . ."

"You could have lied! You fucking idiot!"

She wiped her eyes on the sleeve of her sweater. This man was out to ruin her life from the very beginning. She was so much better off without him. So, why? Why was this so bloody hard?

"Millie, I'm sorry . . ."

He tried to put a hand on her shoulder, but she swatted it away violently.

"Just say what you came here to tell me and be done with it!"

"Millie . . ."

His tone was pleading, and she couldn't stand it. She would not understand. He couldn't make her.

"Say it!" she screamed at him, knowing she looked and sounded like a lunatic.

"I'm going to be with Alice. I'm sorry."

There it was. An eerie calm came over her, as if God Himself reached down and plucked all emotions out of her tiny human body, leaving her empty and hollow.

"Good!" she said flatly. "Y'all deserve each other."

She turned and walked away from him. She didn't look back but walked all the way to the police station, her back as straight as a metal rod. She went out with James the next day and had a wonderful time. She had gotten pregnant with Mina within the first month of them dating, so they married the same year. She never regretted it. Any of it. She got the husband, the family she had always dreamt of. She never wanted for anything. At least, that's what she told herself.

The truth was that there was one thing that she had wanted more than anything. The one thing James couldn't give her. She wanted revenge.

CHAPTER TWENTY-SEVEN

1996
ALICE

She sat in the psychologist's office with a bruised face and hunched back, feeling miserable and incompetent. She wasn't fit to be a real parent. She was an impostor, a phony, someone pretending to be somebody they were clearly not. She didn't feel fit to raise children after what happened. Rosie had elbowed her right on the cheekbone. The bruise itself hurt more emotionally than physically. And she also killed their beloved rooster. If these two things weren't bad enough, she had also tried to attack Emi, her sweet five-year-old sister. It all seemed so surreal. Every time she thought back on what had happened, it felt like a dream. A terrible, ghoulish nightmare in which Rosie was the monster. She had been impossibly strong despite her injured arm. It was as if she had completely forgotten about the pain in her fit or rage.

Rage. Fourteen-year-olds should not be capable of rage like that. Of doing what Rosie had done. Alice kept seeing the mangled body of the dead bird every time she closed her eyes. She hated to think what would have happened to Emi if she hadn't been there—if Noah hadn't been there, for Alice hadn't been strong enough to hold Rosie back. She clutched her arms in front of her stomach and bent over them, feeling sick and displaced. Rosie was sick. It was undeniable at this point. They would get her help. They were doing that right now just by being here at the psychologist's office. Rosie was with the doctor now, hopefully working through her issues. They would find a way to make things right and get their family back. She hoped it was possible.

Alice knew that all this was not her fault. It was genetic. She knew this, and yet, she could not stop blaming herself. When she'd looked at her reflection in the mirror last night, she almost punched it. She wanted to see her own face break and shatter into a million pieces. She wanted to scream at herself, "You did this, you stupid fucking bitch!" She should have never had children. She should have never allowed the gene of mental illness to survive. She told herself she wouldn't from a young age. And yet, she did. She had a baby and then another one. Caution to the wind. She told herself it would be all right even though she knew better. Noah wanted children. But he didn't know what it was like. He had never met her aunt. Never seen the way she lived and the hurt she inflicted. He didn't know, and yet, Alice let him guide her. She wanted to blame Noah for all this. She wanted to blame Rosie. Anyone else but herself, but her sense of truth did not let her. If you knew something was bad, and you did it anyway, did that make you a bad person? Alice leaned back in the cushy leather waiting room chair and closed her eyes. She saw Leon the Terrible, squished and broken. Yes, it definitely did. She was a bad person.

She met with the psychologist the day before. Dr. Lewis Stagner. That name made him sound like a jock, not an intellectual who sat in a small, well-furnished room all day, listening to the mentally weak. She was pleasantly surprised at his appearance. He was a short, thin man who probably weighed less than Alice. He wore a brown suede jacket and dark, almost black jeans. All he needed were some thick, black-rimmed glasses to complete the "psych" look.

They sat down in his colorful office, decorated by strange-shaped pastel furniture and framed pictures of watercolor animals, to discuss the problems at home. Noah couldn't come. He had a work emergency the morning of the appointment. Alice was bitterly disappointed by this, although she didn't tell him. She tried to put on a brave face for her family's sake. For Rosie's sake.

Dr. Lewis was a nice man. He possessed the soothing presence of a sleepy barn owl, blinking slowly at Alice in encouragement with his slightly too-large eyes.

"So, I am going to throw some of the standard questions at you, and we'll kind of branch out from there. Okay?"

Alice nodded, her face set in a severe frown that she believed was appropriate for the occasion.

"Have there been any bigger changes at home? Some kind of stressful or traumatic event, even, that may coincide with the start of Rosie's change in behavior? You can think about it for a bit, if you'd like. No rush."

She nodded again.

"Not quite at home, but I do remember her behaving oddly after she went out horseback riding with two of her friends."

"Define 'oddly.'"

"Upset, I guess, is a better word for it. She seemed to be upset about something, but she wouldn't say what. That was the odd part. She is usually very talkative. She confides in me and my husband."

"Noah, right?"

"Yes."

He looked at the paperwork sitting in his lap. It was presumably Rosie's file that had been sent over from the emergency room. He made a note on it and looked back up at her, blinking slowly.

"So, you believe this was the event that may have started everything?"

Alice shrugged and winced at how inappropriate that probably looked. The last thing she wanted was for this doctor to think she didn't care.

"Most likely. But she wouldn't say what, if anything, had

happened. I think she had a falling out with her best friend."

"Her name is . . ."

"Mina. She's our neighbors' daughter. The same age as Rosie."

Dr. Lewis gave a sound of acknowledgement and wrote another note on the paper.

"So, how would you describe the Rosie from before this event?"

"Oh," she sighed with relief. She usually loved talking about both her daughters. "She is usually very bubby, quite funny. She loves nature. She's constantly outside. Very family-oriented. Like I said, she used to tell us everything. She loves all animals and adores her sister . . ." She trailed off and swallowed hard, blinking back tears.

She would not cry, damn it! She wasn't this weak. She had her shit together. For some reason, it was imperative to her that the doctor understand this. These things weren't happening because of their bad parenting.

"Good, good!"

He was scribbling furiously on the paper with a small, beatific smile on his narrow face.

"Now, tell me how you would describe her now!"

Alice grimaced. It was totally involuntary, and yet, it filled her with shame. Dozens of words came to her lips such as "terrifying," "uncontrollable," and "aggressive," but all of them felt inappropriate to describe a fourteen-year-old girl. She cleared her throat.

"She often looks gloomy or outright sad. I think she has trouble sleeping, but she is so closed off nowadays, I can barely get her to eat breakfast with the family, let alone engage with us. She sometimes says inappropriate things . . ."

"What do you mean by that?"

"She got in trouble at school for upsetting a teacher. But the teacher got into more trouble than she did."

Dr. Lewis arched a manicured brow at her. Did he pluck his

brows, or were they naturally so even-looking?

"The teacher slapped her."

"Wow!"

He was shaking his head, scratching words into the paper. He seemed genuinely upset, which made Alice feel immensely better. Maybe coming here was the best thing they could have done. Maybe Dr. Lewis would be on her side after all.

"I'm so sorry that happened to your daughter. I assume it was quite upsetting to all of you."

"Very."

"Is there anything else you want to add before we wrap up our session?"

Alice hesitated. True to his word, he didn't rush her. He didn't even look at her but pretended to read through his notes, giving her some space to think.

"There is the one thing that happened the other day," she ventured. "Rosie acted . . . She has never done anything like this before." She felt panic rise under her skin at just the memory of it. "She acted very ag . . . agg . . ."

She couldn't say it. She didn't want to. She closed her eyes and, against all her efforts not to, relived that awful morning.

"She acted very aggressively," she said finally, allowing one lone tear to escape.

She told Dr. Lewis all of it. He listened to her patiently and, at the end, handed her a tissue when her tears were running freely down her cheeks.

Today, Rosie was the one being questioned, and Alice had the luxury of sitting on the sidelines. She occasionally heard some muffled voices from behind the closed door of the office, but she couldn't make out any words no matter how hard she strained her ears. As she sat there, left alone with her own thoughts, an unbidden memory came to her. It had been carefully stored away somewhere in the back drawer of her mind, to be kept but not to be seen.

1982

Alice

It was New Year's Eve. Alice could hear thumping music through the walls of her dorm room and merry chatter and hooting from outside. It would be midnight in about an hour, and she would step into the new year as something else than she had been before. She actually didn't know this at the time, but she would soon find out.

She stayed at home despite Nate's pestering to go out because she was feeling ill and drained of energy. Nate was disappointed, but he didn't argue much. He knew she wasn't making it up. She had been feeling sick for some days now. She thought it was the flu. She believed it to be just an ordinary illness until just ten minutes ago, when she went through her calendar. She had missed her period the month before. She had a lot going on with the end-of-the-year exams and meeting Nate's parents during Christmas. She forgot to check. She forgot about it altogether. Her roommate had a test in her nightstand drawer. Alice helped her pick it out when she had a missed period two months before. The box came with two tests. She rooted through the nightstand, feeling awful for going through someone else's stuff. She found the test and peed on it promptly before she could chicken out and pretend this wasn't happening. She sat on the toilet, her head in her hands, with the test sitting on the vanity in front of her. This couldn't be happening! How could have it even happened? They used condoms. The only time she didn't had been with Noah that first and only time. But she'd had a few periods since then. She looked up at the test and, to her horror, saw the second pink line appear in its little window. She was fucked! Sweet Jesus, she was so fucked! She pushed the test away from her so it slid into the sink. *How? How? How? How?*

And then, she recalled that one time around two months ago when Nate took an unusually long time removing the condom. He had his back to her, so she couldn't see exactly what he was doing, but he seemed to be looking down into his lap for a long time. When she finally asked him what he was doing, he snapped out of his trance, got the condom off, only fumbling slightly, and tossed it into the trash. Then, he just turned to her, all smiling and normal, and they went about their day. *You bastard!* she thought viciously. The condom must have torn, and he said nothing. He was probably hoping nothing would come of it, and he would get to skip on buying an expensive morning-after pill. Alice felt his total betrayal hit her in the stomach like an iron fist. This was her life, her body. He couldn't just gamble on all their futures like that. This wasn't just about him. It was about her, and now, this little thing inside her that was making her sick. She would have a baby. *Oh, God! A baby!* She suddenly felt violently ill. Getting up from the toilet, she spun around and vomited into it copiously. When she was done, she pulled up her jeans and sat on the floor in front of the toilet, letting herself sink into hopelessness for a few minutes. Her plan had been not to have children. She could just get an abortion. She wouldn't even have to tell him. He didn't bother telling her about the hole in the condom. She would get the money somehow. This idea was like a beam of light in the darkness that was her life right now. She could make it all go away. She shook herself and stood up. No, she couldn't. She couldn't continue to live her life knowing that she had killed her own baby. Something that was a part of her. A little life only just forming. There was a chance that it would be spared the mental illness. And a chance was all Alice needed.

She would find Nate and tell him, and they would figure it out together. She would go right now. As she was washing her face and brushing her hair, she thought about the nice house that Nate's parents owned. They had money. And while she didn't want to appear like a gold digger, it was a soothing thing to know that they would most likely help them financially. She had really liked his parents when they met this past Christmas. This was a big change in her plans, but maybe, just maybe, it would be okay. As she locked the door behind her and headed down the hall, she thought to herself how unfair life was. If she had to have a baby, why couldn't she have gotten pregnant by Noah? Then, she would be raising this baby with somebody she actually loved. Because she didn't love Nate. She liked him a lot. Cared about him. But after so many years of loving Noah, she knew the difference between love and simple infatuation. Maybe it was better this way. If things went south, at least she wouldn't be burdening somebody she truly loved.

She heard the thumping music of Nate's frat house even before it came into view. There were dozens of students hanging out in front of it, talking, drinking, and horsing around. She blew out a long breath.

CHAPTER TWENTY-EIGHT

1996
LUKE

The Glessner journal made for an interesting read. For a while there, Luke suspected the ghost lady he'd seen on the cliff to be Rosanne, but now, he wasn't sure. As per her own description, Rosanne had chestnut hair. The ghost's hair was most definitely not chestnut. It was a lighter, blonde-ish color.

He and Rosie had tons of phone conversations about their speculations as to what the ghost might want. They talked about every other day to compare notes and ideas up until recently. The last few times Luke called, however, it was always some other member of the family on the other end. Noah had told him that Rosie was having a bit of a rough time and didn't want to talk. It was frustrating not knowing exactly what was going on. He missed Rosie. The absence of even her voice had left an empty void in Luke's days. His mind kept going back to what they had done in the forest. Kissing had, so far, been reserved for adults and much older kids in Luke's understanding. He was fourteen now. Did that make him old enough? What were the rules? Did he even care at this point? He saw Rosie's long, tan legs in his mind's eye, her small breasts through her shirt. There was a disturbance in his nether regions. His face hot, he tugged on the crotch of his pants. *Get a grip!* he thought. *She's not even here.* Come to think of it, it would be much worse if she was. If this were to happen while they were hugging and she felt it or, even worse, saw it . . . he would die. What he was thinking about right now was definitely reserved for adults only. He turned to his side on his bed to hide his shamefully enthusiastic body part in the folds of his pants before his grandfather felt the need to "check on him" again. Focusing on the journal should take his mind off Rosie.

October 31, 1742

I'm sorry, my dear journal, but I haven't much time or energy to write these days. With all the walking and work to do on this journey, I fall unconscious at the end of each day as if bludgeoned by a mallet.

I wanted first to write about meeting my new master. Mr. McCullum is a seemingly nice man in his early forties. He is soft around the waist but not unfortunate-looking altogether. He inspected me with great interest, then told me to sit with him on a log in his campsite. When he told his men to go, I should have been concerned, but I wasn't. I'm no longer afraid of rape. I have no virtue to protect.

To my surprise, he told me that his wife is also a German woman by the name of Greta. They have three little girls, all under the age of ten. His wife had suffered an apoplexy during the birth of the last child and now is unable to speak properly. Her English had always been lacking. Over time, the two older girls had forgotten most of their German, and the smallest, who is three, doesn't speak it at all. This troubles his wife greatly. She had fallen into a deep sadness over not being able to understand her own offspring. This is where I come in, according to him. I had been purchased with the sole purpose to teach the girls German. Mr. McCullum tells me he was delighted when he learned I was not only German but literate. He would have paid twice the price asked just to have me in his possession. This made me smile. It shouldn't have. Being bought like an animal should have been degrading and upsetting. But this was the first time in a long time that I had felt valuable and needed.

He did bed me, of course. I was his possession, after all, and I was made to understand that I was never to say no. It was simply not an option for me. I just nodded and lay back. I found it no need to let him know I had no intentions of refusing him. After the loss of my Heidi and the faceless unknown babe, I long to be a mother again. According to Mr. McCullum, I would have my own quarters within his home, and I would want for nothing so I could best teach and care for his girls. After living in poverty in Germany and enduring life on the ship, this sounded like nothing less than paradise.

Once I was relieved from his presence, I tried to tell my new Black friends what had happened to me. They were eager to know, for most of them haven't even seen our new master. Nono assisted me by translating. They found the part of the bedding most entertaining, for I had made a clumsy attempt at a joke. I had said it was no wonder Mr. McCullum only had female children, for his pecker wasn't big enough to make a son. I demonstrated the size with my own dainty little pinky finger. There were roars of laughter from the men and plenty of cackling from the women. They slapped my back and patted my shoulder, wiping tears from their eyes.

I had learned that night that these dark men and women had given me a name in their own language. They refer to me as Wimbi, which means wave. When I thought back on it, I realized that I had heard them say that word many times before in my presence. Now, it made sense. I understand why they had felt the need for the nickname, for Rosanne is almost impossible for them to pronounce. But why "wave"? When I asked Nono about it, he shrugged and said my long, wavy hair reminded them of the waves of the ocean. During their voyage, that's all any of them could see for weeks on end. I found the reference to be strangely beautiful. I hold the new name dear to my heart. I look at these people, and I am filled with such a bittersweet feeling. They are no animals. They laugh and cry just like us white folk do. And yet, they are treated as so much less. I have seen one of them, a man whose name I do not know, be whipped just for taking an apple from the wrong bag. We who are owned by the master get the fruit fit for pigs. The broken and bruised ones.

The other day, I went to relieve myself behind a bush. The wilderness was dark around me, for the sun had set an hour before. As my eyes adjusted to the light of the campfire, I could make out the silhouette of two people ahead. A white man on top of a Black woman. They were both half naked, the man with his hands around the woman's throat. He was clearly trying to keep her quiet while raping her. I could see how she struggled for air from the way the white circles of her eyes bulged in her dark face. Her teeth flashed as she mouthed at me my given name. My first instinct was to run. I know it sounds terribly selfish, but isn't self-preservation everyone's first thought? I did not want to compromise my future position as governess for the master's girls. Then, I remembered the whites of Kata's eyes in the dark belly of the ship. Her gripping her small pocketknife while I was being assaulted, ready to take on three men for my sake. They would have killed her, and she knew that. My insides burned with shame. How can I do any less for this woman right in front of me? I couldn't tell who she was, but each and every one of the slaves had embraced and helped me these past few weeks. Frantically, I searched the ground for something to throw at the man, and my hand found a big rock with sharp edges. I got the man on the side of the face. He howled in pain as I made my clumsy escape through the shrubs. The woman got away, too. Back at the camp, I realized she was the one who had fixed my shoes.

The next day, I was, yet again, summoned by the master. On my way to the front of the convoy, I saw the man I had struck with the rock. My aim had been true in spite of the darkness. Crusted blood and mottled color covered the left side of his face. He is an ugly beast of a man. He had looked at me with an expression of murder as I passed him. He knew it was I who had thrown the stone. The realization made my insides clench. I was, all of a sudden, filled with a terrible sense of foreboding. I was being taken to the master to be punished.

He did look quite displeased when he saw me. He explained to me that, as his slave, normally, I would have had my hand cut off for striking one of his men. But luckily for me, he needed me whole. In fact, I was much more valuable to him than the man in question, whose name is Ferris, as I've learned. So, from now on, I would be riding in the front of the convoy with him to avoid any "accidents" befalling my person. Apparently, the man who I chose to throw a rock at is the vengeful type. I took a leap and spoke out. I quietly told him that if I had not interfered, Ferris would have surely strangled the poor girl. Then, I got to my hands and knees and apologized for my rudeness and my actions profusely. I was only trying to save the master's property! I sobbed a bit for theatrics. This seemed to annoy him, for he dismissed me. I knew he had spent good money on all the slaves, so I only wanted to point out that Ferris nearly cost him quite a bit with his reckless actions. I do not know what has become of him, but Ferris was not with us the next day.

Luke put the book down and lifted his right hand up to gaze at it. He wiggled and spread his fingers. To lose a hand over throwing a rock at someone. It was hard to imagine. The 1700s had been a harsh time to live in. He imagined Rosanne looking kind of like Rosie, but with wavy brown hair. How brave she had been to embark upon such a treacherous journey. She didn't actually have a say in most of the things that happened to her, but still, she had faced every obstacle with such courage so far. Losing both of her kids and her husband at only nineteen. Still just a kid. He wished he could meet her and tell the girl writing this story that she would have kids again. Or at least one. He wasn't sure how many she actually had, but her family line would live on. More than two hundred years from then, her descendants still lived on the same piece of land she eventually settled on. It was almost unbelievable. Almost . . .

"Too good to be true?" said a woman's voice from right next to his ear.

He sat bolt upright, smashing his head into the low ceiling. Groaning, he scuttled away from the headboard of his loft bed. He stared, saucer-eyed and breathing heavily, at the spot the voice had come from. There was nothing there, but the air in his room felt heavy and humid, like a bathroom after a cold shower.

"Show yourself!" he demanded, surprising himself with his bravery.

He didn't actually want to know who spoke to him, let alone see her. The room was silent. This was stupid. And foolish. He shouldn't call out to spirits like that. It wasn't wise. He felt a soft tap on the top of his head. It made his whole body go rigid with fear. He reached up, his hand shaking, eyes still on the headboard of the bed, and felt the top of his head. His hair felt wet. He brought his fingers in front of his face to examine them. The liquid on them was clear. He gave it a sniff. No smell. Was it water? Swallowing hard, he looked up at the ceiling just to witness another small drop form between two wooden boards. Was there a leak up there? But it wasn't even raining. Confused, he dropped his gaze back down. She was right there, hovering inches from his face. An old woman with tattered clothes and long, gray tendrils of hair. Everything on her moved as if she were submerged under water. She reminded Luke of the picture of a hydra, a mythical snakelike creature with nine heads, that he'd seen in a book about Greek mythology. Only she was much scarier. He held his breath as escape routes flashed through his head. His frantic eyes darted to the ladder that led down from the loft. The woman chuckled, her eyes flashing a cold blue.

"She's the lock, and you are the key," she said in a sing-song tone that wasn't pretty at all.

It was creepy as hell. Then, she opened her mouth wide, showing him the absolute darkness that lay within, and flew right at him. When she went through him, it was as if someone had thrown a bucket of cold water in his face. He gasped and sputtered. His ears were filled with a terrible ringing. He felt water enter his lungs instead of air and flailed his arms in protest. He couldn't breathe—which meant he couldn't cry out for help. Was he actually going to drown in his bed? This wasn't real. He knew it wasn't real. This apparition was using its energy to fool his senses. It was all a trick.

He just had to figure out how to break the illusion. Realizing they were squeezed shut, he forced his eyes open. He could see only darkness. He heard his own heart beating through the awful ringing in his ears. He counted the beats until his heart started to slow, then slowly, measuredly, he blew out the last little bit of air left in his lungs. He saw the rush of bubbles leave his body. Now, he was a clean slate.

With enormous effort, he was able to take a breath, and the sensation of drowning was gone. The ringing ceased, and the darkness receded from around him, revealing his comfortable, warm bedroom. He took another enormous breath and took inventory of his body. He touched his face, his hair, his chest. He was completely dry. Jerking his eyes up, he searched for the leak on the ceiling, but that had been an illusion, as well. There was no water. Anywhere.

He climbed off the loft and went outside to get some fresh air. He decided to walk the bicycle route near his house. He needed to think, and the best way to do it was to walk. He also needed to be out of his bedroom. He wasn't sure where he would be sleeping that night, but it wouldn't be in there. The rhythm of his own steps helped his mind gather itself. He knew what to do. Somehow, instinctively, he knew to slow his breathing. He was also aware the entire time that what he was experiencing wasn't real, that all the sensations weren't real. He had thought at first that the entity had been toying with him or trying to scare him. But something inside him told him that wasn't it. It had some other agenda. The other thing was that the energy the old woman emitted felt . . . familiar? Was that the right word for it? He guessed it was. But where did he encounter it before? He stopped in his tracks and turned sharply on his heels. From where he stood on the wooded path, he could just see the roof of his house above the tree line. And, behind it, the peaked roof of the Glessner house.

"Rosie . . ." he heard himself say in a whisper.

It was the speck. The energy was the same. The blue of the woman's eyes the same as the electric sparks of Rosie's little cloud. He wasn't sure if they were parts of the same entity or not, but they were connected somehow. Maybe Rosie was right. This could all be tied to Rosanne Glessner. There was something in her journal. Maybe something she didn't want Luke to find. "She is the lock, and you are the key." That was what she had said. It sounded like a clue, not a threat. So, maybe she wanted him to find something?

The hairs rose on the back of his neck. He had come to this spot for a reason. He didn't know it when he left the house. His body had made its way here on its own accord. Turning slowly, he lay eyes upon the naked lady of the lake. She stood on the rocks that were meant to break the waves during a storm with her back to him. Her skin was pale, almost white. Tendrils of her wet hair stuck to her shoulders. She stared, unseeing, at the expanse of blue water ahead. Luke walked up to her until there were only a few feet between them. She wasn't as shocking as he remembered. No marks on her. No indicators of how she had died. He examined her profile and was shocked to see how young she looked. She couldn't have been more than twenty when she died.

"Who are you?" he asked.

He expected no answer, and an answer is not what he got. She opened her pale lips and let out a rush of water from inside her.

"Tell my mom I'm sorry!" she said, water continuing to drip from her lips. "I should have listened."

She wasn't looking at Luke, but he had the distinct feeling she knew he was there.

"What's your mom's name?" Luke asked, taking another step toward her.

"Tell her I'm there!"

She pointed out to the water, her voice echoey and desperate.

"What's your name?"

She was fading away, her ghostly particles flying out to the lake on a gust of wind. Luke followed her flight with his eyes. It was a beautiful, sunny day. He could hear people talking in the distance, children running and laughing at the playground nearby. And, amongst the many sounds of life, he could hear the echo of her voice: "I am Lisa."

CHAPTER TWENTY-NINE

1996
ROSIE

Getting up in the morning was stupid. Getting dressed was stupid. Eating was stupid and going to the shrink's office was outright retarded. Yet, here she was. Session number two with Dr. Dumb Big Eyes Lewis. He was a joke. And a bad one at that. He thought he was going to cure her with his pills and meditation exercises. You couldn't cure a haunting. Everybody knew that. The smartass didn't believe her. There were no ghosts. It was all in her head. Such bullshit! Her inner brooding was interrupted by his annoying voice. She could hardly stand it. She could hardly stand anyone talking to her these days. She just wanted peace and quiet so she could sleep.

"You were about to tell me about the dream you had last night!"

"Was I?" Her tone was mocking.

She didn't know why she was talking like this. So disrespectful, but it felt good.

"Yep, you definitely were."

He was just going to pretend Rosie was being normal. He was blinking at her in that sickening slow-motion way of his that made Rosie want to punch him in the face. She imagined herself doing it. Yes. She would knock him out cold. It would be so satisfying. She grinned ear to ear thinking about it. He would bleed just like that dumb rooster. She could do to this dumbass what she did to the rooster. She saw, in her mind's eye, the bucket coming down on that pile of feathers and flesh. She heard the empty plastic *thump* of it and shuddered. As if coming out of a trance, she was hit by the guilt and mutilating sadness she felt that morning.

"No!" she sobbed, covering her ears with her hands and starting to rock back and forth.

She could still hear it, the meaty thumps of the bucket. She could feel warm blood hitting her face. *Stop, stop, stop! Go away!* she chanted in her head. She lived in this waking nightmare now, her consciousness seemingly coming and going as it pleased. It was almost better when it was gone. She could be angry and think terrible thoughts without feeling bad at all. It was almost like it wasn't even her. Like there were two people in her body, playing tag with each other. "Now it's your turn to steer! No, it's your turn!" There was Rosie and Bad Rosie. The problem was that when Bad Rosie left, it was normal Rosie who had to live with all the shit Bad Rosie did. Like killing Leon. That hadn't been Rosie's decision. It was her body that did it, but it still wasn't her. She would never! She loved Leon. She was just so tired. A hand with a tissue materialized in front of her.

"It's okay, Rosie! Bad dreams happen. It's okay to cry."

"What?"

She took the tissue from him and wiped her tear-stricken face. She hadn't realized she was crying. What was this guy even talking about?

"You were going to tell me about your dream. Was it a bad one?"

Her dream. She remembered now. She had mentioned it to him. God knows why. It felt too personal to tell him. But it was much better than thinking about what Bad Rosie had done. So, she grabbed onto that lifeline and pulled herself out of the memory of that terrible morning.

"No." She shook her head and blew her nose. "It was just

very strange. I feel like it meant something. It felt so real."

"Will you tell me?"

"Yeah." She nodded and placed the crumpled-up tissue in the small black bin next to the couch she was sitting on. "I was flying through the forest. At first, I thought I was on my horse, but when I looked down, all I could see was the forest floor rushing by."

She was going incredibly fast, dodging trees left and right. It was kind of fun in a thrilling sort of way. She had known her destination was the homestead, but when she got there, she couldn't believe her eyes. They were alive. The people she had seen in her vision. The main house stood tall and proud. The barn and the springhouse were intact, too. There were chickens scratching in front of the house. She could hear the laughter of children and, a moment later, saw them run out from behind the barn. They startled the chickens, who flew agitatedly in all directions. The old lady who had been sleeping in the rocking chair opened one of the downstairs windows and hollered at the kids good-naturedly. In the distance, someone was chopping wood. Rosie turned her head and saw the man with the long black hair, splitting logs on a stump. They were all here, happy, so full of life. She lowered to the ground, her bare feet touching grass and damp earth. These people were her family. Maybe she could stay here with them. Maybe her ghost wouldn't bother her if she lived here. The braying of a donkey broke the peaceful silence of the day.

"Moonwalk!" she yelled.

She knew it was him. She ran for the tree line, toward the cry of the old donkey. She was moving so agonizingly slowly, getting only barely closer to the cliff. She would be there. Emi would be there. Rosie had to get to her. There was something wrong. An unknown threat. It seemed so far away. The rocks and twigs stabbed at the soles of her bare feet, but she had to keep going. She was almost there. Moonwalk cried again.

"I'm here!" she screamed. "I'm coming!"

The trees opened up, and there they were: Moonwalk with Emi on his old, bowed back, and a woman holding the reins of his bridle. They all had their backs to her, facing out into the abyss.

"Emi!" Rosie called out, and both Emi and the woman turned their heads to look at her.

Moonwalk pranced, agitated, but the woman wouldn't let him move from the spot. Rosie ran up to them and tried to wrench the reins from the woman's hands. She couldn't do it. It was as if the lady had been made from stone. Rosie put her whole weight into it but was unable to move even one of her fingers. *Fine, then!* she thought. *I'll just take Emi, and you can have the donkey, you witch!* She went to grab her sister, who, by this point, had turned her gaze back to the drop-off. A hand on her shoulder stopped her. The woman turned Rosie's body effortlessly to face her.

"Do not fight it!" she said.

"Like hell I won't!" Rosie struggled to free herself from her hand.

"It cannot be helped. It's not your fault!"

Rosie was barely listening to her. She was kicking and punching, but all her strikes went through the woman's body as if she were made of smoke. Winded, she stopped and looked at her more closely. She looked familiar. She kind of reminded Rosie of her mom. That wasn't exceptionally shocking because if she lived here, there was a good chance they were related. She turned her head sharply to look out into the drop-off, giving Rosie a clear view of her profile. She was pretty, in a dated, old-fashioned kind of way. Her dark blonde hair sat in a tight bun at the base of her neck.

"She's here!" she said. "We are out of time."

"Who . . ."

Rosie woke up before she could finish her question. She was standing just inside her parents' bedroom. She backed out as quietly as she could and didn't think she had woken either of them. She did leave this part out. It was really weird and super embarrassing that she, for whatever reason, always ended up sleepwalking into her parents' room. Maybe Dr. Lewis didn't have to know about that just yet.

"It is a very imaginative dream," the doctor said. "Why do you find it so strange?"

"Because . . ." she started and stopped.

Should she be telling him stuff that could get her into trouble? Did he tell everything they talked about to her parents? She frowned, unsure how to proceed. The wretched doctor didn't say anything for what seemed like minutes. He just let her stew in the misery of her indecision. Fuck it! What's the worst that could happen? She already killed their rooster and wasn't grounded for life.

"It happened in real life. The part where I found my sister at the cliff. She wandered off. She couldn't remember how she got there."

Dr. Lewis scribbled something in his notepad.

"Do you think maybe she told you that because she didn't want to get into trouble?" he asked, looking at her imploringly with those sleepy owl eyes of his.

Rosie crossed her arms, not knowing what to make of this question.

"Why would she lie?" she asked, her tone teetering on the edge of rude.

He leaned back in his chair and clasped his hands in front of him.

"Is your sister allowed to go to the cliff on her own? It is a dangerous place, is it not?"

Rosie felt the heat rise in her cheeks. Was the doctor right? Did she have it all wrong? But her dream . . .

"Sometimes, our minds come up with things to explain or rationalize things we can't explain or find out of the ordinary. Sometimes, the explanations can be quite outlandish if our imaginations are vivid. In reality, things are usually a lot simpler than they seem. You were faced with a situation that had no rational explanation, so your brain came up with one. Your dream is a perfect example of that. There is no need to feel silly."

"I do not feel silly," she said with venom.

Oh, no! She could feel herself shifting into Bad Rosie. Could she do something to stop it? She felt her back arch and her body go rigid as she focused every neuron in her brain on holding back this soulless thing that lived within her. It was no use. It was too late.

"This is the biggest load of horseshit I've ever heard! Where did you even get your degree at? The University of Retards?"

He just sat there, looking placidly at her and saying nothing. It made her impossibly angry. How dare he not get offended? He was so stupid, he couldn't even manage that. The moron. She stood up and loomed over him across the coffee table. He didn't react, only picked up his pen and wrote something in his notepad. Rosie's eyes zeroed in on the words. Her focus was laser sharp, so she could see crystal clear the two words on the paper: "irrational anger." She barked out a laugh.

"Irrational? I'll show you Irrational! Let's talk about your marriage! How does that sound?"

For the first time since they met, Rosie saw a negative emotion appear on Dr. Lewis's narrow face. It was fear. *Got ya!* she thought smugly.

"That is not an appropriate topic of conversation. Besides, we are here to talk about you," he said, making an attempt at smoothing out the worry lines on his face and failing.

"Yeah, but what you have going on is much more interesting than my boring ass life."

She flopped back down onto the couch and smiled at him with enthusiasm.

"I know I had been an asshole lately, but you . . . you are cheating on your wife. I'm thinking you are right there with me."

He went an interesting shade of off-white at this. He picked up his pen and poised it above the notepad, then put it back down, leveling his gaze at her.

"How do you know this, Rosie?"

She could hear cold anger in his voice. It sounded so delicious that she licked her lips. She got him, all right. He was nice and pissed. It was only a matter of time before he threw her out and refused to see her again. He couldn't know she was able to see into him. All she had to do was look him hard between the eyes, and all the worst things that ever happened to him came pouring out. It was like cracking a ripe melon. So juicy and sweet.

"Oh, I have my sources."

She crossed her legs in front of her. He clicked his pen angrily and wrote down some quick words. "Empty threats." Wow! Bad Rosie's vision was so much better than regular Rosie's. She definitely wouldn't be able to read it from this far normally. He thought she was guessing. Making things up, hoping she was right. Poor fool.

"Maybe one of your lovers told me," she ventured. "I think his name was Kevin. Does your wife know you like men?"

The pen fell from his grasp. It bounced on the floor before settling next to his right foot. He stared at her in open-mouthed disbelief. His large eyes opened wide enough to look comical.

"I think our time is up," Rosie said, pointing at the wall clock. "So, same time next week?"

CHAPTER THIRTY

1996
ALICE

She didn't know what woke her, just that suddenly, she was wide awake, her heart racing. She lifted her head and peered around the dark room. Her eyes snagged on the silhouette of a person standing at the foot of the bed, and she nearly jumped out of her skin. Sitting up, she flattened against the headboard. Noah grumbled in his sleep next to her. Why wasn't he awake? Freaking log of a man. This was the third time Alice had woken up to her fourteen-year-old daughter standing in their bedroom. She kept wandering in here while sleepwalking. You would think that Alice got used to it by this time, but that wasn't the case. It was really creepy the first time, and it just kept getting creepier and creepier. And God knows how many times she had been in here without Alice noticing. She shouldn't react like this to one of her children surprise visiting her at night. Most parents would be startled but then would just laugh it off. And she probably would do just that if it was Emi who was doing it. There was something wrong with Rosie. Something not normal. Yes, her diagnosis had been bad. Worse than Alice had expected. She was going to have to take multiple medications: one to help her sleep, one to calm her down, and one to balance her mood. She had only been to two sessions with Dr. Lewis, and he insisted they start treatment right away. The seriousness in his voice made Alice's insides clench almost painfully. He had told Alice that Rosie very well may have schizophrenia but that it was too early to tell. He would have to continue seeing her and would be able to give her a final diagnosis in a few weeks. It was a terrible blow, and Noah seemed to take it as badly as she did. He loved their girls so fiercely. Unlike Alice's dad, who often was too busy with his own stuff, Noah was there for every important event in their lives and almost all the less important ones, too. If he could get away from work, he was there.

The medications should be ready for pickup in the morning. Alice didn't tell Noah, but she had the sinking feeling that they wouldn't work on Rosie. She had this aura of doom about her. After the whole rooster incident, Alice really didn't know what she was going to do next. And that is why she was so nervous about finding her in her bedroom at night. It was almost scary. She was almost scared of her teenage daughter. It was awful that she felt that way. She was plenty ashamed of herself, but she couldn't help it. She could almost feel when Rosie's mood was changing. It was a guttural feeling, like being hunted by a cougar. All the hairs on her body prickled, and her asshole clenched. When she saw Rosie running for Emi, it was almost as if it wasn't even her. Even the shape of her eyes looked different. She changed into this intruder, a stranger, in Alice's home. And then, she would change back into her Rosie, her firstborn child. And Alice's body would relax, and her heart would break. She felt personally responsible for Rosie having to go through this.

She never interacted with her when she came into her room at night. Eventually, she would wake up and leave on her own.

Alice sunk down into her pillow and pulled the blanket up to her chin. She was pretending to be asleep. Just one more night of this. Just one more, and then the medications would help Rosie sleep. They had to work. They just had to. A couple of minutes passed, and suddenly, Rosie's posture changed. She lifted her head and glanced around quickly. Realizing where she was, she tiptoed out of the room and shut the door. Alice followed her footsteps with her ears. Once the soft thumping stopped and Alice was sure Rosie was in her room, she got out of bed and, opening the bedroom door a crack, peeked out into the hallway.

Stepping into the hallway from the living room, Emi's door was directly to the right. Rosie's room was on the far left end, with the master bedroom in between the girls' rooms. There was also a bathroom next to Rosie's room that both girls used.

When Alice caught Rosie sleepwalking, she would always make sure that she would go back to her own room and not anywhere else. She and Noah both agreed that Emi needed to lock her door at night for the time being. It wasn't the best solution. It made Emi less accessible in case of any emergency, such as a house fire. Noah did assure her that if he needed to, he could break down Emi's door with no problem. Alice believed him. He was well-built with wide, powerful shoulders. If there was any physical threat, he would protect his family. This simple fact always helped Alice sleep at night. But how could you expect a man to protect people from his own daughter? Noah was the first one to hold Rosie when she was born. He spent sleepless nights with her when she was sick. Taught her how to ride a bike—and a horse, for that matter. Been there for all the highs and lows. How could he even consider her a threat?

Alice got back into bed and curled her body into the fetal position. Would she even be able to sleep now? Her mind was racing. She felt Noah's big body move on the other side of the bed. One strong arm came around her waist and pulled her against him. She sighed and snuggled her body into his. There came a low grunt from behind her. She smiled as he reached under her nightgown to find her breasts. He stroked them one by one. It was a question. Was she up for it? Sex always made her feel closer to him. It was their way of connecting to each other after a hard day or a disagreement. It soothed her nerves and took her mind off the stressful things in life. Yes, maybe she could go for a round. She wiggled her bum against him, and he pulled her even closer.

"Is that a flashlight in your pocket, or are you just happy to see me?"

"I'm not sure. Why don't you investigate?"

His voice was gruff with sleep, his movements slow and soft as he conducted his own investigation under her clothes. Eventually, he did get on top of her, his weight pressing her into the mattress. She did love his large frame. The physical labor of roofing agreed with him. She ran her hands over the toned muscles of his back and along the line of his ribs. She sighed, satisfied by the feel of him. No wonder he was able to convince her to have kids. She wouldn't be able to say no to anything he said when he was like this.

Afterward, she fell asleep with her head on his chest, listening to his heartbeat. And she thought that no matter what happened, she would always have Noah. Her rock and best friend for life.

Rosie came with her to work in the morning. This had been a trend lately. Alice no longer fought her if she didn't want to go to school. She, in fact, didn't think it a good idea to let her go to school while she was so out of balance. Technically, Rosie could have stayed at home by herself, but neither Noah nor Alice thought it a good idea to leave her alone for an extended period of time. The medicine should help. Noah was going to pick it up on his way home from work. Rosie didn't seem too enthused about the prospect of having to take pills every day, but then again, she wasn't particularly happy about anything nowadays.

They parked in front of the YMCA.

"I don't want to go in, Mom!" Rosie whined. "Can I just stay in the car? I won't drive off or anything, I promise! I'll just sleep."

"Nice try, love. No. That's illegal. Come on!"

They made their way inside, Rosie walking like she was dragging a ton weight behind her. Her mouth had this perpetual downward bend to it, so she always looked like she was about to have a tantrum. Like a sleepy toddler.

"There is a bench in the room where we keep the exercise equipment. You can lie down on that!"

Alice settled Rosie in the storage room and conducted her class. She felt distracted the entire time, sometimes forgetting what the next move was altogether. It was frustrating. Part of her thought she should just quit working altogether and take care of Rosie. That's what a good mother would do, said a small, nasty voice in her head. They would survive financially if she didn't work, but they were definitely a lot more comfortable this way. But how comfortable could they possibly be with a sick child who didn't get the attention she needed? She may have to homeschool Rosie if things didn't get any better.

She walked into the storage room after the class was done and found Rosie peacefully dozing on the red storage bench. She was curled up like a cat, one hand under her head and one covering her eyes. Alice smiled, letting love fill her body from head to toe. She used to look at Rosie and get this feeling of all-enveloping love all the time. She missed it. She missed her. Lately, she had been feeling like a failure as a mother. She was making mistake after mistake, and it was terribly disheartening. Her work gave her satisfaction, though. The truth was that she really didn't want to quit. She liked teaching aerobics. She was good at it, and it kept her body looking great. It was selfish of her. She wished she could be more like her mother and less like her father. Her mother would quit working. She would devote herself completely to Rosie until things got better or until there was nothing else she could do. Why couldn't Alice do that? She should sacrifice. Her career, the money, her own health meant nothing if Rosie continued to get worse. So, why? You have sacrificed enough! said the small voice in her head, only it was louder this time. All you did was sacrifice when you were young. To save others. And look what good it did you.

She sat down on the bench next to Rosie's feet and inspected her dainty white ankles above her red converse sneakers. They looked like they belonged to a little bird. Has she lost weight recently? It was hard to tell. Rosie wasn't putting any effort into how she looked nowadays. She wore her baggiest, most comfortable clothes everywhere.

"Come on, love! Let's go home!"

She placed a hand on one of her bony ankles and rubbed small circles on it with her thumb. Rosie came alive slowly. She stretched, almost knocking Alice off the bench, and giggled. Such a sweet sound. This was her daughter. Her smiling, sleepy princess with her golden hair. Alice gave her a big, bone-cracking hug. She almost cried. She wanted her back. She wanted this Rosie all the time.

They parked in front of their house, and Rosie ran inside.

"I'm going to eat some cereal!" she called back over her shoulder and let the screen door slam behind her.

"Okay, love!" Alice said distractedly, pulling letters and magazines out of their mailbox.

She was sorting through it all and walking to the front porch at the same time, so she almost tripped when a letter caught her eye. She righted herself and pulled it out from behind the water bill. It was a light-yellow envelope with her address written on it by hand. It was actually addressed to Noah, not her. No return address. She looked at the back of it, searching for clues as to who may have sent it, but there wasn't anything else on it. The writing looked feminine. She wasn't sure why. The letters were nicely rounded, the spaces so even between them, it looked like the person used a ruler. She and Noah didn't have any secrets between them. They often opened each other's letters like bills and such, so, technically, she could do that right now. She wanted to. Her curiosity had been piqued. It was just . . . this letter looked personal.

"Whatever," she mumbled and tore it open.

As she read, she slowly lowered herself onto the third porch step. Once she was done, her eyes skimmed the paper frantically to find some kind of insignia. There was none. Whoever wrote this wanted to remain anonymous. She read it again, a bit more slowly.

To: Noah Smith

This letter is to inform you that your daughter, Rosanne Smith, isn't biologically yours. She was fathered by a man named Nathaniel Davis. Your wife had been involved with him while attending college in Houston. You, like everyone else, deserve the truth.

Best of luck to you!

That was it. There was no indication as to who wrote it. And even though she thought it may be a woman based on the letters, she couldn't even be sure of that. She looked up from the letter and onto the long, winding dirt road that was her driveway. An autumn breeze made the trees flanking it shiver and drop their colorful foliage. Her grandparents had left her this enormous piece of property while they were both alive. It was almost the most generous thing that anyone has ever done for her. She, in fact, hadn't told anybody about it until she and Noah married, mostly because she didn't actually intend on living here. This had been her wedding gift to him. More of a wedding surprise, really. She felt like she owed him this, a beautiful life on this beautiful land. And they did make a wonderful life. Originally, there was only a shack standing where their house was. Noah built most of it with his own two hands, a show of his dedication to Alice. She did most of the interior design and painting. It was teamwork, really. This structure wasn't just a house that they owned; it was a home they had built log by log, brick by brick, with their own sweat and tears. They had filled it with love and memories over the years, and now, somebody was trying to tear it all down. It seemed to Alice that life had turned against her at some point. First, Rosie, and now, this. She didn't know what she had done to deserve such punishment from God. Her only solace was that it wasn't just her who seemed to be cursed but her entire line of family. Sometime back in the day, an ancestor of hers must have done something so truly horrible that a curse had been placed upon their heads. It trickled down and down and down through the generations until it reached her beautiful, wonderful little girl. Alice felt tears stinging her eyes. She crumpled up the paper in one hand and used the back of her wrist to wipe her face. No need to let Noah know about this little act of terrorism. She would dispose of this paper and act like it never made it into their lives. She would spare Noah this heartache.

She got up and walked the rest of the way up the porch. When she reached for the door handle, it opened seemingly on its own, revealing Rosie inside.

"I can't find Ollie," she said, looking distressed.

"Did you look under my bed?" Alice asked, slowly shifting gears from self-pitying to parenting.

"I looked under all the beds and checked the rest of the house. Can you help me look outside?"

"Of course, love! Let me just put away the mail."

She guided Rosie inside, her hand on her shoulders.

"Can you grab me my work boots from my closet?"

She was uncomfortably aware of the crumpled piece of paper in the palm of her hand. She needed to get rid of it ASAP. Once Rosie was out of the kitchen, she turned on one of the gas burners on the stove and set one corner of the paper on fire. It caught quickly, and soon, the whole thing was ablaze. She dropped it into the sink and washed the ashes away once it was done. This all only took less than a minute. Once it was done, she lit one of the scented candles she had sitting on the kitchen island. When Rosie returned, boots in hand, she took a curious sniff of the air in the kitchen, but then saw the candle and made no comment.

They looked everywhere around the house for the old dog until it was time to pick up Emi from school. It was as if Ollie had been swallowed by the ground. Alice feared the worst. He had more than passed his prime. It was actually quite common for old dogs to wander off and die somewhere hidden. Rosie was devastated. She sat outside on the porch, waiting for Noah to come home so they could ride out together to search the woods. However, it was almost dark by the time his truck rolled down the driveway. Rosie ran to him in the dusky light of the setting sun and jumped into his open arms. They came inside together, Rosie dragging her father by the arm.

"Wait, wait, wait! Slow down, lovebug! What's going on with Ollie?" Noah asked while being dragged through the front door.

"He got lost in the forest," chirped Emi from the table.

She was kneeling on her chair, her face covered in spaghetti sauce. She was feeling all high-and-mighty because she knew something that Dad didn't. She had been briefed about the Ollie situation during the car ride home from school. Alice stepped over to her and cleaned the evidence that she couldn't wait to eat dinner with the family off her face.

"Welcome home!" she said to Noah with a tired smile.

"Yeah, so we have to go find him! Like, right now!" urged Rosie, still pulling on his arm.

"Hold your horses, Rosie! Did you look . . ."

"Yes, everywhere! Let's go! We are wasting time."

"Rosie!"

Noah stopped walking, effectively stopping Rosie in her tracks. He dropped a paper bag on the kitchen counter.

"Ooh, is that candy?" asked Emi, leaning her elbows on the table and licking her lips.

"No, it's your sister's medication," Alice said, opening the bag and examining the contents.

"She needs to take them because she's crazy, right?" Emi asked with the air of somebody who has inside information.

"Don't ever say that again! Your sister is not crazy!" Alice burst out.

She was looking at her younger offspring with disbelief. Where on earth did she get that from?

"Yeah, fuck you! You little dweeb."

"Rosie!" both parents said in unison.

Things were getting out of hand so quickly, it made Alice's head spin.

"We don't have time for this!" Rosie said, raising her voice. "Ollie is out there! We need to find him! We need to go now!"

She was gesturing toward the back door.

"Rosie, it's dark. We can't go tonight. We'll look for him some more tomorrow. Right now, we need to figure out how much of each of these you need to take," said Alice, reading the labels on each of the bottles.

"I can't believe you!" Rosie spread her arms in a gesture of helplessness and let them drop to her side. "Dad! You'll come with me, right?"

Noah shook his head solemnly.

"Your mother is right, girlie. This is more important. We can find Ollie tomorrow."

Rosie's face underwent a remarkable transformation in which it changed shape and color. She had become a snarling red lobster.

"He is our family!" she screamed. "Don't you care? Don't you love him? Would you leave me there overnight if I was lost?"

"They would if you kept acting like this," Emi pitched in with the calm wisdom of an almost-six-year-old.

Rosie turned to her, her face nearly purple with rage.

"You . . ." she started in a voice that was more a growl than anything.

"You will go to your room!" Noah pointed a thick, calloused finger at his younger daughter. "Alice, please help her!"

Thank God! Alice thought as she took Emi by the hand. Noah was going to talk some sense into Rosie. Alice hated confrontation of any kind, so she was more than happy to push this task onto her husband. Emi promptly went limp at her touch and slid bonelessly off the chair. Alice grabbed her by both hands and, grunting a bit, dragged her out of the kitchen, through the living room, and into the hallway, thinking this the path of least resistance in this very moment.

She heard Rosie and Noah arguing in the kitchen.

"I don't want to take the stupid medicine! I don't need it!"

"Yes, you do! This is not up for discussion."

"I hate you!"

Alice shut Emi's bedroom door, cutting off this distressing yelling. She leaned against the door, feeling the vibrations of shouting through it but unable to make out the words. Emi was undressing slowly, her small, round face impassive. Alice knew that look. She was internalizing her feelings in regards to her sister.

"Emi, love, why did you call your sister crazy?"

Emi sighed, flapping her nightshirt in the air.

"I'm sorry, Mom. I won't say that again."

Alice frowned at her. She had a feeling that there was more to this. Neither her nor Noah would ever say that about Rosie. Or did they? Maybe in the past, when she had been acting silly. They might have said it jokingly.

"Don't overthink it, Mom!" Emi ordered her.

Alice grinned at her. That was exactly what Noah would have said to her. He often did when he saw her mind racing.

"Come here, you little weirdo!"

She pulled Emi into her lap and hugged her close. "Weirdo" was probably also not the best word to use. She should definitely reconsider some of the words she used around the kids.

"I heard a teacher say it," Emi said.

"What?"

She had her back pressed against Alice's chest so she couldn't see her face, only the curve of her cheek and the long lashes of her right eye.

"When I was waiting in front of the school for you to pick me up, I heard two teachers talking about Rosie, so I listened. One of them called her crazy."

Helpless fury froze the blood in Alice's veins. She wanted to punch this offending teacher in the face and knock their teeth out. She wanted to scream; she wanted to cry. She wanted to do something other than sit here in Emi's room and pretend that things were okay.

"Was it one of your teachers?" she asked as calmly as humanly possible after hearing about such a thing.

Emi shook her head, her blonde hair rustling against Alice's shirt.

"No. She teaches in the other building, where Rosie goes. She is tall and skinny. And she has glasses."

Norma fucking Lesbith. Maybe it was time for another parent-teacher conference.

CHAPTER THIRTY-ONE

1996
NOAH

Noah was trudging through the forest on top of their big gray gelding, whistling and calling for their elderly dog, his five-year-old daughter on his heels riding their lovely donkey who bit everyone except for her. It was a misty, gray Saturday morning with impending rain above. Rosie couldn't get up this morning. The sleeping pills seemed to work well. A little too well. When they tried to wake Rosie to join the morning search, she was so gung-ho about the night before, she just moaned and swatted them away. It was fine. She needed to catch up on sleep. He really didn't need the kids out here with him, anyway. There was an excellent chance that Ollie had passed away, and if he did manage to find him, he wouldn't be a pretty sight. There were coyotes and hogs out here, and they had the tendency to tear up carcasses. Alice had to work. She had two classes back-to-back this morning. So, Emi was his responsibility for the time being. He didn't mind watching the kids. He just hoped he saw the dog before Emi did.

The old donkey sighed and grunted as he placed one small round hoof in front of the other, ear flopping back and forth. *You've come a long way*, Noah thought with affection, looking down at the scraggly creature carrying his daughter.

When Alice's grandparents left her the property, they told her it came with a rogue donkey. She thought they were kidding. They both thought so until random things started to disappear from outside when they were building the home. They moved into the house while it was still under construction and, in consequence, had to do a lot of things the old-fashioned way, such as washing clothes. Noah's underwear would randomly disappear from the drying rope to be recovered hanging from trees or stomped into the mud with bits and pieces missing from the fabric. They could never catch him in the act, but from the prints, they concluded that the culprit had tiny, round hooves.

Eventually, Alice wobbled over to her grandparents' with her large pregnant belly to ask them about their unwanted guest and learned the sad story behind the lone donkey.

Back when Alice's great-grandparents used to live on the land, they had about fifty of the small-bodied equine roaming freely. It started out innocently enough. They got a few of them, maybe four or five, as pets for the children to play with and ride. The thinking behind it was that donkeys are hardier than horses and require less maintenance. The whole family loved them for their charming personalities and playful demeanors. Over the years, they ended up rescuing and adopting many more of them. Thanks to the lush grass and plenty of space, they also multiplied by the dozens. The Glessner land was like a donkey paradise until one fateful night when everything changed. Something had spooked the herd overnight, and they all ended up running off the cliff and falling into the Red River. They all perished. Alice's grandfather and his older brother were the ones who found them. He was fifteen and his brother eighteen. He said that to this day, he could not get the sight out of his head. All those little bodies down there at the bottom on top of each other. It was a gruesome sight. For many years after that, they could swear they heard the screaming of the long-dead donkeys in the woods. That was actually one of the reasons they had abandoned the small house and moved somewhere else nearby.

At least, that was how they told the story. The truth was that Alice's great-grandmother had to be institutionalized, and the by-then frail great-grandfather couldn't take care of the house and the land by himself. He had moved in with one of his sons.

They still went out to the property from time to time to hunt and visit the old homestead and cemetery where eventually, both great-grandparents would be buried. During one of these visits, Alice's grandfather spotted a lone donkey between the trees and realized that it was he who had been calling for his lost fellows all those years. They had made plenty of attempts to catch him, but none had been successful. Donkeys can live into their fifties, so the lonesome creature still lived on the property when Alice and Noah moved in.

They decided to leave out food for him. At first, he only came to eat the offerings of apples and carrots at night, but eventually, they did start seeing him during the day. It was Rosie who gave him the name Moonwalk when she had been around two or so. They could never figure out why she chose this name in particular, but it stuck. Eventually, Noah had built a pen, and they started placing snacks and hay in there for the skittish animal. One day, they saw him in broad daylight and closed the gate. Moonwalk had been terribly upset by this. He ran around, kicking and bucking and screaming his head off for hours. It was part of his process.

The first step was to get him to eat from their hands. Then, they got a halter on him, which he tore off almost immediately. Over the years, Noah and Alice worked together to tame him. They did succeed in breaking him in to pull a cart and to work under a saddle. His first rider was a tied-on bag of potatoes. When he was steady enough, they let six-year-old Rosie sit on him for the first time. He threw her off, and she twisted her ankle pretty badly. Rosie had been stubborn, though, and as soon as her ankle was fit to ride again, she got back on. For the next five years or so, they continued their love-hate relationship until Rosie got too big to sit on him and, frankly, was fed up with his attitude. Moonwalk got along well with their horses. He finally had companions again that spoke the same language as him, if a different dialect. They had never seen him be affectionate with anyone, though, be it animal or human, until Emi came into the picture. She toddled right into Moonwalk's grouchy old heart with her chunky legs and wispy blonde hair. Noah always thought it was Emi's belly laugh that did it. The first time they met, Emi was only a few months old. The wicked creature had leaned over the rail of the pen and brayed right in Emi's face. Instead of crying, she smiled, showing off her two bottom teeth, and let loose a jingling laugh that would have melted any heart. Turns out, not even donkeys were immune to laughing babies. And the rest is history, as they say.

"We should go to the homestead," Emi said, now catching up to Noah.

"We can," Noah acquiesced, his mouth dry from whistling for the past two hours.

Emi had been strangely quiet this entire ride. She was normally a little chatterbox.

"What's on your mind, my little donkey tamer?"

Moonwalk gave him the evil side-eye. Ain't nobody taming him. He was here because he wanted to be here. Emi shrugged.

"Just thinking about the dog. Sucks that he had to sleep out here."

Noah chose his next words carefully. How do you prepare a five-year-old for the death of a beloved pet? Rosie was right. Ollie was a part of their family. Noah turned inward, remembering last night. It had been rough. This whole thing Rosie had going on was still very new to him. Part of him still didn't want to accept the fact that she was sick. He wanted to treat her like a normal teenager. In his eyes, people were responsible for their actions. Saying that Rosie wasn't responsible for what she did because of her sickness did not sit right with him. He had been down that road before with his dad. It was always everyone else to blame for his problems, mostly Noah's mother. Once his father did take responsibility for his actions, they were able to heal together and mend their bond at least to the point where they were able to work together. But that didn't happen until years after his mother's passing. Noah still blamed him for her death. It had been an everyday struggle not to let that show until the day his father died.

He had never been around a person with mental illness. He did blame Rosie for how she acted and what she had done to the rooster. And he had to keep all those feelings neatly bottled up inside. Now, more than ever, he needed Alice to guide him through this. He trusted her judgment.

"You know, Ollie may not be alive when we find him," he said cautiously. "We might not find him at all."

"We'll find him," she said, urging her mount into a snorting trot.

It had been a minute since he had come up here. The bones of the old homestead stood crumbling before him. They sighed as the autumn winds blew through them. Moonwalk let out a long bray of greeting that bounced back at them from the old buildings and the surrounding trees. The local crows called back, followed by an angry mockingbird. Once the forest went quiet around them, Noah whistled and called out for the dog. They waited in silence.

"Did you hear that?" Emi asked, looking up at him.

"No. What did you hear?"

"He's here."

Noah strained his ears. Emi had much better hearing than he did. She claimed to be able to hear the squeaking of bats as they flew past them in the night sky. There came a soft whimper from somewhere around them. The sound was so weak, it got lost in the wind.

He let loose a booming call. "Ollie! Here, boy!"

"Ollie!" chimed in Emi.

The sound came again, a bit stronger. He was somewhere up ahead. They urged their mounts forward slowly. The dog kept on calling to them. By this time, Noah was sure it was him. He barked softly in between the whining.

"I think he is in there!" Emi said, walking Moonwalk toward the ruins of the springhouse.

Of course he was. Noah hopped down from his saddle and peered into the deep, seemingly bottomless hole that was the corpse of the old springhouse. There were probably spiders in there—and lots of 'em. Ollie was definitely down there. They could hear his frantic barking and his little dog feet scratching at the stones below. Noah shuddered. Well, now he could tick "climb into a deep dark hole full of spiders" off his daily to-do list. Hopefully, it would come off his bucket list, too, 'cause he never wanted to have to do it again.

"Fuck!" he exclaimed and turned guiltily to his daughter. "Don't tell your mother I said that!"

"I won't, Daddy! Don't worry!" She dimpled at him conspiratorially. "In you go!"

He had neglected to bring a flashlight. In hindsight, he wondered what kind of moron he was to do so. There wasn't much left of the stone steps that once led down to the underground cavern. Noah's feet slipped and slid as the earth crumpled under his weight. Once he reached the bottom, he squatted and let his eyes adjust to the darkness.

"Ollie?"

He could hear him. He was whimpering and scratching at the ground.

"Are you stuck, boy?"

He crab-walked toward where he thought he was and soon was able to make out some shapes in the gloom. There was just enough light coming in through the opening behind him for him to see, although not very well. There was a tangle of roots encroaching on the cavern through the sides and the roof. They must belong to those two tall pines that grew next to the opening. Nature was slowly overtaking this place. Soon, it would be swallowed whole if Noah didn't do anything. He could try to save the house. They could maybe rent it out during the spring and summer months. He slowly moved deeper in as he thought. Suddenly, he saw him. Ollie had effectively tangled himself in the roots. He probably came down here chasing something. A fox or a rabbit, most likely. He was wedged between two thick interlocking roots. His upper body had gone through, but his pelvis got stuck. He saw the evidence of his all-night struggle. The poor animal had dug a small hole in front of him and chewed up all the roots he could reach. Luckily, Noah always carried a Swiss army knife. He extricated it from his back pocket.

"Hey there, Ollie boy! You done something stupid? Got yourself stuck, ya old fart?"

Ollie was delirious with happiness in spite of the insults thrown at him. He wiggled his entire body and wagged his short stump of a tail so it thumped against the wall of the cavern. Noah shushed him with a hand and some kinder words and began to saw at one of the roots holding him in place. Once freed, Ollie limp-ran to the opening where the light was spilling in. It took Noah a second to realize that even though the dog wasn't hitting the wall with his tail anymore, he could still hear thumping. He stilled and listened. It sounded like water hitting earth. A wet, hollow sound. He squinted into the darkness ahead. There, in the complete blackness, two lights ignited like tiny blue flames. They were eyes. He knew that for a fact. Without question. His body's response was visceral. All his muscles clenched, and the hairs along his spine stood on end.

"Fuck no!" he said out loud. He was already moving.

He ran to the opening on all fours, stumbling and crawling. He threw the dog upward so it rocketed out of the hole with a startled yelp. Then, he was climbing, propelled by a fear he hadn't felt since he believed the boogie man lived under his bed as a child. Once out, he took a moment to hyperventilate on his knees. He chanced a cautious glance back down and saw something shapeless dart back into the shadows from the print of light. *Holy motherfucking shit!* That thing was in there the whole time. It was some kind of predator, for sure. His gut told him that much. But why didn't it kill Ollie? Was this the thing he had chased down into the hole? Or even worse, did whatever this was lure him down there on purpose?

"You okay, Dad?" Emi asked, hugging the traumatized dog to her. "You threw him kind of hard."

"I guess I just don't know my own strength," he said, feeling shaky and winded.

Ollie had a hard time walking, so he rode in front of Noah in his saddle, all four feet dangling, his tongue lolling out the side of his mouth. He looked about as relieved to be rescued as Noah felt leaving that place. He hadn't felt this scared since his dad used to beat him as a child. This blue-eyed thing, whatever it was, meant him harm. To think he had brought Emi so close to it. The homestead and most of their land would be off-limits to the girls until he figured out what this was and got rid of it. He needed to tell Alice about it. He paused in his tracks and backpedaled. Should he tell her? She had been so stressed with everything involving Rosie, she was getting gray hairs. Should he add one more thing to her plate? Make her feel they were not safe on their own land? Maybe not. He had promised her things when they got together, things he feared that now, he would be unable to keep. He had told her everything would be fine even if mental illness showed its ugly head down the road. He had meant it. He still did. He just had to work on keeping the family together. They had worked so hard to get to where they were, he couldn't let everything just fall apart. No extra stress for Alice. They climbed a small hill, and the house came into view in the distance. It stood so proud in its spot. He remembered the old shack that it once was. Him and Alice standing in front of it. So young. So full of plans for the future. They were always meant to be together. They were meant to be here. On this land.

CHAPTER THIRTY-TWO

1982
NOAH

When Alice left for Houston, it was as if somebody had pulled the rug out from under Noah's feet. He thought he would never get back up again. He had no reason to get up each morning. She left. He had asked her to stay, and she still left. They had sex, and she still left. He had taken her virginity . . . and it was as if it had meant nothing to her. She was dead set on this goal of hers. She told him why, and he understood to a point. She didn't want to hurt the people she loved. She didn't want to be a burden. Blah, blah, blah. It was all bullshit. Okay, maybe he didn't understand. She got so caught up on all these what-ifs that she didn't allow herself to live. She loved him, too. He knew she did, and that's what made the whole thing so much worse. Noah wished he could grab her and shake some sense into her. He should have yanked her out of that car and yelled in her face, "What the hell are you doing? Stay, damn it!" He should have picked her up, carried her into her bedroom on his shoulders, tossed her down onto her bed, and ravaged her. But these were things that his father would have done. And they only lived in his imagination. Noah would never allow them to become reality. He would never force somebody to do something they didn't want to or make them feel bad about any decision they had already made. Like his mother, he would stand by and watch things happen. So, he let Alice go and let his passiveness eat him from the inside.

Millie was the only reason he was able to pull through those first few weeks without Alice. She was a truly wonderful friend. She made him eat when he didn't want to and did her best to take his mind off his grief even though he knew she felt it, too. They both missed her. Millie was just stronger. And just when he started to think that maybe he was becoming stronger, too, she had dropped this bombshell on him.

Millie was in love with him. It was impossible. It was all wrong. He loved her, of course, but as a friend. His heart belonged to Alice, God damn her. It still did, even after she left him. He tried to find the words to explain this to Millie, but he came up short. He also didn't want to upset her. She was the only one he had left.

That night when she gave him the ultimatum was nearly as devastating as when Alice left. Date her or lose her. He had thought about it for two days straight. He didn't want to lose her, too. Was that a good enough reason to date her, though? He wasn't in love with her, and he didn't know if he ever would be. She was very pretty, with her almond-shaped eyes, lush lips, and kinky hair. The fact that she was Black never really bothered him, but on the flip side, he never saw himself dating her. The more he thought about it, the more appealing the idea got. Millie looked so vastly different from Alice, and maybe that was a good thing. He would hate to be thinking about Alice while he was kissing somebody else. It could be sort of therapeutic to date her. It would help him move on with his life. And he could learn to love her the way she needed to be loved. Only time would tell if they worked together. At the end of all of his ponderings was one simple fact: He would lose her altogether if he didn't at least try. So, he did.

It was awkward at first. For him, at least. Millie seemed to be over the moon. He enjoyed making her happy and seeing her smile. It was worth dating her just for that. He couldn't work up the nerve to sleep with her, though. He had only had sex with one person before and wasn't ready for something new to overshadow that first time. He often went back to the memory of that sunny afternoon. He relived the look and feel of Alice's naked body. Their frantic moments. Her cries of pleasure. He just wasn't ready to associate sex with anyone else.

One day just before New Year's, he had gone over to Rosie's parents' house to take a look at the attic. Maggie Glessner had told him a few days prior that she was hearing scampering noises from up there. Mr. Glessner had thrown his back and so was unable to hunt down whatever it was. Noah jumped at the chance to help them out. He loved them as if they were his own parents, and he missed spending time with them now that he didn't have a specific reason to visit their house.

Maggie was on the phone when he got there.

"Oh, hey, Noah! It's Alice. Do you want to talk to her?"

Noah froze. He was still in the process of closing the front door and somehow couldn't complete the action. Talk to Alice . . . Could he? He hadn't heard from her since she left. And now, all of a sudden, he could talk to her? No way this was true. What would he even say? He had walked over to Maggie without meaning to. Suddenly, he was just there, taking the receiver from her. She walked over and closed the front door, then left the room. Just like that. He was alone with her. He pressed the phone to his ear.

"H-hi," he croaked.

"Noah! Hi!" Alice's happy chirping voice hit him right in the heart.

It was her! He wanted to cry. He pressed the receiver closer to his face, wishing it could transport him to where she was.

"It's so good to hear your voice! How is Houston?"

He had no idea where he came up with this. He didn't care about Houston. *Fuck Houston!* He just had to say something, ask her stuff to keep her talking.

"It's very flat and super sunny. It's still pretty warm here during the day."

"That's cool."

"How are things over there?"

"Oh, you know . . ." he paused to think. No, she wouldn't know.

He absolutely couldn't tell her about him and Millie. He didn't want her to know. He didn't want her to think he was over her. He had to talk about something neutral.

"I started working for my dad."

"Really? When?"

"About a month ago."

"And how is it?"

He could hear her shifting gears. She knew better than anyone how Noah felt about his father.

"It's interesting at times. He is still an asshole. But a slightly improved asshole."

She laughed. The sound was a balm to the raw wound that her absence had scratched onto his heart.

"So, why are you working for him, then? You could do something else. What about football?"

"He pays me well. I wanted to get some quick cash so I could come and see you sometime."

He said it without thinking. He got comfortable. He knew he had made a mistake when she went silent on the other end. She had made it clear she didn't want him there before she left. But maybe things had changed. He hoped that with time, she would miss him as much as he missed her. He wanted to be ready. He wanted to be able to drop everything and get on the next bus to Houston.

"Noah . . ." she started to say, her voice thick with agony.

"Just kidding!" he exclaimed, panic raising his voice. "My dad just asked me to work for him. He needed help . . ."

"I have a boyfriend."

Noah swallowed the bitter ball of what tasted like hatred rising up in his throat. *A boyfriend. Already?* Was she some kind of idiot? A slut? Did she not care about him at all? Were all those years together, their entire childhood, just a lie? A big, fat lie? He heard a soft click on the line. Her mother had been listening in on the conversation. She probably had another landline in her bedroom. Noah hung up the phone. He ran out without saying bye. He ran over to his house, slammed the door behind him, and proceeded to trash his bedroom, hollering like a wounded lion as he did it. It wasn't enough to hurt him; she had to tear his heart out completely. She was evil. She was a whore. She didn't care about him. Never cared about him. After he had nothing else to tear or smash, he sat on the ground for a while, leaning against the wall and staring at his extended legs. Dust flakes danced in the stream of afternoon sunlight that came in through his ruined blinds. He counted them absentmindedly. Life was so cruel. He still wanted her. He couldn't hate her, no matter how hard he tried. This should have done it, but instead of stopping, his heart just planned to bleed out slowly, one drop of blood at a time. He got to his feet and looked about him for anything salvageable. He needed a fresh start. He had money. He could redo his bedroom or, even better, move out, get his own place somewhere in town. They had some apartments above some of the shops on Main Street. He could totally afford one of those. He had been pacing round and round in his room but now stopped and looked out the window. He had a girlfriend. Someone who loved him and was eager to see him any chance she got. In his haste to blame Alice for all his sorrows, he had totally forgotten about Millie. It wasn't just her; it was both of them. They were both living their lives and moving on. Millie wanted him. And he was still planning on going to Alice, even if he hadn't said it out loud. What was he doing? He sat down on what remained of his bed and dropped his head into his hands. He was two-timing her, not physically but emotionally. He couldn't just lean on the excuse that going out was Millie's idea, not his. It wasn't fair to her. He needed to do right by her. He had to become a better boyfriend. He would force himself to forget about Alice. She wasn't thinking about him when she was in bed with her new guy. He had to banish her from his thoughts.

So, he made an effort. He focused on being more attentive and loving with Millie. He kissed her more often and reached under her clothes to touch her body when nobody was looking. It was quite thrilling, actually. He was having fun being with her. It was time to rip off the Band-Aid. On New Year's Eve, he slept with her. He never regretted that night. What happened between them had been passionate and beautiful. He was glad he was able to give that to her, that night of true dedication just to her. It was liberating. In the days after, he thought that this may be enough. Life didn't necessarily have to be more. Millie would make him a caring wife. It didn't matter that he wasn't in love with her as long as they loved and respected one another. His heart would heal with time, and he would be happy. He almost succeeded in convincing himself. But then, Alice was back, and this crucial part of him that had lay dormant in her absence came alive. It was like waking up from the dream. He had to go to her. He couldn't help it. Even if she didn't have those bruises on her face, he was helplessly drawn to her. It was shitty. It was one of the worst things he had ever done, betraying Millie like that. But it was the right thing. The only thing. Once he was in her presence, he didn't understand how he could have ever thought to have a life without Alice. He was hers. He had always been hers. He just had to make her understand this.

CHAPTER THIRTY-THREE

1996
DR. LEWIS

Lewis Stagner sat at the dinner table in his beautiful two-story home, gripping his knife and fork as if his life depended on it. His wife, Mary, was busy trying to force food into their four-year-old twin boys. They were notoriously picky eaters who gave her a run for her money at each mealtime. Mary looked quite haggard, with her red curls coming loose from her bun and a colorful array of food smears on her apron. The boys may just turn out to be artists. She was bending over one of the redheaded little monsters and making a valiant attempt at inserting a piece of chicken between his firmly closed lips.

"Come on, Liam! Open up! Just one bite. I promise it tastes good," she pleaded with their offspring.

She huffed out a breath and straightened, hands on hips. Turning her frustrated stare on Lewis, she said:

"Can you please take on David? I'll keep trying with this one."

She poked a fork at Liam, who grinned at him and stuck out his tongue. Lewis nodded and scooted his chair next to David's. Taking a spoonful of mashed potatoes, he offered it to him.

"Come on, little man! Give it a go for Daddy!"

"No!" David exclaimed, turning his head. With a swift, graceful movement of his arm, he knocked the spoon from Lewis's hand.

It flew through the air in a graceful arc and landed in the mouth of their waiting collie, who ran off with it swiftly before anyone could stop her.

"Lily!" Mary yelled after the dog. She threw up her hands in exasperation. "Why does every family dinner have to be a shitshow?"

"Please don't say 'shit' in front of the kids!"

Mary glared at him. But there was a twinkle in her eyes. She cocked her hip to the side and pushed out her chest so she looked like a cocky little bantam rooster.

"You just said it yourself, you terrible hypocrite!"

She was holding her smile in but only barely. Lewis grinned at her.

"We make quite shitty parents, don't we?"

Both of them laughed at this.

Lewis loved his wife. He loved her fire and attitude, both of which she seemed to have passed on to their children. Mary worked as a nurse. Lewis met her when one of his more unhinged patients came to his session wielding a pocketknife. The knife had ended up in Lewis's arm, and he ended up in Mary's care. Their eyes met as she was dressing his wound, and they had an instant connection. This had been a first for Lewis. He had never felt any attraction toward a woman before. He had known from a young age that he had been born different. It became pretty evident in his teens; when most boys his age were lifting up girls' skirts, he had a crush on their young and handsome gym teacher, Mr. Harrison. His little flaw was easy to hide at first, but as the years went by and everyone was dating someone, it became increasingly harder. When he had met Mary, his parents were already actively working on setting him up with someone. He had suffered through countless uncomfortable blind dates and family dinners where a neighbor's daughter had been invited, but he wasn't married yet. His father just shrugged it off as Lewis not wanting to tie himself down yet, but his mother was starting to give him curious looks. It was only a matter of time before she figured out that her perfect psychologist son wasn't so perfect after all. Then, along came Mary. There was just something about her that resonated with him. She was small but strongly built, and her falling curls were shorter back then. He grabbed on to the small shimmer of attraction he felt for her and held on for dear life. They married six months later. On the outside, they looked to be the perfect married couple. And for all intents and purposes, that's what they were. Lewis loved his wife, but the initial attraction only lasted so long, and soon, he became restless. He did not cheat on her with not one man but several. His reasoning was that he did not want a single partner on the side because then he would have gotten emotionally attached to him. Relations with other men became his version of stress release, like eating to calm your nerves. For a while, he felt he found a sort of balance in life. He could have his cake and eat it, too. That was until young Rosanne Smith made him reconsider all his life's decisions. How on earth did she know so much about his personal life? Obsession may be a symptom of her illness. She could have seen his name on the paperwork her doctor gave her mother. She probably researched him. She could have seen him with a man around town. The chance of it was slim, but it was a possibility. And she would have known that he was married once she saw the ring on his finger. Yes, most of the weirdness could be explained, if by a stretch. The only thing was the story about the teacher. Rosie had inside information in her case, too. It was a pattern. Knowledge about the teacher's surgery could have been something Rosie had had for a while and just kept to herself until the opportunity arose to use it. Children tended to have very sharp ears for things they shouldn't be hearing. Curse words, secrets . . . His twins did it often enough. They would come home from pre-K asking the strangest questions. This one time, David had asked him what a lady's muff was. Lewis had straight-up spit out his coffee. When questioned on where he had heard about a lady's muff, he confided in Lewis that one of his classmates had overheard his father say to one of his friends, and I quote, "My wife's muff is as big as Canada."

So, yes, little ears heard all, and so Rosie's inside knowledge could be chalked up to her having sharp ears and eagle eyes. End of story. The only thing was . . . Lewis leaned back in his home office chair and surveyed his computer screen. He was getting ready for his next appointment with Rosie. He read through his notes, adding information and professional thoughts as he went. The only thing was this feeling he got the moment the girl entered the room. The closest he could come to describing it was dread. But that wasn't quite right. It wasn't like he didn't want to work with her—quite the contrary. He found Rosie and her entire case very interesting. It wasn't clean-cut. This made it a challenge, and he liked that. Being in the same room with Rosie was like having to stand next to someone holding a bowling ball, knowing the person could drop it on your foot at any second and with no warning. Rosie was unpredictable but in an almost scary way. The feeling was ridiculous. This was a fourteen-year-old girl he was talking about. She couldn't do much damage to Lewis even if she lunged at him. But there was something about her. Something unnatural.

He sighed. He couldn't put that in the notes. This was too personal. A gut feeling wasn't something you could take as actual fact. He did feel as though Rosie wasn't telling him something. Maybe something crucial, even. He could put that down. He continued his vigorous typing. Once he was done, he looked at his watch. It was quarter to 10. He needed to go to bed. He had a meeting the next day with the ominous teacher. A Ms. Lesbith. He powered off his desktop in hopes that Mary would already be asleep. *"Does your wife know you like men?"* echoed in his mind every time he went to bed with her. No, she didn't know. It would destroy her.

CHAPTER THIRTY-FOUR

1996
ALICE

She sat in her car in front of the school building, gripping the steering wheel, her knuckles turning white. She came here angrily, foolishly, to confront Norma. Was she really going to do it? She didn't want to cause Rosie any trouble. She was finally back in school. The medicines seemed to be working, although the dosage may have to be adjusted. Dr. Lewis told her as much. She could just talk to the principal. But he may just dismiss her complaint at this point. Her third option was to not do anything. Let things be and see if they got better with time. Could she actually do that? She felt firm pushback within her at the thought of leaving Norma unpunished. She shook herself and opened the car door. She would talk to someone. Probably the person who she bumped into first. *Let it be Norma or the principal or . . .*

"Dr. Lewis!" she heard herself say.

Rosie's psychologist had just exited the school building. He looked around with his large eyes, seeming quite startled. His gaze finally found her where she was standing in the parking lot next to her car, and he visibly relaxed.

"Mrs. Smith! I didn't expect to see you here. Is everything

okay with Rosie?"

"Oh, yes! I'm actually here to talk to one of her teachers. You know, the one who slapped her."

She shifted uncomfortably. Dr. Lewis frowned at her. He looked left and right quickly to make sure there were no cars coming and jogged over to her.

"Did something else happen? Between your daughter and the teacher, I mean?"

"No, not exactly. Why do you ask?"

"I just talked to her. I was just wondering if she may have left some things out."

Alice was taken aback. Until just right now, it didn't even occur to her to wonder why Dr. Lewis was at Rosie's school.

"How come? I mean, why did you? Talk to her, that is."

She had a terrible habit of stammering when flustered. She hated that about herself. Dr. Lewis leveled his owlish gaze at her, as if deciding how to proceed.

"Would you like to grab a coffee? I think it would be better to talk somewhere else than in front of the school."

Alice sighed, her body relaxing.

"Yes! That would be great, doctor. Thank you!"

"Quite the unfriendly creature that Norma is," Dr. Lewis said as they sat down at the little cafe down the street from the school.

"That is one way to put it." Alice laughed.

"So, the reason I asked you to have a chat with me today is actually Rosie, not Norma."

"Oh, but I thought . . . because you just spoke to her. "

Alice pointed out the front window of the coffee shop, in the general direction of the school.

"I just wanted to hear her side of what happened. Not because I didn't believe you, don't get me wrong! I was just curious as to how Rosie might know such an intimate detail about her teacher. I was hoping Ms. Lesbith would be able to shed some light on it."

"And?"

"She had no clue. I got the distinct feeling that this is quite embarrassing for her."

Alice took a sip from her latte, hoping it would wash away the bitterness she was tasting right now. Dr. Lewis smiled at her sympathetically.

"I do not agree with what she did," he said softly. "The woman has some deep-rooted issues, and frankly, I don't think she should be teaching."

Alice searched his eyes for earnestness. Did this man truly care about her daughter? He took time out of his own schedule to hunt down answers. Did all psychologists do that? He sipped his coffee, looking calm and relaxed as if they were in the middle of a normal session.

"Well, enough about Norma!" he said, placing his mug down on its saucer. "Let's talk about Rosie! How is she doing with the medications?"

Alice chewed on her bottom lip while she collected her thoughts. She wished she could say that Rosie was great. She wanted to tell Dr. Lewis she had her little girl back. But this wasn't such a simple fix. Things were more complicated.

"I know you told me it would be a little bit before her system got used to the medications and the dosages may need to be changed . . . but she seems a bit washed out."

"What do you mean by that?"

"She doesn't really show emotion. She is there with us physically, but she is zoned out most of the time. She sleeps a lot."

Dr. Lewis drummed on the tabletop with one well-manicured hand.

"Everything you described is a normal side effect. You don't need to worry! I'll adjust the dosage whenever I see her next."

Alice nodded, not totally convinced.

"How is her sleepwalking?"

"She's not doing that right now." Alice brightened. In all reality, she was very much relieved not to have to wake up to Rosie walking around her bedroom. "She has very vivid dreams, though.

It sounds like they feel very real to her."

"I'll make a note of that. She may need a different type of sleep aid."

Dr. Lewis seemed pleased with her answers. He took out a small notebook from his jacket pocket and scribbled something on it. Alice had a minute to think while he was doing that. She had been trying to work up the courage to mention her aunt to the doctor. She should have talked about her before Rosie's first session, but she didn't want him to look at her with any kind of prejudice. The more she thought about it, the more important it seemed to tell him. He seemed like a trustworthy man. He should know this didn't just come out of nowhere. *The more he knows, the better he can help Rosie. Right?*

"Dr. Lewis?"

"Yes?" He looked up at her from his notebook, his owl eyes bright and shiny.

"When I talked to you before the first time you saw Rosie, I . . . wasn't quite telling the truth."

"Oh." He hid his notebook back in his pocket along with the pen he used to write and leaned forward in his seat, seeming eager instead of angry. "Please do tell me now if you left something out!"

"This illness Rosie has, it runs in my family. My aunt had it. She actually spent most of her life in an institution. And according to my mother, there were others, too, before her."

The doctor whistled. He shook his head slightly and took his notebook back out.

"I wasn't expecting that. That's a big one."

"There is one more thing . . ."

He gazed at her quizzically, pen poised just above the paper.

"My aunt knew weird, personal stuff about people, too. We were never able to explain how."

CHAPTER THIRTY-FIVE

1996
LUKE

Joey Schreiber ran ahead of the group of kids walking home from school.

"Hurry, assholes!" He stopped in the middle of the path and yelled back. "I'm telling you, there was an assload of cops out here. Boats and everything."

"If you say so!" said Bill, the oldest of them all.

Bill got held back last year because he sucked at math. He insisted on being called Bill now instead of Billy because he thought Billy sounded like a baby's name. The others in the group were Frank and Rick, and bringing up the rear was Luke. He, of course, already knew about the cops because he knew why they were there. It took him some days to figure out who the ghost on the bank of the lake was. He assumed that her body was never found, and that's why her spirit still lingered here. He knew her first name was Lisa. So, he used the computer in the school library to search for missing women by that name. His whole body broke out in goosebumps when he came across a newspaper article from six years ago. A Lisa Jennings disappeared from the town of Collinsville. She was only eighteen. They didn't have a suspect, and the case went cold. Her mother and father pleaded for anyone with information to come forward, but it seemed like no one had seen her. It was as if she had just fallen off the face of the earth. Except she didn't. Her body was in the lake. It gave Luke full-body chills to think about the fact that people were swimming in the same water her body decomposed in. And he did, too. In a soup of body parts and fish poop. He may actually never again go swimming because of this mental image.

Lisa had disappeared just days before Luke saw her ghost for the first time. All these years, and he had done nothing about her. But he could do something now. And he did. He had gone to the local police station with a story he had come up with. Assuming that Lisa didn't just drown in the lake on her own, there must have been someone else with her. He told the nice lady at the station, the first female officer he had ever met, that he had heard something at the lake six or so years ago, but he was too scared to tell anyone. He heard splashing and screaming coming from the water by the bike trail, and someone—he could not recall if it was a man's or a woman's voice—yelling the name Lisa. He had snuck out of his grandparents' house after dark that night, so he never told them this because he didn't want to get into trouble. The policewoman looked to be extremely skeptical of his story, but two days later, the cops were at the scene, searching the water.

Luke and his classmates stopped behind the police tape to gaze, open-mouthed, out at the proceedings taking place on the water. A diver had just come up from underwater. He was signaling something to the officers waiting in the boat. One of them called back to the diver. Luke thought he asked, "Are you sure?" The diver nodded vigorously and gave a thumbs-up. They pulled the boat around to where the diver was and dropped the anchor. All the people in the boat were bustling about by now. Two of the men on board changed into diving gear, and one of the officers unfolded a large black bag.

"That's a fucking body bag!" Joey exclaimed, almost falling through the police tape in his enthusiasm.

"Why do you always have to curse?" asked Frank, seeming

only mildly annoyed.

As he was the son of the pastor of the local church, it was his role to instill some kind of morals into his group of friends. But his heart wasn't in it today. He was just as interested in what was happening out on the water as the rest of them. This was the most exciting thing that had happened in their town this year.

"A dead body in the water . . . Can you imagine?" asked Rick in what was almost a whisper.

"Yeah . . . and we all swam in the water. It's a good thing we didn't catch cholera or something," said Bill, looking kind of green around the gills.

Luke gave him the side-eye but said nothing.

"Jesus, Bill!" Frank exclaimed, looking horrified. "Did you have to put that in my head? Now I have to go home and take a shower."

"You can't wash away cholera if you already have it!" Joey pointed out all knowingly, and they all snickered—except for Frank, who proceeded to stare at his shoes, looking slightly ill.

"It's hepatitis," Luke said once they all went quiet. They all turned their heads to look at him. "It's hepatitis you catch from a dead body, not cholera."

Frank swallowed audibly. The boys all followed Luke's line of sight to the flurry of bubbles on the surface of the water next to the police boat.

Luke sat down on the worn green couch in the living room. He could hear his grandmother clinking pots on the kitchen and smell the wonderful aromas of her cooking. Plum dumplings on the menu tonight. One of his favorites. He had taken to reading in the living room instead of his bedroom, and most nights, he slept out here, too. He wasn't too proud to admit that the hydra lady had scared the shit out of him, and now, he was too afraid to spend more than five minutes alone in his bedroom. These were facts. There was no use in lying about them. The other day, he screamed like a little girl when he caught the reflection in his bedroom mirror of what turned out to be his black hoodie hanging on his bedpost. He was wound pretty tightly.

Today was a glorious, victorious day. The police had found Lisa's remains. He was sure of it. Now, her family would get some closure, and she would be able to rest in peace after all these years. They may even catch whoever was responsible for her death. It was all thanks to Luke. Maybe his peculiar powers were good for something besides scaring the bejesus out of himself.

He was excited to get on with Rosanne's journal. Last he read, she had made it to the ranch in Texas. She had lived such an interesting life. He picked up the book and thought of Rosie as he always did. He had talked to her over the weekend. She was taking some medication that was making her spacey and slow. Her lifeless voice made Luke's stomach tighten with all the rage he felt. This dumb psychologist she was seeing had diagnosed her with schizophrenia of all things. This whole situation was so stupid. The doctor couldn't see the speck, so therefore, it didn't exist. Everything it did was blamed on poor Rosie. She had to take these useless pills because there was no other explanation for her behavior but illness. *But there is another explanation*, thought Luke bitterly. If only he was a psychologist. He could tell the difference between something like this and actual illness. Whether he could do something about it was a different thing. He had to get stronger, get to know his abilities better. He got Lisa to tell him her name. Maybe he could talk to the speck next time he saw it and ask what it wanted. Or maybe he could get some answers out of Rosanne.

January 8, 1943

We arrived at the ranch ten days ago on the back of an icy winter wind with hail beating on our shoulders. I did think I would lose some toes, but I remain intact, thank the Lord. The master's house is a great, big two-story building that surpassed my wildest dreams. It is blinding white with brown shutters on the windows. Inside, it looks almost like a castle. Upon stepping foot in it, I was whisked away by two Black housemaids. They spoke a mixture of

English and German with a strange, outlandish accent. They took me through the maze of the house, room after room after room, all of them furnished with spectacular detail. I was bathed while the two plump maids clucked and shook their heads at the sight of my skeletal body. "We fatten you up!" was probably the best thing I've heard since boarding that wretched ship. The going had been hard and the rations small. That night was the first time I had meat since leaving Germany. It was steak with stacked potatoes. I will most likely remember that meal until the day I die. Eating red meat was like being reborn. The maids detangled and de-liced my hair and cut my long and broken fingernails. At the end of all of it, I was taken to my room, where I found a small looking glass. I did not recognize myself. I had left Germany as barely more than a girl. Looking back at me was a woman with hard frown lines on her bony face. The longer I looked, the more I recognized of myself. My brown eyes were the same and so was the shape of my now colorless lips. "Hello, Rosanne. It's nice to see you again!" I said to my reflection.

The next day, I met the girls. They are a rambunctious bunch. The two older girls pretended not to speak any German right from the beginning. They then made jokes about me behind my back, thinking that I must not speak any English, for I had introduced myself in German. They whispered to each other that my hair was the color of fresh cow dung. This made me a lot angrier than it should have I admit. They are but girls, one of them only seven, the other nine years old. But I had been purchased to be a governess, and so a governess I shall be. The first lesson had to be on manners. I lashed out at them in German, making sure they knew I understand English just fine, but they are not to speak it in my presence. The older girl went bright red, while the younger one turned pale.

I met the third girl later. She is a bubbly little three-year-old. I worked on teaching her a German lullaby while we threw her cloth ball around the nursery. It was the song I used to sing to Heidi when rocking her to sleep. This beautiful little thing reminded me so much of my Heidi, I nearly cried when first laying eyes on her. I had to work really hard to call her Bertha, not Heidi.

I was taken to meet the mistress of the house the second day after my arrival by the master himself. She had been beautiful once, I can tell, but she lies in a pitiful state now. Half her face is slack and immobile. She tried to talk to me, and for the life of me, I couldn't understand, even though I knew she was speaking German. This had angered her. She gesticulated wildly at her husband with one arm, the other flapping limply against her side. Eventually, Mr. McCullum ordered me out of the room. I could hear the mistress's slurred screaming, even in my own room. I don't know what I had done to upset her so. She seemed to have a great dislike toward me right from the beginning. I truly hope I can turn her. This place could become a comfortable home for me if I play my cards right.

I have had some free time since my arrival, and I have used it to roam the ranch and surrounding countryside. This, what they call Texas, is a truly beautiful place. It has rolling hills and vast, wide-open spaces as far as the eye can see. They breed a type of cattle called a longhorn. True to its name, this breed has the longest horns I have ever seen on a bull or cow. The massive fixtures on their heads surpass the length of their actual bodies. I quite enjoy watching them amble around. They know just how to tilt their heads to fit between objects and trees—most of the time. It is fascinating and sometimes comical. I saw a cow almost knock her own calf over when she turned her head to look for him.

It was during one of the times I was watching the herd that I saw the Indian for the first time. Suddenly, the cows spooked and started moving as one away from the hill behind the pasture. In a minute, a rider appeared on the hilltop. At first, I thought he was a woman, for his long black hair flew behind him as he ran his horse toward me. The horse was beautiful with its spotted gray coat, but the man on its back took my breath away. I had never seen one of the savages for myself, but I had heard tales. Stories that did the man before me no justice. He had clean-cut features, a sharp nose, and flawless bronze skin. His hooded black eyes seemed to look right into my soul. I'm blushing just writing about him. He had asked me who I was, and my jaw nearly dropped. It would have never occurred to me that Indians could learn English. I fumbled halfway between English and German in my ghastly attempt at presenting who I was and why I was here. He smiled, said his goodbyes—in German, of all things—and rode off toward the house as if this were the most everyday thing. I stared after him, open-mouthed, until something flew into my mouth and I had to close it. I honestly don't think I have since fully recovered from that interaction.

Luke lowered the book to his chest, grinning stupidly at his own face reflected on the dark TV screen. So, Rosanne had the hots for some Indian dude. Interesting.

"Luke, honey, will you help me make the table?"

"Yes, Gram. I'll be right there!"

He placed his bookmark in between the pages and snapped the book shut.

He opened the cupboard they kept the plates in. As if on their own accord, his eyes were drawn to the wooden box on the counter in which they kept the family china. He looked over his shoulder at his grandmother still busy at the stove. Decision made, he closed the cupboard door and opened the wooden box. Two of the plates broke the day Luke's parents died. His grandfather had glued them back together the best he could, but they hadn't used the set of plates since then. It was a shame. They were beautifully hand-painted with green vines and orange flowers. Back in the day, when their family was still whole, Luke's grandparents would pull out the old china every time they visited. These places had seen some grand meals over the years. There were originally five of them, which meant three were still intact and waiting to be used. He pulled them out of their wooden slots and set them on the table. He sighed, letting his chest expand with the surprising amount of love he felt for these three inanimate objects. They were like members of the family, and because of him, they had been locked away for far too long. His grandma stepped away from the stove, bearing a bowl full of delicious plum-filled dumplings. She gasped upon seeing the plates on the table and almost dropped her burden. Luke reached out and steadied her with both hands. He took the bowl from her and placed it in the middle of the table. He felt her old arms enfold him and tighten around his middle. He turned and returned her embrace. The first step to healing was always facing the thing you were healing from.

PART 4

CHAPTER THIRTY-SIX

1998
JAMES

North Texas wilderness was not the most hospitable thing in February. The weather had actually been quite mild the night the Smith girls went missing, which bore well for finding them alive. James wiped his nose on his sleeve. He was out here in the underbrush in the fifty-something-degree weather, looking for the bare footprints of a wild woman. He felt silly. For not the first time, he asked himself if he was, indeed, too close to this case and should consider handing it off to someone else. *Or would that be admitting defeat?* His inner monologue was interrupted by the screaming of the Smiths' donkey. It was like listening to nails scratching on a chalkboard.

"Would you quiet down, ya . . ."

His yell was cut off midway as he caught sight of the noisy creature between the trees. It stood there, staring at him intensely, head held high, long ears pricked up. Its breath puffed put in a long white cloud as it opened its mouth and screamed again. James squinted, his ears in pain. *Who on earth would want to keep such an annoyingly loud animal as a pet?* Then, another thought occurred to him. The donkey was supposed to be locked in a pen with the horses, wasn't it? Who let it out?

"Hey! You ugly thing! Come here!"

He started toward the donkey, whistling and clicking his tongue. The cursed animal flattened its long ears along its neck and reared, windmilling small, round hooves at him. Then, it turned and fled between the trees, shrieking wildly as it went. Its cries of indignation echoed through the forest before slowly fading away. James huffed out a long breath. He had never been good with animals. He heard the snapping of a branch behind him and turned sharply just to see something disappear behind a giant sycamore.

"Stop right there!" he yelled and bounded after it.

He wasn't even sure that what he saw was human. It might as well have been a deer. He wowed to leave no stone unturned, though, so he dodged the many small children of the old tree in his pursuit. Rounding the trunk, he saw it again, about twenty yards ahead of him. This time, he was pretty sure what he saw was a human being wearing dark clothes. It went behind another bigger tree. He heaved and puffed running uphill. When he reached this tree, he saw the person disappearing into what looked to be a dip in the forest floor.

"Christ Almighty! You're a quick little bastard!" he grumbled, sweat gathering on his temples.

He reached what looked like an empty riverbed filled with fallen leaves and deadwood. There was no sign of whoever it was he'd seen. He looked to his left and then to his right, trying to decide which way he should go. On the right side, a little bit further down in the riverbed, was an old tree that had died some time ago. It had already dropped most of its limbs, only the ancient trunk remaining. It had a great, big hollow that almost split it into two. And in that hollow was . . . something. He squinted, turning his body toward it. His eyesight wasn't as good as it used to be. Was it?

"Sweet baby Jesus . . ."

He slid more than ran down the bank, taking leaves and twigs with him. Once he caught his footing on the bottom, he ran heedless of snagging branches and slippery rocks. He almost crashed into the old truck. He couldn't believe his eyes. This was truly a day fit for a miracle.

CHAPTER THIRTY-SEVEN

1997
ROSIE

Rosie lived in a cage. The cage was her own body. During the day, her true self was trapped inside, the thick bars only allowing her glimpses of the outside. The worst part was that the thing, this Bad Rosie, was trapped in here with her. And since bad Rosie couldn't get out, she occupied herself doing other things. She gave Rosie weird, very real dreams.

She was walking through a forest in one such dream.

"Where am I?" she asked the trees around her.

There was no answer but the song of the birds. A lone woodpecker was hammering away somewhere in the distance. She whistled and was rewarded with an answer from a mockingbird. Walking along, she suddenly recognized a cluster of boulders. They had the vague shape of a possum. She ran to them and placed both hands on the cool surface of the stones. Backing up a few feet, she walked around the formation. It was the same. This was her parents' land. Possum Rock, as they called it, was about a half a mile from their house. So, why did everything else look different besides the rocks? She had been here about a million times. She knew this area by heart. All the trees were wrong. They were different kinds, and .

. . Was that the big oak she and Mina once put a tire swing on? She walked over to it. It was so small. No branch on it would hold a swing. Is this the place where it actually stood? She gazed around, feeling quite unsure of everything now.

"Hello!" she called out.

Should she head to the house? Her body was slowly filling with a sense of dread. What if the house was different, too? What if it wasn't even there? She shifted on her feet. The decision was made for her when she heard a holler in the opposite direction of where the house should be. It sounded like a child. Thinking he or she may be in trouble, Rosie ran, trying to get there quickly. She stopped after a while and called again. An answering "Hello!" drifted to her again between the trees. She ran for another few hundred feet. For a while there, she had no idea where was going, but suddenly, the shape of the land gave it away. She stopped with some alarm and looked at each tree around her. She was panting and perspiring. If she was right, and she thought she was, she was about to run into the old family cemetery, which meant that the old homestead should be about a mile to her left. She gulped the crisp air of the forest, racking her brain on what to do. Should she go back? She really didn't feel like walking into the cemetery. Nothing good ever happened at cemeteries. Especially in dreams.

"Are you coming?" called the child from somewhere ahead of her.

She sighed, knowing this was a bad idea, and slowly walked through the curtain of shrubs and saplings in front of her.

She emerged into a sunny clearing populated by crumbling gravestones and the occasional ancient tree. It looked a lot less spooky than she remembered.

"Where are you?" she yelled half-heartedly.

It still wasn't too late to turn around.

"Over here!"

A girl in a long floral dress waved at her from under a sprawling oak. She was squatting between four gravestones that stood leaning in the shade of the canopy. "Oh, hell . . ." Rosie muttered and made her way over to her through the waist high grass.

"You took your sweet ass time!" the girl said, not looking at her.

Rosie stepped into the shade of the tree and was instantly horrified when her eyes adjusted after the blinding light of the sun. The girl had short, curly hair. She looked to be a few years younger than Rosie, and she was digging up a grave with her bare hands. She was actually squatting in a two-foot-deep hole.

"What the fuck?" Rosie stepped back. "What are you doing?"

The girl looked at her, a quizzical expression on her narrow face. She clapped her hands together to dust them off. It did virtually nothing. Her palms and fingers remained crusted with dirt. She stood, stretched, and sat down on the lip of the hole, her bare feet still in it.

"That's mighty hard work right there," she huffed, wiping her brow with the back of a wrist, leaving behind a long brown streak.

"Yeah . . ." Rosie said, only halfway creeped out by her at this point. "It looks rough."

This was only a dream. Strange things happened in dreams, but it wasn't like this was actually happening. This wasn't reality. This girl was a figment of her imagination.

"You look different than I imagined," she said, squinting up at Rosie.

There were dapples of sunlight all over her. She took a thin stick from the ground and proceeded to dig the dirt out from under her fingernails with it.

"Do you know who I am?" Rosie asked.

She squatted down next to her to get a better look . Who was this girl supposed to be? The girl in question leaned back and away from Rosie's inquisitive eyes.

"Well, of course I do! Don't you know who I am?"

Rosie shook her head.

"How odd." She leaned back in and looked Rosie in the

face. "You got the prettiest blue eyes. Anywho, I'm Franny. Nice to meet ya!"

She extended a thin, tanned hand to Rosie. She was hesitant to take it. Suddenly, she was uncomfortably aware that she hadn't actually touched this strange girl yet. What if something happened when she did? She could turn into something gross, like a big, hairy spider. Franny tilted her head to the side, grinning at her wolfishly.

"Come on, now! I'm not gonna bite."

Yeah, right! Rosie thought and took her offered hand. They shook, and nothing happened. The world didn't explode, corpses didn't rise from their graves, nothing. They were quiet for a minute, and the song of birds and cicadas filled the air.

"So," Rosie ventured, "how did you know who I was?"

"Oh, she told me."

Franny pointed, arm outstretched to behind Rosie. All the hairs rose along Rosie's spine as she turned to look. She jumped back, flattening her back to the bark of the old tree. The old crone was standing at the far end of the shade. Rosie was, in fact, halfway expecting to see her, but she still freaked her out. She exhaled deeply through her nose. Franny cackled at her reaction.

"Why you so scared, you silly goose? She ain't gonna hurt you. Come here, now!

Rosie turned her head sharply to Franny and back.

"Wha . . . Don't call her over!"

It was too late. The old woman approached then with her slow, measured steps that didn't quite seem to reach the ground. Franny was snorting with mirth.

"Oh, gosh, Rosie. You are too funny."

This girl was insane. Certifiably. For sure. Why would she call this scary ass ghost lady over to them? The crone had her hair pulled away from her face, and to Rosie's immense surprise and discontent, it was changing. One second, it looked the way it did normally, and the next, it was some other old lady's face. She eventually stopped a few feet from them, but her face didn't really want to settle. It kept morphing. Rosie wanted to scream. When it looked like the crone wasn't coming any closer, she let out the breath she didn't know she was holding. Why wasn't Franny afraid of her? The crone started to chant something softly, her ever-changing face moving around the mouth that articulated the words. It was that strange foreign language again. Something occurred to Rosie as she listened to the words that meant nothing to her.

"Franny, what does she look like to you?"

Franny furrowed her brows at Rosie. She didn't understand the question. Rosie tried again.

"Does she look like anyone you know?"

Recognition dawned on her face, and her feathery brows relaxed.

"Oh, well, she's being funny right now. She does weird things like this sometimes. But she normally looks like my meemaw."

"Why was it important for you to know what she looked like?" Dr. Lewis asked.

They were sitting in his office, talking about Rosie's feelings, her dreams, and her daily experiences while living the life of a druggie. Rosie found that the pills loosened her tongue. She had to talk about something while she was here. Dreams were a kind of neutral territory. Having weird dreams did not make one crazy. Since it had already been established that Rosie had a screw loose, she didn't want the doctor to think she was getting worse. So, she opted not to tell him about her daytime stuff, like wanting to bash her own head against the wall or fantasizing about strangling her perfect little sister. She wasn't sure which thoughts were hers and which ones belonged to Bad Rosie.

"I told you that I see her in my dreams. This scary ghost lady."

Sometimes, she saw her when she was awake, too, but there was no need to go into that right now.

"Because her face was changing, I was wondering if Franny saw her as someone else."

"That's an interesting thought. Very creative."

Dr. Lewis was always so rational. Sometimes, Rosie hated him for it. Sometimes, it gave her great peace. In his world, everything had a normal, everyday explanation. Things happened because people made them happen. They weren't brought on by vengeful ghosts. Rosie longed to live in this world. Bad Rosie didn't. In fact, all Bad Rosie did was undermine everything Dr. Lewis said. She had a running commentary going on in Rosie's head just this minute: *"Creative, my ass! You know what's creative, you fool of a shrink? Your marriage! That's what."*

Thanks to the medications, though, she couldn't get out. Rosie was able to hold her back from taking over. She just had to get better at ignoring her ranting. It was very distracting.

"Do you know who she is?" the doctor asked.

"Who?" Rosie shook her head, trying to silence the noise inside.

"Franny? Is she someone you may know?"

"Like a real person? I don't think so. Why?"

"Well, when you talk about your dreams, it's almost like you are reliving memories. That's what it sounds to me."

Rosie took a sip of her water to gain some time to think. They were skating on thin ice here. Because the dreams seemed so real to her, she was sometimes sure that she was actually there doing the things she dreamt about, whether it was gliding into the office or talking to a little graverobber. It all felt real. She could feel the sunshine on her skin and hear the birdsong.

"I know they are just dreams," she said hesitantly. "More like nightmares sometimes. Can we talk about something else?"

"Of course! How are your friends?"

Rosie sank down into the couch, crossing her arms. Here was another thing she didn't want to talk about. Her dead social life.

Once home, she ambled into her room, feeling heavy and exhausted. She dropped face down onto her bed, ready for a nap. *"I'm bored! Let's look into that diary!"* said Bad Rosie in her head. Rosie turned her head on the pillow and peered, bleary-eyed, at her nightstand, where the journal sat.

"Fine . . ." she groaned. "I'll read you just a little bit."

April 11, 1743

Spring has finally come to Texas, and I am in love. There! It's on paper, so it must be true. The beautiful Indian, whose name is John, comes to the ranch more and more often. He always makes it a point to find me and share a few words. I have learned from one of the Black housemaids that he is, in fact, the master's bastard son. The master apparently had a habit of visiting the local tribe to trade goods when he was a younger man. He fathered multiple children to different Indian women, and John is his only son. The maid also told me conspiratorially that the mistress of the house harbors a great anger toward the master for all his infidelity and hates John as if he were the devil himself. A handsome devil, if I say so myself. I never imagined I could fall for such a man, but the way he looks at me with those strange, dark eyes of his makes my insides turn to liquid. There seems to be an undeniable attraction between us that neither of us can do anything about. It is torture of the cruelest and most exquisite kind.

For a few weeks after my arrival to the ranch, the master would visit my room at least a couple of times a week to bed me. The maids tell me that he does the same things to the prettier Black girls he owns and, sometimes, the not-so-pretty ones when he is much with drink. I still can't fathom how us women find the heart to laugh about such things, but apparently, being someone's property strips one's morality away in such ways.

His visits abruptly stopped about a month ago. I suspected the mistress had a hand in it, and I was right. As told to me by the servants, fathering brown bastards is one thing, but if I were to fall pregnant, the master could easily discard his now useless wife and wed me. The color of one's skin bears such power in this country. I suspect the two older girls had heard about this because they continue to be cold and nasty to me. Little Bertha is my only joy, her and talking to my lovely Indian suitor whom I cannot have.

April 20, 1743

My dearest journal! I had to—I just simply had to make time to write. John sent me a letter with the assistance of one of the fieldhands. He wanted me to meet him the next day just before sunset. The place was near where I'd first seen him. I flew over there, my heart in my throat, to find his horse tied to a tree in a small thicket and the furry hide of some great brown beast placed on the ground. He kissed me there, in the half-dark of the trees, for the first time. I pulled him down to the fur in my eagerness, for I knew why it had been placed there the minute I saw it. I have waited too long to be his already. We became one that day, never to be separated. He told me he would purchase me from his father if I wanted to go with him. He would make me his wife and build us a home on the land his father had gifted to him if that was what I desired. He tells me that a beautiful creature such as myself should not live under anyone else's rule but her own. As I gaze into his eyes, I see nothing but truth there. I know my answer. I will go with him if God allows me to. I may still have some say in my destiny after all.

CHAPTER THIRTY-EIGHT
1997
MILLIE

What a dreadful day to be at work. This January had been an especially cold one. Never mind that it was almost over; the cold weather held on to the land with its icy claws. They had a terrible ice storm the other day during which the big oak that provided most of the shade in their backyard dropped a huge branch. It happened to fall right on the boys' clubhouse. There was nothing left of it but useless timber.

The clinic's heater struggled to cope with the unusual cold, coupled with the stream of people constantly opening the front door to bring in their shivering animals. Millie sat at her desk, still in her coat, a chunky yellow scarf wound loose around her face and neck, looking like a pissed-off toad peering out from under a leaf. She had been on edge for days now. Her plan obviously didn't work. Apparently, neither of the men gave a shit who that little nutcase's father was. Millie could not fathom why. Actually, she could. There was a perfectly ordinary explanation for the fact that her letters induced nothing but cricket chirping. Noah most likely knew and didn't mind, the fucking saint he was, and the other guy didn't want to claim Rosie. Or maybe he didn't even live at the same address anymore. Either way, the fact that nothing came of either letter made Millie as sour as a freshly castrated billy goat. She should know, for she had seen her fair share working here.

The door opened again, and Millie rolled her eyes skyward as old little Mrs. Hunter walked in with yet another one of her sneezing chickens. This was the third one this week. She placed the ratty-looking bird on the counter in front of Millie and proceeded to fill out the necessary form with shaking, fat-knuckled hands. The chicken eyed Millie from behind its half-closed lids, breathing heavily. It looked like it was going to drop dead any second. It made a strange gurgling noise, a surprising amount of snot bubbling out of its tiny nostrils. Then, all of a sudden, it took a deep breath and sneezed loudly and explosively. Millie leaned back, but she hadn't been fast enough. Missiles of chicken boogers hit her scarf and face, making it almost impossible for her to stay professional. She blinked rapidly and used her scarf to wipe her face before dropping it to the floor by her chair. Her face set in a mask of professionalism, she snatched the unfinished form from Mrs. Hunter.

"I'll just use the information from the other two to make it easy for you!" she said, smiling with deadly sweetness.

Mrs. Hunter stared at her with wide, watery eyes, her nearly toothless mouth slightly open.

"But her name is different," she protested, lifting a frail hand in the direction of the paper in Millie's hand.

"You can just tell me! I'll put it in!"

"This one is Susan."

Susan sneezed again and stood up uneasily, revealing a tan egg that promptly rolled off the counter to shatter on the floor.

"Micky's got it!" called the man sitting closest to the action.

His German Shepherd was already working on cleaning up the mess. Millie took a deep breath, her chest expanding to maximum capacity. She would not murder everyone in here. She was capable of keeping her shit together. She could do it. At this specific moment, the Smiths blew in through the door. Noah was carrying their elderly dog, who looked worse than Mrs. Hunter's chicken. Behind him were all three of his womenfolk. Millie cursed inwardly and vowed to apologize to God; she'd beg for forgiveness later, when she had time. The hello reserved for all newcomers got stuck in her throat as if it were a whole apple. Mrs. Hunter took her sick fowl and scampered away to sit in the corner. A grim-faced Noah took her place. *Oh, my God! They know it was me*, was her first coherent thought. For a brief, blood-chilling moment, Millie was certain that they had all come here to confront her at work. Then, she remembered the dog. In an attempt to tear her eyes away from all of theirs, she looked down at the animal. It had long strands of saliva hanging from the corners of its mouth that were stretching to reach the floor.

"Oh, dear!" she heard herself say. "Your poor dog! What's going on?"

"He couldn't get up this morning," Alice said, holding her two daughters close.

For a split second, Millie felt bad for the kids. The past wasn't their fault, after all. They had a lot going on, and now, their dog was going belly-up. Maybe it was okay that nothing came of her letters. Maybe this was God's way of telling her to finally let go of her own hurt. Or maybe she just needed to try harder. The second passed, and she shook herself back into work mode.

"I'll see if the doctor can see you guys quickly," she said and gestured for them to take a seat.

They all went—all of them except for Alice. She was looking at something on Millie's desk, totally transfixed. Brows furrowed, Millie followed her line of sight. She froze, cold filling her blood from the top of her head down to her toes. Alice was looking at the envelopes on her desk. Millie had a habit of taking office supplies home. There was never any problem with it 'cause she never took too much. A few papers here, a pen, some envelopes . . . She had used one such envelope to send Noah that letter. Millie turned her head to see that Alice was looking at her with the most severe expression she'd ever seen her wear. Unfiltered fear flashed through Millie's every cell. She righted herself quickly but not quickly enough. Alice had seen it. If only she had been prepared, she would have never made such a blunder. But she wasn't, and so she did. Her lips parted. She should say something. She had to deflect, make Alice doubt what she thought she knew. But her mind was a dry desert of inspiration. All of a sudden, Alice turned from her without a word and went to sit with her family. Millie stood up and hurried to the back to collect herself and talk to the doctor.

About an hour later, the Smiths walked out with the body of their family pet wrapped in a blanket. The girls were crying, the little one holding onto the corner of the blanket, the older one shuffling grimly ahead, her unseeing eyes looking inward. Noah's eyes were dry but red-rimmed, and the tip of his nose was red. All of them displayed their grief in their own way. Except for Alice. She wasn't crying. Her eyes sharp and cold, her face was set in an expression almost resembling hatred. She didn't look at Millie, which was almost worse than if she did.

Once they were gone, Millie took a second to reconsider her recent life decisions. If confronted, she would deny having anything to do with the letters, of course. In spite of the anxiety all this had caused her, she wouldn't change sending them. She needed to know if Noah knew the truth. She simply had to know. If she died without figuring it out, her ghost would haunt the Smith house. She was sure of that. There was the one thing: Alice had read the letter, based on the way she acted. But she didn't think Noah did. It was entirely possible that Alice had gotten to it before her husband and hid it from him. She didn't want Noah to know, which meant that he surely didn't know the truth. Millie smoothed out the paperwork on her desk, feeling a bit more put together. She would make sure that would change one way or another.

CHAPTER THIRTY-NINE

1982
ALICE

She pushed through the crowd of the frat house. The music was booming, the lights were low, and there were more people in here than the house could possibly hold. Not the best place to tell your boyfriend that you're carrying his child, but she could work on that. She would ask him to go outside. She kept telling herself that things would turn out okay if she just did the right thing.

She saw someone she knew. A friend of Nate's. Shoving and ducking, she made her way over to him. Someone spilled something on her. She felt the wetness of it run along the front of her light blue shirt. She stretched the fabric out to look at it. To her horror, it was red wine. It went all the way across her shirt, over one shoulder and across one boob to the bottom. Great, now she would look like a total mess, smelling like a vineyard while she had the most uncomfortable conversation of her life. Whatever. She tapped Nate's friend on the shoulder. She couldn't remember his name but doubted he cared. He looked down at her and grinned with the sweetness of a drunk who's having a great time.

"Where's Nate?" she yelled into his ear through the music.

"Upstairs!" he yelled back and pointed a thumb behind him

at the staircase.

She gave him a thumbs-up and a grateful smile. Squeezing by him, she placed one foot on the first step. She felt a tug on her shirt. Mildly startled, she looked back and saw the same guy she'd just been talking to holding onto the hem of her shirt.

"You're too pretty for him. You know that, right?" he said, leaning against the wall.

Alice's eyes softened. This was a nice thing to hear, even if it was coming from the wrong place. She personally always believed that Nate was out of her league. His jaw was just way too chiseled. Detaching his hand, she gave it a grateful squeeze, then dropped it and ran up the stairs.

There were fewer people up here, and they were mostly kissing and groping one another. Alice got a strange, uneasy feeling in the pit of her stomach. It was almost like a warning. The upstairs was all bedrooms. She went door to door, peeking into each bedroom and seeing things that she definitely shouldn't have. She rounded the corner to the last bedroom and saw him. Her world tilted. He was holding a sloppy, drunken makeout session with some girl, and it was clear they were making their way into the bedroom. Alice's short fuse lit and burned up immediately. How dare this fucking animal do this to her—get her pregnant and just proceed to sling his dick all over campus? And this fucking bitch he was with had almost no clothes on. They shifted their positions slightly, so now, she could see her face. *Oh, God!* It was her fucking roommate. Alice had no idea she was such a skank.

"Melissa, you dirty hoe!" she screamed.

She had no idea why she was calling her roommate out before her boyfriend. Probably because the fact that he was cheating on her with her roommate was more shocking than the cheating itself. They sprung apart, looking at her wide-eyed.

"What the fuck, Nate?" she roared, closing in on them.

Melissa backed away quickly. She bumped into the bedroom door, which opened, slipped inside like a guilty eel, and shut the door behind her. Left alone together, Alice sneered up at Nate, planning on giving him an earful. He was looking down at her in such a way that made her feel like she was no more than dog shit on his new shoe. She had interrupted him, and he didn't like it.

"Is she the only one, or are there more?"

"You know what, Alice?" He threw his hands up and let them drop. "It's none of your fucking business. We're done!"

Ouch! That stung a bit. Now that all the cards were on the table, he didn't have to be nice to her anymore. Gone was her somewhat caring and occasionally funny boyfriend, and in his place was this drunken, horny idiot. He definitely wasn't going to grovel at her feet, begging for her forgiveness. Alice could see that much. All this time, she had been nothing but a convenient fuck to him. And it looked like she ceased to be convenient right about now. He was just going to dispose of her like she was a used condom. A broken, used condom. She was pregnant with this asshole's child. Alice seethed. This shit wasn't going to fly.

"You're not going to get rid of me this easily," Alice howled in his face, raising on the tips of her toes. "I'm pre—"

Her voice was cut off by his hand on her throat. He slammed her into the wall so hard her teeth crunched together. She tasted blood. It was possible she had bitten a chunk out of her tongue. She struggled and shoved at him, but drunk Nathan seemed to be even stronger than sober Nathan.

"Keep your voice down, you little bitch!" he whispered in her ear, his breath hot and moist on her cheek.

She tried to turn her head away. His breath smelled like cheap whiskey. It was gross. It was nauseating. It was . . . Her stomach did a funny little flop and contracted so all its contents came rushing up. She couldn't stop it. Vomit shot out the corners of her mouth, spraying all over both of them. She gagged and coughed, and so did Nate, who let go of her like she was on fire. She crumpled to the hallway carpet and proceeded to heave up some more of her stomach contents.

"Aww! You disgusting fucking bitch!" Nate cried, shaking vomit off the hand he'd used to pin her to the wall. "You're sick!

Fuck!"

He was right about that much. But not with anything that could be fixed with some flu medicine. Alice tried to get to her feet. Nate placed a shoed foot right on the middle of her ass and shoved her forward so she went sprawling to the floor once more. She groaned and instinctively held onto her stomach, where she now knew her baby, their baby, was growing. He took her by the back of the neck and one arm and pulled her to her feet.

"Pull yourself together, you fucking child!" he shouted in her ear and propelled her to a door ahead of them in the hallway.

He shoved her through and let go so she fell inside, unable to catch herself. It was a small bathroom. She fell headfirst into the side of the bathtub. She heard the deep metallic *clang* of it and saw white and red stars as her face made contact. There was a soft crunch, and warm liquid exploded all over her face. Nathan didn't seem to notice that she had been injured.

"Clean yourself up! I'll be back when I'm done. Stay here!"

He slammed the door shut. Alice waited for the ringing inside her head to stop. She pulled her legs up to protect her soft parts in case he came back. One hand still cupping her stomach, she sobbed softly, feeling the blinding pain spread from her face to her entire body. She was afraid of him, and no wonder, but the realization hit her like a bag of bricks—or a bathtub. He was coming back. She didn't want to be anywhere near here when he did. She never wanted to see him again. Her survival instincts kicked in. She had to get up and out of here. Out of this house. Out of the campus. Out of this damn city.

She got on one elbow, then a knee, then, slowly, she pushed herself up using the bathtub that had just crushed her face. There was blood on the side of the tub and on her hands. She turned to face the horror that was her face in the mirror. It was better than she expected. Her nose was broken for sure, her lip busted. There was a copious amount of blood that had run down her face and neck and joined the wine stain on her shirt. But it was still her. Still her face. She cleaned up as best and as fast as she could, leaving the sink and the white bath towel looking pink and the bathroom like a murder scene in general. Then, she fled down the stairs and out of the house. There were some curious glances in her direction, but she was moving too fast for anyone to be able to take a good look at her. She jogged to her dorm, her head pounding. As soon as she was inside of the room, she whipped her shirt off and threw it on her roommate's bed. It landed on her crisp white pillow. Working quickly, she shoved all her belongings into her bags, pulled on a black shirt, and was out the door in less than ten minutes.

She had some money. She would stay in a hotel and take the first bus home in the morning. That was the plan. Lucky for her, there was a hotel on campus she could go to.

The receptionist, a young woman barely older than she, took one look at her face and her bedraggled state, which consisted of still drying blood under her nose and neck, and reached for the phone. Alice lunged forward, her panic rising, and placed both hands on the receiver. The woman stepped back, her manicured fingers curling into tentative fists. A second too late, Alice realized how this must have looked and pulled back.

"I'm sorry!" she said, holding her open hands in front of her. "Please don't call the police!"

The last thing she wanted was for anyone she knew to find out what had happened. If the cops came, they would take her in for questioning, and she wouldn't be able to sneak away. She would have to tell them. She might even have to testify against Nathan in court. She would have to tell him she was pregnant. The thought nauseated her. The second to last thing she wanted to do was let him know he got her pregnant. She would never be rid of him.

"Are you all right?" the receptionist asked. "What happened to you? Do you go here?"

Alice shook her head, allowing one tear slide down her face.

"I just need a room for the night. I'll be out of here first thing in the morning."

The buses didn't start going until five. It was too cold for her to spend the rest of the night outside.

"Where are you going?" the woman asked, surveying her with a strange expression.

"Home," Alice said before she could stop herself.

The woman nodded.

"Come with me!"

They took the stairs up to the third floor. She used a plastic keycard to open room 321. It was dark inside. Alice followed the woman in, suddenly unsure if this was a good idea. The woman saw her hesitation and smiled at her kindly.

"The lights are out in this room. We are waiting on maintenance to replace them, but they won't get to it until sometime tomorrow. The bathroom lights work."

She demonstrated this by flicking them on.

"I'd give you another room, but we are fully booked, it being New Year's and all."

"Thank you!" Alice said, meaning it. "This is great. How much is it?"

The woman shook her head.

"No charge."

"But I have money," Alice protested.

The woman stepped up to her, and it took Alice immense self-control not to step back. She was bruised and battered, tired and weary.

"I sit behind you in Exercise Science 101," she said, and Alice blinked at her in surprise. "It took me a minute to recognize you."

Her eyes darted all over Alice's face. To her surprise, she saw so much sympathy in them, she thought she might actually cry.

"Anyway," she said, placing a delicate hand on each of Alice's shoulders, "you are stronger than you think you are. Everything is going to be okay."

Alice nodded, feeling something lift from her. She became lighter and a bit more sure that what she was doing was, indeed, the right thing. The receptionist gave her shoulders a light squeeze. As she was walking out the door, she called back.

"Try not to let anyone see you leave the room if you can."

And then, she was gone.

Alice took a nice hot bath. Both the soap and the water stung her battered face. Afterward, she curled up on the clean sheets and caressed her still-flat stomach. She drew small circles on it with her fourth finger. She would have to tell her parents something. She had heard stories about students being attacked while walking on campus after dark. There was a story about it on the news just a few weeks ago. She could say that was what had happened to her. She came straight home because she didn't feel safe here anymore. She didn't call the police because she was embarrassed. If the baby stuck—she flattened her palm against her belly—she would tell them it was the consequence of rape. There was no way she would let Nate be a part of its life. Not after the way he acted. She remembered Noah's parents. She knew how much it hurt him to have a family like that. She saw, in front of her, the bruises on his thin boy's body. She would never be with someone like that, someone who beat his wife and child. She would rather die. She would raise this baby on her own if she had to. She drifted off to sleep on that thought and dreamt of a little girl with blonde hair and big blue eyes.

Amy Hotchkins went back to her station behind the reception desk feeling weightless and happy. It had been almost exactly two months since she nearly died here in the University of Houston parking lot. She usually worked the late shift at the hotel because she took her classes during the day. One night while she was walking out to her car at around 11:30 p.m., she was attacked by a man wearing a mask. He held her at knifepoint, the blade pressed against the skin of her neck.

"Open your car!" the assailant hissed at her.

She had heard the stories. People had urged her not to walk to her car by herself. She didn't listen. She never listened to anyone. And now, she would pay the price. There was nothing in her car she could use as a weapon. This man would rape her and kill her as soon as they were inside. She knew that for a fact just as she knew there was nobody around to help her. She was parked under a tree, which meant the streetlight didn't illuminate the spot where they were standing. Still, she looked around, wildly hoping to spot someone to call out to as she searched her pocket for her key. Suddenly, a shout broke the silence of the night. She froze, her key falling from her hand. Her assailant jerked with surprise and nicked her with the blade. A slow trickle of blood made its way down her neck.

"Nathan! Where did you go, you dipshit? Stop trying to scare me!"

A young woman trudged across the parking lot in front of them. She couldn't have been more than fifteen feet away.

"I'm gonna go home!" she yelled again, and her eyes landed right on them as she scanned the parking lot for this Nathan of hers.

To Amy's surprise, the woman was someone she knew. She was one of her classmates from her Exercise Science class. She frowned into the gloom under the tree where they were, evidently not sure of what she was seeing. Amy wanted to scream. She wanted to call out. But she was also afraid of getting her throat slashed.

"I'm leaving! You jerk!" the woman said finally and turned away from them.

As soon as her eyes were away from them, the man withdrew from her, ducked behind her car, and disappeared into the darkness between two campus buildings.

Amy stood there for a second, heart hammering, cold sweat and blood pooling between her breasts. By the time she collected herself, her classmate was gone. She picked up her key, got in her car, and drove home, her hands cold and shaking on the steering wheel.

She never walked to her car alone after that. And she always parked close to a streetlight. She was sure that her classmate had unknowingly saved her life that night. She wanted to thank her every time she saw her in class but didn't know how. How do you tell someone about something like this? "Thanks for saving me from murder!" They didn't even know each other. She would think Amy crazy. She did tell the police, though. Made an official report. She was hoping to repay her classmate one day. So, when she showed up at the hotel during her shift looking the way she did, Amy realized that this was her chance. It was a small thing. A free hotel room in exchange for her life. But she could tell it meant the world to her.

Once her shift was over, the hotel security guard—who, luckily, had been on a bathroom break when the girl came in—walked her to her car. It was just after 1 a.m. Once inside, she locked the doors and waved to the guard. She watched him walk away, and her eyes were drawn up to the window where she knew room 321 was. Amy touched the small scar on her neck. She hoped the girl was able to fall asleep. She started her car and, with her hands on the wheel, wondered, not for the first time that night, if they had been attacked by the same man. She hoped they would catch him one day soon. She hoped he would rot in hell.

CHAPTER FORTY

1996
NATHAN

Nathan Davis ran out to the mailbox to escape the screaming going on in his house. His three small boys were attempting to murder each other over some shitty robot toy, his wife, Melissa, trying and failing to console them. He simply could not deal with the noise anymore. If he was honest with himself, a lot of the time, he wished all four of them would disappear. Then, he could have some peace and quiet. He took the contents of the mailbox and sifted through them. *Bills, bills, bills, a credit card application, more bills.* A soft yellow envelope caught his eye. It was tucked between two magazines. His address had been handwritten on it with no return address. Was it a wedding invitation? Probably. All his idiot friends were getting married even though he always cautioned them not to. It was a trap in which you would have to make money, spend it all on bills, raise some ungrateful brats, and listen to the whining of your bitch wife every day for the rest of your life. At times like this, divorce sounded like the only way to save his sanity, but the child support after three kids would cripple him. If only there were another way. Sometimes, he fantasized about getting a call at work from a solemn police officer. "I'm sorry, sir," he would say. "There's been a terrible accident. Your wife and kids are dead." He would cry, of course. And then, he would move on. He would relocate to Hawaii, marry a beautiful native woman with wide, ever-swaying hips, and teach surf lessons on the beach until he was ultimately eaten by a shark. Were there sharks around Hawaii? He had no clue.

He opened the yellow envelope and read the contents. His eyes bulged, and suddenly, he could feel the onset of a terrible headache. Who the fuck sent this to him? The bastard didn't sign it.

For the eyes of Nathaniel Davis only:
You have a fourteen-year-old daughter called Rosanne Smith. Her mother is Alice Smith, formerly known as Alice Glessner. Your daughter is being raised by her and her husband, Noah Smith. I thought this is something you should know.

Under it was an address that was presumably theirs. *North Texas. Yuck! Nothing but a bunch of cows and rednecks up there.* He knew Alice was from there. He remembered that much. He actually remembered quite a bit about her. She had a really nice body when they were "dating." He wondered if she got fat over the years like Melissa did. He pursed his lips to the side, wondering who could have possibly written this. For some reason, he didn't think it was Alice, although that had been his first thought. She had run away from him like a cat on fire. And yes, that was around fifteen years ago, so the age of the girl checked out. He knew she had been pregnant when she left. Melissa had found the positive pregnancy test in her dorm room sink and showed it to him along with the bloody shirt Alice had left on her bed. He had done her wrong. He knew that. He should have told her about the broken condom so she would have been able to take a morning-after pill. But he was afraid she would have made him pay for it, and he really didn't want to spend the allowance his parents gave him on such a thing. He was pretty sure nothing would become of that little mishap. He and Melissa did it raw-dog once or twice, and she didn't end up pregnant.

He didn't mean to hurt Alice as badly as he did that night.

He was annoyed and drunk, and he lost his temper. She shouldn't have yelled at him, though, cornering him like that. That was her mistake.

He was quite content with never having to see the child she had been pregnant with. He thanked the Lord she took off. One less thing for him to worry about. When he thought of her over the years, he imagined that she may have even gotten an abortion. The thought didn't distress him at all. He couldn't muster up a care. If he was her, he would have gotten rid of the thing before it could develop a human shape. Alice apparently didn't do that. She had the baby and raised it with some other schmuck. So, if this letter was true, Nate had a teenage daughter. He smiled to himself. She may not be the only one. He had fun in those college days, been around the block a few times, unlike right now. This captive life didn't suit him at all.

He studied the letter for a few more minutes and got the distinct feeling that whoever wrote this did it without Alice's knowledge and quite possibly against her will. It was someone who meant her trouble. For a blissful moment, he fantasized about being that trouble. About abandoning his family and showing up on Alice's doorstep. Moving in next door to her. Seducing her and driving her husband mad with jealousy. In his fantasy, she looked exactly as she did fifteen years ago. The image stirred his blood. But the simple truth was that he really didn't want to claim this girl as his own. *One more mouth to feed. One more headache. Let's just leave her and her mother in the past, where they belong.*

The screaming had stopped, so it was safe to go back inside. He crumpled up the letter and tossed it in the garbage can next to the door along with the useless magazines and the credit card application.

1997

Rosie

Rosie watched the man with the angular jaw and sandy hair walk into his grand house. She was having one of those dreams again, like the one with Franny, where everything looks and feels real—except the man couldn't see her, and she couldn't read the letter he had. He was holding it at such an angle that she couldn't see it. He wasn't doing it on purpose. He was just much taller than she, and he also held it close to his face. She tried to move his arm down a bit by hanging on to it like a monkey. But whatever she did had no impact on him. It was frustrating because it seemed like the letter contained something very interesting. He was making all sorts of faces while reading it and afterward, too.

"Who the hell is this guy?" she said out loud once he was inside.

"Wouldn't you like to know?" came a now equally familiar and creepy voice.

She turned to see the crone standing behind her on the sidewalk. It was still a strange sight, seeing her out and about in broad daylight. It was sort of unnatural, like seeing a slug out when the sun was shining bright.

"You don't belong here," Rosie told her in an observational tone.

The old woman smiled at her sweetly. Ooh, it gave her the creeps.

"Neither do you, child."

She had a strange, foreign-sounding accent. Rosie had to admit that ever since her dream with Franny, she was less afraid of the crone. She wasn't sure whether this was a good thing or not.

"Well, no shit!" Rosie said, exasperated. "Then, what am I doing here?"

She gestured to the house, into which he disappeared.

"Oh, wouldn't you like to know?" she said again and snickered.

She managed to even make sarcasm unappealing.

"No. I'm good. I'll just hang out here on this sidewalk until I wake up."

The crone's eyes flashed an icy blue. She flew up to Rosie, stopping only within an inch of her so they were nose-to-nose.

"You'll know soon enough!" she growled like an angry bullfrog.

She opened her mouth unnaturally wide to show Rosie the complete blackness that was her insides. Rosie held her breath. She couldn't move. Of course she couldn't. All this was the old woman's doing. Rosie had no control over anything. She was just going along for the ride. The crone closed the gaping hole on her face and blew a steady stream of ice-cold air into her face. Rosie closed her eyes and gasped involuntarily.

When she dared to open her eyes again, she found herself in her parent's bedroom. *Great . . .* Her shrink changed up her sleep meds, so now, she was sleepwalking again. Not as often as before, but still. She was standing right by her mother's bedside, uncomfortably close to her sleeping face. The nightstand drawer next to Rosie's leg was open, and she was holding what looked to be an old family album. There was a small silver key nestled between the open pages. She picked it up and held it up to her face. It was almost comically tiny. She was so transfixed by the moonlight glinting off its surface, she didn't notice her mother opening her eyes.

"Rosie?" her mother exclaimed, sitting up in bed, an expression of alarm on her tired face. "What are you doing?"

"Sorry, Mom," Rosie whispered, blinking rapidly as Alice turned on her bedside lamp. "I sleepwalked in here again."

She felt bad because she knew her wandering around the house at night upset her mother, even though she never said so. Rosie could see it in her eyes.

"It's all right, love." Her mother sighed, rubbing at her baggy eyes. "It's not your fault. What are you doing with those?"

"Oh, these?"

Rosie looked from the key in her one hand to the album in the other. She did a double take and almost dropped the photo book. Adrenaline surged through her veins so rapidly, she got lightheaded.

"Who is that?"

She pointed to a picture of her grandmother and another older lady. They were sitting on a bench somewhere outside, their heads bent close together. Rosie almost couldn't believe her eyes. The lady had the same face as the old crone who was haunting her.

Alice leaned in to have a better look.

"That's your great aunt Francis. Your nana's older sister."

Rosie's blood ran cold. *What the hell?*

"Why have I never met her?" she asked indignantly and also too loudly.

Her father stirred on the other side of the bed and mumbled something in his sleep. Alice glanced over her shoulder at him.

"Come on! Let's go talk in your room!" she said to Rosie.

"She died in a mental institution when you were six or so," her mother said.

They were sitting on Rosie's bed, flipping through the album together.

"Why was she in there?"

"She had mental issues most of her life. She did something bad when she was only a girl, and her parents couldn't trust her anymore."

Rosie swallowed audibly. She felt tears stinging her eyes.

"Am I like her? Am I going to be locked up?"

"No, love! I will never let that happen." She pulled Rosie in to her chest. "The medicines are working on you. You'll be better in no time. You already are."

Rosie relaxed against her. She smelled like clean linen and warm skin. She felt safe in her arms. She felt wanted and loved. She had almost forgotten how much her mother, her parents, loved her. Her head was so full of confusing things that she almost forgot.

"What did she do?" Rosie asked, her voice muffled by her mother's long nightgown.

Alice shook her head. Rosie couldn't see it, but she felt the movement.

"It doesn't matter, love. That's all in the past."

She released Rosie from the hug and held her at arm's length.

"Time to go back to bed for the both of us. And time for you to give that back."

She was looking at the little key Rosie still held in her hand. "What's it for?"

Rosie held it up between them, and her mother took it from her fingers.

"It's not for anything anymore. It used to open a jewelry box that I don't have anymore. I kept it for sentimental reasons."

"Oh, okay."

"She's lying!" said her great aunt Francis in her head. Her mother turned off the lights on her way out. She had tucked Rosie in like when she was a little girl. She blew Rosie a kiss and quietly closed the door.

When Rosie fell asleep, she dreamed of the open office door. It came closer and closer to her, its dark depths terrifying and enticing her. *"You should know!"* crooned Francis. *"You will know!"* The door shut in front of her face with a windy slam. *"Bring the key!"* Then, her mind finally went blank.

CHAPTER FORTY-ONE

1997
ALICE

The morning had been hectic, to say the least. Rosie was complaining of a hurting stomach. Alice really, really didn't want to let her stay at home from school but eventually gave in. She was way too tired to maintain and win a long argument with her. Then, Emi mysteriously came down with the same ailment. Alice didn't buy it. Emi at least had to go to school. Alice had things to accomplish this morning, and she couldn't do it if she had to watch both girls. There had been screaming both from Emi and Moonwalk, who had evidently heard her and felt he should join in. Accusations of, "You only care about Rosie now!" When Alice felt like her head would burst, Noah finally intervened, looking fresh and quite edible after his morning shower. He scooped the crying Emi off the floor with one strong arm and whisked her off to school. She would be turning six soon, Alice had reminded herself. She wasn't acting much like a six-year-old. More like a toddler crossed with an angry teenager.

Alice had big plans for this morning. She pushed her class back two hours so she could walk to her evil, backstabbing neighbor's house and have a word with her. It was February, and the air was crisp and clean in the forest. Frozen grass and leaves crunched under her boots as she walked along the path connecting the two properties. The trail looked overgrown and neglected. The girls haven't been visiting each other since . . . Alice had no idea when. Some weeks, at least. Rosie still wasn't herself. And her friends, especially Mina, could tell. They didn't like this version of her and stayed away. Rosie didn't make any special effort to reconnect with them, either. Alice hoped that one day soon, things would return to normal for her older daughter. Her common sense told her not to, but she hoped anyway.

She was nearly one hundred percent sure Millie wrote that terrible letter. It made sense. She had always wanted Noah when they were young, and for a while, she had him. Alice sometimes wondered what would have happened if she never left. If she stayed and let the natural course of her relationship with Noah play out like it was supposed to, they would have been high school sweethearts. They would have probably married straight out of high school. Noah always wanted kids, so they would have probably had more than just two. Three, maybe even four. A son. Two sons and two daughters. Instead, she struggled against her destiny. And what did that earn her? A bitch-slap from life that sent her back to reality. It was possible that if she just gave in and dated Noah, she and Millie would have remained friends. Millie would have eventually gotten over her crush and most likely still married James. Because she left and then returned so dramatically, her relationship with Millie was forever scarred. There was hurt there on both sides, unspoken words, for they had never actually talked about what had happened. If they did, if they had stayed friends, Alice would have probably told Millie about Rosie. About Nathan. But neither of them could forgive the other. Millie couldn't forgive Alice for taking Noah, and Alice couldn't forgive Millie for not being there for her in her time of despair. So, they didn't speak, and time moved on. They became neighbors and slowly, tentatively, started talking again as if they were two strangers, neither daring to bring up the past.

The one good thing that came out of her leaving was Rosie.

Even if the illness consumed her and she were never the same again, Alice would still love her. And she wouldn't trade their amazingly beautiful fourteen years together for anything. She would never stop fighting for Rosie's happiness. And she would destroy anything that threatened it.

The envelopes she saw at the veterinary office didn't convince her a hundred percent that it had been Millie. She was acting shady as hell when she saw Alice eyeing them, but still. *How could she know the truth? How did she find out?* Alice had almost forgotten about the letter in her desk. She actually hadn't remembered it until Rosie found the desk key while sleepwalking. That was when it dawned on her. Millie had watched their house. Multiple times. While they were away visiting family, she was snooping around in their home, finding things she had no business finding.

She wanted to move the letter from the desk first thing this morning, but the kids had distracted her, so she forgot. She would move it first thing when she got home. She thought about destroying it altogether, but there was a reason it existed. When Rosie was born, Alice still worried about her own future. Mental illness could hit at any time, and postpartum depression could be an excellent trigger for it. Or maybe she and Noah would become victims of some terrible accident. You never knew what the future held. What if Rosie needed a liver or a kidney, and Alice wasn't a match? All these worries prompted her to write it. It was a "just in case," a last resort. It almost guaranteed that Rosie would be taken care of no matter what. It had been written with the best intentions, not to be used as blackmail. Technically, this wasn't blackmail because Millie hadn't asked for anything. But it was nasty, and it overstepped so many boundaries, Alice couldn't even keep count of them.

She had worked herself into a simmering rage by the time she reached Millie's house.

She knew she was off work. She had called the veterinary office before leaving her house, so Millie should be home if she wasn't out running errands. Alice emerged from the cover of the trees and saw her car was in the driveway. She took a deep breath and blew it out slowly. *Here it goes!* As she walked up the steps to the door, the old porch groaned warningly under her feet. She rapped on the door three times and stepped back, bracing for impact. She heard some shuffling from inside, but nobody opened the door. She was starting to think that Millie was going to go the coward's way and leave her standing outside when she finally swung the door open.

"Alice," she said in a cold, measured tone. "What brings you here?"

"Can I come in?" Alice asked and quickly took a step forward.

Millie instinctively stepped back, opening the door wider. Alice went in and took in the old grace of the two-story home. It was gloomy inside but clean and orderly. She walked along the front hall, looking at the pictures on the wall.

"You have a beautiful family," she said over her shoulder just before stepping into the kitchen.

"Well, thank you." Millie hurried after her. "How can I help you?"

Alice turned around in a circle and took in the charming old kitchen with its original wooden cabinets. There were shelves behind the dining room table, and on them were some books, a potted plant, and a few office supplies such as pens, paper, and a number of yellow envelopes. Alice tuned to face her, trying to keep her face neutral.

"I came to borrow a cup of sugar," she said.

Millie gaped at her with a blank expression.

"Sugar?" she asked dubiously.

"Yeah, and also an envelope. I'm trying to mail out some stuff and realized I ran out."

Millie's eyes flicked over to the shelf holding the office supplies.

"You know you can get them at the post office, right?" she asked, her dark eyes going flat and cold.

"Yes, but you were closer."

They stood there eyeing each other for what seemed like a long time. Who would blink first?

"Alice . . ." Millie started to say, but Alice stepped up to her so they were nose-to-nose, separated by only an inch of air.

"You had no right!" Alice breathed, her voice quivering with tension.

Millie swallowed convulsively, her eyes going as round as saucers. She wanted to move away, but there was a wall right behind her. *I was right*, Alice thought. *It was her.* Alice wanted to hurt her. She wanted to take all her inner pain and frustration out on Millie. She wanted to make her understand how wrong this was. That you couldn't just meddle in other people's lives without consequences. But above all, she wanted Millie to apologize. To admit what she did was wrong and beg for her forgiveness. Millie opened and closed her mouth once, swallowed again, then said:

"I think . . . you need to leave my house!"

"You," said Alice, putting great emphasis on the word, "need to leave my life!"

"You first!"

Millie's voice was shaking—whether from fear or pent-up anger, Alice wasn't sure, but she wasn't getting an apology. She was never getting an apology from Millie. The woman was too stuck-up. Too entitled to admit to any folly. Alice just wasted her time. She shouldn't have come here. She nodded and walked past the person who once had been her friend and out of her life for good.

CHAPTER FORTY-TWO

1997
ROSIE

She watched her mother leave through her bedroom window. Once she was out of sight, swallowed by the trees, Rosie jumped out of bed. Through her partially open bedroom door, she could see the crone, or Great Aunt Francis or whoever she was, disappear into her parents' bedroom. Rosie didn't take her pills this morning. The crone told her not to. She wanted to show Rosie something, and she couldn't do that if she was stuck inside. By now, Rosie realized that the other voice in her head really wasn't her own. It wasn't Bad Rosie. It was the crone. Now that Rosie knew who her face belonged to, something clicked into place. A sort of trust was formed.

She went after her. Peeking into the bedroom, she didn't see her, but that didn't mean she wasn't actually there. "The key!" she heard Francis whisper right next to her ear and felt her wet breath on her cheek. "Get the key!" Rosie walked, soft-footed, to the nightstand and pulled the drawer out. She flipped through the photobook, looking for other pictures of her great aunt, but there was only the one. Now that she had some time to study it, she could definitely see the family resemblance. That's why the crone looked vaguely familiar. This had never been Rosanne Glessner's ghost. She needed to consult Luke on this. He was the only one who could help her figure this out. She needed to tell him what she knew so they could work together.

She grabbed the key and placed the album on the bed. She thought she knew where she needed to go but was reluctant. What if this was some sort of trick?

The office door was closed when she walked out into the living room. That's where Francis wanted her. But should she listen to her? All she did was cause her trouble and pain. She stopped her from sleeping and haunted her day and night. What she should do is put the key away, take her meds, and forget about the whole thing. The office door opened slowly with a loud, whining creak. *Fuck it!* thought Rosie. Maybe if she played along, the ghost would finally leave her alone. She went in, the key clutched in one fist. Once inside, the door slowly shut behind her, making all her down hairs stand straight up. Bracing herself, she spoke out loud.

"What do you want me to do with this?"

She held up the key. Nothing happened. Frustrated, she dropped her hand. The key stayed in place. It hovered there in midair for a second, and then, slowly, gently, as if taken by running water, it made its way to her mother's desk, where it dropped unceremoniously to the ground. Now quite intrigued, Rosie jogged over to where it lay on the floor and squatted to pick it up. When she looked up, key in hand, she was faced with a tiny keyhole just at eye level. A lockable desk drawer. She never knew her parents' desks had those. She never really looked at the stuff in here. This was the world of the adults. Endless boring paperwork, stressful phone calls, and things she and Emi were not supposed to touch. *What could be so interesting in here?* She slid the key in the drawer and opened it.

Heavy footsteps thudded through the house as Rosie ran from the office to her bedroom. Sobbing, she dug under her pillow for the pills she hid away this morning.

"Come on! Come on! Where are they?"

Hot tears blurred her vision and fell from her crumbling

face as she feverishly dug through her bedding. Finally, her fingers closed around the small pills. *"No, child! You don't have to take those! They'll make you silly,"* Francis said in her head.

"Shut up! Shut up! Shut up!" Her screams escalating into animalistic howling, she slapped her hand over her mouth, sending the pills to the back of her throat.

She swallowed, forcing them down as fast as they could go. Arching her back, she shouted her sorrow in a long, raspy wail. Her whole world turned upside down and inside out. She screamed until she ran out of air. Why would the crone want her to know this? What was the point? Curling in on herself like a shrimp, she tried to banish the awful words of the letter from her mind, but they wouldn't go. She fell back against her pillow and cried for a few more minutes until the medication dried her tears, her world once again becoming mellow and manageable. She went quiet, her mind clear and her center hollow. A little while later, she got to her feet and went about hiding her tracks. She put everything back to where she had found it. The damn letter, telling her that the most crucial parts of her life had been a lie, the picture of the man from her dream who was actually her father, the key, the photo album. There. Like it never happened. By the time her mother came home, she was lying on the couch, watching cartoons.

"Are you feeling any better? Can I bring you anything?"

Alice loomed over the back of the couch to look at her. Her mother, the liar.

"No, thanks, Mom."

"Okay. Well, I'm going to head out soon."

She watched the tall, shapely form of her mom walk across the living room. *"What a whore!"*

"Mom!" Rosie called after her.

"Yes, my love?"

"Take me to the lake this weekend! I need to see Luke."

"I'm not sure if we can this weekend, love. Your dad and I both have to work."

Francis snickered. *"Your dad."*

"I have to see him," Rosie insisted with a dull stubbornness.

Her mother smiled at her good-naturedly.

"What's so urgent?"

"I have to tell him I love him," said Rosie and turned her burning face into the pillow.

CHAPTER FORTY-THREE
1743
ROSANNE

June 1

It was hard to say goodbye. I wished desperately to take Bertha with me, or if not her, then maybe one of the Black women I had gotten so close to. It couldn't be so. John is no rich man. I know I myself had cost him greatly. He never spoke of my price, though, and I did not ask. Of course, taking Bertha was only a fantasy. She is not my child and never will be. It was time for me to leave the ranch and her with it. She started calling me Mama. The mistress, as jealous as she was, would have had me killed sooner or later. At least, that's what I gathered from the looks she gave me with her grotesquely drooping face. And all these things aside, John will never treat me as his property. His mother is an Indian woman, and their people treat women differently. Indian women can choose freely who they wish to be married to. And if their husband doesn't suit them any longer, they can put him out and marry another man. Just like that. I gaped at him when he told me. I asked him what he would do if I chose to leave him for another man. He grinned at me with that white, wolfish smile of his and told me he would kill my new man and do his best to woo me back. The concept is strangely romantic, I must say.

We rode out at dawn on the 28th of May. John had brought a pretty roan mule for me to ride on. She has a delicate, narrow face and long, shapely ears like a rabbit. I asked him if she already has a name. He grinned at me and spoke in his native tongue. The word is simply not pronounceable for me, so I promptly decided to call her Bunny.

The countryside is beautifully alien. We passed by an area covered in orange sand and giant, protruding stones of the same color, and rounded, spiky plants grown from between rocks. This is called a desert, I'm told. John's land is forested. It backs up to a wide river called the Red River. It is called so because it carries with it the orange sand of the desert. There is plenty of game here. Deer by the dozens. And great, big, furry creatures that look like cattle but are called buffalo. I saw one not even a hundred yards from us and thought it was a bear. John tells me not to fear them unless they charge. Apparently, the fur we spent our first night together on belonged to a buffalo. John laughs at me quite a bit. But good-naturedly. He tells me that the wonder with which I look upon this land is truly charming. I cannot help it. Everything surprises me. There is something I haven't seen before, around every corner, behind each tree. I feel as if I'm a child again.

Speaking of child, I do wonder if I may be carrying one under my heart. I have missed my courses this past month. It would truly be a lovely thing. A wonderful new start. The babe would have John's black hair, I'm sure. I dream about it. In my dreams, the babe is a little girl. She runs through the forest with me, wild and free, our feet bare and our hair flying loose. I wish I could tell Kata about it. About everything. She would be so pleased to hear I'm doing well. She would approve of John. I think about her a lot. I wonder where she ended up. If she is treated well. If she is happy.

Yesterday, we arrived at the house, or what will be the house once it's finished. John had started on the framework, but it's far from having a roof. He assures me we'll have a waterproof shelter before winter comes again, and if not, we can go stay with his people for a season. I'm pleased by the idea of living with the Indians for a time. They sound like good people. John has two sisters still living back where he came from. One from his mother, by an Indian man, and one fathered by Abel McCullum to another tribe woman. I imagine them to be just as beautiful as he is.

I rode Bunny the mule out to the cliff today. The view is breathtaking. I saw a herd of buffalo drinking from the river below. The forest is green and teeming with life. I can hardly believe that this land, this untamed wilderness, is my new home.

1997

Luke

He was just finishing up with a chapter of the famous journal when he heard the Smiths' car pull into the gravel driveway next door. He knew they were coming this time because Rosie had called to tell him. She sounded strange over the phone, her voice hollow and distant, like she was holding something in. Something big. She said she had something important to tell him, so he guessed he would find out what it was shortly. He waited for her, his anticipation and anxiety building.

He ambled outside and peered through the bushes by the fence dividing the two properties. Rosie's grandparents had come outside, and they were all hugging and removing small pieces of luggage from the back of the car. Emi ran straight to the water, shrieking as she went.

"The water is too cold, you loon!" Noah boomed, one hand next to his mouth.

Emi didn't stop. No surprise there. She rid herself of her shoes while running, picked up a stick, and was already wading in the shallows by the time her grandfather caught up with her. Luke spotted the tall, thin frame of Rosie, and the bottom of his stomach dropped out. There was the dark silhouette of a person hovering just behind her. It moved with her as if they were tethered together by a short rope. He was right. The speck and the spirit lady weren't just connected. They were one and the same. Does the fact that it— she—grew in size mean that her influence over Rosie had gotten stronger, too? He moved without making the conscious decision to do so. He had to at least try to do something for Rosie, however small of a difference he could make.

Alice let him into the home. He found Rosie in her grandparents' living room. She was looking up at a large painting of three children on the wall. There was a little boy and a slightly older girl, both with wispy blonde hair and one older girl with a short mane of curls. The oldest one reminded Luke of Rosie a bit. They had the same shaped eyes and lips. Rosie's eyes seemed to be fixed on her.

"Who is that?" he asked, standing next to her.

He gave the silhouette of the ghost lady a weary side-eye. She had no distinct shape to her body parts. But he knew it was her. He felt her energy on his skin like electricity.

"Franny," Rosie breathed, still looking at the painting.

She looked to be in a trance, her eyes glazed and unfocused.

"A family member of yours?"

Luke placed a hand on her shoulder. He made a fist with his other hand and imagined all his muscles contracting all the way from that fist, taking his inner power through his core and arm and into Rosie through the hand on her shoulder. The silhouette flared to the side as if hit by a strong gust of wind. It sparked agitatedly. *Take that, you fucker!* Luke thought spitefully. Rosie shook herself. She blinked and turned her beautiful face toward Luke. Her expression was unreadable.

"It's my Great Aunt Francis," she said and took Luke by the hand. "Come on! We got stuff to talk about."

Luke thought she was going to lead him to the boulders in the forest, but they walked down to the dock at the end of the yard instead. It was hard for him to hide his disappointment. His main objective was to help her figure out her haunting situation, yes, but he also wouldn't have minded some alone time with her. There weren't any trees here to hide them from prying eyes. Looking over his shoulder, he could actually see Alice looking at them from the big bay kitchen window. Rosie seemed to read his mind, for she gave him a half-smile.

"Sorry!" she said, shrugging slightly. "She wanted to be by the water."

"Who?" he asked, his brows knitted. He could still feel Rosie's own energy through her hand, but it was muted somehow. They sat down on the dock.

"Francis," she said matter-of-factly. "She's my ghost. I know you can see her. She told me."

Luke's mouth opened and closed. He swallowed.

"Can you see her now?"

She shook her head. She was looking at him with this eerie, calm expression, her eyes big and shiny.

"I can hear her. Like, in my head." She shifted her focus to her shoes.

She knocked the toes together contemplatively. The speck had always stayed right behind her, so Luke wasn't surprised that she had no idea it was always hovering just behind her. He wondered if she could see it in the mirror. Probably not. She most likely only saw her when she wanted to be seen. He didn't think telling her about Francis's constant presence was a good idea. He didn't want to distress her any more than she already was.

"I figured it out the other day. That it was her and not Rosanne. I don't think she has anything to do with Rosanne at all. So, us reading the journal is probably meaningless."

"It's still a good read," Luke said, meaning it. "How come you didn't know who she was until now?"

Rosie gave her one of her radiant smiles, and his heart did a weird fluttering motion.

"This is what I love about you. You are always on my side, Luke. You don't think I'm lying or that I'm crazy."

For a moment, Luke was speechless. He could feel heat rising in his face.

"Of course! You are my best friend!" he burst out, his voice cracking a bit.

And I love you, he thought but did not say.

"Anyway, I didn't know who she was because I have never met her. My great aunt, I mean. My mom said she had some mental illness. She died in a mental hospital."

Suddenly, her face went serious.

"The thing is . . ." She searched his eyes, making him blush even harder. "Okay, this is going to sound crazy, but I think I did meet her."

"What? Like, in the hospital?"

"No, in a dream. It's hard to explain."

She chewed on her bottom lip, her cheeks turning a healthy pink.

"If we kiss, will you stop staring at my mouth and focus?"

Luke's head nearly exploded with the amount of blood rushing to it. He had been stealing glances at her lips, but he didn't think she noticed. He cleared his throat.

"Maybe," he said quite hoarsely.

Their heads bent together in the light of the late afternoon sun. After Rosie leaned her forehead against his, her eyes closed.

"I'm a little scared sometimes," she whispered. "I feel her getting stronger, and I don't know what she wants and where it will stop."

"No matter what happens, I'll be here. Just tell me what's been happening, and we'll figure it out together."

She nodded against him and leaned back, looking severe.

"I have these dreams where I go places and meet people. I think . . . I'm actually there. At first, I thought the ghost was just making me see things, but I think I actually met my great aunt when she was a little girl."

Luke nodded, trying to look encouraging.

"So, you traveled to the past?"

"I think so."

"That's way cool!"

The theory of it was very interesting. But also scary. What if Rosie were to accidentally change something that caused her not to exist? Was that even possible?

"I didn't recognize who she was until I saw the painting just now."

"Do you think there is a reason you saw her when she was little? Were you supposed to do something or tell her something?"

"I don't know!" Rosie groaned. "It's all a huge shitshow. I honestly don't know what's going on. I probably have to do something. There has to be a reason why her ghost is ruining my life."

"There are three kids in the painting. The other girl must be your grandma, but who is the third? The boy."

Rosie sat up straight, her spine stiffening. She looked at Luke with an expression somewhere between excitement and alarm.

"He is my great uncle Harry."

"Why have I never seen him?"

The strangest array of emotions flickered over Rosie's face; her eyebrows looked like they were doing a fun little dance. Luke feared he already knew the answer but still waited for her to speak.

"Because he's dead," she said finally. "I think."

Luke lay on his bed, looking at the ceiling and contemplating the information given to him by Rosie. He wasn't going to lie, it was some scary stuff.

She told him about her grave digging dream and how young Francis saw the ghost lady, too, but to her, she looked like somebody else. "She wasn't afraid of her at all," Rosie had said in astonishment. *That's probably why the entity was able to grab a hold of her at such an early age*, Luke thought. Francis was most likely not mentally ill but plagued by the same thing as Rosie. When he told Rosie this theory, she went as white as a ghost. She agreed with him. Luke had hesitated to say his second theory out loud, but it had to be done. If both Francis and Rosie saw the same thing but with a different face, that would mean it was neither the ghost of Francis's grandmother nor Francis herself. It must be something different entirely. And it wears the face of someone you know—or, in Rosie's case, should have known. It made sense why the ghost lady didn't let Rosie sleep. Why it fucked around with her mind. It had to break her down to get in. To grab a hold of her.

Chills broke out on Luke's arms, and he rubbed his hands over them, feeling his arm hairs rasp against his palms.

Rosie had cried a bit on his shoulder. She told him about this nagging feeling she had that something bad was going to happen. She had no idea what and when, but it was coming. The medication was helping. "It traps her inside," she'd said, pointing at her temple. "I can still hear her, but she can't make me do stuff. She uses my bad emotions. If I feel angry or sad or even just annoyed, she bends it out of shape." She told him then about killing their beloved rooster without meaning to. She described it as not being in control of her own body.

It was hard to even imagine such a thing, something taking over one's mind and body. Luke shuddered. He wanted to help her, but whatever this thing was, it was more powerful than he initially thought. It would chew him up and spit him out if he gave it the chance.

He remembered Rosie's lovely face, her eyes, red-rimmed from crying, pleading with him to believe all this. He did. He believed her, and still, he couldn't help her. And that killed him.

"I love you!" she had said, making this one of the best and worst days of his life. "I just wanted you to know in case I can't tell you later. In case this thing makes me disappear."

Luke's eyes filled with tears, and he blinked them away. He rubbed at his eyes with his fisted hands. This was so unfair. So incredibly, impossibly unfair. Rosie didn't think she could beat this thing. And that already gave it the upper hand.

CHAPTER FORTY-FOUR
1997
ROSIE

They were sitting at the breakfast table the morning after she had the talk with Luke. Rosie had no appetite. She pushed the eggs around on her plate, sneaking glances into the living room where the painting of the three children hung above the fireplace. The childhood rendering of Francis kept eyeing her. She was following Rosie with her mud-brown eyes. It was creepy and rude. She was trying to eat. She shifted her focus to her parents. *Oops! Parent,* she corrected herself. She only had one parent in this room. *"And she's a lying whore!"* Francis hissed and then cackled. *"Both of them are lying sacks of shit!"*

Oh, give it a rest! thought Rosie, even though she was right. They lied to her all her life. It was shitty. Her dad, the man who had raised her, wasn't even related to her. He was a stranger. Did he even know? Did her mother hide this from him, too? Was he aware he was raising another man's child? Rosie had a sour taste in her mouth. She couldn't stop thinking about that letter, and it was driving her mad. She pushed her plate away, eggs untouched.

"You have to eat!" her mother said, taking a sip of her coffee, a piece of egg delicately balanced on the fork she was holding.

"What happened to Harry?" Rosie asked, partly because she did want to know and partly to distract herself from the other thing.

All heads around the table turned to look at her. Her mother looked blank for a moment, then recognition hit, and she nearly choked on her coffee. The piece of egg slid off her fork and landed on the table with a tiny splat. Her grandmother blinked at Rosie, round-eyed like a surprised owlet. There was silence in which you could clearly hear Emi's small teeth working hard at a piece of toast.

"Harry?" Rosie's grandfather frowned at his wife.

"My brother."

"My uncle."

Rosie's mom and grandma said at the same time. Rosie snickered, although she wasn't sure why. Her mother looked at her sharply, her mouth folded into a thin line.

"I didn't know you had an uncle. Rosie's da . . ." Noah said, looking just as confused as Grandpa.

"I don't," her mother said, her face looking weary and very tired all of a sudden.

"He disappeared when he was just a boy. It happened a long, long time ago," Grandma supplied, clearly trying to shut this topic of conversation down.

"He's dead, right? How did he die?" Rosie said, not really paying attention to her family's discomfort.

She had her eyes locked on the painting, but what she saw were small fingernails packed with dirt. Bare feet dangling in a shallow grave.

"Rosie! Where . . . why . . ." her mother sputtered.

Rosie glanced at her. Her face was as red as a ripe tomato.

"They never found him," her grandmother said, looking down at her plate.

Her half-eaten breakfast would never be finished, Rosie thought, and for a second, she felt bad for the obvious hurt she had caused. Then, it passed. Her mother, having collected herself, placed both her hands on the table and stood up.

"Come on, love!" she called to Rosie, tilting her head

toward the back door. "Let's take a walk!"

They strolled along the old bike trail next to the houses, their hands in their pockets to avoid frostbite. It was a cold morning, and a chilly wind blew at them from the lake. Rosie's mind was blissfully blank. Being near water always made her inner demon quiet down. Maybe she should start taking long baths. Maybe she should live in a bathtub. Her mother put an arm around her shoulders.

"Harry is a touchy subject for your grandma," she said, her breath puffing out in front of her face. "What made you bring him up?"

Rosie shrugged. Long-dead family members shouldn't interest her. She knew it was weird that she was suddenly so curious.

"I was just looking at the painting, and I realized the only thing I know about him is his name."

She turned her face up to her mother and tried to seem nonchalant.

"What happened to him?"

Her mother sighed, her chest expanding inside her coat.

"Nobody really knows. Like Grandma said, they never found him. Her sister, Francis, was suspected of having something to do with it, but they couldn't prove it. She was taken away anyway. Locked up in what you kids call a loony bin."

"We don't say that, Mom. That's so lame!"

She was only teasing. She actually loved when her mom tried and failed to be cool. Alice gave Rosie a half-smile and shrugged.

"Anyways, her parents didn't trust Francis after that. That's why they got rid of her. And your grandma went from having two siblings to having none in just a few days. It's a very traumatic memory for her."

Rosie was quiet for a minute. How would she feel if she lost Emi? It would be so quiet and depressing at home without her rambunctious little sister. Their parents would never be happy again. Francis stirred within her, shoving and poking. Rosie realized she was feeding off her negative feelings, her fear and anxiety brought on by the thought of such loss. She shook herself and tried to think of other things. Something good. Like Luke. Warmth flooded her face. She should kiss him again before they left today. Maybe she should do a bit more than just kiss, just in case things went south with her. Francis was making her crazy, and the medication was making her a zombie. Her future seemed pretty bleak just right now. *Why not live in the moment and do something reckless and risky?* She imagined herself taking her shirt and bra off in front of him and thought there might be steam coming from her ears. How could she? It would be so awkward and embarrassing, and yet . . . *Luke would like it, wouldn't he? Boys like boobs.* She wanted to shock him, to see the color rise in his cheeks and hear his breath hitch. *Oh, my God!* She could never! She wasn't ready to show a boy her boobs. Even if it was Luke. Even if she knew she would be dying tomorrow. She wouldn't be able to do it.

"So, did you get to tell Luke what you wanted?"

How on earth did she know she was thinking of Luke? Her mom was using that sixth sense only mothers had. She wasn't playing fair. Rosie wriggled out of her grasp.

"We talked," she mumbled.

She only said what she said to her mom to ensure she would bring her here. She didn't actually intend to tell Luke she loved him. But then, she did because it was true. She loved him. She had been feeling frightened and emotional, and it just slipped out. She didn't regret it, though. He needed to know so he could remember it for the both of them in case Francis decided to keep growing inside her and one day swallow her whole.

Her mom didn't press her, for which she was grateful. They walked around for a few more minutes and then decided to head back to warm up in front of the fireplace, under the watchful eyes of Francis.

CHAPTER FORTY-FIVE
1997
MILLIE

Millie and her daughter had their heads bent over Mina's math homework. Millie had never been great at math. Who was she kidding? That was an understatement. She barely skimmed by the last two years of high school with a D. Noah was the only reason she didn't fail. Math had come so easy to him. He'd tutored Millie when he had the time. Those tutoring sessions had been the few rare occasions when it was just the two of them. No Alice. Just Noah and some terrible, confusing numbers. Back then, Millie had been ecstatic to be bad at math just because it gave her an extra reason to see Noah. Now, not so much. Mina was supposed to turn a written problem into some complicated equation, and she had no idea how to do it. Millie was right there with her. The more times they read the problem, the less they seemed to understand it. Mina groaned and laid her head on the table.

"This is hopeless!" Her muffled voice came from under her mane of curls.

"Sit up straight!" Millie slapped her on the shoulder. "I didn't raise a quitter."

No, what she did raise was a math idiot. A regular chip off

the old block. She wondered fleetingly if James had also been bad at math. She really had no idea. They hadn't known each other in high school. He usually worked long hours, so it really wouldn't make a difference if he was better at this than Millie. He still wouldn't have the time to help the kids with homework.

Noah probably helped his girls with their math homework. He probably made it seem easy and fun, just like when they were kids. Her stomach clenched with the familiar pain of envy, and she had to fight to regain control of her face. She knew how she must look with her brow all wrinkled and the corners of her mouth drooping. Like a cow with indigestion. *Stop it, Millie!* she told herself. *You need to let this go! You've been bitter for long enough.* It was no use. She felt the way she felt. And what she was feeling right now, right this second, was hatred. Bitter, sour, smelly hatred.

Alice had come into her home and nearly attacked her. The nerve of her. She should have told James. Have her arrested. But then, she would have had to admit to writing the letters, and she wanted to avoid that if possible. Still, the thought of Alice hauled off in handcuffs gave her goosebumps. The bitch was just as crazy as that daughter of hers. Rosie was seeing a shrink now. Millie had heard it through the grapevine. What she would give to know what unhinged things they talked about. To get her hands on Rosie's file and plaster it all over town. That would show them! Alice would die from embarrassment. *She would probably beat you to a pulp, you flaming idiot.* It would be worth it. Her rage eventually simmered down to a manageable level, and she focused on turning it against the math problem.

They wrapped up doing homework in another hour. They did solve the math problem, although Millie was pretty sure the answer they came up with was wrong entirely.

"What are you going to do for the rest of the day?" Millie asked her daughter, moving toward the sink. There were some dishes in there from this morning that needed washing.

"I don't know," Mina said automatically. "Can I call Sam?"

Millie pursed her lips, pulling on her bright yellow rubber

gloves. Sam and her annoying mother lived some miles away. That meant driving. She had housework to do, and honestly, she wasn't thrilled about the idea of interrupting her boys. They were trying to rebuild their smashed clubhouse, which meant they were out of the house and currently not underfoot. It would be nice to keep it that way until she finished vacuuming and mopping.

"Why don't you see what Rosie is up to?"

She said it without thinking. She squeezed her eyes shut, grimacing. After what happened between her and Alice, she wasn't sure if Mina was even welcome at their house. She sure as hell didn't want Rosie to bring her craziness over here, and Alice was probably on the same page. She suddenly felt enormously selfish for not considering Mina's friendship with Rosie when she did what she did. Those two girls did everything together, kind of like her and Alice when they were young. Before all the jealousy and anger.

"That's okay, Mom. I'll just call Sam if you don't mind."

Millie whirled around to face her. Mina was looking inside her school bag like there was something extremely interesting in there. She was giving Millie an out, a chance to drop the topic of Rosie and save them both some heartache. She couldn't do it. Millie was physically incapable of not digging. She had to ask.

"Is everything okay with you two?"

Mina shrugged her skinny teenage shoulders.

"We are not really friends anymore."

She picked up her bag and tried to flee the kitchen, but Millie stopped her.

"Hang on! What's this all about? You girls used to be thick as thieves."

Her heart in her throat, Millie stripped her gloves off and stood in front of her daughter. There was a small frown line on her normally smooth young forehead. *Shit!* she cursed inwardly. Maybe Mina already knew about what had happened between her and Alice. Rosie probably knew and was now shunning her. Or even worse, what if Alice herself confronted Mina at school? She could just imagine her pointing a finger at Mina's chest and saying, "You and your whore mother stay away from Rosie! You hear me?" *Would she dare do that? Would the school not say anything? Maybe nobody saw.* Mina shrugged again.

"She's not the same. I know she's sick, but it's like she's not the same person. Sometimes, when I talk to her, it's like she's a stranger or something. It's weird."

"But she is taking medication now. That didn't help?"

Mina shook her head. Millie only knew about the pills because of the history teacher, Ms. Lesbith. That woman is a terrible gossip and an excellent source of information. She relished the dirt she had on Rosie; Millie could see it in her eyes. Where she had gotten the scoop from, Millie could only guess. Alice must have told the principal. Ms. Lesbith must be close with him to be able to get such juicy details. Maybe Millie should invite her out for coffee sometime. *The woman looks like she could use a friend. And some good home cooking. Skinny as a rod, that one. Maybe a dinner instead of a coffee, then.* Mina shifted uncomfortably in front of her, and she realized she'd been silently thinking for way too long.

"Mom, can I tell you something?"

"Of course, baby. What's the matter?"

"She scares me . . ."

"Who?"

The teacher? It wouldn't surprise her. The woman was scary. And she had those strange-colored eyes.

"Rosie," Mina said with a tinge of impatience. "The way she looks at me sometimes. It's scary."

Mina frowned up at her, and she could see worry turn her hazel eyes green. She was such a heartbreakingly beautiful child. Even in a time like this. Millie herself had never been this beautiful. Not even in her prime. She placed both her hands on Mina's shoulders and said to her in a tone that called for no argument:

"Just stay away from her, baby girl! You definitely don't have to keep being friends with someone like that. Go ahead and call Sam! I'll drive you over if she is available!"

Mina left the room, and Millie went back to doing dishes,

her shoulders slumping with relief. Things just got a lot easier. If the girls weren't going to be friends anymore, there was no reason for her and Alice to run into each other. They may still see one another at school, but they could just pretend not to know each other. There was no use for pleasantries and "Oh, how are you?". She watched the soap suds slowly dripping from her gloves. If only they weren't neighbors. That was what made things tricky. Maybe they should move somewhere more bustling and interesting, like Dallas, or Austin, even. Plenty of receptionist jobs in a big city. Plenty of crime, too. Any police district would welcome a fine detective like James. Finished with the dishes, she turned, leaned back against the sink, and looked around her charming old house.

They had bought the house and the land, not knowing that the adjacent big property belonged to Alice's grandparents. She never told Millie that her family owned land here. Never even mentioned it. So, it had been a terrible shock when one day after moving into the old two-story, she went for a nice walk in the forest and stumbled upon Alice and Noah. They were living in this shitty little shack, but the framing for the expansion that would become their new house already stood. At first, she only saw Noah. He was working on a roofbeam. He was shirtless, his tan body stretched upward as he hammered away, totally unaware of her presence. He looked good enough to eat. Millie did a bit of mouth breathing as she watched the lean muscles of his back work. She was four months pregnant with Mina and was definitely showing. She stroked the small curve of her stomach meditatively. Her libido had been out of control for the past month along with her appetite. All she could think of was what his nether regions would look like here in the warm light of the sun. She still remembered the feel of him. Felt the ghost of his kisses on her body. She could have him one last time. Nobody had to know. Not her husband, not stupid Alice. Nobody. All she needed was one last feverish coupling out here in the wilderness, and she would be satisfied. She would have the last word. Then, later, she could throw it in Alice's face if the opportunity arose. Could she seduce him, pregnant as she was? She could give it a go. She wouldn't know unless she tried.

Silently, she walked up to the construction site, not taking her eyes off his narrow, sculpted hips on which the shorts rode a bit too low. It was his tool belt, ladened heavily with miscellaneous things that made his shorts dip oh so erotically low. She opened her mouth to say some witty greeting when a sharp, vulgarly loud sound split the air behind her. She whirled to see a donkey of all things staring at her with its large, long-lashed eyes. It stomped with one little hoof and brayed again, making her flinch before taking off into the forest and stirring up a small dust cloud in its wake. Millie squinted after it, momentarily forgetting about any romantic fantasy she may have had.

"Millie?" came a strained grunt from Noah.

She turned back to see Noah hanging off the roofbeam he had been working on, his ladder flat on the ground. She gasped and ran to his aid. The damn ladder was a lot heavier than it looked, and she struggled to get it standing against the framework. Once in place, Noah placed one foot, then another on it cautiously. He climbed down and rubbed his shoulders, squinting back up at his handiwork.

"At least it held," he said good-naturedly, making Millie relax. "I see you've met the donkey."

"That I did."

She smiled at him appreciably and watched his eyes take her body in for the first time in over half a year. He did a double take at her stomach and grinned with what looked like genuine joy.

"I see a congratulations is in order."

Millie looked down at her bulging abdomen and blushed prettily, partially with pride for the simple reason that she was carrying new life and partially because of the things she had been thinking just a minute ago. He was looking at her body and noticing things.

"Thank you!" she said and then fell silent.

How did pregnant women flirt? Was it even allowed? Did men even find pregnancy attractive? Noah didn't seem displeased.

"So, what brings you here?" he asked conversationally.

Sweat was glistening on his shoulders and pecs and running down his abs. Down, down, all the way down. *Does he take his shirt off on all his job sites?* she wondered.

"Oh, I live here now," she indicated at the tree line, "just on the other side of the woods."

A strange expression crossed Noah's handsome face. It almost looked like concern. Was he worried because she was walking around in the forest all by herself? It would be so like him to worry about stuff like that.

"Don't worry; it's just a short walk. And you are working on my neighbors' new house, I see. Are they nice people?"

"No!" he said, then cleared his throat. "I mean, this isn't for someone else."

Now, he was turning an interesting shade of red under his stubble. He looked around for inspiration and seemed to find none.

"This is my house. Or it's going to be once it's done."

Millie gaped at him, her brain not processing what she'd just heard. These pregnancy hormones were making her so ditsy.

"What? You mean this is yours? "

She gestured at the wilderness around them. Was he messing with her?

"Mine and Alice's."

As if summoned, Alice stepped out of the shack with a tall glass of iced tea in one hand. The sun glinted off her honey-colored hair that fell loosely around her shoulders and down her back. Millie hadn't seen her in so long, her beauty was like a punch to her baby-ladened gut. She looked absolutely radiant. She also had a gargantuan pregnant belly.

"Oh, Millie!" she gasped in surprise.

She must be at least six months pregnant by the looks of her, the analytical part of Millie's brain informed her. Which would mean that Noah had jumped from her bed straight into Alice's. Probably the same night they saw her in front of the bookstore.

"S-Sorry, I didn't expect to see you. I mean, I-I didn't expect to see anyone but Noah," Alice stammered slightly and placed a slim hand over her huge statement of a belly.

She always stammered when she was nervous, Millie recalled in a detached sort of way. She used to find it cute, a harmless little flaw in her otherwise perfect friend that made her seem more approachable and human. Now, she found it overplayed and childish.

"I'm your new neighbor," she heard herself say and felt the color drain from her face.

Her eyes caught the glint of something shiny on Alice's hand. It was a thin, gold wedding band that suited her perfectly. Her head turned to look at Noah's large left hand, where she found the slightly wider pair to Alice's ring.

"And you guys are married." Her voice sounded as colorless as her face.

She thought she had one-upped them. She found a decent man, a police officer, in no time after Noah broke it off with her. She got pregnant with his child almost immediately after they started sleeping together. They got married. They bought a house. They were happy. So insanely happy. She rode off into the sunset with James and had left Alice and Noah behind. In the dust.

Only she didn't. Alice had fallen pregnant before she did. They most likely married as soon as a pastor was available. They had a bigger property and would have a brand-new house on it that Noah built with his bare hands. She felt her world tilt and her stomach squeeze painfully.

Alice was saying something, but it was somewhere in the background. She felt a hand on her shoulder, and Alice's golden, glowing face swam before her eyes.

"Are you okay? You look like you're about to be sick."

Indeed she was. Alice had great observation skills, as always.

"I have to go!" she blurted and turned to flee.

They didn't try to stop her. Or maybe they did, but she had been too quick. She started running the moment she was inside the cover of the woods, her hands protectively cradling her meager baby bump that shied in comparison to Alice's. She couldn't keep the phase up for too long and soon found herself leaning against a tree, breathing heavily. To her horror, there were tears running down her face. She wasn't a crier. It was these damn pregnancy hormones. The same ones that told her to seduce Noah. *Oh, God!* She almost did it, too. She must be some kind of stupid to think that had been a good idea on any planet. *Poor Jim. Poor, humble, loyal, caring Jim.* He didn't deserve her acting this way. He had been nothing but good to her, and here she was, fantasizing about infidelity. And with Noah of all people—the man who had broken her heart, then stomped on it and threw it to the wolves. *Wow!* These hormones were no joke. Her emotions were flying all over the place, from anger to disgust and all the way to despair. She had to center herself. Her baby was squirming gently within her. She placed a loving hand over her.

"Hush, little girl! Everything is all right."

Her heartbeat slowed as she hummed softly to her tiny unborn child.

Maybe they could move. No, they couldn't. They had just put all their money toward this house. A fence was an option, although not a very good one. She was about to be a mother. She needed to be a grown-up about this. Make logical, grown-up decisions. So what if they were neighbors? It didn't mean they had to have tea parties every weekend. They could avoid each other. And what was that saying? "Keep your friends close and your enemies even closer." Living so close to those assholes gave her an excellent opportunity to observe the Smiths and find any weak points in their relationship. She would bide her time. Be a good neighbor. And when the opportunity arose, she would make her move. She would make both of them pay for the way they treated her. You bet your bottom dollar!

She came back the next day, carrying a freshly baked apple pie. She explained that she needed to throw up, and she was most embarrassed to do it in front of other people. So, she ran. They seemed to buy her story, and so the roleplay began. Millie and Alice both played their parts as friendly neighbors perfectly. Up until now.

And now, the curtains were down, and the masks were off.

She wasn't moving anywhere. There was no way she would show weakness in front of either Alice or Noah. It wasn't happening. She wasn't finished with them just yet.

CHAPTER FORTY-SIX

1997
ROSIE

Rosie wondered vaguely what year she was in. In place of her house stood this little shed-looking thing that looked like it was about as big inside as her living room. Was she getting any actual sleep during these waking dreams of hers? Probably not. She normally woke up feeling like washed shit nowadays, but after a dream like this, she always felt exceptionally worn out.

There was smoke coming from the great big river stone chimney. So, this is what it had looked like. It was pretty neat. She overheard her parents talking about it one time, how they both wanted to save the old chimney and incorporate it into the new house, but it hadn't been salvageable. She wished she could show it to her dad so he could see what it had looked like in its pride. Her dad . . . Her heart squeezed. Was there a way for her to get past this? She wished she'd never found out. She couldn't look at her life the same way. She wasn't his flesh and blood. He probably didn't know, and if he ever found out, he would abandon her. She would be the cause of her parents' divorce. Noah would move out of the house and take Emi with him. She is his actual daughter. She and Emi are only half sisters. This gave her pause. This had never occurred to her before. Her mom, Noah, and Emi made a perfect little triangle. A perfect little family. And Rosie was an outsider. A black sheep. The ruiner of everything good. Maybe she should just run away. Nobody would miss her. Especially the way she was right now.

She peeked in through the window of the small house. There were people inside. Three kids and one lady. The two smaller kids were sitting on the floor and playing with some wooden figurines. The bigger girl was sitting on a bench by the kitchen table. It was Franny. She was swinging her legs back and forth, back and forth, back and forth with perfect timing, like a pendulum. Her gaze flat, her eyes dull, she looked to be deep inside her own head.

The other girl must be Rosie's grandmother. She had been an exceptionally cute little girl with her round face and large eyes. So, this meant the small boy was Harry. The woman turned from the stove, and Rosie was shocked at how much Franny resembled her. The only difference was their hair. The woman had straight hair, and Franny's was very curly. The woman said something to the kids and left the room. In a moment, the back door swung open, and she stepped outside. Rosie froze where she was by the window. The woman walked right past her without reacting to her presence in any way and made her way over to the chicken coop. So, she couldn't see her. Neither could the man in her other dream. She turned her face back to the window just in time to see Franny lift the boiling pot of soup from the stove and hold it above the head of her brother.

"No!" Rosie screamed and banged on the glass.

It was a totally involuntary reaction. Franny stopped mid-motion and looked around until her eyes found Rosie in the window.

"Put it down and come outside!" Rosie beckoned to her, mouthing her words in an overexaggerated way to make sure she understood.

Franny took one more look at her brother, shrugged, and placed the soup back on the stove. Rosie sagged against the wall of the house with relief.

"What the fuck, Franny?" She gawked at her when she came outside.

"What?" she asked, crossing her arms.

"What do you mean, 'what'? You think it's normal to try to boil your brother alive?"

"Did you just come here to yell at me?"

"I don't know why I'm here," Rosie retorted through her teeth. "I don't have a choice. I come here in my sleep."

Franny nodded as if this was a completely normal thing to say. A gust of wind ruffled her wild curls. Rosie wondered if she was hearing the crone right now. If she was listening intently to her every word.

"Come on! I wanna show you something."

She started walking before Rosie could protest. It was a nice day for a walk in the past, but she wanted to talk rather than walk. There must be a reason she was here. She just had to figure out what it was. *"Two can play that game,"* said dear Great Aunt Francis in her head. She squeezed her eyes shut. *Go away, you ugly, old bitch!* she thought savagely. The crone cackled in response. She was having fun with them, a grand old time, making them do evil things. What if she could change the past? If she could stop Harry from disappearing, maybe poor Franny wouldn't be taken to the loony bin, and maybe, just maybe, all their futures would be better somehow.

"Do you hear her right now?" she asked Franny. "Your ghost."

"Yeah, she is chattering away. She says you're having some naughty thoughts." She gave Rosie the side-eye.

"I bet she is. Does she ever talk about Harry?"

Franny pressed her lips together and shook her head.

"Are you lying to me? You know I'm older, so you have to tell me the truth!"

"No, you ain't. My Meemaw tells me that I'm already dead in your time, so that makes me older. By a whole bunch.

She said it so matter-of-factly. *"I'm already dead . . ."*

"Doesn't that scare you? Death, I mean?"

She shrugged, looking down at where her feet were hitting

the ground.

"Not really. Everybody dies someday. My Meemaw did. But she loved me so much, she never really left."

She looked so young and so sad at that moment, Rosie wanted to hug her. She didn't, though. She was still a bit wary of touching her.

"I'm not my father's," she said suddenly, making Rosie stumble and nearly fall on her face. "We have that in common, you and I. He doesn't know. Nobody knows but my mom and my Meemaw. I wasn't supposed to know, but my Meemaw took me to see how it happened."

"In a dream," Rosie said softly, and Franny nodded, her face solemn.

"She was coming home from the market when a man attacked her. He told her to be still if she wanted to live, so she did. She had never seen him before and never saw him after. She was already married, so she wasn't sure who my true father was. Not until I grew this."

She took a handful of her curls.

"The man who took her there on the forest path had the same hair I do. She never told her husband, afraid he would turn her out or make her get rid of me. I think he knew anyway. He never loved me like the other two."

She smiled. A sad, tired smile.

"My Meemaw spoiled me. Even when she was losing her mind, she did everything she could for me."

"Wait! Franny, did you day she lost her mind?"

She nodded.

"Went as crazy as a cuckoo bird, my Pawpaw used to say, just before Meemaw stuck a knife in him. God rest his soul. They are buried together."

"Holy shit!" Rosie exclaimed for various reasons.

Franny eyed her curiously, a faint smile playing on her lips. They all had it. Franny, her Meemaw, and Rosie, too. They were all connected somehow by this thing. This ghost demon motherfucker.

This wasn't a mental illness. It was a haunting that plagued Rosie's family line. Only God knows how many more came before the three of them. She was so engrossed in her thoughts, she hadn't noticed that Franny had stopped and bumped into her.

"Watch your step!"

Franny put out an arm to stop her from tumbling forward. They were at the edge of a ravine. Some shallow water was trickling lazily at the bottom of it. A little further off, she saw a big old oak tree, the water forking around its big roots. It had sprawling, low-hanging branches and a hollow in its wide trunk that looked almost big enough to fit a person. It was like something straight out of a story book.

"I know where we are," Rosie said in awe. "I come here sometimes in my free time to look for newts. But the ravine is dry, and that big tree is dead."

Franny dipped her curly head in acknowledgement, as if she expected her to say just that.

"It dies during a big flood. About twenty years from now, give or take."

"Why did you bring me here?"

Franny's eyes remained fixed on the big old oak.

"Meemaw likes to sleep here. She likes being near the water."

A chill ran through Rosie's spine, making her small hairs stand on end. There was a something inside the hollow of the tree. The crone unfolded first one grayish leg from it, then a stick-thin arm, and, slowly, all the rest of her. Rosie took an involuntary step backward. Her foot landed on a small branch, and it broke with a loud snap that echoed across the ravine. The crone's face slowly rotated upward, and she looked straight at them.

"Franny, you know that's not really your Meemaw, right?"

Franny turned to her, feathery brows furrowed.

"Well, of course she is, silly goose."

"No, she just looks like her so you wouldn't be afraid of her."

"You're talking all sorts of nonsense today, Rosie."

Meanwhile, the crone walked across the water without actually touching it. Small droplets separated from its surface and floated gently around her feet. She was coming over to them. Rosie had this mostly irrational thought that she had to get her point across to Franny before she reached them.

"She's going to make you do something bad. I think she wants you to kill your brother."

"She doesn't want me to kill him. It's not like that. She just needs him with her in heaven."

Rosie placed both hands on Franny's small shoulders and turned her body away from the ravine.

"You don't have to do as she says! You can choose not to! You can choose to ignore her."

"We all have a part!" Franny yelled in her face with surprising furiosity. "I have to send Harry to heaven, and my sister needs to carry the family line."

"You are just a tool for her! She's using you."

"It's all for you, Rosie. Don't you understand? You are the special one!"

All of a sudden, Franny deflated, all her anger flowing out of her like a stream. Rosie felt her presence before she saw her. The crone was right behind her. She whirled around to face her, righteous anger burning her chest.

"Leave her alone!" she screamed. "She's just a g . . ."

Her shouting was cut off by the bony, long-fingered hand of the crone on her face.

She woke up with a gasp. She was standing outside in the dark chill of the night. Panting, she rolled her eyes about. Where was she? A cold wind blew through, and she realized she was wet. She looked down and saw her body was covered in some sort of dark liquid. It looked black and shiny in the moonlight. It was all over both her legs and her arms, too. It went up past her elbows and stopped just below her shoulders. There was a coppery stench in the air. She heard a grunt from the ground, took a step back, and bumped into a warm, wet body. She whirled, a scream already in her throat. It came out as a startled squeak when she realized that what she was looking at was a light-colored foal standing on unsteady, spindly legs. Sand must have given birth. This was her baby. She squatted and hugged the wobbly little creature to her. The colt welcomed her affection. It stuck its small muzzle into Rosie's ear and started to nibble on it. It was still soaking wet. Sand was supposed to clean it off, and it was supposed to suckle. Where was Sand? She then remembered the grunt from the ground. She stood up slowly, turned, and, this time, did scream.

"Everything always has a price, child," said the crone.

Rosie swatted a fly away from the still, unseeing eye of her mare. They had called the vet, but it was already too late. She had bled out. Dr. Arnolds examined her giant, blood-covered body and determined that the colt, for the new foal was a little stallion, had been too big for her to birth. She tore on the inside and had started to die even before the colt was born. If it hadn't been for Rosie, who apparently reached in and pulled the colt out, they both would have died. This was little consolation for Rosie, who would much rather have Sand live than her baby. There could have been other foals. There had been only one Sand. She cried endlessly while caressing the cooling body of her beloved pet. She wouldn't look at the colt, not even when it came to suckle from the teats of its dead mother.

Dr. Arnolds put them in contact with another family who had lost a foal but managed to save the mare just a few days ago. They agreed to lend the mare to them, given that it would accept and nurse their newborn colt.

Rosie felt nothing when they told her this. She still hadn't showered in spite of her mother's attempts to send her inside. Sand's blood was mostly dry and crusty on her now. She didn't quite remember what she had done to save the colt, for she apparently did it while sleepwalking, but she did get some flashes of memory. Her pushing against Sand's butt with one bloody hand while the other was inside her. Her hand pulling out one tiny hoof, then another. The wet splat of the colt's body hitting the ground. She saw Sand's eyes looking at her in the dark. She knew she was going to die. Rosie finally looked at the colt through her swollen red eyes. His eyes were the same color as his mother's, a strange light hazel. The same pink nostrils. He came over to her, one unsteady step at a time, and sniffed her hair. *I wish you would have died instead*, she thought, but she did pet the side of his face gently.

"What do you want to name him?" Noah asked, standing next to them. "*We may as well call him Death.*"

"His name is Soul," Rosie said and stood.

She had decided on this name for a colt months before. There was no need for her to think on it any further. She went inside to stand under the shower, ridding herself of the life force of her friend, watching it make its rusty way down the drain.

CHAPTER FORTY-SEVEN

1997
ALICE

They celebrated Emi's sixth birthday on a sunny April day. It was a great turnout. They had rented a bouncy castle, and Alice baked a giant red velvet cake with vanilla frosting. Eleven of Emi's classmates showed up with their respective parents. There was squealing aplenty. Noah had made a donkey-shaped piñata, which proved to be way too sturdy to be beaten to death by the weak hands of six-year-olds. He was such a perfectionist when it came to building things, he couldn't manage a flimsy piñata. The thought made Alice smile. It felt good to smile. Things had been tense around the house after Sand died. She watched the horde of kids bring the piñata to the ground to try and break it open by stomping on it. Moonwalk, witnessing this horror, had run to the back of the pasture and brayed angrily from the cover of some bushes. Little Soul was definitely the star of the day. The kids flocked to him and his surrogate mother, a large bay Clydesdale named Cindy, to offer treats and pets. The little colt came out a delightful cream color. He was slightly darker than her mother had been, but Alice suspected he would end up looking just like Sand by the time he was grown.

Rosie didn't seem to be recovering from the loss of her

horse. She was withdrawn and mopey 24/7. Nothing seemed to interest or excite her anymore. Even today, she hid in her room. When Alice went to check on her, she was just sitting on her bed, wrapped in a blanket, looking pale and fragile.

Alice thought Rosie may be taking more of her medication than she was supposed to. They kept running out before time. She tried to hide the bottles, but pills still went missing. She had no idea how Rosie was able to find her hiding place every time. It was as if she had cameras all over the house. At one point, she did consider that it may not be Rosie who was stealing the pills, but she did seem like she was taking a higher dosage than necessary. She was spacey and rarely paid attention to things happening around her. Alice should say something about it to Dr. Lewis, shouldn't she? But she couldn't quite prove that it was Rosie. It was still a possibility that she had the count wrong. Or that Emi was stealing the pills and hiding them somewhere. She wouldn't put it past her. Dr. Lewis did say that there was a possibility Emi would find a way to act out since her sister was receiving some special attention. When she had questioned her family, everyone denied messing with the meds. So, she needed to catch someone in the act. She would get a small camera and not tell anyone. Not even Noah. That way, if she didn't catch anything incriminating on it, at least nobody would call her paranoid. So, she did just that the day after the party.

She put it up on top of their fireplace mantel and left the pill bottles on the coffee table so they were in plain view. Then, she waited. She let some days pass before she pulled up the recorded footage on the computer. There were a lot of hours to go through, so after a bit, she hit fast-forward. She sat there, eyes glued to the screen, for some minutes before she came across something strange. The bottles seemed to move. She paused the footage and rewinded it. *There!* It happened the first night she placed the bottles on the table, around 3:20 a.m. The footage cut out, and then, when it came back on, two of the bottles had switched places. Was she seeing it right? She rewinded it again. There was the malfunction. The screen went black and grainy for twenty-eight seconds. When it came back on, the two bottles were definitely switched. She paused the footage and leaned back in her chair, arms crossed. *Some waste of money this camera was.* It cut out right at the most crucial moment. It was a pretty big coincidence. A little too big, maybe. She frowned at the pill bottles portrayed on her computer screen. She would just have to keep at it. She'd catch the culprit soon enough.

That night, she was awakened from sleep by a long *creak.* She sat up in bed to see what had made it. Her bedroom door was open. *Did Noah leave the room?* Her tired eyes couldn't see in the dark. She placed her hand on his side of the bed and felt warm, hairy flesh under her fingers. So, it hadn't been him who opened the door. Alice sighed and contemplated just laying her head down on her pillow and going back to sleep. The thought was very tempting. But leaving the door open as it was just didn't sit right with her. Grunting softly, she swung her legs off the bed and padded over to the door. She pulled it shut, then opened it again. It was moving silently. So, what made the creak? Maybe she should go check the rest of the house. No. She needed to get some sleep. If she walked the whole house, she would be fully awake by the end of it. She shut the door and turned to go back to bed. The door opened with a creak before she even reached the bed. Chills broke out on her entire body. This wasn't normal. Was she dreaming one of those super-realistic dreams? She stepped out of her room and looked left and right down the hallway. There seemed to be nothing out of the ordinary. The house was quiet. Her motherly instincts told her to check on her children, so she did. Emi was peacefully sprawled across her bed, one foot casually hanging off the edge. Alice closed her door gently and headed over to Rosie's room. Her bed was messy, her covers strewn in all directions, and void of Rosie. Alice's heart sunk into what seemed like a bottomless pit. Was she in the bathroom? Nope. Alice groaned. Why did she have to deal with this right now, in the middle of the night? Why couldn't Rosie just sleep through the night? It annoyed her. It was unfair.

No, *she* was being unfair. Her daughter couldn't help it. She'd been through a lot recently and needed her support. It was the middle of the night, and Alice was just tired and grouchy. She would find Rosie, escort her back to bed, and be done with it. She would feel much better knowing Rosie was safely tucked into her bed. She walked out into the living room. The temperature of the air dropped several degrees as soon as she stepped foot in there. Alice stopped and squinted. Ahead of her was what looked to be a person's dark silhouette. Was that Rosie? It had to be. She was probably sleepwalking. Some sleepwalking this was. She was just standing there, motionless. Something wasn't quite right. She appeared to be much taller than usual. Was it just a trick of the light? Or the lack of light? She had her back to Alice, her long hair falling straight down her back. That was definitely Rosie's hair. She could recognize it anywhere. She had such pretty hair. Alice took a few steps to the left, and Rosie's feet came into view behind the couch. They were not touching the ground. Cold fear gripped Alice's insides. She had an instant fight-or-flight response, but she couldn't explain why. What she was seeing didn't make sense, and it terrified her. *Dear God.* She wasn't hanging from the ceiling, was she? Her eyes flew up to Rosie's head just in time to see it fall from her shoulders. It bounced on the hardwood floor and rolled in a leisurely fashion toward her like a large, hairy melon. Alice bolted, a scream of primal terror stuck in her throat. She ran straight into her bedroom, shut the door as quickly and quietly as possible, and jumped into her bed, making Noah snort and shift in his sleep. She pulled the covers up and over her head. "This isn't real! This isn't real!" she chanted feverishly, curling her body into a tight ball. "I'm dreaming. It's only a nightmare." The bedroom door opened with a soft click and that long, foreboding creak. There were no footsteps, but Alice could feel an ominous presence creeping over her like an icy fog. It was here. In the room. That thing. It couldn't possibly be her daughter. Could it? No! There was no way. No way in hell. This wasn't real. She squeezed her eyes shut to the point where it was nearly painful, working desperately to shift gears inside her brain and think happy thoughts. She thought of the velvety cream coat of their new colt. The way he played with the old donkey, running from one end of the pasture to the other. Unbidden came the image of its mother lying in a pool of her own blood. Rosie standing next to her, smeared from head to toe in the same substance. Her hoarse, undulating scream that seemed to go on and on to the ends of time. It still echoed in her mind, that horrible sound of despair, her child tearing apart at the seams with grief. Alice could do nothing to fix it. No amount of hugging would heal the wound opened by what Rosie had seen. No amount of words would bring the horse back to life. Alice felt a tear escape the corner of her eye and run down across the bridge of her nose. It dropped onto her pillow next to her face. *Oh, my little Rosie, I wish I could take the hurt from you!* she thought, clasping her hands in front of her. The cool fog was suddenly lifted from her, and she saw in her mind's eye the big bay mare seeing the orphan colt for the first time. They tied her to a post and walked little Soul up to her on unsteady legs. The mare's belly was still distended from the pregnancy, her hind quarters swollen from the birth. She had lost her filly. Born too early, the doctor had said. Alice thought she could see the grief in those large, moist eyes. The mare gave the colt a deep sniff, taking in that powdery baby smell. Her teats, so incredibly full of rich milk for her offspring, released their contents in two thin, white streams. Her decision was made. She wanted this baby. The colt had nursed then, drawn in by the sweet smell of spilled milk. The mare had reached down with her huge head and licked the rump of her new baby with such tender care, Alice almost cried. When she turned to look for Rosie, she saw that she had walked off, the screen door of the house just slamming shut behind her.

CHAPTER FORTY-EIGHT

1997
ROSIE

Who is Rosie? She is a girl. An ordinary girl and a girl like no other at the same time. For the most part, she is stuck inside, to the point where she doesn't experience the outside world. It is the medication. Rosie hates it, but she also needs it to keep the demon at bay. She needs more and more of it every day. The problem is that she isn't supposed to take more than the doctor said. Her mom hides the pills. The thing is, Rosie has a way to know where they are. It is a gift from the ghost. It lets her see above and beyond. She can see the past, the present, and the future at the same time. She can see through walls and read people's innermost thoughts. She can do all this, if only she asks. The demon gives her the gift readily because there is a price. There is always a price. Not now, but there will be. She can feel it. The demon's anticipation. The more Rosie asks to use the gift, the bigger her debt becomes. And once it reaches the appropriate size, she will have to pay. She will have to do the crone's bidding. An awful thing. Rosie doesn't know what, but that's the game. The crone likes her not knowing.

They had tricked her mother. The crone feeds off of fear and despair. She told Rosie how to do it. It got her curious. Could she actually do such a thing—make her mom see something that wasn't actually happening? First, she had to get inside her head. That was easy enough. Rosie saw her thoughts. They were going round and round in a circle. Her mother was tired. She was looking for Rosie. She was also pretty annoyed. Rosie annoyed her. That wasn't really nice. It's not like this was her choice. Rosie didn't want to get out of bed every night and wake up feeling like she hadn't slept a wink. *"Time to give her a little scare!"* the crone said with relish. Rosie grabbed on to her mother's internal monologue with her long, imaginary hands and imagined what she wanted her to see. She twisted and bent them into a new shape, just like the ghost instructed. And *voila*! Her mother saw a vision of Rosie's head falling right off her skinny little neck. She had reacted immediately, fleeing into her bedroom like a fox chased by a pack of hounds. *That was mean*, Rosie thought as her body lifted higher into the air. *I didn't like that at all.* Her head reached the ceiling, and in response, her body shifted into a horizontal position.

"Let's apologize, then!" the crone instructed, and Rosie's nightgown-clad body moved forward.

She was like a long board, floating across her home just under the ceiling. Her head bumped softly against her parents' bedroom door, and it clicked open. She floated in as silently as a cloud, settling just above her mother's form under the blanket. Her eyes beamed through the blanket, and she saw her, curled up on herself as if she were a scared child. Rosie's long hair hung down toward her mother like the roots of a flower freshly pulled from the earth.

"I'm sorry, Mom. I'm so sorry I'm turning into this monster."

She peeked into her mother's thoughts and saw that she was thinking about her. She was remembering that night when she ran out into the yard to find Rosie standing next to her dying horse, covered in her blood. Alice felt an almost physical pain at not being able to make things better. *She loves me so much*, Rosie thought in awe. *Even after all this.* She loved her even when Rosie couldn't love herself.

Let's let her sleep! she told the crone.

She slinked out of the room the way she came. Her hair and nightgown fluttering toward the ground, she made her way into her bedroom.

"The night is young, child. It isn't time to rest yet!" The crone clicked her tongue disapprovingly.

Rosie rotated belly-up in a slow, leisurely fashion and lowered neatly to lie on top of her bed.

"Take me to see Franny, then!" she said, clasping her hands on top of her chest and closing her eyes.

She found herself running through a dark forest, a cold rain beating down on her scalp and back. She had no clue why she was running, but it may have something to do with the weather. She was probably looking for shelter. In her haste, she smacked straight into a tree. She gasped with the pain of the impact and held on to the offending tree as her feet were sliding alarmingly out from under her. She looked about herself, wet hair flying, to see where on earth she was. The forest had a sense of urgency about it, the canopies of the trees scraping and bumping one another with a force resembling anger. *There!* She spotted something familiar. Down in the bottom of the ravine she was standing on the lip of stood the big old oak tree with its gaping hollow. Water spilled down to join the small creek on the bottom. Now, it roared, foaming on either side of the old trunk. Lightning struck and thunder clapped, shaking the very earth beneath her feet. She cowered, leaning against the tree.

"Franny!" she screamed, trying to be louder than the rain. "Franny, it's Rosie! Where are you?"

Her answer came in the form of another bolt of lightning. It struck jagged across the dark sky, and in its light, Rosie saw a disturbance in the thick mud of the riverbank. *Footprints.* She dropped to the ground and fixed her eyes on the marks, waiting for the next shine of light. When it came, she saw what appeared to be one or two sets of small prints. They were all over the place, sliding and going on top of one another. It almost looked as if the people who left them were dancing. She followed their progress on the forest floor, moving each time lightning struck. She lost the track briefly, then picked it up again: two little bare feet and what looked to be drag marks this time. Rosie stood tall against the rain and wind and peered deliberately into the darkness. Lightning struck, and she saw where she was. The cemetery wasn't far, and she was headed straight for it.

"Son of a bitch!" she spat and took off in a slip-slide run.

The rain was cold, but the blood heating her cheeks and the working of her muscles warmed her. Roots and rocks tripped her. Branches snagged her hair. She burst through the shrubs at the edge of the clearing.

"Franny!" she screamed and saw her lonely silhouette flash alive under the sprawling oak with the next burst of light.

She ran, dodging headstones. She missed one that lay resting in the tall grass and fell headlong just before reaching the cover of the tree. She saw Franny's dirty bare feet just in front of her. Behind her lay the black hole of the hand-dug grave.

"What did you do?" Rosie gasped.

She spat dirt and blades of grass. Franny was wearing only her thin floral dress. *She must be freezing out here.* Rosie got shakily to her feet. She'd skinned both her knees. Her jeans torn, blood and mud oozed down her shins. Franny's face was a white mask of desolation, her eye sockets black holes. She looked like her own ghost.

"I . . ." she said, her voice breaking. "Rosie . . ."

A flash of lightning showed her crumpling face and, behind her, the shape of a small person in the makeshift grave. Instinctively, Rosie pulled Franny to her, hugging her tight. She felt protective toward this poor, fragile soul. Even now, even in a situation like this, she was family. Franny hugged her around the waist and sobbed into her shirt, adding her tears to the wet of the rain, her small shoulders shaking. Rosie let her cry for a few seconds, her eyes fixed on the dark hole behind her, then held her at arm's length and searched her face.

"Is that Harry?" she asked, even though she already knew.

Franny nodded.

"Is he dead?"

Franny nodded, then shook her soaked head. She buried her face in her hands. Rosie peeled them off to look her in the eyes.

"Did you do it?"

For some reason, it was imperative she know the truth. For Franny, the memory of her great aunt. For her grandmother, who loved her so. And for herself. Franny's mouth opened and closed. The light went out of her eyes, and she stared, dazed and unseeing, at Rosie. She shook her head once.

"I don't know," she said. "I don't remember."

"Focus, Francis!" Rosie shook her so her head bobbed back and forth. "It's okay if you don't remember all of it, just some parts. Concentrate!"

Franny gazed at Rosie's extended arms, her eyes going in and out of focus. She swallowed.

"I took him out of bed. Outside. Nobody heard us leave 'cause of the rain. I remember holding his hand. I remember pulling him. He was crying because he was getting wet."

She shook her head rapidly, new tears falling from her lashes and becoming one with the rain.

"He was scared," she sobbed. "Then, he was in the water. By the big tree. He can't swim."

"Did he fall in? Or did you push him?"

Franny shook her head so violently, water flew from the ends of her hair like a sprinkler.

"I don't know," she whined, her voice escalating. "I jumped in and pulled him out, but it was too late. He was . . . He was already . . ."

She sagged against Rosie, overtaken by the memory. *She must have done it*, Rosie thought. *She must have pushed him in. But she had no control. The crone made her do it. The crone did this! All of it.*

You are pure evil! she said to the old witch inside her head and heard the distant echo of her laughing, like the call of a crow.

She turned to Francis. "Then, what happened?"

"Then, I brought him here."

Rosie nodded. Her mind was racing. What would happen to Franny now? She would take the fall for this. This poor, innocent little girl. She would be shunned by everyone. Her family, the entire town.

"I have to tell Maa. Maybe she can fix it. Maybe she can wake him up."

She tried to push past Rosie, but she grabbed her skinny arms again and held her firm.

"No! Franny, you can't tell anyone where he is."

"But they'll know he's missing. They'll figure out he's dead when he never comes home."

Rosie shook her head.

"They'll never know for sure. If you just play dumb, they'll never find him."

Franny looked searchingly into her eyes. Lightning struck, and her pupils shrank to pinpoints in her big, mud-brown eyes. Rosie could see her fear as clear as day.

"They won't know it was me? Everything will be okay?"

Rosie hesitated. She knew the truth, Franny's terrible future. Her family would still suspect her of making Harry disappear. Deep in their hearts, they would know he was never coming home. A trust would be broken, never to be forged again. Franny would be sent away. But they would visit her, at least. Over the years, her family would at least remain in contact. If she told them the truth, or the fractions of it, they may abandon her altogether. She wanted to spare her that.

"Yes," she said definitively. "Everything will be as okay as can be."

Franny nodded. She turned, and they both looked at the small, hand-dug grave only big enough for a little boy. Franny took a step toward it, then another. Rosie followed, their feet squishing in the muddy grass. By morning, the rain would have washed away all remnants of digging, and Harry would remain here until the end of time.

Rosie awoke in the morning crusty-eyed and with an inside so hollow that she felt like no more than a husk, like the butterfly inside of her had flown away overnight, leaving behind nothing but the brittle shell of its chrysalis. She expected to see dirt all over her hands and under her fingernails, but there was nothing. Not yet. She hopped out of bed and exited the house as quietly as a mouse.

CHAPTER FORTY-NINE

1997
NOAH

Noah rode his big gray gelding to the traps he had set up on his property. He didn't know what he was hunting for, not exactly, only that he didn't think it was human. He borrowed some hog-sized live traps from a friend and set them up all over the area around the homestead. So far, he had only trapped raccoons and foxes and, on one occasion, Emi, who had thought being locked in a huge cage was hilarious.

What he saw might have been a mountain lion. Maybe—if one had walked through some nuclear waste dump and was now roaming around spreading radioactivity. He thought of those glowing blue eyes and shuddered. Perhaps not a mountain lion. But maybe someone's exotic pet that had escaped captivity. Like a tiger. White tigers had blue eyes. That would explain why it didn't eat the dog. It may have been raised with dogs.

He wished he could tell Alice about what had happened down in the black hole of the springhouse, about the visceral fear that had gripped him that day and every day since when he thought of it. But she had no space in her life for a new fear such as this. She needed to concentrate on Rosie and only Rosie. So, when he was unloading the traps from the back of his truck, he told her he had seen some feral hogs on the property, and that was that. He worried about her. Alice was the glue that held their little family together. He knew what was happening was one of her worst fears coming to life. She was becoming unsteady in her role as a mother, and in consequence, small but visible cracks began to show in the foundation of their household. Just this morning, he found out she had placed a camera in the living room. It didn't necessarily bother Noah. He wasn't doing anything worth catching on it. It was more the fact that she didn't think she could trust the children. And by children, she meant Rosie.

The footage she had been looking at was black and white. On it, he could see the living room table and Alice's bare legs. "I had this terrible dream," she had said. "It seemed so real." She looked tired and shaken. When questioned, she would not say exactly what the dream had been about, only that in it, she was in the living room, just like on the footage. "Looks like I've started sleepwalking, too. I had no idea it was catching," she'd said, looking equal parts defeated and relieved.

To Noah's knowledge, sleepwalking wasn't an infectious disease. Alice was probably just stressed and worn out both mentally and emotionally. They both were. They needed to get away for a bit, maybe leave the kids with the grandparents and take a short weekend trip. The idea was so appealing, he nearly let himself believe they could actually do it. In reality, this was a terrible time to leave. Rosie was spiraling. She was doing it quietly, but it was happening all the same. He had been with her since birth. He could see all the signs and changes in her behavior so clearly. And he couldn't blame her. First, Ollie, their beloved dog, died, shortly followed by Rosie's horse. They were both so important to her. She was so badly affected that she hardly looked at the new colt, as if she couldn't bear even the sight of him. Her looking and acting depressed was a totally normal response. She just had her little "issue" on top of everything. He hated referring to her daughter as someone mentally ill. Part of him still didn't believe it. Part of him hoped that one day, the problem would just magically disappear if he just treated Rosie as he did before it all started.

He stopped at the last trap of the day, just south of the old Glessner cemetery. He normally left a piece of raw chicken as bait that could be enticing to a number of carnivores in the area. He dismounted, looped the reins loosely around a strong tree branch, and went to investigate. Inside the trap lay a distinctly plump-looking possum with its mouth gaping wide open, its neat rows of sharp white teeth glinting in the afternoon sun. The little bastard ate the whole breast all by itself. It was obviously playing dead, its beady black eyes fixed on a spot far away and its scruffy little body curled around itself. Noah opened the entrance of the cage and began searching for a suitable poking stick. Once found, he prodded the possum gently, clicking his tongue.

"Come on, you little fucker! I know you ain't dead."

He received no response. This little critter was committed to being a corpse. Noah sighed, eyeing the inert marsupial with his hands on his knees. He could just leave the trap open and let the possum find its way out on its own time. But then, he wouldn't be able to reset the trap. Maybe he should just give up on this wild goose chase. Whatever he saw in the springhouse must be out of the area by now.

His horse suddenly lifted its head, a green, leafy branch sticking casually out of the corner of his mouth. His ears pricked, he listened.

"What is it, Pilot? Friend or foe?"

Noah surveyed the woods around them. He heard the snap of a twig. The rustling of a bush. Whatever it was, it was coming toward them. Instinctively, he stepped closer to his mount. He should probably get on, right? He was just being paranoid. It was most likely an armadillo rooting around for food. Nothing more. The bushes in front of him parted, and from their depths emerged the graceful form of Millie Walker. Noah exhaled audibly. It was just his neighbor. No threat. He had to stop hunting for this thing. It was messing with his head.

"You gave me a fright," he said with only a touch of irritation.

He was aware of the disturbance between his wife and Millie. Alice had been vague on the details, but she did say she and Millie had a falling out. When Noah pressed her, she just shook her head and said it wasn't even worth talking about. He suspected it had something to do with Rosie. Everything did these days. Mina and Rosie no longer seemed to be friends. The conflict was most likely over that. Noah's philosophy was to stay out of Alice's affairs until she requested his assistance. This stance formed over the long years of their marriage. Alice was normally capable of handling most things, and if Noah tried to help, he usually just got in the way. As far as the two women went, their relationship never truly recovered from what happened all those years ago. It was all Noah's fault. He should have never dated Millie. He knew from the start that if Alice only whistled, he would go to her. Millie did give him an ultimatum when he had been in a weak state: Either date her or lose her altogether. He should have stuck to his guns and told her he couldn't, that it felt wrong to start something new when he was still hung up on Alice. But he had been afraid. He was scared of being left completely alone. If Alice never returned and he lost Millie, too, he would have had nobody. And still, it was the wrong decision to make.

"Should I be afraid of whatever these are for?" Millie asked, nudging the cage with her foot.

"Probably."

Noah tossed the poking stick he just realized he was still holding and went to untie his horse.

"There is some kind of predator out here. You probably shouldn't be walking around by yourself." He approached her, the hulking horse trudging behind him. "Come on. I'll walk you back to your house!"

Millie didn't move. Instead, she gazed at him with this darkly intimidating expression. The woman made him uncomfortable. He realized this early on, shortly after they found out they were neighbors. At that time, he chalked it up to the fact that they had history, and he wanted to avoid acting inappropriately around her even by accident. He preferred to stay as far away from her as possible for Alice's sake. That way, there would be no jealousy or doubt poking their ugly heads up. But different cards were dealt, and he had to resign himself to awkwardly polite conversation.

"Why are you always so damn nice?"

She sounded almost angry. Noah was taken aback. Wasn't being nice the neighborly thing to do? Besides, he was inherently a pleasant person. He got that from his mother, who had always been like a ray of sunshine. Before the drinking started, that is.

"What do you mean?" He put up his hands, the ends of the reins dangling from one of them. "Never mind! I just wanted to warn you. You are free to walk back home alone or stay. You and your family are always welcome on my land."

He had no time or mental capacity for small talk or arguing right now. He just wanted to check the traps real quick and then get back to his family. Besides, if Alice and Millie were at odds, he didn't want to be secretly talking to her in the woods. That just looked bad. He turned to leave in the direction he came from.

"You mean Alice's land!" she called after him.

"What?"

"Well, the land was technically hers before you guys married. The legendary Glessner family land."

"Okay. That's true. Why are you bringing it up?"

He turned to her with what he knew was an incredulous expression on his face. If he didn't know any better, he would have thought she was trying to pick a fight with him.

"No reason." She walked up to him with those slow, measured steps of hers. "You still haven't answered my question."

Noah leaned slightly back, adding distance between them without actually moving.

"I'm sorry. Which was?"

"Why are you always so damn nice to me?"

Her words were measured and well-articulated. There was

no chance of him missing any of them. Exasperated, he fisted his hand with the reins in it against his hip and looked down at his boots. This was not a conversation he wanted to have. It could potentially go places he didn't want to go. He ran his tongue over his teeth. *Fine.*

"I care about you, obviously. We used to be friends. Now, we are neighbors. I am only acting accordingly."

"We used to be more than friends."

Noah looked skyward. Anywhere else but at her. Why on earth was she bringing that up now? He had thought the past safely buried. They had never talked about it. Any of it. It was meaningless to bring it up. It made no sense. Unless . . . Unless the beef Alice and Millie had wasn't about Rosie after all.

"What is this about? You didn't come out here just to walk around. You were looking for me, weren't you?"

"It's about the truth."

Millie pursed her lips in that peculiar way of hers that was almost flirtatious. *Oh, God!* Noah had a bad feeling about this. If Millie was about to confess some tender feelings to him, he didn't want to hear it.

"Listen," he said almost pleadingly. "I don't know what happened between you and Alice, but she and I are happily married. So, I don't need this." He gestured at the air between them. "So, can we go back to being good neighbors?"

"I am a good neighbor," Millie said, stepping up uncomfortably close to him. "And I care about you, too. As a friend. Nothing more."

Noah deflated with relief. He took a step back, with the pretense of wanting to pet Pilot's shoulder.

"Well, good," he said, looking at his horse rather than her. "Sorry if I misunderstood anything."

Millie smiled at him, but there was something wrong about it. It didn't reach her eyes.

"As a good neighbor and a friend, I thought I should tell you that you are being lied to. It's only the right thing to do."

"Okay . . . By who?"

"Alice."

The bottom of Noah's stomach dropped out. *Lie? Alice?* Those two didn't even belong in the same sentence. He trusted her completely. There was no lying between them. However, Alice had been acting oddly. She looked stressed and tired, and in consequence, she was a bit more irritable than usual. But that was all because of Rosie. This was just a thing they were all going through. The entire family was involved. She wasn't unhappy. She wouldn't go out and do something stupid like cheat on him. No. Way. She wasn't like that. Them two were solid. But still, the moment the thought of her cheating occurred to him, his chest squeezed painfully, and cold sweat appeared on his temples. Millie would relish telling him something like that. He knew she would. She still harbored that old hurt within her. He could see it in her eyes. He could also see how much it pleased her to be the bearer of bad news to him. He swallowed dryly. His first instinct was to protect his wife. To tell Millie off and not even hear what she had to say. But his curiosity and the ever-so-slight amount of doubt he had within him won.

"What is she lying about?"

For a moment, Millie gazed into his eyes. In hers, he could see a touch of the longing she used to have for him. Those dark, dark eyes. They possessed a foreign beauty that used to bewitch him, if only briefly. She leaned close, as if to whisper in his ear, and brought the knife down.

"Rosie is not yours. Alice was already pregnant when she came back from Houston."

She took a step back, no doubt to be able to see the entire effect her words brought. For a moment, Noah felt nothing. His body hummed with an eerie stillness, such that came before any disaster. Then, red-hot rage exploded within the confines of his skull. He staggered back and bumped into his horse's chest.

"I'm sorry, Noah!" Millie said, reaching for him with one of her slim, delicate hands.

"No, you're not! You're a fucking bitch is what you are!"

The look of utter hatred he gave her made her pull her hand back and hold it against her chest. He turned and quickly got on his mount. The horse snorted under his weight and, feeling his energy, danced, ready to take flight.

"Stay away from my family! You hear me? I will tell your husband what a nosy bitch you are. How about that? He and I can have a nice chat about it just like this."

Millie's eyes were as round as saucers, and her plump lips opened and closed so she looked almost exactly like a fish out of water. Noah turned his horse homeward, then, over his shoulder, he said,

"Oh! And Millie, I hope whatever is out here eats you!"

And then, he was off. He pricked the sides of his horse with his heels, and the big animal bolted. Around him, he could see the blur of vegetation and hear the crack and snap of small branches. Beyond all these earthly things hovered a vision of young Alice, broken and bruised, sitting on her bed, waiting for judgment.

CHAPTER FIFTY

1982
ALICE

They came inside from the impending storm. Under the soft yellow light of her bedroom lamp, Alice turned her radio low and sat down on her bed, inviting Noah to do the same. He shut the bedroom door behind him and froze mid-step to the bed as he saw all the pills on the floor. He couldn't have known what she was about to do before she saw him standing there on the driveway. Could he? He was staring at the cluster of small white tablets like he knew exactly what they were and why they were on the floor. Alice had all but forgotten about them in her relief that he was here. They were like the many pieces of her shattered life. She forgot her situation and the fact that she was thinking about killing herself and her unborn baby just mere minutes ago. Now, it all came rushing back, and fresh tears welled in her eyes.

"What are those?" Noah asked, his voice trembling slightly.

She buried her face in her hands and sobbed, unable to put into words the devastation that was her life. All of a sudden, she wished he hadn't come so she could have finished the job and been done with all this. The task ahead of her was too daunting, and she was too tired and scared to complete it. To become a single mother to the child of a monster. Okay, she was going overboard. The baby would be totally normal. Innocent. But Alice would become a washed-out, tired mother to a fatherless child. Nobody would want her. Especially not Noah. He had the lovely Millie now. She would give him beautiful, exotic-looking children. And Alice would get to watch them from the outside while she cursed herself for her own stupidity. He came to her. Sitting right next to her, he wrapped both arms around her shaking shoulders and pulled her in tight.

"What happened to you? Can you please tell me?"

She shook her head, doing her best to fight back the tears. She breathed in deeply. Her split lip hurt. Her whole face hurt. She remembered the hollow *ding* of the bathtub as she collided with it. It echoed in her brain. She saw again Nate's angry, drunken face. Felt the same terror she felt knowing he was coming back. For her. To finish her off.

"You are still my best friend, Alice. Am I not yours?"

Noah loosened his arms so she could lean back and look at him. Ashamed of how her face looked, she slowly met his eyes and was struck by how handsome he was. Was it possible that he had gotten even more attractive while she was away? The injustice of it was heartbreaking. There was stubble on his cheeks, his hair messy from the storm that still roared outside. Alice was suddenly overcome by a totally inappropriate want for him. She lowered her gaze to hide her internal turmoil.

"Of course you are," she whispered, her voice sounding strangely husky.

"Then, tell me! Let me help you!"

She wanted to. Oh, how nice it would be to share her burden, to spill her guts and be free of this secret. But shame burned her insides and sealed her mouth shut. She had chosen to go to bed with a man who didn't care about her at all, who irresponsibly knocked her up and cheated on her. He hurt her. She could have died. He could have killed her. Her death would have been an accident— but an accident brought on by his carelessness and violence. Noah's eyes roamed her face. He was looking at her bruises. With gentle fingers, he stroked the tender places: her nose, under her eyes, and, finally, her lips. Then, he took her face in both hands and bent his head to press a soft kiss to her mouth. His lips seemed to sear hers in the best possible way. Desperately hungry for more, she leaned into him, her mouth opening, inviting him in. Gone was the constant pain, burned away by his touch. His arms came around her waist, and hers settled behind his neck as the memory of what they had done on this very bed came alive and gave way to new possibilities. She wanted him more than anything she had ever wanted in her life. Sleeping with him would make her forget and make her feel alive. An idea, a solution to all her problems, came forth from somewhere in the deepest, darkest crevices of her mind, somewhere in the fog of lust. *Sleep with Noah, and tell him the baby is his.* She wasn't far along. Noah wouldn't question her. He would be delirious with joy. Her mother might have doubts. She could see through Alice most of the time as if she were a piece of glass. But she wouldn't say anything. She would just be happy for her. And that's what Alice could be. Happy. She just had to tell this one lie. By this time, Noah had her on her back and was exploring her breasts with one huge, calloused hand under her shirt. She was unknowingly unbuttoning his jeans, her fingers working on their own accord. She could do it. They stopped kissing, and their eyes met, their rugged breaths mingling between them. To Alice, Noah just about looked like a god. A shiny beacon. The perfect man. She loved him. She had always loved him. One of her hands let go of the waistband of his jeans to travel to his face. She stroked his cheek, feeling the rasp of his fledgling beard on her palm and fingertips. She couldn't do it. She couldn't do this to him. He deserved better than to live a life perched atop such a lie. He deserved better than her. She began to sit up, and he followed suit.

"Sorry," Noah said, his voice still thick with his want for her. "You have a lot going on. I didn't mean to . . ."

"It's okay."

She tasted coppery blood and knew she must have opened the gash on her mouth in her frenzy. She grabbed one of his hands for support and proceeded to stare out her bedroom window. The trees were being whipped by the wind and beaten by the rain, but to her, it almost looked like they were dancing.

"When you and Millie saw me today in front of the bookstore . . . I was there looking at baby books."

She swallowed and chanced a quick glance at his face. He looked completely blank, a small smear of red just above his lips. Her blood.

"I am pregnant."

The words seemed to hang in the air in front of her, slowly turning like a dead body hanging from a tree.

"How . . . How far along are you?"

His voice was hesitant and so full of hope, it broke her heart. She did sleep with him just before she left. She shook her head.

"It's not yours. But I wish it was."

She didn't know why she said that last part. It just came out, like her tears. She squeezed her eyes shut, trying to hold them back.

"So, it's your boyfriend's?"

She shook her head. Not in negation but in shame.

"No? It's not his?"

His brows drawn together, he was looking all sorts of confused.

"No. I-I mean yes," she sputtered. "It's h-his, I just haven't told him. He doesn't know I'm pregnant."

Her face was burning scarlet. She couldn't believe she was actually talking to Noah about this.

"Why?"

Alice sighed. She started, but her voice shook so hard that she had to stop and collect herself.

"B-because when I tried to tell him, this happened." She gestured to her battered face and let her hand drop back into her lap. "I don't know if he meant to do this, but the end result is the same."

Noah was as still as if he'd been carved out of stone. Then, suddenly, he came alive. He jumped to his feet and started for the door.

"I'm gonna kill him!"

Alice ran after him and caught him by one arm.

"No! Stop! Wait! He can't find out! I don't want him to know!"

Noah did stop, but he didn't turn back. Alice could see his jaw working under his skin. Suddenly, he whipped his head around to face her.

"I can still beat his ass and not tell him why. Where does he live?"

She could see the crazed lust for violence inside his widened pupils. A gift from his father, no doubt. A strange sound, somewhere between a laugh and a sob, erupted from inside her. She pulled Noah to her and squeezed him hard around the middle.

"Thank you," she said into his chest. "But I came back so I could cut ties with him completely. I am never going back, and neither are you!"

"So, you don't want him to know? Ever?" he said after a long pause of silence.

His arms were around her by now, and she shrugged within their confines. There were so many reasons why she would never tell him, but the number one reason was the baby itself.

"No. If he could do this to me, I don't want him anywhere near my baby."

"My baby." It was the first time she had said it out loud. She was going to have a baby, and she was going to do it all alone. *"What a disgrace!"* the tiny voice inside her head said. *"People will talk. They will spew their venom and make your life miserable."*

Let them! Alice answered defiantly. *I will turn my back and hold my head high.*

Her lip trembled.

"Oh, fuck . . ." she mumbled and pulled back.

She wiped her eyes with the heels of her hands. She could do this. She would do this, damn it!

Noah was looking out her window, seemingly captivated by the dance of the trees.

"So, nobody knows you're pregnant?" he said musingly.

"Nope," Alice said, wrapping her arms around herself. "I haven't told my parents yet. As far as they know, I came back because I was attacked on campus. If the baby stuck . . . I was planning on telling them it was rape."

There was another beat of heavy silence in the small room, in which they could hear the wind howling outside and the rain beating the side of the house angrily. Somewhere in the background, the muted sound of "The Chain" by Fleetwood Mac played on repeat.

"Don't tell them that!" Noah said softly.

"I have to tell them something. And it won't be the truth . . . You can count on that."

"Then . . . tell them it's mine."

Lightning struck, illuminating half of him in stark white light as he turned to face her fully. Alice's lips parted. New tears pricked the back of her eyes. She shook her head violently.

"No! I can't let you do that for me. It's too much."

"You have done so much more for me in my life than this. Let me repay you!"

"No!" Alice cried, pushing away from him.

"Yes, Alice!" He grabbed her by both arms. "I love you! I always have and always will. And this baby . . ." He put a hand to her stomach. "This baby is a part of you, which means I'll love it, too. I'll love you both if you'll just let me!"

Alice's whole body was shaking. Whether with fear or relief, she wasn't sure. The world was melting around her, the details fading into each other. The only clear thing was Noah right in front of her. His earnest face. His broad, heaving chest. He would. She knew. He would love them both. All she had to do was let go of the reins of her life and give them to him. Let him take her pain, her burden, her worries onto his strong, capable shoulders.

"I love you, too," she sobbed, and the fresh tears spilled over.

He pulled her into him and held the back of her head against him as if she were a small child.

"I know," he whispered into her hair. "Now, can you please stop fighting it and be with me?"

"Okay." She nodded against him. "Yes."

They slept in her bed that night tangled in each other, his big body like a wall between her and reality. In the morning, they walked hand in hand out into the kitchen, where Alice's parents were eating breakfast and reading the paper. They were still wearing yesterday's crumpled clothes, but Noah wore the expression of a man who had just won the lottery. Alice's hair looked like she had just walked through a hurricane from the countless times they made love throughout the night. That, coupled with the bruises she already had and her freshly split lip, made her look like the worst kind of bum you didn't want to meet in a dark alleyway.

"Alice!" her mother exclaimed in wide-eyed shock. "Noah! Dear, I didn't know you were . . . you . . . were here," she finished lamely.

Her father lowered the newspaper, a piece of toast carelessly dangling from his mouth. He removed it.

"What's cooking, kids?" he asked as if this were a normal, everyday occurrence.

"We," Noah gestured between them, "are getting married."

Alice's mother screamed. She jumped up with confused joy and came to hug them both around the neck. Her father folded the paper and slapped it over his knee.

"It's about damn time!" he said and got up somewhat more slowly—he had bad knees—to hug them in congratulations.

Alice and Noah looked at each other over the graying heads of her parents. Noah glowed with happiness. His shine melted away any last doubts Alice had about their situation, and she grinned back at him, squeezing his hand tight.

They married three weeks later. The location was a surprise to Noah. Alice's dad had walked him out, blindfolded, to the cliff above the Red River, where Alice, her mother, and the priest were waiting. The view was stunning from up there, Alice knew, but once the blindfold was removed, Noah only had eyes for her. She wore her mom's old wedding dress, altered slightly to fit her taller frame. It surprised even her how pretty she looked. For what seemed like the first time in her life, she was full of hope, her worries lost far behind her.

After the ceremony, her parents walked the priest back to his car, and the new couple took a stroll in the forest.

"So, why this place?" Noah asked, lifting her hand to his lips. "You still haven't told me why you chose to get married here. Was it the view?"

He winked, and she chuckled. He hadn't taken his eyes off her the entire ceremony. She doubted he saw anything of the view. She nudged his shoulder.

"It was part of it. I chose this place because it's our new beginning."

"What do you mean?"

Alice stopped and gazed ahead of them. Noah followed her line of sight to the small, shack-like house that sat in a picturesque little clearing ahead of them.

"This land belonged to my grandparents. They left it to me. So, now, it's ours."

"Holy shit!" Noah said a little breathlessly. "Did I just marry into money?"

Alice laughed, and he noted with satisfaction that her joyful giggle was back. She seemed to only laugh like this with him.

"No. Not quite. The house actually needs a lot of work to make it livable. I was actually wanting to use you for slave labor."

She hooted with surprise as he lifted her into his arms to carry her over the threshold of the shack. It had no door, so that was one less obstacle.

"You have my services. But it will be a labor of love."

And he stepped inside, trailing her veil behind them.

CHAPTER FIFTY-ONE

1997
MILLIE

She paced her living room like a caged animal. She had made a fatal error. The problem was that she couldn't quite place her finger on where. There may have been multiple places, really. Noah's reaction was quite unexpected and undecipherable. In all the scenarios she had played out in her head, he was either sad and shocked or pretty much indifferent. Never angry. His rage surprised her. In the history of their relationship, she had never seen such animosity in his eyes. It seemed like she had touched a nerve. Not only that, but she still was no closer to the answer. Did he know, or didn't he? Was his rage toward Alice, and was what Millie had witnessed simply an example of "Don't kill the messenger"? Or did he already know and was just angry that the secret was out?

He had called her a bitch. Such an ugly word to describe a woman. The information given to him was shocking, so Millie could forgive that. What he had said about telling James about her nosiness was the most troubling part. Millie's husband explicitly told her not to interfere with the Smiths' business. But she did just that. Such open defiance cannot be good for her marriage. James wouldn't leave her over it, but she would be in the doghouse. She was chewing on the thumbnail. It was a gross habit that she seemed to be doing more and more these days. She was ruining her manicure. It had to stop. How could she have miscalculated so immensely? The only thing worse than James finding out what she had done was him finding out from someone else. In that case, there was no way for her to bend the situation into a more pleasing light. She had to come clean. Today.

She made burgers and fries and sent the children away to friends' houses. Maybe she should put some beer on the table. She usually didn't do that. Would it look suspicious? She heard the front door rattle and creak. She was out of time.

James walked in with both his uniform and his face rumpled from a long day's work. He did look quite haggard. For a second, cold fear spread through Millie's body from head to toe. Was she too late? Did Noah already tell James what she had done? He could have gone to him at work. When James looked at her, he smiled his tired, grateful-to-see-you smile. So, no. She wasn't too late.

"What's this?" he asked, looking over the spread on the table.

"I sent the kids away. I figured we'd have ourselves a little date." She smiled at him conspiratorially and a little suggestively. "Just my idea of fun."

He hugged her from behind as she was putting out plates and kissed her neck. His mustache tickled her skin, sending waves of expectant pleasure through her body. For a second, she forgot all about her mission and allowed herself the thought of taking him to bed before dinner. Maybe she should. There was no possibility of them having sex after she said out loud what she had to. As soon as she thought about Noah's angry face, the toe-curling pleasure was gone, replaced by cold fear. She turned and placed a gentle hand on his chest.

"Wash up, and let's eat! The meat will get cold."

She allowed him to finish his meal before broaching the subject. She also brought him a beer and watched him take two big gulps before letting out a huge sigh and folding her hands on the table. Her cuticles looked like shit.

"What's wrong?" James asked, placing his glass on the table. "You hardly touched your food."

"I have something to tell you, and I'm afraid you're not going to like it."

James looked thoughtfully down into his lap.

"I was afraid this surprise dinner had to do with something unpleasant. In fact, I would have bet money on it." He met her eyes. His expression was one of disappointment. "All right, tell me! Rip the Band-Aid off!

Millie leaned back in her chair. She wished he didn't know her so well. Now, she felt like all her efforts for a pleasant evening were in vain. If he knew from the beginning that she was planning something, why not just say so? Why let her put on this whole dog and pony show?

"Remember the talk we had about the older Smith girl? How Noah isn't her actual father?"

"Yes . . ." He drew out the word. "I remember going to that nice burger joint. I should have guessed this had something to do with that the moment I saw you made burgers." He shook his head, looking like he was smelling something distasteful. "I also remember telling you to stay out of their business!"

"Well, I didn't."

James threw up his hands.

"Of course you didn't, for why would you listen to your husband when he tells you something? What did you do?"

"I told him. I told Noah."

James looked as if he was going to be sick. His face went pale, then bright red under his mustache. He opened his mouth to speak, then thought better of it.

"I'm sorry, James, but he has a right to know."

"You are right," he said, so quietly she almost didn't hear it.

"What did you say?"

She hardly believed what she'd just heard. It was looking like she was making a habit out of misjudging situations.

"I said a man has a right to know if he is being dicked around." There was hurt in his eyes and a boiling anger in his voice. "The thing is, you shouldn't have been the one to tell him. You know who should have told him? His wife! Are you his wife, Millie?"

"No," she whispered, her face flaming.

He was chiding her as if she was one of the children.

"No! You're not his wife. You're *my* wife! So, how do you think it makes me feel when I see you so hung up on another man?"

"I'm not hung up . . ."

"Why can't you leave the damn bastard be? Why, Millie? Haven't I given you enough? Enough love? Enough comfort? Beautiful, healthy children? Hell, I actually feel really bad for Noah right about now, no matter how he did you wrong in the past."

"You don't understand!" Millie hissed, her pot ready to boil over.

"You're right. I don't. Their daughter is sick. Their family is near falling apart because of it. Why tell him now? Why tell him at all? Isn't this enough? Just think about it, Millie! What if it was Mina? Wouldn't that be enough heartache?"

To her immense surprise, Millie felt tears on her cheeks. She had no idea when they started. Suddenly, she just felt one drop on top of the back of her hand.

"You don't understand," she said again, wiping her face with a napkin.

"Then, make me!"

James leaned in, only his fingertips resting on the tabletop.

"I want him to feel as cheated as I did!"

"Okay, and then what?"

"Then, he would know!"

"Know what?"

"That he made the wrong choice!"

She looked him in the face, feeling like the shame would split her own in two. It was an awful thing to say. James was right. All he had ever done was give to her. Always loving, always patient. And here she was, unable to let go of the past. She disgusted herself.

"Do you love me, Millie?" James asked her, sounding damn near close to tears himself.

His eyes remained dry, though. He was a real man who stayed strong even in the face of devastation. His anger had gone. As suddenly as it appeared, it was gone, leaving him looking tired and sad.

"Of course I do. You know I do."

He shook his head once. "Do you love our children?"

She nodded. "Yes."

"Then, stop! I will have no more of this."

He pushed away from the table and, without another word, left the room.

Later, sometime late that night, Millie lay in their bed, James's side cold and empty beside her. Her mind would not, could not, turn off. James had gone out. He came back some time ago. She heard the telltale creak of their front door. He really needed to oil that thing. It had been a couple of hours since the creak of the front door, and still, he did not come to her. Maybe she misjudged this, too. Maybe her rash decisions would ruin their marriage after all. She didn't want Noah. She just wanted to hurt him. Him and Alice both. But that's not how this was coming off. She could see it now from James's point of view. And it could be that a small, very small part of her did want Noah. She hated to even think of it, but it was true. Hate and revenge weren't the only players in her game. But she would never in a million years give up James to achieve her goals. He came first. Her knight in shining armor. She just lost sight of that somewhere along the way. She had to fix this somehow. Whenever James was ready to speak to her again, she would do whatever he wanted. Give him anything. She was just about to doze off when he came into the room. She sat up, relief flooding her.

"Jim!" she exclaimed.

He placed a finger in front of his mouth and crawled into bed with her, smelling of beer and the day's sweat. She didn't care. He was here. That's all that mattered. He took her—fast and hard at first, but eventually, he slowed, settling into their usual rhythm. He would forgive her. In fact, he already started. He loved her too much to stay mad, and Millie gave thanks for that. Afterward, they lay together, her head on his chest.

"Did he know?" he asked out of the blue. "Before you told him, did he already know about Rosie?"

Millie shifted and placed a hand on his chest. She curled his wiry hair around one finger.

"I don't know. He didn't say. He just stormed off."

James was quiet. Millie could hear the slow, steady beat of his heart within his ribcage.

"I'm going to transfer to Dallas in a few months. I confirmed it today."

Millie sat up to look at him.

"So, we're going to move?"

"Yes. It's for the best."

His eyes were closed. He was pretending to fall asleep. There it was: her punishment. And she had no room to fight it. Not if she wanted to keep him. After a minute, Millie lay her head back down onto his chest, but her eyes remained open for a long time.

PART 5

CHAPTER FIFTY-TWO

1998
ROSIE

She was looking out the window of the school bus on one of the coldest January mornings she could remember. Fog covered the glass from all the warm bodies packed inside. Rosie drew on the glass, sitting alone. She always sat alone now. The others were too afraid to catch her crazy to even come near her. She should have been the loneliest fifteen-year-old in her school, but she actually always had company. Even now, the crone sat in the seat next to her, wearing her late great aunt's face. She pressed a bony hand to the glass. When she took it away, instead of a handprint, the word "Harry" was left sketched into the moisture. Or did Rosie write that there? There was no real way to tell. Sometimes, it was hard to know where she ended and where the crone began. She had moved in and was here to stay.

Today must have been a special day, for Mina came to sit beside her. The form of the crone burst and scattered like sand in water as she hopped down onto the vinyl seat.

"Hey," Mina said in a whisper.

Rosie didn't look at her. She was way too busy drawing on the glass. Mina peeked over her shoulder to see her artwork. She was getting way too close. Concentrating her energy to the tip of her shoulder, Rosie zapped her. Just a little.

"Ouch!" Mina leaned slightly back, rubbing at her chin where the strike landed. "There is so much static in the air today."

Rosie snickered. She had learned to do this just recently. It seemed to her that the more in tune she got with the crone, the more of her "powers" she got access to.

"What's that?" Mina asked, pointing to her drawing.

"It's bones."

"Oh . . ."

Rosie saw a thick packing of dirt under her fingernails, although she knew it wasn't actually there. She had scrubbed her hands clean after digging that day.

Now, she heard the early morning birdsong of late summer. Felt the dew on her legs from the tall grass. She was standing there again. In front of the hole she just dug. Her filthy hands hanging by her sides. Her nightgown smeared with all that nature had to offer.

"So, why did you dig a hole?" Dr. Lewis asked.

"What?"

Rosie looked up at him, only slightly confused.

"You started telling me how one morning, you snuck out of the house before school to dig a hole. Why did you do that?"

That's right. She wasn't actually on the school bus. She was at the shrink's office. Time and space seemed to bend around her these days. That conversation with Mina had already happened. Or was it going to happen still?

"I wanted to know. I needed proof."

"I have to tell you something," Mina said.

The word "Harry" had already bled away into unrecognition. Only the bones remained. Rosie looked at her friend in her shiny maroon coat. She liked that coat. If she concentrated on it hard enough, would it burst into flames? She imagined it doing just that. In front of her mind's eye, Mina and her shiny coat began to burn. Her hair caught on fire and her skin, too. Yet, she still kept on talking. Rosie reached out to grab the fabric. It was cool to the touch. *"You're not quite there yet,"* said the crone.

"Nice coat," Rosie said, rolling the fabric of the sleeve between her fingers.

"Thanks . . ." Mina said uncertainly. "Anyways, what I was saying . . . Rosie, are you listening?"

"I suppose I am."

They locked eyes, and for a moment, she saw Mina as a little girl. Life was so simple back then. So stupid.

"Listen, I know I have been a shitty friend to you. I should have been more . . . sensitive. I should have been there for you."

"It's okay. I needed the space."

"Proof of what?"

Dr. Lewis leaned forward in his seat, looking intrigued. This was a bit annoying. Rosie felt almost like the three of them were in the same place, which meant there were two entirely different conversations that she needed to follow. She was still sitting on the bus seat, but now, she was in Dr. Lewis's office. *Can we pick a time and place? This is a bit hard to follow,* she asked the crone in her mind. In the dark corner of her brain, she saw the mouth of the crone pull into a wide grin, her crooked teeth gleaming like spears. *"Sure thing!"*

A drop of morning dew landed straight on the crown of her head, making her shudder. Above her, a blue jay shrieked and took flight, releasing more droplets of water from a thin branch of the tree. They landed scattered around her. The hole in front of her gaped only a couple of feet deep.

"I needed to know whether what I was seeing was real or a figment of my imagination," she said to Dr. Lewis, who was standing under the oak with her.

"And?"

Now, she saw, barely covered with dirt, the curve of a small skull, some scattered ribs, and the side of an off-white hipbone. She looked down at her hands, covered in scrapes and fresh mud.

"It was all true. All real. All of it."

"We're moving," Mina said, and to Rosie's surprise, she

grabbed one of her hands.

Her hands were so soft and warm. Rosie thought about zapping her again. That would teach her a lesson about just touching her without being invited to.

"Not now. In a few months. My parents told me yesterday. We're moving to Dallas. Can you believe that?"

Back when they still hung out, they often talked about moving to a big city when they grew up. Dallas was their number one choice because it was the closest option. They fantasized about moving into an apartment together and getting a small, barky dog that they would both take care of. In this fantasy, they would also have equally handsome boyfriends, possibly twin brothers. That way, if they married, they would become part of the same family. *Wouldn't that just hit Mina's mother right in the gullet?* Rosie thought, amused.

"I'm happy for you," Rosie lied.

"Thanks."

Mina smiled, looking relieved and pleased with her answer.

"It's kind of scary, to tell you the truth. I always thought that when I moved to Dallas, you would be right there with me."

"Things don't always work out the way we want them to."

"Yeah . . ."

Sensing her distance, Mina released her hand.

"I know I haven't been there for you like I should have. But I wanted to say . . . I was hoping we could be friends again. And then, you could come visit me in Dallas when you were feeling better."

She was afraid of being alone, of being the new girl at some strange school in some strange neighborhood. Rosie could tell her that she need not be afraid. She had seen her future filled with many new friends and excitement. She would fall in love over and over again, and she and her new best friend, Tanya, would end up dating a set of tall, handsome cousins when they were eighteen. She would still think of Rosie—with pity. Rosie could have told her all of this to reassure her, but sticky, green envy flooded her insides, resulting in an ugly frown on her face. So, instead, she just said:

"Sorry, but I won't be available to be your friend anymore."

And she turned back to the window.

"We have to talk about your medication intake," Dr. Lewis said, a bit more sternly than Rosie would have liked.

"What about it? I'm a good girl. I take my meds. Right. On. Time."

"You are taking more than necessary."

"Who told you that? My mother? She's a little snitch, isn't she? Kind of a bitch, too. Did I tell you she's been lying to me my entire life? I guess I can't blame her. My real dad is kind of a dick."

"Rosie, I will ask you kindly to stop deflecting and concentrate on the problem at hand. Why are you taking more pills than prescribed? A higher dosage can result in health problems. It's dangerous."

"Yeah, yeah. You know what's dangerous, Doc?"

"Rosie . . ."

"Releasing the demon that's inside me."

"You know there isn't an actual demon inside you. You just use the word 'demon' or 'crone' to describe your illness. But a separate entity does not exist within you."

"You know what your problem is, Doc?" Rosie leaned forward, an eager grin on her face. "You are small-minded. You can't see the big picture."

"Which is?"

He was pinching the skin between his eyes with two fingers. He had lost amusement for Rosie's antics long ago, which meant he was a terrible bore.

"I take the meds to keep this thing inside me from getting out. It's getting harder and harder because the sadder I get—and I have to tell you the truth: I'm pretty fucking sad nowadays—the stronger she gets. So, I need more meds."

"Like I told you, taking a higher dosage is hazardous to your health."

"You still don't get it! She is banging on the cage like some crazed ape, and I can't control what happens if she gets out!"

Rosie was shouting as she imitated a monkey banging on some imaginary cage. The doctor shook his head slightly as he scribbled something onto his notepad.

"Great!" Rosie exclaimed, throwing up her hands. "You're not even fucking listening to me. This is serious stuff."

"I'm going to switch you to a different medication starting next week."

"No!"

"We'll start you off with a low dosage and work our way up depending on any side effects."

"But these meds are working! I just need more!"

"You will also have to go to the pharmacy twice daily for the time being to receive accurate dosage since your parents can't seem to be able to keep you out of the bottles at home."

Rosie balled her hands into fists and spoke through her teeth.

"Somebody is going to end up getting hurt!"

"As long as we manage to keep you safe, Rosie, that's all that matters."

He crossed his legs and gave her a professional little smile. The bastard actually thought he had just won some sort of a game. The poor sap had no idea this decision would haunt him for the rest of his life, affecting every professional decision he would make during his career.

CHAPTER FIFTY-THREE

1998
LUKE

Luke dreamt of Rosanne Glessner. In his dream, she was walking around the forest with her chestnut hair flowing behind her like a veil, her big, pregnant belly protruding ahead of her as if she were carrying a ripe watermelon. It was no wonder he dreamt about such a thing because he fell asleep reading her diary. In it, she talked endlessly about her developing pregnancy and the building of her new house. It was sort of a boring chapter that lulled Luke to sleep within a few minutes. In his dream, he was the father of her baby. He had to build a house overnight because a storm was coming. It was very stressful. He was chopping wood and stacking logs for what seemed like eternity. In reality, he had no idea how to build a house. But his imagination made up for what he did not know. Amidst his feverish work efforts, someone had arrived at the homestead. A young woman with dark blonde hair. Luke saw her talking to Rosanne. The women hugged each other, and the newcomer came over to where Luke was working.

"How are you, my friend?" she asked, sitting down on a tree stump.

"Do I know you, lady?" Luke grunted with the effort of

lifting a log into place.

She laughed, showing him two rows of straight, white teeth.

"Indeed. We have met before."

She was looking at him expectantly. She had a nice face. Freckles. Symmetrical features. Kind brown eyes. She was vaguely familiar, but from where? He did a double take. It was the lady from the cliff. The one who scared the shit out of him just after his first kiss. She noticed the angry flush developing on his face and smiled at him kindly. He was perhaps right, and she had lived here at one time. It was odd remembering her ghostly countenance just behind Rosie's face. She looked so normal now. So alive.

"You ruined my first kiss," he burst out and went an even deeper crimson.

She laughed again. Not an entirely unpleasant sound.

"Sorry for that, although I'm sure you had many more after that one."

"Not many . . ." he mumbled and bent to pick up another log. "What do you want? I'm kind of busy."

She didn't answer. After a while, Luke thought she might have left, but when he looked up from his work, he saw her still sitting on the stump, just staring at him.

"What?" he said. "Why are you looking at me like that? It's creepy."

"Sorry, friend. It's just been a while since I've seen you. I have come to convey a message."

Luke clapped his hands together to rid them of dirt.

"Okay. What is it?"

He had no time to waste. There was a rumble of thunder in the distance. He had to finish this house before those dark navy clouds reached them. The lady looked back over her shoulder at Rosanne, who was sitting in a patch of flowers, talking animatedly to her round stomach.

"She's a good mother, you know," she said to Luke.

"And how would you know that?"

"I'm her daughter."

"Oh." Luke looked from one woman to the other, hands on hips. "It's just hard to imagine 'cause you guys look the same age."

"That's because this is a dream, silly."

"That would explain it, I guess."

"I'm the only child she will have. Isn't that sad?"

"I don't think so. I'm an only child."

Luke took up the hatchet and started to hack away at a young pine. This was hard work. It was almost unimaginable that people did this on a day-to-day basis in this time period.

"I died young," the lady said. "Childbed. My mother was still alive to bury me."

"I'm sorry," Luke said, dropping the hatchet and coming over to sit on the fallen tree next to her stump. "Sorry you had to die like that."

She shrugged.

"It was hard for her. My mother. Really hard. But I did leave behind three children to comfort her."

Luke searched her face. There was no sadness or bitterness there. She seemed to be at peace with her fate.

"What is the message you have for me?"

"It's not for you. But for your friend. Tell her, if you will, that everything happens for a reason. She need not worry."

"That's it?"

"No, there is more."

She opened her mouth, and out of it came a creak and a slam.

Luke opened his eyes. The screen door. Someone either came in or had just left the house. He sat up and peered through the haze of sleep. His watch on the nightstand said it was 5:05 a.m. It was still dark out, it being February. The weather had warmed this past week, and instead of snow, their area received copious amounts of rain. He heard muffled voices from outside. Trepidation ran over his spine like cold fingers. Whatever was going on, it could not be good. No good news ever came at this time. He climbed off his loft just about as quick and as swift as a newborn rhinoceros. His foot slipped on the ladder, and he almost knocked over his bedside lamp. His body refused to work with him this early in the morning. After this unseemly descent, he ambled to the front door to investigate. He got there just in time to catch his grandmother coming inside. The wind that blew in after her had Luke's knees knocking together. She held her robe together with one hand against the chill of the night.

"What's going on?" Luke asked in a whisper.

His grandmother hooted with surprise.

"Luke, darling, you scared the living daylights out of me!"

"Sorry! Who was that?"

His grandmother flapped her free hand dismissively, her other one hanging onto the front of the robe for dear life.

"Oh, just Mrs. Glessner. Nothing for you to be concerned about."

The words she said were meant to be nonchalant, but her face was anything but. The wrinkles on her forehead had arranged themselves in the perfect imitation of a worried cartoon character.

"What did she want?"

He craned his neck to try and catch a glimpse of their neighbor.

"Just for me to watch the house and feed their cat for a few days. They are going up north to visit family."

"It's kind of early. They are leaving right now?"

His grandmother nodded solemnly. She was a terrible liar. Suddenly, there was a click, and the small Tiffany lamp came on in the living room behind them. Luke's grandfather sat in the armchair next to it.

"Heavens!" his grandmother exclaimed, placing a hand over her heart. "How long have you been sitting there?"

"Long enough," he grunted. "Just tell the boy what happened! You'll have to eventually. Why wait?"

"I . . . I just wanted to let him sleep some more." She wrung her hands.

"Gram? What's wrong? Is it Rosie?"

Luke's stomach felt hollow and raw with sudden fear. His

grandmother nodded.

"Her and Emi, too. They have gone missing."

Luke felt like someone had just pulled the rug out from under his feet. He stumbled, then collected himself and ran into his bedroom. He clumsily pulled clothes on top of his pajamas.

"What are you doing?" his grandmother asked from the doorway.

"I'm going with them."

"Oh, honey, I don't think . . ."

He pushed past her, placing a quick kiss onto her worried forehead. Then, he was out the door, running to their neighbors' house. He had to go. He was the only one who knew the truth about Rosie. He could help. He could do something. He got to their driveway just in time to see their little black car drive off. He ran after it, but they didn't stop. They hadn't seen him. It was too dark outside. Panting, he watched the red taillights of the car get smaller and smaller until they were gone, vanished into the endless darkness of the night.

"Rosie . . ." he said breathlessly. "Hang on! I'm coming!"

CHAPTER FIFTY-FOUR

1998
JAMES

One down and one to go, thought James as he stood before the door of the small, private hospital room that housed Rosie Smith. The door had a small window on eye level that allowed him to observe her without actually being inside. He still couldn't believe she was alive. Her body had been wedged in that tree hollow so tightly that they had to use a saw to free her. When he first saw her body folded into the fetal position, her cheek touching her knees, he was sure he was looking at just that: a body. Her skin had been ice-cold. Her temperature barely registered on the thermometer. But underneath the corpse-like countenance was a pulse. Surprisingly strong. James's skin broke out in goosebumps just thinking about how he felt that beating of her blood under his fingertips when he expected nothing. She was alive. And with some luck, she would stay that way and would be able to tell the tale of what happened to her and her sister.

Her mother, Alice, sat by her bedside, holding her hand and occasionally stroking her immobile face. Alice was allowed to come see her because currently, she wasn't a suspect. Her footprints were not found outside alongside Noah's and the girls'. The house had been searched for blood, and none was found except for some of Alice's and Rosie's in the shower. That was no surprise since both of them bled monthly. James personally didn't believe Alice had anything to do with this. His money was on Noah, who was still being detained at the police station.

James hated to think that the fact that his meddling wife told Noah his daughter wasn't actually his had something to do with all this. A secret like that could drive a man to do something irrational and stupid. James had seen it before. And apparently, from what he'd heard, Noah's father had been a piece of work. People talked, and it was well known that there had been domestic abuse in the household, but no police report was ever filed. The wife had probably been too scared to call for help. Instead, she drank herself into an early grave. A sad tale and not at all uncommon, unfortunately. The tendency for violence was inheritable. Although the talk between Millie and Noah happened a couple of months earlier, it was possible that Noah kept the knowledge to himself and plotted his revenge. Maybe he wanted to get rid of both the children to get back at his wife and start anew. Alice still swore she'd seen someone in the woods, but she could have mistaken an animal for a person. The mind plays tricks sometimes, especially if people's lives are at stake. So far, he hadn't mentioned his knowledge of Rosie's paternity to either of her parents. He was holding on to that particular card until he thought he really needed it. Rosie had been found alive, so there was a chance that Emi would be, too, if he acted quickly. He left Jeffrey to guard the hospital room with strict instructions to notify him if Rosie woke up and headed back to the station.

Noah was lying on the floor, his hands covering his face, when James entered the room. For a moment, James thought he may be sleeping, but he got up immediately when he heard him come in.

"Any news?" he croaked, looking like he hadn't slept in days.

His beard was well on its way, his hair tangled and unkempt. James almost felt bad for not allowing him a shower. Almost.

"Sit!" he said, gesturing to one of the chairs.

Noah did as he was told. With baggy eyes, he watched James take a seat.

"I found Rosie," he said without preamble.

Shocking a suspect was an excellent way of getting a genuine reaction. He watched Noah's face go pale. He swallowed and opened his mouth to speak. His lips were chapped, his voice raspy.

"Is she . . ." He cleared his throat. "Is she okay?"

"She's alive and being treated at the hospital. Your wife is with her."

Noah dropped his face in his open palms and heaved a giant sigh that almost sounded like a sob.

"And Emi? Did you find her?"

He leaned across the table, his bloodshot eyes bulging. He looked strange to James, not quite like himself, as if he'd just shed his skin, allowing a glimpse at the raw, real Noah underneath. The one who'd been hidden away carefully all this time.

"No. Not yet."

"Did Rosie say anything? Anything about Emi?"

And there it was. An abnormal behavior. Noah looked worried, his eyes roaming James's face nervously. Was he perhaps worried that Rosie would tell the truth? If Noah had taken his girls and tried to make them disappear, even one of them found would make him nervous.

"I haven't spoken to her yet. She's in a weakened state. But I should be able to soon."

There was no need to let Noah know that Rosie was, in fact, unconscious, and they had no idea if and when she would awaken.

"Listen, Noah, let's cut to the chase. Now that we have Rosie, we'll know the truth soon enough. Sooner would be better than later, though, so why don't you come clean?"

Noah leaned back in his chair, crossing his arms. A classic defensive position.

"I want to see her!"

"I'm afraid that's impossible due to the fact that you are a suspect in the case of her disappearance."

"Like I said, I had nothing to do with that. I went out to look for them."

"To me, it looks very much like someone wanted both girls to disappear. Rosie was barely alive when I found her. Time is of the essence when it comes to your younger daughter. If you care about her at all, I suggest you speak!"

Noah's jaw worked under his skin. James could almost hear his teeth grinding.

"Rosie wasn't well. You know that, James. Everybody did."

"So, you are going to try and blame this on her?"

"No!" Noah's voice went up an octave. "I really, really didn't want to. I was hoping that she was just a victim in this, but . . ."

"Go on!"

"She did show some aggressive tendencies leading up to this."

"And you didn't think to mention this because?"

"Because she's my daughter! And I wanted to protect her."

"Only she isn't your daughter. Not really."

There was silence in the room. Noah's face became smooth and expressionless, like the surface of water just before a storm. James could see his muscles bunching in his neck, his chest, his arms. And then, he did something totally unexpected. He smiled. A toothy, wolfish smile. A sneer, really.

"Millie . . . she told you."

"Yes."

Noah shook his head, looking down into his lap. And this was the reason James saved this card for last. In order to use it, he had to involve his wife.

"I have to ask you the obvious question," James started to say, but Noah didn't seem to be listening. He had that thousand-mile stare.

"Noah, did you . . ."

"I should have told you to put a muzzle on your bitch."

"You watch your mouth!" James sputtered.

He would have been outraged if he had the time. But it seemed like Noah was on top of him in the moment it took him to blink. One moment, he was in the chair across the table; the next, his enraged face was just mere inches from James's. He had lunged as quickly and as unexpectedly as a jungle cat. They had toppled the table and his chair over with their combined weights. The fall backward had knocked all the wind from James's lungs, and now, there was no chance of him taking another breath due to the fact that Noah's hands were wrapped tight around his throat. He tried to fight him off, but he had no leverage from his position.

"It's all her fucking fault!" Noah hissed in his face. "She told her!"

Black spots danced in James's vision. Another few seconds, and he would have passed out. In a few more, his lungs would have strained for their last breath that would never come. But just in the nick of time, two officers burst into the room and wrestled Noah's solid body off of him. A bit of commotion ensued, of which James didn't notice much because he was too busy coughing and gasping for air. How could he have been so stupid, allowing himself to be put in this situation? The signs were there if only he cared to look: Noah's bunched muscles, the color creeping up his neck. But James was too preoccupied to see what was right in front of him. A dangerous man. The two newcomers sat Noah back down in his chair with his hands cuffed behind his back. He spat blood onto the floor. He had a split lip and an eye that was quickly swelling shut. The rescue team did a number on him.

"Shit, Noah! Why the hell did you do that?" James coughed a few more times while getting to his feet.

He didn't answer, just stared at him from under dark brows with his one good eye.

"Can you get me a water?" James asked one of the two men.

The younger one nodded and went out. The other stayed, eyeing Noah warily. He was a big guy, James realized with some unease. His plaid shirt had torn at one shoulder during the scuffle.

Besides his obvious injuries such as the black eye, Noah didn't look hurt. He looked like he could spring up and take them both, hands cuffed or not. A man of action. A strange, foreign sensation pulsed inside James's core, and it took him a minute to realize it was jealousy. His wife was still hung up on this man who was younger and in better physical shape than him. It hurt. Why couldn't have Noah gotten fat and irritable like most men his age? Instead, here he was, all hulking and mysterious. No wonder Millie could never let him go. For a while, James truly believed he had won. But his careful, patient love could not compete with whatever Noah had given her in the end.

"You are a fool," Noah said, looking at the fallen table. "But you are the same kind of fool I was. I guess I shouldn't have done what I did."

"Elaborate!" James said, testing his chair by pressing on it with one hand. It was clearly broken and unsuitable to bear any weight.

"Millie gets what she wants, no matter the cost. I should have never gotten involved with her."

Fresh rage bubbled up within him. This man had no right to talk about his wife. His wife! He wasn't going to just hand her over, God damn it!

"Leave her out of this!"

"Are you blind?" He pinned James with his eye then, finally looking miserable and worn out. "This is all her fault."

"First, you blame your daughter; then, you blame my wife! Tell me something, Noah! Did you know Rosie wasn't yours? Because if you didn't, that's quite the motive."

"Of course I did!" he burst out, and, to James's surprise, a tear rolled down his cheek.

"It was my idea to raise her as mine. Her father had beaten Alice, so we never told her the truth. There was no need to tell her. We were happy."

There was a sinking feeling in James's stomach. He knew what was coming, but the words still cut him because he feared them to be true.

"I'm afraid Millie may have told her."

"No . . ." James said, but there was enough uncertainty in that one word to drown a cow. "Why would she?"

"For revenge," Noah said simply. "She wants me to pay for what I did. She's using you as a tool. I hope you know that."

This was the single most disrespectful thing anyone had ever said to James in his adult life, that his wife was using him as a tool. And he had no comeback. He just stood there, slightly bent over and feeling lightheaded, looking at his only suspect. Was he telling the truth? Or was what he said just a convenient cover? James had no idea. Some people, the more intelligent psychopaths, waited for a convenient occurrence of events to aid in covering their crime. For example, the one case when a man only killed during hunting season and left the bodies of his victims in thickly forested areas. At first, the victims, all shot in the chest and stomach, were written off as unlucky hunting accidents. Noah could have done the same thing if he was wanting out of family life but didn't want to go through an ugly divorce and many years of child support. Millie finding out about their secret and Rosie's mental illness may have just been the lucky break he'd been waiting for. Alice may have been next. A convenient fall from the attic stairs or a horse riding "accident" would have taken care of her. Or Noah could be telling the truth. But that would put most of the blame on Millie. Telling a mentally unstable teen that her entire life had been a lie might have sent her over the edge. James suddenly realized that some time had passed since Noah spoke. He really should say something. He opened his mouth at the same time the door of the room swung open. It was the young deputy he had sent out for water.

"You have a phone call, sir! It's from the hospital."

CHAPTER FIFTY-FIVE

1998
ROSIE

There was cotton in her mouth and lead in her skull. The insides of her bones felt painful, as if someone had run hot wires through them. The cotton turned out to be her own tongue. She wiggled it around in her mouth. It rasped against her teeth painfully. Her head and limbs were impossibly heavy. She tried to move any part of her besides her tongue, but even her eyelids weighed way too much. What happened to her? The last thing she remembered was . . . Her brain worked sluggishly. She had floated out of bed. Totally normal. And then, she was in her sister's room. Why on earth was she in there? These new meds messed her up big time. Her memory was total shit. They weren't nearly enough to keep the crone at bay, either. She was gathering strength. Rosie could feel it. Payday was upon her. *"Soon, soon . . ."* she would croon to Rosie just before she fell asleep each night for days now. She felt somebody squeeze her hand. *No!* she thought groggily. *Leave me alone! Let me sleep. Please . . .*

"Rosie! Can you hear me, love?"

The voice was familiar. Soothing. A childhood memory came to her: her mom waking her up to go to school. Her bed was impossibly warm and so comfortable. Her mother shook her gently both then and now.

"You have to wake up!" her mother said, sounding strangely urgent.

"You don't have to do anything. Not anymore," the crone rasped in her ear. *"The deed is done."*

Rosie opened her eyes. At first, she couldn't see anything. Tears flooded her vision, and her surroundings swam with it. She blinked and tried to wipe them away, but one of her hands had something stuck in it. The other was held firm by her mother. After a while, her vision cleared on its own, and she was able to see. The dim light in the room made everything look gray. Gray walls, gray sheets, her gray mother. She wasn't at home. This realization came as a shock to her.

"Where are we?" she croaked.

Her mom reached over to a bedside table and gave her a sip of water from a plastic cup through a straw.

"We are at the hospital."

Rosie looked around again. She had no recollection of coming here. Was she dreaming? It was a possibility. She blinked rapidly and squeezed her eyes shut, opening them wide to see if things would change. They did not.

"Is this a dream?" she asked, unsure who she expected the answer from.

"No, honey," her mother said, placing a hand on her shoulder.

"That depends. Do you want it to be?" the crone chimed in, in her usual fashion.

"Listen." Her mother leaned in close to her face. She didn't look good. "Rosie, the police are coming. I need you to tell me what happened before they get here."

"What? The police?"

None of what she was saying made sense to her. A sharp burst of pain flashed through the front of her brain, making her wince and leaving her dizzy.

"I don't feel too good," she said, feeling impossibly weak.

She felt like her head was a basketball wobbling atop a matchstick that was her neck.

"You are dehydrated, and you got hypothermia. You are going to be okay, but I need you to tell me where your sister is!"

Her mom was squeezing her arm uncomfortably tight, her whispering voice bordering on hysterical. She looked like a mental patient with her baggy eyes and unbrushed hair. Rosie leaned away from her slightly.

"What do you mean? Isn't she in her room? Did she come here with us? Why are we at the hospital?"

The thoughts whizzed through her mind one after another. Some she was able to catch to say out loud, some she wasn't. There was another flash of blinding pain inside her skull.

"Ah!" she gasped and tried to bat her mother's hand off her arm, but there was an IV in her wrist preventing her from reaching over. "Let go! You're hurting me!"

Alice loosened her grasp but did not let go completely.

"You guys have been missing for two days. They found you in the forest a few hours ago, but Emi is still missing. Was she with you? Did somebody take you?"

"Mom, you're not making any sense!"

She wasn't. This had to be one of those dreams where nothing made sense.

"I'm ready to wake up now!" Rosie said out loud.

"You are awake! her mother said pleadingly. "Please focus!"

The door opened, and in walked Mina's dad. Her mother finally released her.

After a seemingly endless and mostly one-sided conversation, Rosie was made to understand that she was, indeed, awake, as much as this reality sucked, and that they had been looking for her for almost two days before she was finally found.

"When is Mina coming?" she asked Mr. Walker.

He sighed, rubbing his forehead with the back of a hand. He was sitting right next to her bed, in the chair her mother previously occupied. Alice refused to leave the room, so she was banished to the far corner, where she sat hunched over, a tall, young police officer looming over her.

"She's not," Mr. Walker said, looking endlessly irritated.

"Oh . . . Well, then, why are you here?"

"It's because I'm a police officer. Rosie, we've been over this a few times now. Let's just drop it and focus on whatever happened to you."

"I told you I don't know! The last thing I remember was standing in Emi's room. Then, I woke up here."

This was getting to be annoying. She really had no memory of being out in the woods. She had apparently wedged herself inside a tree. It was ridiculous. It all sounded made-up.

"You are telling me that you are missing two days of memories?"

Mr. Walker sounded aggravated. Rosie didn't like his tone. Could she zap him from this distance? She tried but could not gather her energy. It was all over the place, just like her brain. When she tried to sit up, she realized her whole body hurt. It was as if someone had placed her into a bucket, put a lid on top, and given it a good shake.

"Rosie, I need you to work with me here! We have to find your sister! I need your help!"

"Have you looked at home? She is probably still asleep. What time is it?"

Mr. Walker threw up his hands, rolling his eyes skyward. Rosie didn't appreciate this gesture. She didn't appreciate it at all. He was insinuating that she was stupid. And she wasn't. It was just that her head hurt like a bitch, and things kept going in and out of focus around her. Rage filled her, and she concentrated it in her fingertip. She reached out and touched the pen he was holding to take notes with. His reaction was instantaneous. He yanked his hand back and shook it vigorously. He looked at her with the oddest expression from under lowered brows. She recognized it as him trying to rationalize what just happened.

"Was your father with you?" he asked after some time.

"Don't ask her that!" Alice burst out.

She stood up to come over, but the other cop stepped in front of her.

"Ma'am, please sit down!"

"No! This is not right! She says she doesn't remember. Don't put things in her head!"

Mr. Walker turned to stare at her moodily.

"I'm going to have to ask you to refrain from interrupting!"

"But . . ."

"Do you want your other daughter found or not?"

Alice slowly lowered herself back down onto her chair, a cornered, wounded look on her face. Watching her, Rosie suddenly got a flash of memory. She and Emi were standing in a dark forest, her sister wearing the exact same expression as her mother. "I don't want to go without him!" she had yelled. "You told me I could take Moonwalk with me!" "I lied," Rosie had said.

"What did you say?"

Mr. Walker clicked his pen and scribbled something in his notepad. Rosie didn't realize she had spoken out loud. "I lied" must have sounded awfully suspicious when placed into this context. Mr. Walker was looking at her expectantly. *Damn the nosy bastard.*

"A memory just came to me. Emi was with me. I think she wanted to go riding. She was asking about her donkey."

"Okay, this is good!" He scribbled furiously. "Anything else? Anything you can remember? Maybe the place or the time of day."

Rosie thought a bit.

"It was dark and windy. I don't think we were far from the house. But I'm not sure."

"Anything else?"

Rosie shook her head.

After a few more minutes, Mr. Walker left to allow Rosie some time to rest. He would be back, he assured her. Rosie felt drained and slightly nauseated. That sharp pain in her head still came and went. It was like unexpectedly getting punched. You never knew when the pain would hit, only that it was coming. Her mother made it clear, though, that this was no time to rest. She came to sit by her immediately after they were left alone.

"I know this is scary," she said.

You don't know shit, Rosie thought wearily.

"But you can tell me the truth! I'll help you. We'll figure it out together."

"Oh, my God!" Rosie gawked at her. "You think I did something to her! You think I'm responsible!"

"What? No! Of course not!"

"You've already decided. I can see it in your face."

Her mother looked as if she had slapped her. The truth did hurt sometimes.

"No, honey! I just want to find your sister."

"You have me! Isn't that enough?"

Why on earth did she say that? She wanted to find her sister just like everybody else, but she felt like all the fingers were pointed at her—"Rosie did it! She's at fault!"—and that made her angry. The crone used her anger to take her tongue and run away with it. Alice was speechless. Her mouth opened and closed soundlessly. She cleared her throat.

"You and Emi are both my children. I love you equally. I want to have you both."

Rosie could see her anger rising under her skin. It had a bright, reddish light. It made the hairs on her arm stand up. If only she could get a hold of that anger . . . Just imagine what she could do.

"What about Dad? Does he even care that I was found? Or is he still out there, looking for Emi?"

"Of course he cares! Why are you asking these questions?"

Alice's voice was loud enough now that Rosie was sure all the nurses could hear from outside the room.

"You know why."

Rosie was as calm as still water, which seemed to aggravate

her mother even more.

"What are you saying?" she panted, her chest rising and falling within the confines of her shirt.

"You know. Dad knows, too. Is that why he isn't here?"

Alice stood up rapidly. She looked like she was about to hit her. Her rage was pouring off her in thick, red waves, like smoke. It mingled with something else. Rage and fear. Rosie could see her thoughts. They came at her in rapid succession: *You ungrateful brat! How does she know? We gave you everything! Oh, God! My child is evil. I should have gotten rid of her. What's wrong with me? I love her! Emi! Emi! Emi! She did something to her! I know it! I'm gonna make her tell me! I'm gonna . . .*

She started forward, and at the same moment, her waves of emotion reached Rosie. She felt it. A prickle on her skin, a rushing in her veins. She grabbed hold of it, an invisible force in her hands, and whipped it so it lashed right back at Alice. It caught her across the face. She staggered back, her eyes wide, as a red mark appeared on her face. The band of impact went from one side of her jaw across her nose and one eye to her temple on the other side. She just stood there, dumbfounded. A thin trickle of blood appeared from one of her nostrils. She touched it, smudging it on her upper lip, and held her hand in front of her face.

"What?" she said breathlessly as she surveyed the room for the something that had hit her.

When she found nothing, her eyes, filled with horror and bewilderment, landed on Rosie.

"I think it's best that you go! Like Mr. Walker said, I need my rest."

CHAPTER FIFTY-SIX

1998
JAMES

Things were getting out of hand. If it turned out that Millie had told Rosie about their little family secret and that had caused her to fly off the handle, well, that would be very bad, indeed. At that point, James would have to step back and give the case to someone else. His instincts were thoroughly confused. Who was telling the truth, and who was lying? He had to talk to Millie. He stopped by their house just now, but she wasn't there. *She must be at the vet's office today.* James cursed himself for not knowing her schedule better. Ideally, he would have gone there next, but he had just gotten the go-ahead to speak with Rosie's psychologist, a Dr. Lewis. He was waiting for James at the station. He would be able to give James a clear, unbiased view of Rosie's mental health, which he, at this point, needed desperately.

Jeffrey was waiting for him in the front lobby.

"Speak!" James barked at him as he made a beeline for the coffee machine.

"We had to let Noah Smith go."

"What?" James stopped to glare at him.

"We had no choice. His wife turned up with a lawyer. We

don't have enough cause to hold him . . ."

"Yeah, yeah. Tell me something I don't know!" He poured himself a cup, took a sip, and swished it around in his mouth. "Tail him!" he ordered, pointing at Jeffrey with his free hand. "I want to know where he goes and what he does. He may actually lead us to the other girl if I'm right and he is our guy."

"Sir!" Jeffrey nodded and scurried away.

Dr. Lewis was exactly what James expected, meaning he looked like a psychologist. He was short and thin, with large, kind, owl-like eyes.

"Dr. Lewis," James said, sliding onto the chair across the table at which he sat. "My name is James Walker. I'm handling the case involving your client, Rosanne Smith."

"It's a pleasure to meet you, Mr. Walker, even under these unfortunate circumstances."

"I'm guessing you were briefed on why you are here?"

The shrink nodded, his face growing shadowy and serious.

"Yes, I have been told . . . How is Rosie?"

"She's stable and awake."

Dr. Lewis visibly relaxed at this.

"And her sister?"

"We haven't located her yet, which is why I must cut to the chase. Did Rosie confide in you about any thoughts or plans of harming her sister?"

"No!" The doctor shook his head definitely. "She never talked about her sister. She, in fact, had a clear aversion to the topic. She liked to change the subject whenever I brought her up."

"I see. And what do you make of that?"

"It's hard to say what her reasons behind that may be. I did get the impression that there is some jealousy between the two girls."

"Rosie being jealous of her younger sister?"

Dr. Lewis nodded. He touched his fingertips together, searching for the right words.

"These sessions were about Rosie. Talking about her sister would take the spotlight off of her."

"I see."

James did see. Being a father of multiple children, he had the inside scoop on sibling rivalry, having experienced it firsthand. For example, when his middle child, Jason, was born, Mina went through a weird stage of having nonexistent physical aches. She would complain of her stomach or her head hurting, knowing it would get her some pampering. So, the fact that Rosie would enjoy only talking about herself during therapy made sense. But if she did harm her sister in any way, why now?

"Did Rosie ever mention anything about her father?"

Dr. Lewis shifted in his seat, his thin, weirdly perfect eyebrows pushing together in thought.

"She talked about both her parents, actually. But not in a good way. She was developing some animosity toward both of them, I'm afraid. But I believed it to be mainly focused on her mother. She would often call her a liar or a bitch, for example."

This was new and interesting information. Problems at home, sibling rivalry. If Rosie had knowledge about her parentage, that would give her an excellent excuse—a motive, if you will—to take her sister out of the picture.

"Did she say why she was angry with them?"

Dr. Lewis shook his head.

"Rosie is quite a complicated case, I'm afraid. Despite the medication, her condition has been getting worse. She has developed quite a few delusions. She also has a hard time telling the difference between reality and these delusions. So, there is a real possibility that she thinks her family members have done something against her when, in fact, they did not."

"What kind of delusions are we talking about?"

Paranoia is a very powerful thing. It definitely has the potential to drive someone to do strange or even harmful things. This definitely did not bode well for Rosie.

"Her strongest and most often mentioned one was about traveling back in time and talking to her great aunt when she had been around twelve or so." The doctor smiled crookedly. "She really believed she was there, but the strangest thing was that she would speak of these occurrences with such detail that I almost found myself believing her, too."

James frowned into his notes. Rosie's great aunt. It rang a small bell inside his skull. He couldn't remember why, though.

"Did she mention what her aunt was called?"

"She called her Franny. I did ask her if she had ever met her while she had been alive. She has been dead for many years, you see. But she said she hadn't because her mother didn't want to take her to the mental hospital."

"Hold up! What mental hospital?"

James was missing something crucial. A piece of the puzzle he hadn't known was there.

"Her great aunt had lived most her life in the old psych building just outside of town."

"The one that closed down about . . . six, seven years ago?"

"That's the one!" The doctor looked pleased with James's knowledge. "She apparently had exhibited eerily similar symptoms as Rosie but was diagnosed earlier in life. Such a shame. With some of the medications we have in hand today, she may have lived a more normal life."

"So, the family has a history of this illness? Rosie isn't the first one?"

"Yes, I'm afraid."

Dr. Lewis looked James deep in the eyes, evidently pondering something.

"Mrs. Smith didn't tell me of this family history at first. She seems to be . . . frightened of Rosie's illness, almost as if it were her own. It is a bit of an unusual reaction. I did report to her on the sessions I've had with her daughter, and at times, I got the impression that she was actually scared of Rosie herself."

James envisioned Rosie Smith's scrawny teenage body as he saw her wedged inside a tree. He shook his head slightly.

"She's only a girl," he said, more to himself than to the doctor.

"While that's true, mental illness does have the capacity to change one's personality. She did beat their rooster to death with a bucket."

James looked up at him sharply. *What the actual fuck?*

"Oh, you didn't know?"

"No . . ." James said after a while. He had the sinking feeling that there were many things he didn't know but was about to find out.

CHAPTER FIFTY-SEVEN
1998
MILLIE

Embarrassment burned Millie's cheeks in the cold air as she walked out of the forest to return to her home. She did go snooping around, yes, but it was just harmless curiosity. She had heard Noah had been released and wanted to know if he had come home or had gone somewhere else. She wasn't going to go up to his door and knock. *Heavens, no!* That would be a terrible idea. No. She was just going to get a quick peek of the Smith house from the cover of the trees. She had run into some yellow police tape before she reached her favorite peeking spot. She was too far. She couldn't see anything from there. So, after a moment's hesitation, she looked left and right like a well-raised child at a crosswalk and ducked under the tape. It would be fine. Her husband was a police officer. She was allowed to break the rules just a little bit. She made it to her usual spot, where her brown skin and coat blended in perfectly with the dry underbrush. Both Noah's and Alice's cars were up front and one extra car. *Maybe the lawyer's?* As she watched, a tall, skinny, gray-haired man stepped out onto the front porch to smoke a cigarette. She'd seen him before, she was sure, but it took her a minute to place him. *Alice's father. Yes!* That's who he was. So, her parents had come for moral support. *How sweet.* However, no amount of good intentions or family values was going to fix whatever fuckery was going on behind the walls of that house.

"Ma'am!"

Millie started at the intrusion of this disembodied voice. She whirled to see a police officer in full uniform weaving through trees to approach her.

"Oh, my God!" she exclaimed, her hand on her thumping heart. "You cared the bejesus out of me!"

"Ma'am, this is a restricted area. I'm going to have to ask you to leave!" the officer said in a clipped tone that left no space for argument or excuses.

Millie didn't like his tone at all. She had always had free range in this area, and a stranger wasn't going to tell her otherwise. She squared her shoulders and held her head high.

"It's quite fine. I'm their neighbor, you see. I come around here all the time. I . . ."

"It doesn't matter who you are," the snooty officer cut her off. "This area is closed off for investigation and to protect the privacy of the family living here."

"I understand, sir," Millie said through her teeth. "The family is good friends with mine. I only came to check on them."

She glanced back to the house, but the old man was no longer on the porch.

"Ma'am, you are standing in the middle of a crime scene!"

Millie looked down at where she was standing, slightly startled, fully expecting to see blood or bones or something equally gruesome.

"Oh. Well, there is nothing here . . ."

"If you do not leave, I'll be forced to handcuff you and take you down to the station."

Cold fury mixed with equal parts fear flooded Millie's chest. This was escalating very quickly.

"No need for that! I'm just the neighbor," she breathed, her voice breaking on the word "neighbor."

The officer reached for the shiny silver cuffs dangling from his belt. Millie turned without another word and started speed-walking down the deer path leading toward her property. From behind her came the officer's voice, thick with sarcasm.

"Next time you want to 'check on your neighbors,' you might want to try their door instead of snooping around in the bushes, ma'am!"

Millie's face burned with righteous indignation. She walked furiously ahead, her rage propelling her. How dare this asshole threaten her? Her husband is the head detective on this case. She should tell James what this lunatic did. She should . . . She tripped on a protruding root and nearly fell headlong into a thorny bush. That would have been quite bad. *Calm down, you fool!* she chided herself. She couldn't tell James. What was she thinking? She was already on thin ice with him. He can't know.

She reached her house in just under ten minutes and walked in to the sound of the phone shrieking in the kitchen. She ran to reach it.

"Walker house. Millie speaking."

There was silence on the other side.

"Hello?"

Was this a prank call? She was really not in the mood. She was just about to slam the phone down on the receiver—that'll show the damn bastard not to mess with her—when she heard a stirring on the other line.

"Millie . . ." her husband's voice crackled through the distance.

It gave her goosebumps, and not in a good way. He sounded worn and irritated. Just that one word told her so much.

"Jim, why did you wait so long to speak? I almost hung up."

There was another brief period of silence that made her toes go cold with uneasy anticipation.

"I . . ." He cleared his throat. "I didn't know what to say. How to start . . ."

Uh-oh. This definitely wasn't good.

"Why do you do this to me, Millie?"

She saw a flash of fire behind her closed eyelids as she blinked in surprise.

"Do what? I haven't done anything."

Was he going to bring up the Noah thing? Did he call her just to argue? She had thought all that had settled. She stepped out of line, and he was punishing her by moving the whole family to a strange, new place.

"You were caught walking all over my crime scene, for one!"

Instantly, a giant lump formed right in the middle of her throat. *Shit!*

"I didn't . . ." she started to say but was cut off by his roar.

"This town, my district, is not your personal playground! God damn it, Millie! This is my case, and you've embarrassed me in front of the whole station."

"Don't be so dramatic! I just went to take a look."

"You are not above the law!" he shouted, putting equal emphasis on each word.

She held the receiver away from her ear. In their entire marriage, he had never raised his voice with her. Never. This was now the second time in two months. Was she causing this? Or was he just falling apart at the seams? When she placed the phone to her ear again, all she heard was his heavy breathing.

"Jim, I didn't mean . . ."

"I need to ask you something, and I need you to be honest with me!"

There he went again, cutting her off. And implying she might lie, to boot. She knew she was in the wrong, but it still made her angry.

"Of course," she said, quite testily.

He heaved a giant sigh.

"Did you tell Rosie Smith that Noah wasn't her father?"

Millie felt like she had just received a kick to the gut. She reached blindly for a nearby kitchen chair and, upon locating it, pulled it to her and sat down.

"No. I only told Noah."

A little lie. She did send that letter to the actual father, but James didn't need to know that unless the man himself showed up pointing fingers. James made a strange huffing sound, and Millie could just see him trying to smooth the deep frown lines on his forehead.

"Millie," he said so suddenly, it made her jump.

"Yes, James?"

"Stay away from our neighbors! At least until we figure out whether the younger girl is dead or alive. Can you manage that?"

There was a strange, breathless feeling in Millie's throat, as if she had swallowed a whole apple.

"Yes . . ." she squeezed out.

"Good!"

He hung up. Millie listened to the dial tone for a bit longer, then, slowly, mechanically, she hung the phone onto its base on the wall. She stared ahead of her at nothing in particular. *Little Emilia may be dead. No. That couldn't happen, could it? That wild, dirty-faced little girl with her flying blonde hair.* The last time Millie had seen her, she was riding her annoying donkey. They flew through the frozen meadow near the edge of her property, the donkey's nostrils wide and puffing white, hot air like a small steam engine. Emi was wearing adorable, small chaps, and her wide-brimmed hat had been swept off her head so it dangled in the wind behind her. *That child is going to go places*, Millie had thought to herself. *Such a wild spirit. Such an innocent soul.* Millie had always thought Emi was the most innocent in her family. She never thought about punishing her. And now, she was maybe dead. Millie recalled Noah's enraged face just after she told him the truth. She saw his wide, powerful shoulders as he rode off atop his horse. *Oh, Millie, what have you done?* She buried her face in her hands.

CHAPTER FIFTY-EIGHT

1998
ALICE

She remembered the lawyer's words long after he had left their house: *"You shouldn't have gone out there. Your footprints are all over the woods. This is going to be hard to fix."*

And what was Noah supposed to do? she asked herself, now enraged. *Just sit around and wait for help to come?* He was not that type of person. He was a doer. A fixer. Alice walked into her bedroom, leaving her parents in the living room. Her mother was baking Rosie's favorite white cream-filled cookies, and her dad was probably smoking. Noah was in the shower. He refused food, saying that his stomach would not take it. But he finally agreed to a shower. Now, with nobody around her, Alice was free to have the meltdown her body desperately needed. She sank to the floor by her bedside and allowed her dry, bloodshot eyes to fill with tears. It was a wonderful, almost euphoric release. She didn't sob. She had no energy left for that. She merely tilted her head forward and watched silently as her tears dropped onto the bedside rug one by one. She had never cried like this, not even when she found out she was pregnant. Not after Nathan pushed her into the bathtub. And that was one of the worst days of her life. There was something unnatural about this cry. But there was also something unnatural about thinking you just might bury one of your children. Or the possibility that your other child was evil. *Stop thinking that, you dumb bitch!* She took a shaky breath. *This isn't Rosie's fault. She's sick. It's your fault. You should have never had children. You should have never dragged Noah into the sewage pit that's your life.* Maybe not, but here they were. She couldn't go back in time and undo things. She couldn't do anything but sit here and be useless.

Noah emerged from their bathroom. He was damp and pink from the hot water. He saw her and came to sit on her side of the bed. The mattress creaked under his weight. His presence was a comfort. Alice lifted her tear-stricken face and saw, to her surprise, that he seemed to have shrunk in the past couple of days. His chest looked smaller, as if it was slowly caving in. *No, it actually has been almost three days since . . . since . . .* Her insides clenched painfully, so she hugged herself.

"Do you think Rosie knows?"

Alice instantly understood his meaning and remembered the day Noah galloped up to the house around two months ago.

Alice had been taking grocery bags from the car. She was having a good day. She was going to make lamb and brown rice casserole, which both girls loved. And after, they would have brownies and ice cream. She promised herself she would make an effort to bake more. And she was sticking to it. When the girls got home from school, the house would smell of delicious food, and it would make them sigh with happiness. She was just about to carry the last few bags inside when she heard the beating of hooves coming from behind the house. Frowning, she took a few steps to the side and saw that it was Noah and Pilot. They were approaching her at a full gallop, kicking up dust and small rocks. Once she was able to make out Noah's face, she knew immediately that there was something wrong. Quickly, she dumped the groceries on the porch and jogged to meet him. Pilot was foamy with sweat. Alice could clearly see the tender pink membrane inside his nose as he took large, trumpeting breaths. Noah had ran him hard.

"What's wrong?"

Noah hopped off the horse's back and turned to her, a crazed look in his eyes that frightened her.

"How does Millie know about Rosie?" he asked without preamble.

At first, Alice's mind went blank. Then, with a rush, she remembered the envelope and the confrontation in Millie's dark, outdated kitchen. She had told him. Alice explicitly told her to stay out of her life, and she still went to Noah. A fury bloomed in her chest, so all-encompassing that it made her lightheaded.

"That nasty bitch!" she heard herself say as she turned, grabbed the first thing she saw—which was an old, rusty hoe—and headed straight in the direction of Millie's house.

She was stopped short by Noah's viselike grip on her arm.

"Oh, no, you don't!" he said, turning her to face him.

"Let me go!" She struggled.

"What are you going to do with that?" He gestured to the barely operational hoe in her hand.

"What do you think? I'm going to cave her skull in."

He shook his head, seemingly finding some humor in this even though she was dead serious. He dragged her to the porch, pushed her down to sit next to the bags of food, and, crossing his arms, sat down next to her.

"I gather you knew she knew," he said, arching a brow at her.

His temper was dissipating by the moment after seeing her reaction. Alice dropped the hoe and covered her face with both hands.

"God, this is such a shitshow!" she groaned into her palms. "I'm sorry! I should have told you. But I didn't think . . . I told her . . ."

She couldn't quite finish. She rubbed her hands over her face and into her hair, making the wispy hairs of her bangs stand up. Noah was looking down at her with a kind expression. He wouldn't blame her, although it was technically Alice's fault.

"How did she find out?"

"She found the 'in case of an emergency' letter I wrote when Rosie was born. And not accidentally, I might add. It was pretty well hidden, locked in my desk drawer."

Noah shook his head slowly. His gaze was faraway, and Alice knew he was thinking of the time in his life when she had left him, and so, he found solace in Millie. Although now, in hindsight, Millie looked to be more of a curse than anything.

"I can't fucking believe it . . ." he said, his voice trailing off.

"She wrote you a letter."

Noah turned sharply to look at her.

"What?"

"I burned it. She didn't sign it, but I know it was her. She used the same envelope they have at the vet clinic. When I put two and two together, I confronted her and told her to keep away from us. I guess she didn't listen."

Noah was gaping at her, his face showing utter bewilderment and a bit of hurt, too.

"Why didn't you tell me?"

Alice shrugged, a nervous habit.

"I didn't want to worry you. With Rosie going through this . . . this . . ." Her voice broke, and she gestured vaguely at the air in front of her. "I just didn't want you to be reminded that she's not yours. Especially at a time like this." Her voice shook ever so slightly.

He put an arm around her shoulder and pulled her into his side.

"But she *is* mine," he said after a moment. "And there is nothing that will ever change that."

There was a warm, fuzzy feeling in Alice's chest, as if she'd just drank some good champagne.

"I love you so much," she said and tilted her face up for a kiss.

"And I love you," he said and delivered it.

They sat there for some minutes, observing nature and

enjoying the ability of being able to lean on one another.

"Rosie cannot find out," said Alice after some time. "She's not old enough and definitely not in the right mindset. I'm afraid she wouldn't be able to handle it."

"Agreed," Noah said and placed another kiss on the crown of her head.

"You don't think Millie would tell her, do you?"

"I made it pretty clear she wasn't welcome on our land anymore. So, I don't think she'll come around again."

"How'd you do that?"

"I told her I hope she gets eaten by something while walking home."

Alice burst out laughing.

"It's the only time I wished we had mountain lions around here," he added, grinning at her.

Now, here in the present, as they sat in the midst of the ruins of their life, Alice felt the cold fingers of nearby death drumming on her spine. What if Millie told their daughter the secret in spite of both of them telling her to keep quiet? What if she still did? And what if Rosie, in response, did something truly terrible? She saw in her mind's eye Emi's small, sleeping face as she last saw her. Long lashes curling against her cheeks. Her golden hair splayed over her pillow. Her little wild child. It was a strange thing, really. Rosie had always been calm and well-behaved. A quiet little girl. Alice and Noah had this inside joke that she got her personality from Noah. As impossible as it was, it seemed to be so. And Emi got her strong will and quick temper from Alice. She saw so much of herself in her that it was sometimes scary. And deeply unfair. Joke all they might, it wouldn't make Rosie genetically Noah's. Didn't he deserve a child who not only acted like him but looked like him, as well? She imagined a little boy with big brown eyes and sandy hair. It wasn't too late. They could have one more to even out the scales. *No! No more children, you flaming idiot! Look at what happened!* Her inner voice was right, of course. She was stupid. One of her children was still missing. They would find her, of course. They had to. She would come home alive and well. She had to. That was the only option. Emi would come home, Rosie would be fixed, and then things would go back to normal. They would get their family back.

She realized Noah had asked her a question a while ago, and she never gave him an answer. She didn't really have one. She only had hopes.

"I really hope she didn't."

That night, Alice walked out into the embrace of the cold winter air. She waited until everyone was asleep. At first, she didn't know why she wanted to go outside, just that she had to. Standing on her back porch, she caught the whiff of the horses on the evening breeze. *Yes!* The donkey. She wanted to see Moonwalk. She needed to have a talk with him. It may sound absurd—stupid, even—but that animal loves Emi so much, he would know if she was all right. Maybe there was some way he could tell Alice, too, so she may know and have some peace.

She approached the paddock and spotted the old donkey right away. He was standing a little ways away from the other horses, his rump to Alice. His demeanor was odd. Alice expected him to be asleep with the others who stood in a small, uneven circle, long necks drooping as they dozed. The colt was sprawled on its side, his adoptive mother lying next to him with her legs tucked neatly underneath her. Moonwalk looked to be wide awake. Long ears pricked, he stared into the darkness ahead of him. When Alice was close enough, she heard him give a low, raspy nicker. The blood froze in her veins. She heard that sound many times before, mostly when Emi was tending to him. But she wasn't here.

"No!" she whispered.

This isn't the sign she wanted. She should turn and leave here. Run back to the house and sleep. She was just imagining things. The donkey turned his head to look at her, and at the same time, a gust of warm breeze caressed Alice's cheek. She dropped to her knees, hugging her middle, and howled like a wounded animal.

CHAPTER FIFTY-NINE

1998
JAMES

He sat, leaning heavily on his desk, and waited for the forensics report on some of the findings from the past few days. The reports should be ready any minute now. In the meantime, he went through his theories on what could have happened.

Theory Number One:

Noah didn't actually know Rosie wasn't his biological daughter and had snapped after Millie told him. He planned out his revenge. He most likely thought he had killed Rosie and then placed her inside the hollow of the tree. Since Rosie had no visible bruises on her, such as strangulation marks on her neck, it is possible Noah had used a pillow to try and suffocate her. As for Emi, she may have walked in on the act, and Noah thought best to dispose of her, too.

Theory Number Two:

Noah planned to kill off both the girls as punishment for Alice's lie. Alice most likely doesn't know this and is standing by her husband's side like a blind fool.

Theory Number Three:

Alice and Noah worked together to rid themselves of their children. Noah convinced his wife either by emotional blackmail or threatening to be a part of it. She came up with the story of the homeless woman to cover for them both.

Theory Number Four:

Now, James was getting into dangerous territory. Rosie found out about her family's little secret and lost her shit. Aided by her unstable state of mind, she either acted on impulse or planned out the murder of her sister. Unfortunately, at this point in time, there was a real chance Emi wasn't alive anymore. Then, stricken with guilt, Rosie wedged herself in a tree and waited to die from cold and starvation. This one was a little out there. It would take some dedication on Rosie's part. If this theory turned out to be true, there was the really strong possibility that Millie was lying and did tell Rosie the truth. Or her parents were lying, and they had told her. She could have read the same letter Millie did, even though Alice swore up and down that she had disposed of it.

Theory Number Five:

The least likely, in James's opinion. Rosie simply reached some breaking point due to her mental illness and decided to off her little sister, whom she supposedly loved dearly.

Theory Number Six

Emi fell victim to some horrible accident, and the whole family tried to cover it up. Rosie could not take the pressure, so she ran away and ended up in the tree.

Now, the findings.

The guys had found some kind of blood on a flat stone in the woods near the cliff. Noah's boot prints were all over the area as well as the girls' bare footprints. The blood could belong to some animal. So, the results of the DNA test are crucial. The bloodhound that followed Emi's scent kept on losing it and picking it back up but finally lost it completely near the edge of the cliff. They did search for her extensively at the bottom but turned up nothing. If she did fall or was pushed off the cliff, there was a chance they would never find her. The current is quite strong there, so her little body would have been swept away. If that was the case, she would probably be located in another state if ever found.

James leaned back in his chair and rubbed both hands over his face. He had to talk to Rosie again. She was the key in all of this. James just knew that she would remember what happened. Her mental illness made her a not-so-reliable witness, but she may be the only witness he's got.

The gangly form of Jeffrey popped up in his office doorway.

"The results are in, sir."

He looked bright-eyed and bushy-tailed as he waved a thin stack of papers at him.

"Did you read it?" James asked, taking the papers from him.

"I brought it straight over, sir."

James gave him a quizzical look through his reading glasses. Jeffrey cleared his throat and pulled at the collar of his uniform with one finger.

"I skimmed it, sir. "

James lowered the paperwork onto his lap.

"Well, then, please do tell!"

He only needed to know the most important thing. He'd read the whole thing later.

"The blood on the rock matched the DNA of Emilia Smith."

James felt the blood drain from his face, even though he was fully expecting this to be the result.

"Traces of her blood were found on the right boot of Noah Smith and the ankle of his jeans on the same side."

James grimaced. They may have just located their murder weapon. He had seen serious wounds inflicted on someone by stomping and kicking. A well-placed boot could very well kill a child or render her unconscious. At that point, it would be easy to carry the small, unresponsive body to the edge of the cliff and toss it over. He had to speak to Rosie. Immediately.

"Get an arrest warrant for Noah Smith!" he barked at Jeffrey and gave him the papers back.

He took them and held them to his chest. James stood slowly, his knees creaking.

"There is one more thing, sir," he said hesitatingly.

"What is it?"

Jeffrey's mouth worked, but no sound came.

"Speak! I haven't got all day." His aching knees made him cross.

"During the search of the property, an open grave site was located, containing some old bones."

"So? Isn't there an ancient cemetery on the property?"

Jeffrey nodded. God, the boy was dense sometimes.

"Yes, sir, and that is where the bones were located, but . . ." Jeffrey jogged after him as he exited his office and headed toward the front of the building. "This grave is pretty shallow," he said, huffing. "No more than two feet."

People used to bury their dead at least four feet deep, even back in the day, so this was a bit unusual. His interest piqued, James stopped and faced him.

"It also looks to have been dug up fairly recently, sir," he finished, relief settling onto his face.

James ground his teeth together, thinking. There was that same little tickle in the back of his brain, like this had to do with something. *Another missing puzzle piece.* It didn't seem to be related to this current case, but what if it actually was?

"Bring in the bones for age, gender, and DNA testing!"

Jeffrey blinked and opened his mouth to say something, but James had already turned away, intent on his decision.

"Whose DNA are we testing it against?" he heard Jeffrey call after him. He smirked.

"I don't know yet," he said but didn't look back.

CHAPTER SIXTY

1998
ROSIE

Rosie was tormented by small, starburst-like flashes of memory. She tried so hard to remember what had happened, but this was all she got. Glimpses. And she couldn't even trust that what she was seeing was from three nights ago or sixty or so years ago. One moment, she was dragging Emi through the dark woods near their house; the next, she was following Franny to wherever she was going. The same forest, sixty-odd years apart. It was very confusing. And terribly aggravating. Mr. Walker was coming back, and she wanted to be ready, but the crone wouldn't let her see. She was tampering with her brain and having a damn good time doing it.

"I hate you, you ugly witch!" she said to the empty room.

"Ha-ha-ha! Delicious hate," her constant companion crooned inside her skull. Her mother hadn't come back, and Rosie didn't blame her. She almost believed at times that it was she herself doing the bad things, such as slapping her mom. But then, eventually, the crone would recede, and it was as if a dirty, nasty fog was lifted from her, and she was Rosie again. Plain Jane, fifteen-year-old Rosie. She can't escape this demon now. She knew that. She used her misery and tiredness to take over. The transition was

seamless now. Nobody would believe her if she told them the truth. Maybe not even Luke. Definitely not her father. He didn't even believe in ghosts. Her father . . . He never came to see her. Rosie's face crumpled, and she buried it in her blanket-covered knees. He must think she made Emi disappear. He must hate her even though Emi is the best little sister and Rosie wouldn't do anything to hurt her. Not in a million years. *"Tsk, tsk, tsk,"* the crone clicked her tongue. *"He only cares about Emi. You are only a burden to him."*

"No . . ." Rosie groaned into the blanket.

"You are not even his child. He never loved you."

"Shut up!" Rosie screamed, and the tray of food she never touched flew off the table next to her bed.

It smashed against the wall, leaving a colorful array of stains in its wake. Rosie stared at it, breathing heavily and feeling both terrified and exhilarated. Did she just do that? She looked at her hands. They were pale and clammy. Her plastic cup full of water was still on the table. She reached for it but stopped her hand about ten inches short and focused on moving it with her mind. The cup didn't move, but the water inside it sloshed and swirled like a miniature lake during a storm. She gaped at it, fascinated.

The door opened, and in came Mr. Walker. His eyes immediately drifted to the food on the wall, and his eyebrows went up to his hairline.

"Well, it's nice to know I'm not the only one having a bad day," he said quizzically.

"That was an accident," Rosie clarified.

"Like what happened to Emi was an accident?"

Here we go! The fucker hadn't even sat down, and he was already at it. Rosie could feel the crone grab on to her anger. She had to control herself. She took a deep breath and blew it out through her nose. Mr. Walker pulled up a chair and sat down uncomfortably close to her.

"Have you found Emi? Is she all right?" Rosie's voice trembled slightly.

Mr. Walker gave her a hard stare that she did not like or

appreciate. At all.

"Listen, honey! Now that you've had some time to rest, I'm going to be honest with you. I believe you know what happened to your sister. And now, today, during this visit, you will tell me! Understand?"

"You haven't answered my question." She sounded like a mouse. Was his aim to scare and confuse her? "Is she all right?"

"No, she's not all right, Rosie! Come on!"

His booming tone scared her. His words were like tiny knives penetrating her brittle skin.

"Your sister has been missing for three days. We found her blood on the forest floor. This is not looking good for her."

A memory, as sharp and quick as a bee sting, hit her. She was dragging her sister through the thick underbrush. Emi was sobbing softly, but she didn't resist. And then, a scream.

"Rosie, stop! It hurts!"

Rosie looked back at her sister dispassionately. The jagged edge of a fallen tree branch had dragged across Emi's calf. It made a deep cut. Her dark blood welled and ran down her milky white skin. It reached her foot and ran between her toes.

"It really hurts," she cried again.

Her little face, her lovely little face, was scrunched up in pain and fear. Rosie didn't care. She had been so cruel.

"Stop being a baby!" she had said. "Come on! We need to go!"

She yanked on her sister's hand, and she came and limped after her.

Rosie blinked, the memory receding.

"She cut her leg on a tree branch," she said in a raspy whisper. "I remember. I was there."

"Was your father there?"

Rosie thought on that.

"No. I don't think so."

"You sound uncertain."

Her tongue felt thick in her mouth, and her throat felt raw

with oncoming tears. *Emi*. Her dear Emi. Why did she do that, take her out into the woods like that? *It doesn't make sense. None of this makes sense.* She didn't have the answers. Mr. Walker wanted something from her she didn't have, so she couldn't give.

"Here is what I think happened: Your father hurt Emi. Maybe even killed her. He tried to do the same thing to you, too."

"No . . ." she whispered, shaking her head.

"We found Emi's blood on his clothes."

"No," she said, fixing him with her blue stare.

"There is a good chance your sister didn't make it, so now, I need you to help me put the person responsible away!"

"No!" she screamed.

It was a throaty, feral sound. The cup of water tipped over, soaking Mr. Walker's pants. He jumped up and started dabbing at it with a tissue from the nightstand.

"That was odd . . ." he murmured.

He was going to blame this on her dad—the man who raised her, who had loved her unconditionally, even though he didn't have to. A slideshow of memories ran through her mind. She was six. She fell with her bike on their long driveway. Her mother placed a Band-Aid on her knee, and her dad had wrapped her up in his big arms. Fast-forward, and they were riding up to the house. She was nine. Her dad was just ahead of her, riding Pilot. Rosie was on Sand. Oh, her dear Sand.

"Look!" her dad said, pointing toward their home.

Her mom was there, standing on the back porch, a chunky baby Emi in her arms. She picked up the baby's arm and made her wave to them. *She is radiant.* Her beautiful mother.

"You look just like your mom," her dad said to her, turning in the saddle. "Y'all are the two prettiest girls I know."

Warmth flooded Rosie's chest. She believed him. Her dad knows all. If he said she was pretty, then it had to be true.

Another skip, and Rosie was thirteen. She was standing on the deck over the water at her grandparents' house. Suddenly, her dad grabbed her from behind, lifted her as if she weighed no more than four-year-old Emi, and tossed her into the water. Rosie bobbed back up and took a large gulp of air, ready to deliver some insults, only to be met with her father's falling form. She screamed and ducked to the right as he hit the water. She laughed hysterically, splashing water in his face as he came up for air.

"Oh, my God, Dad! You are such a loser!"

But she didn't think that at all. She secretly loved him even more when he was being goofy.

Her dad. Her loving, caring, funny dad. He couldn't have done anything to either of them. *He didn't make Emi disappear. He didn't hurt her.* Rosie knew these things for a fact. And yet, her knowledge was useless. If only she could remember what happened that night. Then, she could tell Mr. Walker the truth, whatever that may be. *"Help me, you evil twat! Let me see what happened!"* She pleaded with her demon, but she seemed to retreat into the dark hollows of her mind. If she was going to save her father, she would have to do it alone. She would have to give Mr. Walker a different culprit. That was the only way.

"It was me," she heard herself say.

Mr. Walker furrowed his eyebrows at her sternly.

"I know you want to protect your dad . . ." he started, but Rosie cut him off.

She had to say this out loud before her nerves failed her.

"I took her out into the forest and pushed her off the cliff."

A huge teardrop slid from her bottom lid, followed by another and another until there was a shower of tears running down her cheeks.

"You know this counts as a confession, right?"

Of course she knew. She wasn't stupid. But the debt had to be paid. Noah Smith raised her and loved her as his own daughter. The least she could do was not let him go to prison for something he didn't do. She would tell this lie and take the fall. It didn't matter that she did not know this to be true. It would become her truth. She wiped her face with a corner of her blanket and looked up to see Mr. Walker staring at her with the oddest expression. He looked sad.

A moment of silence passed between them in which he was most likely allowing her to take back her statement if she chose to. She didn't. She stared him down with cool blue eyes.

"Why would you do such a thing?" he asked after a while, looking like he didn't actually want to know the answer.

It was simple, really. The solution, the motive, was there all along. Rosie just had to reach for it and use it as if it were a tool she had kept in her pocket, knowing that one day, it may come in handy. She knew now, at this moment, that this had all been carefully, meticulously planned by the crone. Her dreams of the office. The letter that she had helped her find. It was all a part of her plan.

"I found out that my dad isn't really my dad," Rosie said and felt an eerie calm settle into her bones.

She shrugged, feeling weightless and quite heavy at the same time. It was over. She had reached her destination on this journey.

"I got really jealous . . ." She couldn't finish the sentence.

What else was there to say? She had taken this lie as far as she could. Now, it was up to the ones around her to make of it as they pleased. Mr. Walker cleared his throat. His color wasn't quite right. He looked pale and clammy. Actually, he looked like he was about to be sick.

"How did you find out? Who told you?"

Rosie noticed that he wasn't looking at her. He was staring at the food on the wall as if that was the most interesting thing he'd ever seen. There was something there, something Rosie was meant to find. She could feel it. So, she dove into his brain, and in there, she saw his biggest fear. *Ah!* she thought. *"Ah!"* said the crone. Rosie took a moment to contemplate what she should do. On the one hand, this man was her once best friend's father, her neighbor, an innocent man doing his job. On the other hand, he was about to put Rosie's father in jail. He was over here interrogating a hurt little girl. That wasn't cool. That wasn't cool at all. So, why not?

"It was your wife," she said.

CHAPTER SIXTY-ONE

1998
JAMES

He drove to the police station, his hands white-knuckled on the steering wheel. He was inside a weird sort of bubble where he couldn't really hear the outside world. There was a very loud humming in his ears. Millie had lied to him. Made a fool of him. It was either that, or Rosie was full of shit. There was something about that girl, something not right. His head was all over the place. He needed a sign, something to tell him he was looking in the right direction, because nothing made sense to him at the moment. His own life seemed to be falling apart alongside the Smiths'.

He walked into the station moving like a zombie, not really knowing why he'd come here. He really didn't want to go home. Maybe that was it. He heard his name called and peered around dazedly.

"Detective Walker!"

It was the bubbly receptionist. She was waving him over with unusual enthusiasm. He went, his feet dragging on the tiles, each step an effort.

"What is it . . .?"

He realized a bit too late that he'd forgotten her name. He

searched the depths of his mind for it and came up empty. He closed his mouth and tried to look at her in an inventive sort of way. In reality, he felt numb and wanted nothing but to fall asleep right that second.

"I found the file you were looking for, I think. There is only one unsolved case from that time period. Here you go!"

James stared dumbly at the offered pieces of paper. *Unsolved case?* What was this girl even talking about? Then, it hit him, and his eyes widened. He snatched the papers out of her hand so quickly, she took a wary step pack.

"I'm sorry . . ." he started and realized he still didn't know her name. "I'm sorry!"

He zoomed into his office, passing a startled-looking Jeffrey in the hallway.

"Sir?" He stuck his weaselly head into James's office. "Is there anything new?"

"Bring me coffee!" he barked and slammed the door with a swift kick, almost decapitating Jeffrey, who only pulled his head back in the nick of time.

James read the file and, at the end of it, knew that his cop's instincts had not abandoned him after all. Goosebumps broke out on his arms. It was Harry Glessner. Disappeared at age seven. Body never found. His older sister, Francis, was accused of his murder, but there wasn't enough evidence found. James thought about the bones in the shallow grave and was almost a hundred percent sure that, if tested, they would come back as belonging to Harry. The two cases were eerily similar, down to the point of Francis having a different father than the man who had raised her. It was in her mother's statement. James dropped the papers onto the table. Same mental illness, same destiny, it seemed.

It was no surprise that the bones came back as Harry's. James had solved the age-old case that his old partner couldn't. Rosie was charged with the murder of her sister and was locked up in a brand-new mental institution in Dallas. Things seemed to have come full circle. And still, none of it gave James any satisfaction.

He felt he had been cheated somehow. Even after everything was settled, the feeling wouldn't go. After the verdict, Rosie's condition deteriorated. Or so James heard. People in town talked. They talked way too much. His move to Dallas close upon him, he was ready to put this case and many other things in life behind him.

CHAPTER SIXTY-TWO

1998
ROSIE

Rosie was in a black hole. She lay in the fetal position and gently rocked on top of soft, dark waves.

That awful day in the courtroom, when they told her she was guilty of killing her sister, something snapped in her. Now, she knew it to be the last weak string of her humanity, but then, she only perceived it as the smallest, sharpest pain she had ever felt. Her parents were in the room somewhere behind her.

"We find the defendant . . . guilty!" said the representative of the jury.

From just behind Rosie came a raw, animalistic wail. It was her mother. Her poor, poor mother. An innocent woman who had birthed a monster. Rosie knew her father was there, too. She could feel his misery spreading through the room like black smoke. He was probably holding her mother, gently rocking her. He would take care of her, that remaining his only job in life. Rosie wanted to turn around. She wanted to see them, tell them she was sorry. So, so incredibly sorry. But at the sound of her mother's cry, she felt that sharp pain, and then her eyes rolled back in her head, and she fell, and she kept falling for what felt like the ends of time.

She had lost everything, and finally, she was at peace.

She came to sometime later in a small white room, where she lay tied to her bed with thick leather straps. Her mouth felt dry and her throat raw, as if while in the dark hole, she had been screaming the whole time. Sometime later, a nurse in cream-colored scrubs came in and was quite startled to hear Rosie speak.

"How long has it been since the trial?" Rosie croaked.

She had no real concept of time while lost in the dark. She could have been in there for an hour or a hundred years.

The nurse, a heavyset woman in her late forties, took a step back and stared at her, her red-rimmed lips agape.

"What?" she asked, turning her head slightly so her ear was closer to Rosie.

"How . . . how long . . ." Her voice failed her.

Her tongue felt brittle and unused, like old, weatherworn plastic. The nurse shook herself as if coming out of a trance.

"I'm sorry, dear!" She hurriedly picked up a cup with a straw dangling from it and held it to Rosie's mouth at arm's length.

It was quite comical how she was making an effort to stay as far away from Rosie as possible while still tending to her.

"I have just never heard you speak like that. Normally, I mean. What did you say?"

Rosie drank the whole cup's worth of water, and her body already ached for more.

"How long since the trial?"

"Oh . . . Just about . . . twenty-seven days, I believe."

"What?"

Rosie tried to sit up, but, of course, she couldn't because of the straps. The nurse, however, reacted as if she was fully capable of tearing the leather to shreds and jumping on her. She danced back, dropping the cup in her haste. It rolled lazily to the corner of the room. They both watched it with fascination.

"Don't!" The nurse put out a chubby finger at her and slowly backed out of the room, slamming the door behind her.

What the fuck? Rosie felt as if she had been placed in a

weird alternate reality in which she was actually a tiger or something equally as dangerous. She looked at the fallen cup and wondered if she could somehow get it to go back on the table. It bothered her the way the nurse just left it there. To her surprise, the cup lifted effortlessly from the floor, followed by the straw. Rosie swiveled her eyes to the table, and the two objects followed her line of sight. They settled peacefully and silently in their previous spot, the straw landing precisely in the middle of the cup.

"Oh . . ." breathed Rosie.

After another week or so, she was allowed some visitors. Apparently, her behavior had been so erratic and, frankly, dangerous—the resident shrink's words, not Rosie's—she had to be placed in solitary confinement. Rosie remembered nothing from those twenty-seven days. And that was fine with her.

Her first visitor was her mother, and Rosie was so nervous about seeing her, she almost declined.

They chained her to the floor using leather handcuffs and placed her into a small room, this one with a highly placed window with the view of a tree's canopy. It was windy outside. The branches of the tree swayed gently from time to time, showing off their new spring buds. Then, her mother came in, and Rosie no longer saw anything, for the tears came and the world dissolved into a blurry mess. They weren't allowed to touch, so they just sat there awkwardly for some minutes, not saying anything.

"How are you feeling?" her mother asked finally.

She looked older. Tired. Her lips moved stiffly. Rosie shook her head.

"I'm so sorry, Mom."

Alice shook her head, too. Her eyes were dry and red as if she had already cried all her tears and had no more left.

"No, *I'm* sorry, love. I should have been a better, more attentive parent. It's all my fault."

"That's not true . . ."

Her mother didn't correct her, just looked at her with a mingling of pity, fear, and revulsion. Rosie wished she couldn't see all these feelings flowing forth from her. It was hurtful. Even though she knew her mom couldn't control the way she felt, it still hurt her feelings.

"Is Dad gonna come?" she asked hopefully.

Her mom shook her head ever so slightly.

"Not just yet, love. He's . . . still mourning Emi."

And the hurt just kept on coming. Rosie felt the black fingers of the crone on the back of her scalp and knew she didn't have much time until she made her appearance.

"I mourn her, too," she said, sulking.

Alice looked as if she had just slapped her, and rightfully so. Rosie could see her thoughts racing one another to reach her mouth: *How dare you? You did this! Evil, evil child . . .* She cleared her throat.

"Luke sent you a package. I had to leave it at the front so they could examine it, but they should give it to you sometime today."

"Is he gonna come visit me?"

Excitement rose in her chest at the thought of being able to tell him the truth: that she didn't actually remember what happened. She said what she said to protect her dad. He would believe her. For sure, he would.

"No, love," her mom said quietly.

"Why not?"

Rosie felt like she was a balloon, and her mom had just taken a sharp pin and jabbed her. Her chest caved inward, and there was a bitter taste at the back of her throat. *This isn't fair!* At least they could allow her to see her friend. Her mom should fight for her. She should make sure Rosie was at least treated like a human being.

"Because you are dangerous!"

Her mother seared her with her narrow, foxlike gaze, and Rosie didn't need the ability to see into her. She knew exactly what she was thinking.

Later in the evening, she was brought the package. They

opened it, but originally, it had been a letter and a book wrapped in brown wrapping paper. She tore into the envelope, hungry for some kind words and compassion.

Dear Rosie,

I know you didn't do it.

Rosie let out a huge breath she didn't know she was holding. She hugged the letter to her chest for a brief moment before continuing.

I wanted to come see you, but they will not let me until I turn eighteen. It's not so far away. I will wait. I will not forget you! I love you! When you are feeling down, just remember that I believe you. I think of you every day.

I sent in the copy of Rosanne Glessner's journal you gave me. I finally found the evidence we've been looking for. I know it's too late, and I know it doesn't make much difference now, but I wanted you to be able to read it for yourself if you haven't already. I have marked the passage you are meant to read.

I will write to you often. You can write back if you feel like it and if they let you. I would like that.

Love, Luke

Rosie placed the precious letter carefully next to her on the bed and ran her fingers over the words "I love you" before taking up the book.

Luke had marked the page with a small, grainy photo of the two of them. Rosie grinned tearily as she picked it up and held it close to her face. They were about eight at the time it had been taken. They were sitting on the dock, both of them cross-legged. Luke was showing her how to tie a hook onto her small fishing rod. She remembered that day. His glasses kept on sliding down his nose while he was working the thin fishing line. He didn't get frustrated, though, just kept on pushing them back up. His grandfather had just gotten a new camera for his birthday, and he had been hell-bent on documenting everything. He was the one who took the picture. It was a good memory of a warm summer day. She placed the photograph on top of the letter, grateful for the thought on Luke's part to send it, and began to read.

February 11, 1744

I was saved today by the merciful hand of God. I had lost faith in Him for a while there, I have to admit. But let me start from the beginning.

I went into labor these two months past. I knew the babe would not be born live. It was much too early in the pregnancy. Still, holding his still form in my arms was such a shock. He was tiny, his skin a translucent gray. There are no words to describe the agony I felt that day, so I will not even attempt it. John was there. He helped me during the birth. I have never seen such a thing—a man who isn't a trained doctor assisting in the birth of a child. But there he was. The little boy who will never be had the beginnings of a black mane. Just like John's. Life is cruel.

We buried the babe, whom we named John Manfred Glessner, the same day he was born. John wanted us to use my last name instead of his father's, whom he had always disliked. I went to his grave today, and then, as if in a trance, I started to walk toward the cliff. I felt I had no life left in me, no life left to give. God was telling me that I shall never bear another child, and thus, I am useless. John would be better off without me. If I disappear, he can find another wife and have many beautiful children who will all bear his shiny black hair. I would jump from the edge of the cliff and cease to exist. It would be a quick death, hopefully instant. And then, the red blood of the river would mingle with mine. The water would welcome my body and take it far away from here. Quite poetic. Quite sad.

I was almost to the edge when I heard it.

Rosie read, her lips silently moving.

"What?" she breathed, her eyes turning as round as saucers.

Was it possible? She tried to remember what date it had been, and yes, it was the same. She read it again, and in the middle of it, the floodgates of her memory finally opened.

She had been telling Emi for days that the two of them were going to go on a nighttime adventure—only it wasn't really her. It was the crone using her body. Emi was okay with it. She had said that the ghost had told her what was going to happen and that she should just go along with it. But the night of February 11, when Rosie had gone to her room to collect her, she got cold feet. So, Rosie had cruelly promised her that she could take the donkey with her. It had been a lie. Rosie had marched her through the dark woods. Emi was crying. She made a few attempts at stopping them by throwing herself on the ground. During one of these fits, she injured her leg on a jagged branch. She bled everywhere. It was no wonder their dad ended up stepping in it. Rosie didn't care about her injury, though, or more like the crone didn't care. She dragged Emi's protesting little body right up to the cliff, and . . .

I heard somebody calling my name. "Rosie! Rosie!" she yelled. My mother used to call me that. That is one of my only childhood memories of her. I believed the voice to be her ghost. She was calling me from the other side, waiting for me. So, I ran, the cold wind whipping my hair and shift. I ran to get to her, but when I arrived at the edge, my mother's ghost was not what I found.

Rosie lifted her hand, and a blue light, like lightning, appeared at her fingertips. She sliced into the air, and the air opened. She had never seen anything like it. Even the memory of it was so shocking, she had to keep blinking. A jagged scar appeared in front of her, and through it, she could see another cliff, another night sky. Then, she took Emi by both shoulders. "Off you go!" Rosie said and pushed Emi into the opening in the air. Emi landed on the other side and gave Rosie a scared, wide-eyed look before the scar closed up like it was never there.

There stood a little girl. I could hardly believe my eyes. How on earth did she get here? The cold winter wind was blowing her long blonde hair every which way. She looked scared out of her mind. She only wore a long shirt, so I could see a big, bloody cut on one of her skinny little legs. When she finally saw me, she asked who I was. I told her that I am Rosanne Glessner, my husband and I own this land, and she was safe here. I was so afraid that the little thing might try to run off and fall right into the river valley. I asked her for her name, and she told me the most wonderful, unbelievable thing. "My name is Emilia," she said, "and I have come to be your daughter."

Life is a truly fascinating thing. I went out to the cliff wanting to end my life, thinking that it had no meaning, and came back with a strange little daughter. I swore to myself that I would not question where she came from, for I already knew the answer. God had sent her to me, and God is great.

Rosie let the book fall from her hands.

CHAPTER SIXTY-THREE

1998
MILLIE

She walked up the steps of the large, cream-colored building, her red high heels clicking with each step. She got some curious looks, as expected. She did come dressed in her best. She wore a fitted navy suit jacket embroidered with red roses and a matching knee-length pencil skirt. She had straightened and curled her kinky mane of hair, so now, it fell in thick waves over her shoulders and back. Yes, most people didn't dress up to visit the loony bin, but she had another, much more important appointment after. Two birds, one stone and all that. She had been meaning to see Rosie Smith for a while now, and since Millie's court hearing was only a few streets from where she was locked up, it made sense to come today. She had heard ghastly stories of the girl's condition. Millie was in the courtroom when they announced her verdict. Rosie had fainted and then had a full-blown seizure on the floor. It was quite frightening, actually. Her body had bent in strange, impossible-looking angles. When the two security guards tried to carry her out of the room, they had both dropped her almost immediately. Afterward, both men claimed that her skin was hot to the touch; touching her was like grabbing a pan out of a working oven without any oven mitts. They had to get a stretcher and roll her onto it. They had covered their hands with their jackets so as to not have to touch her again. This wasn't even the most fascinating part. Apparently, she got really violent after being taken to the asylum. Millie heard some very juicy stories of Rosie tearing off her restraints and jumping on the nurses, or that she constantly threw things at the workers seemingly without touching them. One lady at the grocery store had told her that Rosie had been placed into solitary confinement because of all of this. She had inside scoop because her daughter-in-law worked at the facility. Millie hoped it was true. The little rat deserved the punishment.

"I'm here to see Rosanne Smith," she said to the lady at the desk.

"How are you related to her?" she asked without much interest.

"I'm not!" Millie spat with such disdain that now, she did receive an interested look. "My daughter is best friends with her," she clarified, suddenly feeling very self-conscious. "I'm here because she can't visit. I need to deliver a message."

She had a message to deliver, all right, but it wasn't from Mina. The lady pressed some buttons on her keyboard and took her sweet ass time to read whatever was on the computer screen.

"Okay, I see she has no other restrictions besides the visitor being over eighteen, so I will have someone ask her if she wants to see you. Please have a seat!"

She gestured at the row of uncomfortable-looking metal chairs against the wall. Millie obediently took a seat and observed the workings of the building as she waited. People came and went, but everyone had to go through a set of heavily fortified metal doors guarded by two security guards. One of them had a mustache so similar to James's that, for a second, Millie thought it was actually him. But, of course, it wasn't. There was no reason why he would come here. He said himself that he was done. Done with this case. For a second, though, cold fear had run through Millie's veins, thinking James figured out what she was up to and was here to stop her.

"Ma'am!"

Her head snapped back to the reception desk. The lady was pointing at the security doors with a phone held to her ear.

"She'll see you. You can go in!"

This was a bit of a surprise. Millie had halfway expected to be turned away. She stood and clip-clopped through the heavy doors in her shiny new shoes.

What awaited her was a skinny, tired-looking little girl. Rosie was much smaller and paler than she remembered. Her wrists looked delicate and so breakable inside her leather handcuffs. Her white shirt hung on her as if she were merely a coat hanger. She looked up at her like a little lamb waiting for slaughter, dark rims under her delightful blue eyes. For a second, Millie felt sorry for her. But only for a second. Then, she stomped the feeling down and smushed it into the ground with her red high heels.

She sat and laced her perfectly manicured fingers on top of the table. *That's right, little girl, take it all in! You will never be able to go to a nail salon or go shopping. You will rot in here in your plain white uniform with all the other crazies and unkind nurses.* Rosie's mouth twitched, and her pupils seemed to dilate just a fraction. Millie wondered if what she thought was plain on her face, for the girl seemed to sense her animosity.

"Hello, Rosie, dear!" she said, smiling at her with fake radiance.

She didn't answer, but Millie heard chains rattling. She glanced under the table and saw that Rosie was actually chained to the ground. Millie had a flash of panic run down her spine like cold fingers. For whatever reason, the staff felt that this little girl needed to be handcuffed and chained to the ground. And Millie was locked in here with her. Her hands found her purse in her lap and gripped it for comfort. *Don't be stupid!* she chided herself. *She is merely a girl. You are a fully grown adult woman. You have no need to fear . . .*

"I was wondering when you'd come," Rosie said in a timid little mouse voice.

This is all an act, Millie reminded herself. *She isn't this harmless in real life. She killed her sister, for God's sake.* Her heart squeezed at the thought of that. *That innocent, wild little girl.* She would never ride her annoying donkey by Millie's house again.

"So, what brings you here?"

Rosie laced her fingers on the table and squared her shoulders, mimicking Millie's posture perfectly. Anger rose within Millie's chest, white and hot. *The little witch!* As if she didn't know.

"I think you know exactly why I'm here! You told my husband a lie! A terrible, unjust lie that ruined my marriage."

Her voice had risen a few octaves in spite of her every effort to keep calm and collected. Rosie laughed. It started off as a jingly little sound that quickly morphed into an ugly, raspy cackle. Millie grimaced and leaned slightly back in her chair. This little bitch was crazier than she thought. *The nerve of her.* She would definitely deliver her a good, open-handed slap to the face if she wasn't aware that she was being watched by the staff.

"Oh, sorry!" Rosie said, slapping a hand over her mouth, her eyes widening. "I didn't mean to laugh. It just came out."

"You little devil's spawn!" Millie spat, her voice vibrating with anger.

"Okay, okay!" Rosie put up her hands in surrender. "It was a terrible lie, I'll admit, but it wasn't unjust."

"James left me because of what you said!" Millie burst out.

It was true. In fact, she was going to their divorce hearing after this. Since James thought she told Rosie her family's little secret, he also believed her to be responsible for everything that came after. It was unjust. It wasn't Millie's fault that this little psychopath pushed her sister off a cliff. There it was again, that slight pain in her chest. It wasn't her fault, damn it!

"I thought he might."

Rosie scratched at a small speck on the table. Millie's mouth fell open. Did she just hear that correctly? Did Rosie lie even though she knew what the repercussions might be? She ruined her marriage on purpose.

"You will go to hell for this!" she breathed, pointing a finger at her.

"Already there, dear Millie."

"And you will address me as Mrs. Walk . . ."

Her lips clamped shut, for after today, she would no longer actually be Mrs. Walker. She would be a sad, fat divorcee; nobody would want her. Rosie had this shit-eating grin on her face. She swayed side to side in her chair, softly clicking her tongue. Her behavior was unnerving. Her face looked strange—her eyes too big, her mouth too wide. Her pupils were so big that the blues of her irises didn't even show anymore. She stopped swaying and clicking and fixated on Millie with this wide-eyed stare that made her skin crawl.

"You know what?" she said, her eyes large and unblinking. "This isn't actually what hell looks like. That was a bit harsh. Here, they feed you, and there are windows and sunshine and other people. Hell is a dark hole full of pitch-black water that you are meant to spend eternity in. Alone."

She slowly stood during this strange monologue, and now, she was bent over the table, balancing on her thin hands, her neck outstretched toward Millie.

"What on earth are you talking about?"

To her surprise, Millie felt a visceral fear grip her insides. Maybe this girl was, in fact, a demon. And she was locked in a room with her. She had to get out. She glanced toward the door.

"No, no! Not just yet!"

Rosie dropped back into her seat, and at the same time, Millie's chair scooted closer to the table as if by its own accord, pinning her to the table uncomfortably. She wriggled, but it was no use. The table was fixed to the floor, and her chair wouldn't budge.

"What the . . ." she grunted, trying to free herself.

"You dare to say my lie was unjust when you yourself worked diligently for years to destroy my parents' marriage."

"I did no such a thing!" Millie squeaked with indignation.

She was being squeezed so hard, it was getting hard to breathe.

"Don't you lie to me, young lady! I see all."

Rosie's eyes were dark pools of black tar. Her hair floated around her as if she were submerged in water. She was a demon! Here to grab her and drag her down to hell.

"I'm sorry!" Millie screamed breathlessly, feeling her eyes bulge with the effort of breathing.

"Do you think that matters now, you dumb wench!? Your 'sorry' isn't going to wipe away all the meddling you have done. Your 'sorry' isn't going to make things right. Besides, you're not even sorry. You are scared."

Millie felt her ribs crunch under the pressure of this unimaginable force. She would die here because she was stupid enough to think she could get away with anything. Because she was stupid enough to come here. People would say that her own stupidity had killed her, and they would be right. She gave the table one last futile shove, and her chair slid back effortlessly this time. She gasped and coughed as air—wonderful, sweet air—flooded her bruised lungs.

"What . . . What are you?" she coughed, bending forward and hugging her aching sides.

Rosie stared down at her dispassionately.

"I'm only a wronged soul. Just like you are."

Suddenly, Millie's chair slid all the way back to the wall with her in it. Her whole body shook. Should she stand up and run out? Would she let her? Rosie wasn't even looking at her. Her gaze was on the high window and the flowering tree behind it.

"I'm done with you. Get the fuck out!" she said without moving her eyes from the window.

Millie stood on shaking legs. She felt like a newborn giraffe just learning how to walk. She banged on the door, and as soon as it opened, she scurried out like the cockroach she felt she was. She fell into the arms of the guard, and to her surprise and immense relief, she saw it was James. She clung to him as he held her unsteadily with one arm, closing the door with the other.

"Are you all right?" he asked.

"Oh, Jim!" Her words were laced with her oncoming tears. "I'm so sorry, so incredibly sorry! Let's not get divorced! I'll move with you to Dallas! I'll be good. I promise!"

"Ma'am?"

That wasn't his voice. She pushed away from him, and to her horror, she saw that it wasn't James at all. It was the security guard from before. The one with the mustache. He wore a knowing expression on his face, as if he knew what she went through in there. Mortified, Millie pulled a handkerchief from her purse and made an attempt at fixing her makeup.

"Excuse me!" she said, dabbing at her eyes.

This was the single most embarrassing moment of her life, groveling like that in front of a complete stranger, hanging on to him so intimately. She almost wished Rosie did crush her with the chair. The guard shrugged.

"She has this effect on people."

"What?" Millie looked up at him and saw that he had kind blue eyes.

"That one in there. She's a bit nasty. Not even her own parents will come see her."

Millie blinked up at him, a bit baffled. He was being so nice to her, and he didn't even know her.

"Can I walk you out?"

Millie stepped out into the bright sunshine and walked quickly down the steps. The heel of her right shoe snapped off on the second step. She looked down at it furiously. Slowly, carefully, she turned her head back and searched the side of the building with her eyes. *There!* There it was: a tall jacaranda tree, covered in purple flowers. And just behind it, placed high on the second-story wall, was a long, rectangular window. She saw the flicker of a blue spark in there, like a tiny burst of electricity. Goosebumps broke out on her arms and legs in spite of the warm weather. Rosie pushing her sister off a cliff was not the full story. Millie was sure of that. There was a secret there, hidden within the innocent girl that was Rosie Smith. Behind her pretty mask lay something unearthly and sinister. It was terrifying and thrilling. Such power. Millie told herself that one day, if she got the chance, she would get her hands on the truth. Nobody loved a good secret more than her. She picked up her broken heel and limped down the rest of the stairs, turning her back on this mystery only for the time being.

EPILOGUE

Luke sat on a fallen log and looked out into the open sky that lay before the cliff on the Glessner land. He and his grandparents came to show their respects and give support to the Smith family. They would leave in only a few hours, so Luke wanted to use his time to come out here and see if he could find some answers. He missed Rosie desperately and Emi, too. It was Noah's idea for him to bring the donkey: "Moonwalk could use some attention. He barely touches his food lately."

So, Luke walked him out here on a long lead. He was peacefully grazing behind him now, his long ears gently swaying in the warm spring breeze.

Luke had no idea if she would show, but one minute, he was alone, and the next, she was sitting right there on the log next to him. The young woman with the blonde hair. The one who scared the crap out of him after his first kiss. The one who he saw in his dream.

"Why didn't you tell me who you were?" he asked her, feeling tears prick the back of his eyes.

The woman had a beatific smile on her face. Her edges blurred and swirled as she gave a small shrug.

"You would have tried to change things, and that could not be," she said, her ghostly voice coming in and out of focus.

Neither of them said anything for a moment. Luke just looked at her, trying to take in all her details. He knew there was no guarantee he would see her again. That's just how ghosts worked. He wanted to remember her so he could tell Rosie about her. About

443

how beautiful she would become.

"I miss you, Emi," he said and sniffled as he wiped his nose with the back of his hand.

Moonwalk poked his long head between them and nickered softly at his master's ghost. Emi smiled tenderly at him and reached out a fading hand to stroke his nose.

"He sees you!" Luke said in wonder.

"Yes. He has always seen me. My dear old friend."

Luke reached out to pet him, but the donkey flattened his ears along his neck and attempted to remove one of his fingers with his flat teeth. He yanked his hand out of the donkey's mouth. Emi laughed. It was a jingly sound that reminded Luke so much of Rosie, it hurt his heart.

"Tell Rosie that all is well. And that I was happy. Up until the very end," she said. And then, she was gone, picked up by the winds of the cliff.

"I will," Luke said to the emptiness next to him. He stood, wiped some loose tears from his cheeks, and picked up Moonwalk's lead. They walked back to the house side by side, the only two who knew the truth and were still allowed to walk free.

WRITER'S NOTES

As I said before, a book, to me, is an organic, almost live thing. I sat down to write a story about a girl, and soon, everywhere I looked, new characters popped up. They populated this imaginary world and took on lives of their own. I say this because I never really thought hard on what a character would look like or what their personality would be like. Each character appeared suddenly before my mind's eye, like a wildflower on a meadow, already carrying their story with them. My job was to write everything down as I saw and perceived it.

Each person in the book is like a tiny seedling. They grew as I tended to them. Some grew bigger than others.

My husband asked me if I have a favorite character, and upon thinking on it, I found that I do. Can you guess who it is? Come on! Have you guessed? It isn't an obvious one. My favorite character is Millie, the reason being that she was one of my smallest seedlings, and she ended up growing the tallest. She started off as nothing but a name and a face, the wife of the detective. Then, she wanted a backstory, so I gave it to her. She asked for feelings, so she got those, too. Then, she was asking for her own chapters, and at that point, I couldn't deny her. She grew so powerful, seemingly on her own, that she became a complex main character. And that is why she is my favorite. She taught me that a story can have multiple faces and various truths depending on whose eyes you are viewing it through, an invaluable lesson.

Thank you, dear reader, for enjoying this book with me! Till next time!

I dedicate this book to my husband, Mike, who was the first reader to enjoy it and who taught me that life is short and precious; and to our daughter, Annika, who taught me to step past my limits and to look at things from more angles than just one. Without them, this book wouldn't exist.

ABOUT THE AUTHOR

I was raised in a small country called Hungary that sits smack in the middle of Europe. Moving to Houston in my early twenties, I was full of hopes and dreams for my future but had no concrete plan. Writing is one thing that I have always enjoyed through my life, and it is something I kept coming back to. Growing up in Europe, I was always surrounded by stories of ancient mysteries. I love folklore and the unexplained. I have also always enjoyed coming up with solutions to mysteries, and sometimes, I would find that I had stumbled upon a great storyline.

At 32, I decided, with the encouragement of my husband, to put all my unfinished manuscripts behind me and actually finish and publish a book. Life gets in the way, but I felt in my gut that now is my time.